JULIE

"Undoubtedly Garwood is a pro."

—*Kirkus Reviews*

"Julie Garwood attracts readers like beautiful heroines attract dashing heroes."

—*USA Today*

"If a book has Julie Garwood's name on it, it's guaranteed to be a meticulously written . . . and thoroughly engaging story."

—*Sun Journal*

"Julie Garwood creates a highly enjoyable feast for her readers."

—*Romantic Times*

"[Garwood is] the Rembrandt of romance novels."

—*The Kansas City Star*

## CASTLES

"A charming, sweet, funny romance, brimming with sparkling dialogue, delightful characters, and a story that flies."

—*Romantic Times*

"The story is splendid, the characters are wonderful, and the dialogue is excellent. . . . The secondary characters are marvelous and there are many from which to choose, including some of our friends from Ms. Garwood's earlier books. . . . A keeper."

—*Rendezvous*

"*Castles* is Julie Garwood at her best. It is witty, sexy, romantic, and has enough danger to keep things moving quickly."

—*All About Romance*

## REBELLIOUS DESIRE

"Julie Garwood is a spectacular storyteller."

—*Affaire de Coeur*

"Caroline and her duke are perfectly matched. . . . Read this book!"
—*All About Romance*

## COME THE SPRING

"Julie Garwood has become a trusted brand name in romantic fiction . . . [featuring] characters of the Old West, especially the ruggedly handsome gunslingers and the sassy, beautiful women who love them."

—*People*

"What began so beautifully in *For the Roses* and continued with the Clayborne Brides series comes to a truly lovely conclusion in *Come the Spring*. . . . You'll find it as hard as I did to say farewell to a family you have come to love like your own. Thank you, Ms. Garwood, for Mama Rose and her children."

—*RT Book Reviews*

"With its tremendous prose and building suspense, this book [is] a long-term literary classic."

—Harriet Klausner

"Garwood does her usual superb job. . . . [A] fascinating tale of western romance and adventure."

—*Abilene Reporter-News*

## THE CLAYBORNE BRIDES

### *One Pink Rose • One White Rose • One Red Rose*

"Utterly charming."

—*The Philadelphia Inquirer*

# JULIE GARWOOD

# CASTLES

POCKET BOOKS

*New York   London   Toronto   Sydney   New Delhi*

Pocket Books
An Imprint of Simon & Schuster, Inc.
1230 Avenue of the Americas
New York, NY 10020

This book is a work of fiction. Any references to historical events, real people, or real places are used fictitiously. Other names, characters, places, and events are products of the author's imagination, and any resemblance to actual events or places or persons, living or dead, is entirely coincidental.

This Pocket Books paperback edition March 2017

POCKET and colophon are registered trademarks of Simon & Schuster, Inc.

For information about special discounts for bulk purchases, please contact Simon & Schuster Special Sales at 1-866-506-1949 or business@simonandschuster.com.

The Simon & Schuster Speakers Bureau can bring authors to your live event. For more information or to book an event, contact the Simon & Schuster Speakers Bureau at 1-866-248-3049 or visit our website at www.simonspeakers.com.

Manufactured in the United States of America

30   29   28   27   26   25   24   23   22

ISBN 978-0-671-74420-5

For Sharon Felice Murphy,
an easy listener, an inspiration,
a source of joy.
What would I do without you?

# CASTLES

# Prologue

### England, 1819

*He was a real lady killer.*

*The foolish woman never had a chance. She never knew she was being stalked, never guessed her secret admirer's real intent.*

*He believed he killed her with kindness. He was proud of that accomplishment. He could have been cruel. He wasn't. The craving eating away at him demanded to be appeased, and even though erotic thoughts of torture aroused him to a fever pitch, he hadn't given in to the base urge. He was a man, not an animal. He was after self-gratification, and the chit certainly deserved to die, yet he'd still shown true compassion. He had been very kind—considering.*

*She had, after all, died smiling. He deliberately caught her so by surprise he only glimpsed one quick spasm of terror in her cow brown eyes before it was over. He crooned to her then, like any good master would croon to his injured pet, letting her hear the sound of his compassion all the while he was strangling her, and he didn't stop his song of sympathy until the killing was finished and he knew she couldn't hear him.*

*He hadn't been without mercy. Even when he was certain she was dead, he gently turned her face away from him before he allowed himself to smile. He wanted to laugh, with relief because it was finally over, and with satisfaction because it had gone so very well, but he didn't dare make a sound now, for somewhere in the back of his mind lurked the thought that such undignified behavior would make him seem more monster than man, and he certainly wasn't a monster. No, no, he didn't hate women, he admired them—most anyway —and to those he considered redeemable, he was neither cruel nor heartless.*

*He was terribly clever though. There wasn't any shame in admitting that truth. The chase had been invigorating, but from start to finish he had been able to predict her every reaction. Granted, her own vanity had helped him immensely. She was a naive chit who thought of herself as worldly—a dangerous misconception—and he had proven to be far too cunning for the likes of her.*

*There had been sweet irony in his choice of weapons. He had planned to use his dagger to kill her. He wanted to feel the blade sink deep inside her, craved the feel of her hot blood as it poured over his hands each time he slammed the knife into her soft, smooth skin.* Carve the fowl, carve the fowl. *The command echoed in his mind. He hadn't given in to his desire, however, for he was still stronger than his inner voice, and on the spur of the moment he decided not to use the dagger at all. The diamond necklace he'd given her was draped around her neck. He grabbed hold of the expensive trinket and used it to squeeze the life out of her. He thought the weapon was most appropriate.* Women liked trinkets, this one more than most. *He even considered burying the necklace with her, but just as he was about to pour the clumps of lime over her body he'd gathered from the cliffs to hurry the decay, he changed his inclination and put the necklace in his pocket.*

*He walked away from the grave without a backward glance. He felt no remorse, no guilt. She'd served him well and now he was content.*

*A thick mist covered the ground. He didn't notice the lime powder on his boots until he had reached the main road. He wasn't bothered by the fact that his new Wellingtons were probably ruined. Nothing was going to blemish his glow of victory. He felt as though all his burdens had been lifted away. But there was more, too—the rush he'd felt again, that magnificent euphoria he'd experienced when he had his hands on her. . . . Oh, yes, this one was even better than the last.*

*She'd made him feel alive again. The world was once again rosy with choices for such a strong, virile man.*

*He knew he would feed on the memory of tonight for a long, long while. And then, when the glow began to ebb, he would go hunting again.*

# Chapter
# 1

Mother Superior Mary Felicity had always believed in miracles, but in all of her sixty-seven years on this sweet earth, she had never actually witnessed one until the frigid day in February of 1820 when the letter arrived from England.

At first the mother superior had been afraid to believe the blessed news, for she feared it was trickery on the devil's part to get her hopes up and then dash them later, but after she had dutifully answered the missive and received a second confirmation with the Duke of Williamshire's seal affixed, she accepted the gift for what it truly was.

A miracle.

They were finally going to get rid of the hellion. The mother superior shared her good news with the other nuns the following morning at matins. That evening they celebrated with duck soup and freshly baked black bread. Sister Rachael was positively giddy and had to be admonished twice for laughing out loud during evening vespers.

The hellion—or, rather, Princess Alesandra—was called into the mother superior's stark office the following afternoon. While she was being given the news of her departure from the convent, Sister Rachael was busy packing her bags.

The mother superior sat in a high-backed chair behind a

wide desk as scarred and old as she was. The nun absentmindedly fingered the heavy wooden beads of her rosary, hooked to the side of her black habit, while she waited for her charge to react to the announcement.

Princess Alesandra was stunned by the news. She gripped her hands together in a nervous gesture and kept her head bowed so the mother superior wouldn't see the tears in her eyes.

"Do sit down, Alesandra. I don't wish to talk to the top of your head."

"As you wish, Mother." She sat on the very edge of the hard chair, straightened her posture to please the superior, and then clasped her hands together in her lap.

"What do you think of this news?" the mother superior asked.

"It was the fire, wasn't it, Mother? You still haven't forgiven me that mishap."

"Nonsense," the mother superior replied. "I forgave you that thoughtlessness over a month ago."

"Was it Sister Rachael who convinced you to send me away? I did tell her how sorry I was, and her face isn't nearly as green anymore."

The mother superior shook her head. She frowned, too, for Alesandra was inadvertently getting her all riled up over the reminders of some of her antics.

"Why you believed that vile paste would remove freckles is beyond my understanding. However, Sister Rachael did agree to the experiment. She doesn't blame you . . . overly much," she hastened to add so the lie she was telling would only be considered a venial sin in God's eyes. "Alesandra, I didn't write to your guardian requesting your leave. He wrote to me. Here is the Duke of Williamshire's letter. Read it and then you'll see I'm telling you the truth."

Alesandra's hand shook when she reached for the missive. She quickly scanned the contents before handing the letter back to her superior.

"You can see the urgency, can't you? This General Ivan your guardian mentions sounds quite disreputable. Do you remember meeting him?"

Alesandra shook her head. "We visited father's homeland several times, but I was very young. I don't remember meeting him. Why in heaven's name would he want to marry me?"

"Your guardian understands the general's motives," the mother superior replied. She tapped the letter with her fingertips. "Your father's subjects haven't forgotten you. You're still their beloved princess. The general has a notion that if he marries you, he'll be able to take over the kingdom with the support of the masses. It's a clever plan."

"But I don't wish to marry him," Alesandra whispered.

"And neither does your guardian wish it," the superior said. "He believes the general won't take no for an answer, however, and will take you by force if necessary to insure his success. That is why the Duke of Williamshire wants guards to journey with you to England."

"I don't want to leave here, Mother. I really don't."

The anguish in Alesandra's voice tugged at the mother superior's heart. Forgotten for the moment were all the mischievous schemes Princess Alesandra had gotten involved in over the past years. The superior remembered the vulnerability and the fear in the little girl's eyes when she and her ailing mother had first arrived. Alesandra had been quite saintly while her mother lived. She had been so very young—only twelve—and had lost her dear father just six months before. Yet the child had shown tremendous strength. She took on the full responsibility of caring for her mother day and night. There was never any possibility her mother would recover. Her illness destroyed her body and her mind, and toward the end, when she had been crazed with her pain, Alesandra would climb into her mother's sickbed and take the frail woman into her arms. She would gently rock her back and forth and sing tender ballads to her, her voice that of an angel. Her love for her mother had been achingly beautiful to see. When at last the devil's torture was finished, her mother died in her daughter's arms.

Alesandra wouldn't allow anyone to comfort her. She wept during the dark hours of the night, alone in her cell, the

7

white curtains surrounding her cubicle blocking out none of her sobs from the postulants.

Her mother was buried on the grounds behind the chapel in a lovely, flower-bordered grotto. Alesandra couldn't abide the thought of leaving her. The grounds of the convent were adjacent to the family's second home, Stone Haven, but Alesandra wouldn't even journey there for a visitation.

"I had thought I would stay here forever," Alesandra whispered.

"You must look upon this as your destiny unfolding," the mother superior advised. "One chapter of your life is closing and another is about to open up."

Alesandra lowered her head again. "I wish to have all my chapters here, Mother. You could deny the Duke of Williamshire's request if you wished, or stall him with endless correspondence until he forgot about me."

"And the general?"

Alesandra had already thought of an answer to that dilemma. "He wouldn't dare breach this sanctuary. I'm safe as long as I stay here."

"A man lusting for power will not care if he breaks the holy laws governing this convent, Alesandra. He certainly would breach our sanctuary. Do you realize you are also suggesting I deceive your dear guardian?"

The nun's voice held a note of reproach in it. "No, Mother," Alesandra answered with a little sigh, knowing full well that was the answer the nun wished to hear. "I suppose it would be wrong to deceive . . ."

The wistfulness in her voice made the mother superior shake her head. "I will not accommodate you. Even if there was a valid reason . . ."

Alesandra jumped on the possibility. "Oh, but there is," she blurted out. She took a deep breath, then announced, "I have decided to become a nun."

The mere thought of Alesandra joining their holy order sent chills down the mother superior's spine. "Heaven help us all," she muttered.

"It's because of the books, isn't it, Mother? You want to send me away because of that little . . . fabrication."

"Alesandra . . ."

"I only made the second set of books so the banker would give you the loan. You refused to use my funds, and I knew how much you needed the new chapel . . . what with the fire and all. And you did get the loan, didn't you? God has surely forgiven me my deception, and He must have wanted me to alter the numbers in the accounts or He never would have given me such a fine head for figures. Would he, Mother Superior? In my heart, I know He forgave me my bit of trickery."

"Trickery? I believe the correct word is *larceny,*" the mother superior snapped.

"Nay, Mother," Alesandra corrected. *"Larceny* means to pilfer and I didn't pilfer anything. I merely amended."

The fierce frown on the superior's face told Alesandra she shouldn't have contradicted her, or brought up the still tender topic of the bookkeeping.

"About the fire . . ."

"Mother, I have already confessed my sorrow over that unfortunate mishap," Alesandra rushed out. She hurried to change the subject before the superior could get all riled up again. "I was very serious when I said I would like to become a nun. I believe I have the calling."

"Alesandra, you aren't Catholic."

"I would convert," Alesandra fervently promised.

A long minute passed in silence. Then the mother superior leaned forward. The chair squeaked with her movement. "Look at me," she commanded.

She waited until the princess had complied with her order before speaking again. "I believe I understand what this is really all about. I'm going to give you a promise," she said, her voice a soothing whisper. "I'll take good care of your mother's grave. If anything should happen to me, then Sister Justina or Sister Rachael will tend to it. Your mother won't be forgotten. She'll continue to be in our prayers every day. That is my promise to you."

Alesandra burst into tears. "I cannot leave her."

The mother superior stood up and hurried over to Alesandra's side. She put her arm around her shoulders and patted her. "You won't be leaving her behind. She will always be in your heart. She would want you to get on with your life."

Tears streamed down Alesandra's face. She mopped them away with the backs of her hands. "I don't know the Duke of Williamshire, Mother. I only met him once and I barely recall what he looked like. What if I don't get along with him? What if he doesn't want me? I don't want to be a burden to anyone. Please let me stay here."

"Alesandra, you seem determined to believe I have a choice in the matter and that simply isn't true. I too must obey your guardian's request. You're going to do just fine in England. The Duke of Williamshire has six children of his own. One more isn't going to be a bother."

"I'm not a child any longer," Alesandra reminded the nun. "And my guardian is probably very old and weary by now."

The mother superior smiled. "The Duke of Williamshire was chosen and named guardian over you years ago by your father. He had good reason for naming the Englishman. Have faith in your father's judgment."

"Yes, Mother."

"You can lead a happy life, Alesandra," the mother superior continued. "As long as you remember to use a little restraint. Think before you act. That's the key. You have a sound mind. Use it."

"Thank you for saying so, Mother."

"Quit acting so submissive. It isn't like you at all. I have one more bit of advice to offer you and I want your full attention. Do sit up straight. A princess does not slump."

If she sat any straighter, she thought, her spine might snap. Alesandra thrust her shoulders back a bit more and knew she'd satisfied the nun when she nodded.

"As I was saying," the mother superior continued. "It never mattered here that you were a princess, but it will matter in England. Appearances must be kept up at all times. You simply cannot allow spontaneous actions to rule your life. Now tell me, Alesandra, what are the two words I've asked you again and again to take to heart?"

"*Dignity* and *decorum,* Mother."

"Yes."

"May I come back here . . . if I find I don't like my new life?"

"You will always be welcomed back here," the mother superior promised. "Go now and help Sister Rachael with the packing. You'll be leaving in the dead of night as a precautionary measure. I'll wait in the chapel to say my good-bye."

Alesandra stood up, made a quick curtsy, then left the room. The mother superior stood in the center of the small chamber and stared after her charge for a long while. She had believed it was a miracle the princess was leaving. The mother superior had always followed a rigid schedule. Then Alesandra came into her life, and schedules became nonexistent. The nun didn't like chaos, but chaos and Alesandra seemed to go hand in hand. Yet the minute the strong-willed princess walked out of the office, the mother superior's eyes filled with tears. It was as though the sun had just been covered with dark clouds.

Heaven help her, she was going to miss the imp and her antics.

# Chapter
## 2

*London, England, 1820*

They'd called him the Dolphin. He'd called her the Brat.
Princess Alesandra didn't know why her guardian's son
Colin had been given the nickname of a sea mammal, but
she was well aware of the reason behind his nickname for
her. She'd earned it. She really had been a brat when she was
a little girl, and the only time Colin and his older brother,
Caine, had been in her company, she'd misbehaved shamefully. Granted, she had been very young—spoiled, too—a
natural circumstance given the fact that she was an only
child and was constantly being doted upon by relatives and
servants alike. But her parents had both been gifted with
patient natures, and they ignored her obnoxious behavior
until she finally outgrew the temper tantrums and learned a
little restraint.

Alesandra had been very young when her parents took her
with them to England for a short visit. She had only a vague
memory of the Duke and Duchess of Williamshire, didn't
remember the daughters at all, and only had a hazy recollec-
tion of the two older sons. Caine and Colin. They were both
giants in her mind, but then she had been very little and they
had both been fully grown men. Her memory had probably
exaggerated their size. She was certain she wouldn't be able
to recognize either brother in a crowd today. She hoped

Colin had forgotten her past behavior as well as the fact that he'd called her a brat. Getting along with Colin would make everything so much easier to endure. The two duties she was about to undertake were going to be difficult, and having a safe haven at the end of each day was really quite imperative.

She had arrived in England on a dreary Monday morning and had immediately been taken to the Duke of Williamshire's country estate. Alesandra hadn't been feeling well, but believed her queasy stomach was due to anxiety. She was quick to recover, for she was welcomed into the family with sincerity and affection. Both the duke and duchess treated her as one of their own. Her awkwardness soon dissipated. She wasn't given special consideration, and was even allowed to speak her own mind every now and again. There was only one argument of substance between Alesandra and her guardian. He and his wife were going to escort her to London and open their town house for the season. Alesandra made over fifteen appointments, but just a few days before they were scheduled to leave for the city, both the duke and duchess became quite ill.

Alesandra wanted to go alone. She insisted she didn't want to be a bother to anyone and suggested that she rent her own town house for the season. The duchess had palpitations over the mere thought, but Alesandra held her ground. She reminded her guardian she was an adult, after all, and she could certainly take care of herself. The duke wouldn't hear of such talk. The debate raged for days. In the end it was decided that Alesandra would take up residence with Caine and his wife, Jade, while she was in London.

Unfortunately, just the day before she was supposed to arrive, both Caine and Jade came down with the same mysterious ailment currently afflicting the duke and duchess and their four daughters.

The only choice left was Colin. If Alesandra hadn't already scheduled so many appointments with her father's associates, she would have stayed in the country until her guardian had recovered. She didn't want to inconvenience

Colin, especially after hearing from his father about the terrible past two years he'd had. She imagined the last thing Colin needed now was chaos. Still, the Duke of Williamshire had been most insistent that she avail herself of his hospitality, and it wouldn't have been polite for her to refuse her guardian's wishes. Besides, living with Colin for a few days might make the request she was going to have to make of him easier.

She arrived on Colin's doorstep a little past the dinner hour. He had already gone out for the evening. Alesandra, her new lady's maid, and two trusted guards crowded into the narrow black and white tiled foyer to present her note from the Duke of Williamshire to the butler, a handsome young man named Flannaghan. The servant couldn't have been more than twenty-five years of age. The surprise of her arrival obviously rattled him, for he kept bowing to her, blushing to the roots of his white-blond hair, and she wasn't at all certain how to ease his discomfort.

"It is such an honor to have a princess in our home," he stammered out. He swallowed hard, then repeated the very same announcement.

"I hope your employer feels the way you do, sir," she replied. "I don't wish to be an inconvenience."

"No, no," Flannaghan blurted out, obviously appalled by the very idea. "You could never be an inconvenience."

"It's good of you to say so, sir."

Flannaghan swallowed hard again. In a worried tone he said, "But Princess Alesandra, I don't believe there's room for all of your staff." The butler's face was burning with embarrassment.

"We'll make do," she assured him with a smile, trying to put him at ease. The poor young man looked ill. "The Duke of Williamshire did insist I bring along my guards, and I couldn't travel anywhere without my new lady's maid. Her name's Valena. The duchess personally chose her for me. Valena has been living in London, you see, but she was born and raised in my father's homeland. Isn't it a wonderful coincidence she applied for the position? Yes, of course it is," she answered before Flannaghan could get a word in.

"Because she's only just been hired, I can't let her go. It wouldn't be at all polite, would it? You do understand. I can see you do."

Flannaghan had lost track of what was being explained to him, but he nodded agreement anyway just to please her. He was finally able to tear his gaze away from the beautiful princess. He bowed to her lady's maid, then ruined his first show of dignified behavior by blurting out, "She's just a child."

"Valena's a year older than I am," Alesandra explained. She turned to the fair-haired woman and spoke to her in a language Flannaghan had never heard before. It sounded a little like French to him, yet he knew it wasn't.

"Do any of your servants speak English?" he asked.

"When they wish to," she answered. She untied the cord at the top of her white fur-lined burgundy cloak. A tall, muscled guard with black hair and a menacing look about him stepped forward to take the garment from her. She thanked the man before turning back to Flannaghan. "I would like to get settled in for the night. The journey here took most of the day, sir, because of the rain, and I'm chilled to the bone. It was horrid outside," she added with a nod. "The rain felt like sleet, didn't it, Raymond?"

"Aye, it did, Princess," the guard agreed in a voice surprisingly gentle.

"We're all really quite exhausted," she told Flannaghan then.

"Of course you're exhausted," Flannaghan agreed. "If you'll follow me, please," he requested. He started up the stairs with the Princess at his side. "There are four chambers on the second level, Princess Alesandra, and three rooms on the floor above for the servants. If your guards will double up . . ."

"Raymond and Stefan will be happy to share quarters," she told him when he didn't continue. "Sir, this is really just a temporary arrangement until Colin's brother and his wife recover from their illness. I'll move in with them as soon as possible."

Flannaghan took hold of Alesandra's elbow to assist her

up the rest of the stairs. He seemed so eager to help that she didn't have the heart to tell him she didn't require his assistance. If it made him happy to treat her like an old woman, she would let him.

They had reached the landing before the servant noticed the guards weren't following. The two men had disappeared toward the back of the house. Alesandra explained that they were looking around the lower level to familiarize themselves with all of the entrances to the house and would come upstairs when they were finished.

"But why would they be interested . . ."

She didn't let him finish. "To make it safe for us, sir."

Flannaghan nodded, though in truth he still didn't have any idea what she was talking about.

"Would you mind taking over my employer's room tonight? The linens were freshly changed this morning and the other chambers aren't ready for company. There's only Cook and me on staff, you see, because of the difficult financial time my employer is suffering through, and I didn't see the need to put linens on the other beds because I didn't know we would . . ."

"You mustn't worry so," she interrupted. "We'll make do, I promise."

"It's good of you to be so understanding. I'll move your things into the larger guest room tomorrow."

"Aren't you forgetting Colin?" she asked. "I would think he'll be irritated to find me in his bed."

Flannaghan imagined just the opposite, and immediately blushed over his own shameful thoughts. He was still a bit shaken, he realized, and surely that was the reason he was acting like a dolt. The surprise of his guests' arrival was not the true cause of his sorry condition, however. No, it was Princess Alesandra. She was the most wonderful woman he'd ever met. Every time he looked at her, he forgot his own thoughts. Her eyes were such a wondrous shade of blue. She had the longest, and surely the darkest, eyelashes he'd ever noticed, too, and her complexion was exquisitely pure. Only a sprinkle of freckles across the bridge of her nose marred her skin, but Flannaghan found that flaw absolutely wonderful.

He cleared his throat in an attempt to unscramble his thoughts. "I'm certain my employer won't mind sleeping in one of the other chambers tonight. There is a good chance he won't even come home until tomorrow morning anyway. He went back to the Emerald Shipping Company to do some paperwork, and he often ends up spending the night there. The time, you see, gets away from him."

After giving her the explanation, Flannaghan began to tug her along the corridor. There were four rooms on the second level. The first door was wide open and both she and Flannaghan paused at the entrance.

"This is the study, Princess," Flannaghan announced. "It's a bit cluttered, but my employer won't allow me to touch anything."

Alesandra smiled. The study was more than cluttered, for there were stacks of paper everywhere. Yet it was still a warm, inviting room. A mahogany desk faced the door. There was a small hearth on the left, a brown leather chair with a matching foot rest on the right, and a beautiful burgundy and brown rug took up the space in between. Books lined the shelves on the walls, and ledgers were stacked high on the wooden file cabinet tucked in the corner.

The study was an extremely masculine room. The scents of brandy and leather filled the air. She found the aroma quite pleasant. She could even imagine herself curled up in front of a roaring fire in her robe and slippers reading the latest financial reports on her holdings.

Flannaghan tugged her along the hall. The second door was to Colin's bedroom. He hurried ahead of her to open it.

"Is your employer in the habit of working such long hours?" Alesandra asked.

"Yes, he is," Flannaghan answered. "He started the company several years ago with his good friend, the Marquess of St. James, and the gentlemen have had a struggle staying afloat. The competition is fierce."

Alesandra nodded. "The Emerald Shipping Company has an excellent reputation."

"It does?"

"Oh, yes. Colin's father wishes he could purchase shares. It would be a sure profit for investors, but the partners won't sell any stock."

"They want to maintain complete control," Flannaghan explained. He grinned then. "I heard him say just that to his father."

She nodded, then walked into the bedroom, dismissing the topic. Flannaghan noticed the chill in the air and hurried over to the hearth to start a fire. Valena skirted her way around her mistress to light the candles on the bedside table.

Colin's bedroom was every bit as masculine and appealing as his study. The bed faced the door. It was quite large in size and was covered with a dark chocolate brown quilt. The walls had been painted a rich beige color, an appropriate backdrop, she thought, for the beautiful pieces of mahogany wood furniture.

Two windows flanked the headboard posters and were draped with beige satin. Valena removed the ties holding the material away from the window panes so the room would be closeted from the street below.

There was a door on Alesandra's left that led into the study, and another door on her right, next to a tall, wooden privacy screen. She walked across the chamber, pulled the door wide, and found an adjoining bedroom. The colors were identical to those of the master suite, though the bed was much smaller in size.

"This is a wonderful house," she remarked. "Colin chose well."

"He doesn't own the property," Flannaghan told her. "His agent got him a good price on the rental. We'll have to move again at the end of the summer, when the owners return from the Americas."

Alesandra tried to hide her smile. She doubted Colin would appreciate his servant giving away all of his financial secrets. Flannaghan was the most enthusiastic servant she'd ever encountered. He was refreshingly honest, and Alesandra liked him immensely.

"I'll move your things into the adjoining room tomor-row," Flannaghan called out when he noticed she was looking into the other chamber. He turned back to the hearth, tossed another log on the budding fire, and then stood up. He brushed his hands on the sides of his pant legs. "These two rooms are the larger bed chambers," he ex-plained. "The other two on this floor are quite small. There's a lock on the door," he added with a nod.

The dark-haired guard named Raymond knocked on the door. Alesandra hurried over to the entrance and listened to his whispered explanation.

"Raymond has just explained that one of the windows in the salon below has a broken latch. He would like your permission to repair it."

"Do you mean now?" Flannaghan asked.

"Yes," she answered. "Raymond's a worrier," she added. "He won't rest until the house is secure."

She didn't wait for the servant's permission but nodded to the guard, giving him her approval. Valena had already unpacked her mistress's sleeping gown and wrapper. Alesandra turned to help just as Valena let out a loud yawn.

"Valena, go and get your sleep. Tomorrow will be time enough to unpack the rest of my things."

The maid bowed low to her mistress. Flannaghan hurried forward. He suggested the maid take the last room along the corridor. It was the smallest of the chambers, he explained, but the bed was quite comfortable and the room was really rather cozy. He was certain Valena would find it suitable. After bidding Alesandra good night, he escorted the maid down the hall to help get her settled.

Alesandra fell asleep a scant thirty minutes later. As was her usual habit, she slept quite soundly for several hours, but promptly at two o'clock in the morning she awakened. She hadn't been able to sleep a full night through since returning to England, and she'd gotten used to the condition. She put on her robe, added another log to the fire, and then got back into bed with her satchel of papers. She would read her broker's report on the current financial status of Lloyd's of

London first, and if that didn't make her sleepy, she'd make a new chart of her own holdings.

A loud commotion coming from below the stairs interrupted her concentration. She recognized Flannaghan's voice and assumed from the frantic edge to his tone that he was trying to soothe his employer's temper.

Curiosity got the better of her. Alesandra put on her slippers, tightened the belt around her robe, and went to the landing. She stood in the darkness of the shadows, but the foyer below her was ablaze with candlelight. She let out a little sigh when she saw how Raymond and Stefan were blocking Colin's way. He was turned away from her, but Raymond happened to look up and spot her. She immediately motioned for him to leave. He nudged his companion back to his station, bowed to Colin, and then left the foyer.

Flannaghan didn't notice the guards' departure. He didn't notice Alesandra either. He never would have gone on and on if he'd known she was standing there listening to his every word.

"She's just what I imagined a real princess would be," he told his employer, his voice reeking with grating enthusiasm. "She has hair the color of midnight, and it's full of soft curls that seem to float around her shoulders. Her eyes are blue, but a shade of blue I've never seen before. They're so brilliant and clear. And you're certain to tower over her. Why even I find myself feeling like a giant, a bumbling one at that, when she's looking directly up at me. She has freckles, milord." Flannaghan paused long enough to take a breath. "She's really wonderful."

Colin wasn't paying much attention to the servant's remarks about the princess. He had been about to put his fist into one of the strangers blocking his way and then toss both men back into the street when Flannaghan had come running down the stairs to explain that the men came from the Duke of Williamshire. Colin had let go of the bigger of the two men and was now once again sorting through the stack of papers in his hands, looking for the report his partner had completed. He hoped to God he hadn't left the thing at the office, for he was determined to transfer the numbers into the ledgers before he went to bed.

Colin was in a foul mood. He was actually a little disappointed that his butler had interfered. A good fistfight might have helped him get rid of some of his frustration.

He finally found the missing sheet just as Flannaghan started in again.

"Princess Alesandra is on the thin side, yet I couldn't help but notice how shapely her figure is."

"Enough," Colin ordered, his voice soft, yet commanding.

The servant immediately stopped his litany of Princess Alesandra's considerable attributes. His disappointment was apparent in his crestfallen expression. He'd only just warmed to his topic and knew he could have gone on and on for at least another twenty minutes. Why, he hadn't even mentioned her smile yet, or the regal way she held herself. . . .

"All right, Flannaghan," Colin began, interrupting his servant's thoughts. "Let's try to get to the bottom of this. A princess just decided to take up residence with us? Is that correct?"

"Yes, milord."

"Why?"

"Why what, milord?"

Colin sighed. "Why do you suppose . . ."

"It isn't my place to suppose," Flannaghan interrupted.

"When has that ever stopped you?"

Flannaghan grinned. He acted as though he'd just been given a compliment.

Colin yawned. Lord, he was tired. He wasn't in the mood to put up with company tonight. He was exhausted from too many long hours working on the company books, frustrated because he couldn't make the damn numbers add up to enough of a profit and extremely weary fighting all the competition. It seemed to him that every other day a new shipping company opened its doors for business.

Added to his financial worries were his own aches and

pains. His left leg, injured in a sea mishap several years ago, was throbbing painfully now, and all he wanted to do was get into his bed with a hot brandy.

He wasn't going to give in to his fatigue. There was still work to be done before he went to bed. He tossed Flannaghan his cloak, placed his cane in the umbrella stand, and put the papers he'd been carrying on the side table.

"Milord, would you like me to fetch you something to drink?"

"I'll have a brandy in the study," he replied. "Why are you calling me your lord? You've been given permission to call me Colin."

"But that was before."

"Before what?"

"Before we had a real princess living with us," Flannaghan explained. "It wouldn't be proper for me to call you Colin now. Would you prefer I call you Sir Hallbrook?" he asked, using Colin's knighted title.

"I would prefer Colin."

"But I have explained, milord, it simply won't do."

Colin laughed. Flannaghan had sounded pompous. He was acting more and more like his brother's butler, Sterns, and Colin really shouldn't have been at all surprised. Sterns was Flannaghan's uncle and had installed the young man in Colin's household to begin his seasoning.

"You're becoming as arrogant as your uncle," Colin remarked.

"It's good of you to say so, milord."

Colin laughed again. Then he shook his head at his servant. "Let's get back to the princess, shall we? Why is she here?"

"She didn't confide in me," Flannaghan explained. "And I thought it would be improper for me to ask."

"So you just let her in?"

"She arrived with a note from your father."

They had finally gotten to the end of the maze. "Where is this note?"

"I put it in the salon . . . or was it the dining room?"

"Go and find the thing," Colin ordered. "Perhaps his note will explain why the woman has two thugs with her."

"They're her guards, milord," Flannaghan explained, his tone defensive. "Your father sent them with her," he added with a nod. "And a princess would not travel with thugs."

The expression on Flannaghan's face was almost comical in his awe of the woman. The princess had certainly dazzled the impressionable servant.

The butler went running into the salon in search of the note. Colin blew out the candles on the table, picked up his papers, and then turned to the steps.

He finally understood the reason for Princess Alesandra's arrival. His father was behind the scheme of course. His matchmaking attempts were becoming more outrageous, and Colin wasn't in the mood to put up with yet another one of his games.

He was halfway up the steps before he spotted her. The banister saved him from disgrace. Colin was certain he would have fallen backward if he hadn't had a firm grasp on the railing.

Flannaghan hadn't exaggerated. She did look like a princess. A beautiful one. Her hair floated around her shoulders and it really did look as dark as midnight. She was dressed in white, and, Lord, at first sight, she appeared to be a vision the gods had sent to test his determination.

He failed the test. Although he gave it his best effort, he was still powerless to control his own physical reaction to her.

His father had certainly outdone himself this time. Colin would have to remember to compliment him on his latest choice—after he'd sent her packing, of course.

They stood staring at each other for a long minute. She kept waiting for him to speak to her. He kept waiting for her to explain her presence to him.

Alesandra was the first to give in. She moved forward until she stood close to the top step, bowed her head, and then said, "Good evening, Colin. It's good to see you again."

Her voice was wonderfully appealing. Colin tried to

concentrate on what she had just said. It was ridiculously difficult.

"Again?" he asked. Lord, he sounded gruff.

"Yes, we met when I was just a little girl. You called me a brat."

That remark forced a reluctant smile from him. He had no memory of the encounter, however. "And were you a brat?"

"Oh, yes," she answered. "I'm told I kicked you—several times, in fact—but that was a very long time ago. I've grown up since then and I don't believe the nickname is appropriate now. I haven't kicked anyone in years."

Colin leaned against the banister so that he could take some of the weight off his injured leg. "Where did we meet?"

"At your father's home in the country," she explained. "My parents and I were visiting and you were home from Oxford at the time. Your brother had just graduated."

Colin still didn't remember her. That didn't surprise him. His parents were always entertaining houseguests and he'd barely paid any attention to any of them. Most, he recalled, were down on their luck, and his father, kindhearted to a fault, took anyone begging assistance into his home.

Her hands were demurely folded together and she appeared to be very relaxed. Yet Colin noticed how white her fingers were and knew she was actually gripping them together in either fear or nervousness. She wasn't quite as serene as she would have him believe. Her vulnerability was suddenly very apparent to him, and he found himself trying to find a way to put her at ease.

"Where are your parents now?" he asked.

"My father died when I was eleven years old," she answered. "Mother died the following summer. Sir, would you like me to help you collect your papers?" she added in a rush, hoping to change the subject.

"What papers?"

Her smile was enchanting. "The ones you dropped."

He looked down and saw his papers lining the steps. He felt like a complete idiot standing there with his hand grasping air. He grinned over his own preoccupation. He really wasn't any better than his butler, he thought to himself, and Flannaghan had an acceptable excuse for his besotted behavior. He was young, inexperienced, and simply didn't know better.

Colin should have known better, however. He was much older than his servant, in both years and experience. But he was overly weary tonight, he reminded himself, and surely that was the reason he was acting like a simpleton.

Besides, she was one hell of a beauty. He let out a sigh. "I'll get the papers later," he told her. "Exactly why are you here, Princess Alesandra?" he asked bluntly.

"Your brother and his wife are both ill," she explained. "I was to stay with them while in the city, but at the last minute they became indisposed and I was told to stay with you until they are feeling better."

"Who gave you these instructions?"

"Your father."

"Why would he take such an interest?"

"He's my guardian, Colin."

He couldn't contain his surprise over that little bit of news. His father had never mentioned a ward to him, although Colin guessed it wasn't any of his affair. His father held his own counsel and rarely confided in either one of his sons.

"Have you come to London for the season?"

"No," she answered. "Although I am looking forward to attending some of the parties and I do hope to see the sights."

Colin's curiosity intensified. He took another step toward her.

"I really didn't want to cause you any inconvenience," she said. "I suggested I rent my own town house or open your parents' London home, but your father simply wouldn't hear of it. He told me it wasn't done." She paused to sigh. "I did try to convince him. 'Tis the truth I couldn't outargue him."

Lord, she had a pretty smile. It was contagious too. He

found himself smiling back. "No one can outargue my father," he agreed. "You still haven't explained why you're here," he reminded her.

"I haven't, have I? It's most complicated," she added with a nod. "You see, it wasn't necessary for me to come to London before, but it is now."

He shook his head at her. "Half-given explanations make me crazed. I'm blunt to a fault—a trait I picked up from my partner, or so I'm told. I admire complete honesty because it's so rare, and for as long as you are a guest in my home, I would appreciate complete candor. Are we in agreement?"

"Yes, of course."

She was clutching her hands together again. He must have frightened her. He probably sounded like an ogre. God only knew he was suddenly feeling like one. He was sorry she was so obviously afraid of him, yet pleased, too, because he'd gotten his way. She hadn't argued with him over his dictate, or tried to act coy. He absolutely detested coyness in a woman.

He forced a mild tone of voice when he asked, "Would you mind answering a few pertinent questions now?"

"Certainly. What is it you wish to know?"

"Why are there two guards with you? Now that you've reached your destination, shouldn't they be dismissed? Or did you think I might withhold my hospitality?"

She answered the last of his question first. "Oh, I never considered you would deny me lodging, sir. Your father assured me you would be most gracious to me. Flannaghan has his note for you to read," she added with a nod. "Your father also insisted I retain my guards. Both Raymond and Stefan were hired by the mother superior of the convent where I used to live to travel with me to England, and your father insisted I keep them on. Neither guard has family back home to miss, and both are very well paid. You really shouldn't worry about them."

He held his exasperation. She was looking so earnest now. "I wasn't worried about them," he replied. He grinned then and shook his head again. "Do you know, trying to get answers out of you is proving to be very difficult."

26

She nodded. "Mother Superior used to say the very same thing to me. She considered it one of my greatest flaws. I am sorry if I confuse you. I don't mean to, sir."

"Alesandra, my father's behind this scheme, isn't he? He sent you to me."

"Yes and no."

She quickly held up her hand to waylay his frown. "I'm not hedging. You're father did send me to you, but only after he found out Caine and his wife were ill. I don't believe there was a scheme involved, however. As a matter of fact, your father and your mother wanted me to stay in the country until they were recovered enough to escort me to the city. I would have, too, if I hadn't made all of my appointments."

She sounded sincere. Colin still scoffed at the notion that his father wasn't behind this plan. He'd seen him at the club only a week before and he'd been perfectly healthy then. Colin remembered the inevitable argument too. His father had oh so casually brought up the topic of marriage, then become relentless as he once again nagged Colin about taking a wife. Colin had pretended to listen, and once his father had wound down, he told him he was determined to remain alone.

Alesandra didn't have any idea what was going through Colin's mind. His frown was making her nervous, however. He certainly seemed to be a suspicious sort. He was a handsome man, she thought to herself, with rich, auburn-colored hair and more green- than hazel-colored eyes. They had fairly sparkled when he smiled. He had an adorable little dimple, too, in the left side of his cheek. But, heavens, his frown was fierce. He was even more intimidating than the mother superior, and Alesandra considered that an impressive feat.

She couldn't stand the silence long. "Your father planned to speak to you about my unusual circumstances," she whispered. "He was going to be very straightforward about the matter."

"When it comes to my father and his plans, nothing's ever straightforward."

She arched her shoulders back and frowned at him. "Your father is one of the most honorable men I've ever had the pleasure to know. He's been extremely kind to me, and he only has my best interests at heart."

She was sounding incensed by the time she finished her defense of his father. Colin grinned. "You don't have to defend him to me. I know my father's honorable. It's one of the hundred or so reasons why I love him."

Her stance relaxed. "You're very fortunate to have such a fine man for a father."

"Were you as fortunate?"

"Oh, yes," she answered. "My father was a wonderful man."

She started backing away when Colin came up the rest of the steps. She bumped into the wall, then turned and slowly walked down the hall to her room.

Colin clasped his hands behind his back and fell into step beside her. Flannaghan was right, he thought to himself. He did tower over Alesandra. Perhaps his size intimidated her.

"You don't have to be afraid of me."

She came to a quick stop and turned to look up at him. "Afraid? Why in heaven's name would you think I was afraid of you?"

She'd sounded incredulous. Colin shrugged. "You backed away rather hastily when I reached the landing," he pointed out. He didn't mention the fear he'd glimpsed in her eyes or the fact that she'd been wringing her hands together. If she wanted to pretend she wasn't afraid, he'd let her have her way.

"Well, I'm not very afraid," she announced. "I'm not used to . . . visiting while in my nightgown and wrapper. In fact, Colin, I'm feeling quite safe here. It's a nice feeling. I have been a little jumpy lately."

She blushed, acting as though her confession was embarrassing her.

"Why have you been jumpy?" he asked.

Instead of answering his question, she turned the topic. "Would you like to know why I've come to London?"

He almost laughed then and there. Hadn't he been

diligently trying to find out just that for the past ten minutes? "If you want to tell me," he said.

"I really have two reasons for my journey," she began. "They're both equally important to me. The first involves a mystery I'm determined to solve. I met a young lady by the name of Victoria Perry over a year ago. She stayed at the Holy Cross convent for a spell. She was touring Austria with her family, you see, and she became quite ill. The sisters at Holy Cross are well known for their nursing skills, and once it was determined that Victoria would recover, her family felt it safe to leave her there to recuperate. She and I became fast friends, and after she returned to England, she wrote to me at least once a month, sometimes more. I do wish I'd saved the letters, because in two or three of them she made references to a secret admirer who was courting her. She thought it was all very romantic."

"Perry . . . where have I heard that name?" Colin wondered aloud.

"I don't know, sir."

He smiled. "I shouldn't have interrupted you. Please continue."

She nodded. "The last letter I received was dated the first of September. I immediately wrote back, but I didn't hear another word. I was concerned, of course. When I reached your father's home, I told him I was going to send a messenger to Victoria to request an audience. I wanted to catch up on all the latest happenings. Victoria led such an exciting life and I so enjoyed her correspondence."

"And did you get your audience?"

"No," Alesandra answered. She stopped and turned to look up at Colin. "Your father told me about the scandal. Victoria was supposed to have run off with a man from a lower station. They were married in Gretna Green. Can you imagine such a tale? Her family certainly believes it. Your father told me they've disowned her."

"Now I remember. I did hear about the scandal."

"None of it's true."

He raised an eyebrow over the vehemence in her voice. "It isn't?" he asked.

"No, it isn't," she said. "I'm a good judge of character, Colin, and I assure you Victoria wouldn't have eloped. She simply isn't the sort. I'm going to find out what really happened to her. She may be in trouble and need my help," she added. "Tomorrow I shall send a note to her brother, Neil, begging an audience."

"I don't think the family will want their daughter's embarrassment drudged up again."

"I shall be most discreet."

Her voice reeked with sincerity. She was a dramatic thing, and so damned beautiful it was difficult to pay attention to anything she said. Her eyes mesmerized him. He happened to notice she had her hand on the doorknob to his room. He was further distracted by her wonderful scent. The faint smell of roses floated in the air between them. Colin immediately took a step back to put some distance between them.

"Do you mind that I'm sleeping in your bed?"

"I didn't know you were."

"Flannaghan's going to move my things into the adjoining chamber tomorrow. He didn't think you would be coming home tonight. It's just for one night, sir, but now that he's had time to put linens on the bed next door, I'll be happy to give you your bed back."

"We'll change in the morning."

"You're being very kind to me. Thank you."

Colin finally noticed the dark smudges under her eyes. The woman was clearly exhausted and he'd kept her from her sleep by grilling her.

"You need your rest, Alesandra. It's the middle of the night."

She nodded, then opened the door to his bedroom. "Good night, Colin. Thank you again for being so hospitable."

"I couldn't turn my back on a princess when she's down on her luck," he said.

"I beg your pardon?" She didn't have the faintest idea what he meant by that remark. Where had he gotten the idea she was down on her luck?

"Alesandra, what was the other reason for coming to London?"

She looked confused by the question. The second reason must not have been very important, he decided. "I was merely curious," he admitted with a shrug. "You mentioned you had two reasons and I wondered . . . never mind. Go to bed now. I'll see you in the morning. Sleep well, Princess."

"I remember the reason now," she blurted out.

He turned back to her. "Yes?"

"Would you like me to tell you?"

"Yes, I would."

She stared up at him a long minute. Her hesitation was obvious. So was her vulnerability. "Do you want me to be honest with you?"

He nodded. "Of course I do."

"Very well then. I'll be honest. Your father suggested I not confide in you, but since you have insisted upon knowing and I did promise I would be honest . . ."

"Yes?" he prodded.

"I've come to London to marry you."

*He was suddenly hungry again. It was peculiar to him the way the craving burst upon him all at once. There was never any warning. He hadn't thought about a hunt in a long, long while, and now, at the midnight hour, while he was standing in the doorway of Sir Johnston's library listening to the latest gossip about the prince regent, sipping his brandy with several other titled gentlemen of the ton, he was nearly overwhelmed with his need.*

*He could feel the power draining away from him. His eyes burned. His stomach ached. He was empty, empty, empty.*

*He needed to feed again.*

# Chapter
# 3

Alesandra didn't get much sleep the rest of the night. The expression on Colin's face when she had blurted out her second reason for coming to London had made her breath catch in the back of her throat. Lord, he'd been furious. No matter how hard she tried, she couldn't seem to block the image of his anger long enough to fall back to sleep.

So much for honesty, she thought to herself. Telling the truth hadn't served her well at all. She should have kept silent. Alesandra let out a loud sigh. No, she had to tell the truth. Mother Superior had drummed that fact into her.

Her thoughts immediately returned to Colin's expression of fury. How could a man with such an adorable dimple in his cheek have eyes so frigid? Colin could be dangerous when he was riled. She really wished his papa had mentioned that important fact to her before she had embarrassed herself so thoroughly and infuriated Colin so completely.

She dreaded her next encounter with him. She took her time getting dressed. Valena assisted her. The maid kept up a constant chatter while she brushed Alesandra's hair. She wished to know all the details of her princess's day. Was she going out? Would she wish her maid to accompany her? Alesandra answered her questions as best she could.

"We may have to find another lodging after today," she remarked. "I shall share my plans with you as soon as I've formulated them, Valena."

The maid finished buttoning the back of Alesandra's royal blue walking dress just as a knock sounded at the door.

Flannaghan requested the princess join his employer in the salon as soon as possible.

Alesandra didn't think it would be a good idea to keep him waiting. There wasn't time to braid her hair, and she didn't want the bother anyway. She didn't have a lady's maid while living at the convent and found the formality a nuisance. She had learned to do for herself.

She dismissed Valena, told Flannaghan she would be downstairs in just a moment, and then hurried over to her valise. She pulled out the notecard her guardian had given her, brushed her hair back over her shoulders, and then left the room.

She was ready to take on the dragon. Colin was waiting for her in the salon. He stood in front of the hearth, facing the door, with his hands clasped behind his back. She was relieved to notice he wasn't scowling. He looked only mildly irritated with her now.

She stood in the entrance, waiting for him to invite her to join him. He didn't say a word for a long while. He simply stood there staring at her. She thought he might be trying to get his thoughts under control. Or his temper. She could feel herself blushing over his close scrutiny, then realized she was being just as rude scrutinizing him.

He was a difficult man not to notice. He was so attractive. He had a hard, fit body. He was dressed in fawn-colored riding buckskins, polished brown high boots, and a sparkling white shirt. His personality came through in the way he wore his apparel, she decided, because Colin had left the top button of his shirt undone, and he wasn't wearing one of those awful starched cravats. He was obviously a bit of a rebel who lived in a society of conservatives. His hair wasn't at all fashionable. It was quite long—shoulder length at least, she guessed—although she couldn't tell the exact

Julie Garwood

length because he had it secured behind his neck with a leather thong. Colin was definitely an independent man. He was tall, muscular in both shoulders and thighs, and he reminded Alesandra of one of those fierce-looking frontiersmen she'd seen charcoal sketches of in the dailies. Colin was wonderfully handsome, yes, but weathered-looking too. What saved him from being unapproachable, she decided, was the warmth of his smile when he was amused.

He wasn't amused now.

"Come in and sit down, Alesandra. We have to talk."

"Certainly," she immediately replied.

Flannaghan suddenly appeared at her side. He took hold of her elbow to assist her across the room. "That isn't necessary," Colin called out. "Alesandra can walk without assistance."

"But she's a princess," Flannaghan reminded his employer. "We must show her every courtesy."

Colin's glare told the butler to cease his comments. Flannaghan reluctantly let go of Alesandra.

He looked crushed. Alesandra immediately tried to soothe his injured feelings. "You're a very thoughtful man, Flannaghan," she praised.

The butler immediately latched on to her elbow again. She let him guide her over to the brocaded settee. Once she was seated, Flannaghan knelt down and tried to smooth her skirts for her. She wouldn't allow his help.

"Is there anything more you require, Princess?" he asked. "Cook will have your breakfast ready in just a few more minutes," he added with a nod. "Would you care for a cup of chocolate while you wait?"

"No, thank you," she replied. "I do need a pen and inkwell," she added. "Would you be kind enough to fetch them for me?"

Flannaghan ran out of the salon to see to the errand.

"I'm surprised he didn't genuflect," Colin drawled out.

His jest made her smile. "You're fortunate to have such a kindhearted servant, Colin."

He didn't reply. Flannaghan came rushing back inside with the items she requested. He placed the pen and inkwell on a narrow side table, then picked up the table and carried it over to her.

She thanked him, of course, and that bit of praise made him blush with pleasure.

"Close the doors behind you, Flannaghan," Colin ordered. "I don't want to be interrupted."

He was sounding irritated again. Alesandra let out a little sigh. Colin wasn't a very accommodating man.

She turned her full attention to her host. "I've upset you. I really am sorry . . ."

He wouldn't let her finish her apology. "You haven't upset me," he snapped.

She would have laughed if she'd been alone. The man was upset, and that was that. His jaw was clenched, and if that wasn't a giveaway to his true feelings, she didn't know what was.

"I see," she agreed just to placate him.

"However," he began in a clipped, no-nonsense tone of voice, "I believe we should settle a few pertinent issues here and now. Why in heaven's name did you think I would marry you?"

"Your father said you would."

He didn't even try to hide his exasperation. "I'm a grown man, Alesandra. I make my own decisions."

"Yes, of course you're a grown man," she agreed. "But you'll always be his son, Colin. It's your duty to do whatever he wants you to do. Sons must obey their fathers, no matter how old they are."

"That's ridiculous."

She lifted her shoulders in a dainty shrug. Colin held on to his patience. "I don't know what kind of bargain you struck with my father, and I'm sorry if he made promises on my behalf, but I want you to understand I have no intention of marrying you."

She lowered her gaze to the notecard she held in her hands. "All right," she agreed.

Her quick agreement, given in such a casual tone of voice, made him suspicious. "You aren't angry over my refusal?"

"No, of course not."

She glanced up and smiled. Colin looked confused. "I'm disappointed," she admitted. "But certainly not angry. I barely know you. It would be unreasonable for me to be angry."

"Exactly," he agreed with a quick nod. "You don't know me. Why would you wish to marry me if you . . ."

"I believe I've already explained, sir. Your father instructed me to marry you."

"Alesandra, I want you to understand . . ."

She wouldn't let him finish. "I accept your decision, sir."

He smiled in spite of himself. Princess Alesandra looked so forlorn.

"You won't have any trouble finding someone suitable. You're a very beautiful woman, Princess."

She shrugged. She was obviously unaffected by his compliment.

"I imagine it was difficult for you to ask me," he began then.

She straightened her shoulders. "I didn't ask," she announced. "I simply explained to you what your father's primary objective was."

"His primary objective?"

He sounded as though he was laughing at her. She could feel herself blushing with embarrassment. "Do not mock me, sir. This discussion is difficult enough without having you ridicule me."

Colin shook his head. His voice was gentle when he spoke again. "I wasn't mocking you," he said. "I realize this is difficult for you. I hold my father responsible for both your discomfort and mine. He will not give up on trying to find a wife for me."

"He suggested I not say anything at all about marriage to you. He said you tend to develop a rash whenever that word is used in your presence. He wanted me to give you time to get to know me before he explained what he wanted. He thought . . . you might learn to like me."

"Look, I already like you," he said. "But I'm not in a position to marry anyone right now. In five years, according to my schedule, I'll be in a strong financial position and will be able to take a wife."

"Mother Superior would like you, Colin," Alesandra announced. "She loves schedules. She believes life would be chaotic without them."

"How long did you live in this convent?" he asked, anxious to turn the topic away from marriage.

"Quite a while," she answered. "Colin, I'm sorry, but I can't wait for you. I really must get married right away. It's unfortunate," she added with a sigh. "I believe you would make an acceptable husband."

"And how would you know that?"

"Your father told me so."

He did laugh then. He couldn't help himself. Lord, she was an innocent. He noticed she was clutching the notecard in her hands then and immediately forced himself to stop. She was already embarrassed. His laughter was only adding to her discomfort.

"I'll talk to my father and save you that ordeal," he promised. "I know he put these ideas into your head. He can be very convincing, can't he?"

She didn't answer him. She kept her gaze on her lap. Colin suddenly felt like a cad because he had disappointed her. Hell, he thought to himself. He wasn't making any sense.

"Alesandra, this bargain you made with my father surely involved a profit. How much was it?"

He let out a low whistle after she told him the exact amount. He leaned back against the mantel and shook his head. He was furious with his father now. "Well, by God, you aren't going to be disappointed. If he promised you a near fortune, then he's going to pay. You kept your part of the bargain . . ."

She raised one hand for silence, unconsciously mimicking the mother superior's behavior.

Colin obeyed without even realizing it. "You misunderstand, sir. Your father didn't promise me anything. I promised him. He wouldn't accept my bargain, however, and was in fact appalled I even suggested paying for a husband."

Colin laughed again. He was certain she was jesting with him.

"This isn't at all humorous, Colin. I must get married in three weeks' time, and your father is simply helping me. He's my guardian, after all."

Colin needed to sit down. He walked over to the leather chair facing the settee and sprawled out.

"You're going to get married in three weeks?"

"Yes," she replied. "And that is why I asked your father's assistance."

"Alesandra . . ."

She waved the notecard in the air. "I asked for assistance in preparing a list."

"A list of what?"

"Suitable candidates."

"And?" he prodded.

"He told me to marry you."

Colin leaned forward, braced his elbows on his knees, and frowned at her. "Listen carefully," he ordered. "I'm not marrying you."

She immediately reached for the pen. She dipped it into the inkwell, then drew a line across the top of her notecard.

"What did you just do?"

"I crossed you off."

"Off what?"

She looked exasperated. "My list. Do you happen to know the Earl of Templeton?"

"Yes."

"Is he a good man?"

"Hell, no," he muttered. "He's a rake. He used his sister's dowry to pay off a few of his gambling debts, but he still haunts the tables every night."

Alesandra immediately dipped the pen into the inkwell again and scratched through the second name on her list. "It's peculiar your father didn't know about the earl's gambling vice."

"Father doesn't go to the clubs anymore."

"That would explain it," she replied. "Heavens, this is turning out to be more difficult than I anticipated."

"Alesandra, why are you in such a hurry to get married?"

Her pen was poised in the air. "I beg your pardon?" she asked, her concentration directed on her notecard.

He repeated his question. "You told me you had to get married in three weeks' time. I wondered why."

"The church," she explained with a quick nod. "Colin, do you know the Marquess of Townsend perchance? Does *he* have any horrible vices?"

His patience was gone. "Put the list down, Alesandra, and start answering my questions. What in God's name does the church have to do with . . ."

She interrupted him. "Your mother already reserved it. She made all the other arrangements, too. She's the most wonderful lady, and heavens, she's so organized. It's going to be a beautiful wedding. I do hope you can attend. I've decided against a large wedding, much to your parents' frustration, and settled instead on small and intimate."

Colin wondered if his father realized his ward was out of her mind. "Let me get this straight," he began. "You've taken care of all the arrangements without a man to . . ."

"I can't take the credit," she interrupted. "As I just explained, your mother did all the work."

"Aren't you approaching this from the wrong angle? It's usual to find a groom first, Alesandra."

"I agree with you, but this isn't a usual circumstance. I simply must get married right away."

"Why?"

"Please don't think me rude, but since you've decided against marrying me, I think it's best you not know anything more. I would still appreciate your help, however, if you're inclined to give it."

Colin didn't have any intention of letting the matter drop. He would find out the real reason why she needed to get married, and he'd find out before the day was over. He decided to use a little trickery now and ease back to his question later.

"I would be happy to assist you," he said. "What is it you need?"

"Would you please give me the names of five—no, make

that six—suitable men? I'll interview them this week. By Monday next, I should have settled on someone."

God, she was exasperating. "What are your requirements?" he inquired mildly.

"First, he must be honorable," she began. "Second, he must be titled. My father would twist in his grave if I married a commoner."

"I'm not titled," he reminded her.

"You were knighted. That qualifies."

He laughed. "You've left out the most important requirement, haven't you? He'll have to be wealthy."

She frowned at him. "I believe you've just insulted me," she announced. "Still, you don't know me at all well and for that reason I'll forgive you your cynicism."

"Alesandra, most women looking for husbands want to live a comfortable life," he countered.

"Rich isn't important to me," she replied. "You're as poor as a serf and I was willing to marry you, remember?"

He chafed over her bit of honesty. "How would you know if I'm rich or poor?"

"Your father told me. Do you know, Colin, when you frown, you remind me of a dragon. I used to call Sister Mary Felicity a dragon, though I was too cowardly to say it to her face. Your frown is every bit as fierce, and I do believe the nickname is more appropriate for you."

Colin refused to let her bait him. He wasn't going to let her switch topics either. "What else do you require in a husband?"

"He'll have to leave me alone," she replied after a moment's consideration. "I don't want a man who . . . hovers."

He laughed again. He immediately regretted that action when he saw her expression. Hell, he'd hurt her feelings. Her eyes got all teary, too.

"I don't particularly want a wife who would hover either," he admitted, thinking his agreement would ease her hurt.

She wouldn't look at him. "Would a rich woman appeal to you?" she asked.

"No," he answered. "I determined a long time ago to make my own fortune without any outside help, and I mean to keep that promise to myself. My brother has offered to lend my partner and me funds and of course my father has also offered to help."

"But you refused them," she countered. "Your father believes you're too independent."

Colin decided to change the subject. "Will your husband share your bed?"

She refused to answer him. She lifted her pen again. "Begin your list, please."

"No."

"But you said you would help me."

"That was before I realized you were out of your mind."

She put the pen back on the table and stood up. "Please excuse me."

"Where are you going?"

"To pack."

He chased her to the door. He took hold of her arm and turned her around to face him. Damn, he really had upset her. He hated to see the tears in her eyes, especially since he knew he was the cause of her distress.

"You're going to stay here until I decide what to do with you," he said, his voice gruff.

"I decide my future, Colin, not you. Let go of me. I won't stay where I'm not wanted."

"You're staying here."

He added a glare to his order so she would back down. It didn't work. She wouldn't be intimidated. In truth, she glared back. "You don't want me, remember?" she challenged.

He smiled. "Oh, I want you all right. I'm just not willing to marry you. I'm being completely honest with you and I can see from your blush I've embarrassed you. You're too damn young and innocent for this ridiculous game you've taken on. Let my father . . ."

"Your father is too ill to help me," she interrupted. She jerked her arm away from his hold. "But there are others who will come to my aid. You needn't be concerned."

He couldn't explain why he felt insulted, but he did. "Since my father is too ill to see to his duty of looking out for you, the task falls on my shoulders."

"No, it doesn't," she argued. "Your brother, Caine, will act as my guardian. He's next in line."

"But Caine's conveniently ill too, isn't he?"

"I don't believe there is anything convenient about his illness, Colin."

He didn't argue the point with her, and in fact pretended he hadn't heard her. "And as your guardian during this period of family illness, I will decide where you go and when. Don't give me that defiant look, young lady," he ordered. "I always get my way. By nightfall I'll know why you think you have to get married so quickly."

She shook her head. He grabbed hold of her chin and held her steady. "God, but you're stubborn." He tweaked her nose, then let go of her. "I'll be back in a few hours. Stay put, Alesandra. If you leave, I'll come after you."

Raymond and Stefan were both waiting in the foyer. Colin walked past the two guards, then stopped. "Don't let her leave," he ordered.

Raymond immediately nodded. Alesandra's eyes widened. "They're my guards, Colin," she called out. Damn, he'd treated her like a child when he'd tweaked her nose and talked so condescendingly to her, and now she was behaving like one.

"Yes, they are your guards," Colin agreed. He opened the front door, then turned back to her. "But they answer to me. Isn't that right, boys?"

Both Raymond and Stefan immediately nodded. She was a bit piqued, and almost blurted out her opinion of his high-handed methods.

*Dignity* and *decorum*. The words echoed in her mind. She could feel the mother superior standing behind her, looking over her shoulder. It was a ridiculous feeling, of course, for the nun was an ocean away. Still, her lectures had taken root. Alesandra forced a serene expression and simply nodded agreement.

"Will you be gone long, Colin?" she inquired, her voice quite calm.

He thought she sounded hoarse. She looked like she wanted to shout at him. Colin smiled. "Probably," he answered. "Will you miss me?"

She matched his smile. "Probably not."

The door closed on his laughter.

# Chapter
## 4

She didn't miss him at all. Colin didn't come home until well after the dinner hour. Alesandra was thankful he stayed away because she didn't want his interference, and the man certainly did seem to interfere.

She was kept busy with her appointments. She spent the remainder of the morning and all afternoon entertaining her father's old friends. They called, one after another, to pay their respects and to offer her assistance while she was in London. Most of the visitors were titled members of the ton, but there were also artists and laborers as well. Alesandra's father had had a wide range of friends. He had been an excellent judge of character, a trait she believed she had inherited, and she found she liked every one of his friends.

Matthew Andrew Dreyson was her last appointment. The elderly, potbellied man had been her father's trusted agent in England, and he still handled some of Alesandra's assets. Dreyson had held the coveted position of subscriber on the rolls of Lloyd's of London for over twenty-three years. His standards as a broker were of the very highest. He wasn't just ethical; he was also clever. Alesandra's father had instructed his wife, who in turn had instructed his daughter, that in the event of his death Dreyson should be leaned upon for financial advice.

Alesandra invited him to stay for dinner. Flannaghan and Valena served the meal. The lady's maid did most of the work, however, as Flannaghan was busy listening to the financial discussion at the table. He was astonished that a woman would have extensive knowledge of the marketplace, and made a mental note to tell his employer what he had overheard.

Dreyson spent a good two hours going over various recommendations. Alesandra added one of her own, then completed her transactions. The broker used only her initials when placing his slips before the underwriters at Lloyd's, because it was simply unthinkable for a woman to invest in any venture. Even Dreyson would have been appalled if he'd known the suggestions she gave him actually came from her, but she understood the man's prejudice against women. She'd gotten around that obstacle by inventing an old friend of the family she called her Uncle Albert. She told Dreyson the man wasn't really related to her, but she held such great affection for him she'd begun to think of him as her relative years ago. To ensure Dreyson wouldn't try to investigate the man, she added the mention that Albert had been a close personal friend of her father's.

Dreyson's curiosity had been appeased by her explanation. He didn't have any qualms about taking stock orders from a man, although he did comment more than once how odd it was that Albert allowed her to sign her initials as his ambassador. He wanted to meet her adviser and honorary relative, but Alesandra quickly explained that Albert was a recluse these days and wouldn't allow company. Since he'd moved to England, he found visitors a distraction to his peaceful daily routine, she lied. Because Dreyson was making a handsome commission on each order he placed with the underwriters, and because Uncle Albert's advice to date had been quite on the mark, he didn't argue with the princess. If Albert didn't wish to meet him, so be it. The last thing he wanted to do was alienate his client. Albert, he decided, was simply eccentric.

After dinner they returned to the salon, where Flannaghan served Dreyson a glass of port. Alesandra sat on the settee across from her guest and listened to several amusing stories about the subscribers who haunted the floors of the Royal Exchange. She would have loved to see for herself the gleaming hardwood floors cluttered with wooden stalls they called boxes where the underwriters conducted their business. Dreyson told her about a quaint custom that had begun way back in 1710, referred to as the Caller in the Room. A waiter, he explained, known as the Kidney, would step up into what looked very like a pulpit and read the newspapers in a loud, clear voice while the audience of gentlemen sat at their tables and sipped their drinks. Alesandra had to be content to picture the events in her mind, however, as women were not allowed in the Royal Exchange.

Colin came home just as Dreyson was finishing his drink. He tossed his cloak in Flannaghan's direction, then strode into the salon. He came to a quick stop when he spotted the visitor.

Both Alesandra and Dreyson stood up. She introduced the agent to her host. Colin already knew who Dreyson was. He was impressed, too, for Dreyson's reputation was well known in the shipping community. The broker was considered by many to be a financial genius. Colin admired the man. In the cutthroat business of the market, Dreyson was one of the very few who put his clients' affairs above his own profits. He was actually honorable, and Colin considered that a remarkable quality in an agent.

"Have I interrupted an important meeting?" he asked.

"We were finished with our business," Dreyson replied. "It's a pleasure to meet you, sir," the broker continued. "I've been following the progress of your company and I must compliment you. From ownership of three ships to over twenty in just five years' time is quite impressive, sir."

Colin nodded. "My partner and I try to stay competitive," he said.

"Have you considered offering shares to outsiders, sir? Why, I myself would be interested in investing in such a sound venture."

Colin's leg was throbbing painfully. He shifted positions, winced, and then shook his head. He wanted to sit down, prop his injured leg up, and drink until the ache went away. He wasn't about to pamper himself, however, and shifted positions again until he was leaning against the side of the settee, then forced himself to think about the conversation he was engaged in with the agent.

"No," he announced. "The shares in the Emerald Shipping Company are fifty-fifty between Nathan and me. We aren't interested in outsiders gaining possession."

"If you ever change your mind . . ."

"I won't."

Dreyson nodded. "Princess Alesandra has explained you are acting as her temporary guardian during the family illness."

"That is correct."

"You've been given quite an honor," Dreyson said. He paused to smile at Alesandra. "Protect her well, sir. She's a rare treasure."

Alesandra was embarrassed by Dreyson's praise. Her attention was turned, however, when the broker asked Colin how his father was doing.

"I've just seen him," Colin replied. "He's really been quite ill, but he's on the mend now."

Alesandra couldn't hide her surprise. She turned to Colin. "You didn't . . ." She stopped herself just in time. She was about to blurt out the obvious fact that Colin hadn't believed her and had in fact tried to catch his father in a lie. She found his behavior shameful. Private affairs, however, should never be discussed in front of business associates. She wasn't about to break that sacred rule, no matter how pricked she was.

"I didn't what?" Colin asked. His grin suggested he knew what she was about to say.

She kept her expression serene, but the look in her eyes had turned frigid.

"You didn't get too close to your father or your mother, did you?" she asked. "I believe the illness might be the catching kind," she explained to Dreyson.

47

"Might be?" Colin was choking on his laughter.

Alesandra ignored him. She kept her gaze directed on the agent. "Colin's older brother visited his father for just an hour or two several days ago, and now he and his dear wife are both ill. I would have warned the man, of course, but I had gone out riding, and by the time I returned, Caine had come and gone."

Dreyson expressed his sympathy over the family's plight. Both Alesandra and Colin walked with the agent to the entrance. "I'll return in three days, if that fits your schedule, Princess Alesandra, with the papers ready for your signature initials."

The broker left a moment later. Colin closed the door after him. He turned around and found Alesandra just a foot away, glaring up at him. Her hands were settled on her hips.

"You owe me an apology," she announced.

"Yes, I do."

"When I think how you . . . you do?"

The bluster went out of her anger. Colin smiled. "Yes, I do," he said again. "I didn't believe you when you said my brother and my father were both too ill to watch out for you."

"You had to find out for yourself, didn't you?"

He ignored the anger in her voice. "I admit I believed it was all a scheme," he told her. "And I really thought I'd be bringing my father back with me."

"For what purpose?"

He decided to be completely honest. "To take you off my hands, Alesandra."

She tried to hide her hurt feelings from him. "I'm sorry my staying here is such an inconvenience for you."

He let out a sigh. "You shouldn't take this personally. It's just that I'm swamped with business matters now and I don't have time to play guardian."

Colin turned to his butler before she could tell him she most certainly did take his remarks personally.

"Flannaghan, get me a drink. Something hot. It was damned cold riding today."

"Serves you right," Alesandra interjected. "Your suspicious nature is going to get you into trouble someday."

He leaned down until his face was just inches away from hers. "My suspicious nature has kept me alive, Princess."

She didn't know what he meant by that remark. She didn't like the way he was frowning at her either, and decided to leave him alone. She turned to go up the stairs. Colin followed her. He could hear her muttering something under her breath, but he couldn't catch any clear words. His concentration was too scattered to pay much attention to her remarks anyway. He was thoroughly occupied trying not to notice the gentle sway of her hips or acknowledge how enticing he found her sexy little backside.

She heard a loud sigh behind her and knew he was following her up the stairs. She didn't turn around when she asked, "Did you look in on Caine, too, or did you accept your father's word that your brother was also ill?"

"I looked in on him."

She whirled around to frown at him. She almost bumped into him. Since she was on the step above, they were now eye to eye.

She noticed how tanned his face was, how hard his mouth looked, how his eyes sparkled green with his incredible smile.

He noticed the sexy freckles on the bridge of her nose.

Alesandra didn't like the path her thoughts were taking. "You're covered with dust, Colin, and probably smell like your horse. You need a bath."

He didn't like her tone of voice. "You need to quit glaring at me," he ordered, his voice every bit as curt as hers had been. "A ward shouldn't treat her guardian with such disrespect."

She didn't have a ready comeback for that statement of fact. Colin was her guardian for the time being, and she probably should be respectful. She didn't want to agree with him, however, and all because he had made it perfectly clear he didn't want her there.

"Is your brother feeling better?"

"He's half dead," he told her quite cheerfully.

"You don't like Caine?"

He laughed. "Of course I like my brother."

"Then why did you sound so happy when you said he was half dead?"

"Because he really is sick and isn't in league with my father and his schemes."

She shook her head at him, turned around again, and ran up the rest of the steps. "Is his wife feeling any better?" she called over her shoulder.

"She isn't as green as Caine is," Colin answered. "Thankfully their little girl wasn't exposed. She and Sterns stayed on in the country."

"Who is Sterns?"

"Their butler-turned-nanny," he explained. "Caine and Jade will remain in London until they're recovered. My mother's feeling better, but my sisters still can't keep anything in their stomachs. Isn't it odd, Alesandra, that you didn't get sick?"

She wouldn't look at him. She knew she was responsible and hated having to admit it. "Actually, now that I think about it, I was a little bit ill on the journey to England," she remarked casually.

He laughed. "Caine's calling you The Plague."

She turned around to look at him again. "I didn't deliberately make everyone sick. Does he really blame me?"

"Yes." He deliberately lied just to tease her.

Her shoulders slumped. "I had hoped to move in with your brother and his wife tomorrow."

"You can't."

"Now you think you're going to be stuck with me, don't you?"

She waited for his denial. A gentleman, after all, would have said something gallant, even if it was a lie, just to be polite.

"Alesandra, I am stuck with you."

She glared at him for being so honest. "You might as well accept the situation and try to be pleasant."

She hurried down the hallway and went into his study. He

leaned against the door frame and watched her collect her papers from the table by the hearth.

"You aren't really upset because I didn't believe my family was ill, are you?"

She didn't answer him. "Did your father talk to you about my circumstances?"

The fear in her eyes surprised him. "He wasn't up to a long talk."

She visibly relaxed.

"But you're going to tell me about your circumstances, aren't you?"

He kept his voice low, soothing. She still reacted as though he'd just shouted at her. "I would prefer your father explain."

"He can't. You will."

"Yes," she finally agreed. "I will have to be the one to tell you. You're blocking Flannaghan's way," she added, her relief obvious over the interruption.

"Princess Alesandra, you have a visitor. Neil Perry, the Earl of Hargrave, is waiting in the salon to speak to you."

"What does he want?" Colin asked.

"Neil is Victoria's older brother," she explained. "I sent a note this morning requesting him to call."

Colin walked over to his desk and leaned against it. "Does he know you want to question him about his sister?"

Alesandra handed Flannaghan her papers, asked him to please put them in her room, and then turned back to Colin. "I didn't exactly explain the purpose of the meeting."

She hurried out of the room so Colin wouldn't have time to berate her for using trickery. She ignored his summons to come back inside and went down the hallway to her room. She had made a list of questions to ask Neil and she didn't want to forget any of them. The sheet of paper was on her nightstand. She folded it, smiled at Flannaghan, who was straightening her bed covers, and hurried downstairs.

Flannaghan wanted to announce her. She wouldn't let him. Neil was standing just inside the salon. He turned when Alesandra reached the foyer and bowed low in greeting.

"I do appreciate you coming so soon," she began as soon as she had finished with her curtsy.

"You mentioned the matter you wished to discuss was quite important, Princess. Have we met before? I feel sure that if we had met, I certainly would have remembered."

Victoria's brother was trying to be charming, Alesandra supposed, but the smile he gave her looked more like a sneer. The Earl of Hargrave was only an inch or two taller than she was and he held himself so rigid it appeared his clothing had been starched stiff. Alesandra couldn't see any resemblance in his thin face to Victoria other than the color of his eyes. They were the same shade of brown. Victoria had gotten the pleasing features in the family, however. Her nose was short, straight. Neil's was long, very like a hawk's, and extremely narrow. Alesandra thought he was a thoroughly unattractive man and she found his nasal voice to be grating.

Appearances, she reminded herself, meant nothing. She prayed Neil had a sweet disposition like his sister. He looked persnickety. She hoped he wasn't.

"Please come inside and sit down. I wanted to talk to you about a matter that concerns me and beg your indulgence with a few questions."

Neil nodded agreement before turning to walk across the room. He waited until she had taken her place on the settee and then sat down in the adjacent chair. He folded one leg over the other, stacked his hands on top of one knee. His nails, she noticed, were quite long for a man and immaculately manicured.

"I've never been inside this town house," Neil remarked. He looked around the room. There was scorn in his voice when he added, "The location is marvelous, of course, but I understand it's just a rental."

"Yes, it is," she agreed.

"It's terribly small, isn't it? I would think a princess would require more suitable quarters."

Neil was a snob. Alesandra was trying not to dislike the man, but his remarks were making it difficult. He was

Victoria's brother, however, and Alesandra needed his assistance in locating her friend.

"I'm very happy here," she remarked, forcing a pleasant tone of voice. "Now then, sir, I wanted to talk to you about your sister."

He didn't like hearing that announcement. His smile faded immediately. "My sister is not a topic for discussion, Princess Alesandra."

"I hope to change your mind," she countered. "I met Victoria last year," she added with a nod. "She stayed at the Holy Cross convent with me when she became ill on her journey. Did she by chance mention me?"

Neil shook his head. "My sister and I rarely spoke to one another."

"Really?" Alesandra couldn't hide her surprise.

Neil let out a loud, exaggerated sigh. "Victoria lived with our mother. I have my own estate," he added, a hint of a boast in his voice. "Of course, now that she's gone to God knows where, mother has moved in with me."

He started tapping his fingers on his knee, his impatience apparent.

"I apologize if this is difficult for you to talk about, but I'm concerned about Victoria. I don't believe she would ever run off and get married."

"Don't be concerned," he countered. "She isn't worth anyone's concern. She made her bed . . ."

"I don't understand your callous attitude. Victoria could be in trouble."

"And I don't understand your attitude, Princess," Neil retaliated. "You haven't been in England long and you therefore don't understand what a scandal can do to one's social standing. My mother was almost destroyed by Victoria's thoughtless actions. Why, for the first time in fifteen years, she wasn't invited to Ashford's bash. The humiliation sent her to bed for a month. My sister threw it all away. She is and always has been a fool. She could have married anyone she wanted. I know of at least three titled gentlemen she turned down. Victoria only thought about herself, of course. While our mother was worrying and fretting over a good match, she was sneaking out the back door to meet her lover."

Alesandra struggled to hold on to her temper. "You can't know that for certain," she argued. "As for the scandal . . ."

She never got to finish her argument. "You obviously don't care about a scandal either," Neil muttered. "No wonder you and my sister got along so well."

"Exactly what are you implying?" she asked.

"You're living in the same house with an unattached man," he said. "There're whispers going around already."

Alesandra took a deep breath in an attempt to control her temper. "Exactly what are these whispers?"

"Some are saying Sir Colin Hallbrook is your cousin. Others believe he's your lover."

She dropped her list in her lap, then stood up. "Your sister rarely mentioned you to me and now I understand why. You're a despicable man, Neil Perry. If I weren't so concerned about Victoria's welfare, I would throw you out this minute."

"I'll take care of that chore for you."

Colin made the announcement from the entrance. He was leaning against the door frame, his arms folded casually across his chest. He looked relaxed, but his eyes . . . oh, Lord, his eyes showed his fury. Alesandra had never seen Colin so angry. She shivered in reaction.

Neil looked startled by the interruption. He quickly recovered, awkwardly unfolded his legs, and stood up.

"Had I known the true reason you wished to see me, I never would have come here. Good day, Princess Alesandra."

She couldn't take her gaze off Colin long enough to speak to Neil. She had the oddest notion Colin was getting ready to pounce.

The notion proved true. Flannaghan held the door open for their guest. Colin moved to stand next to his butler. His expression was masked, and for that reason Neil had no idea that he really meant to throw him outside.

If she'd blinked, she would have missed it. Neil only had time to let out a squeal of indignation that sounded very like a pig's howl of distress. Colin grabbed him by the back of his neck and the back of the waistband to his trousers, lifted him up, and threw him outside. Neil landed in the gutter.

Alesandra let out a little gasp, picked up her skirts, and went running to the front door. Flannaghan let her see the Earl of Hargrave sprawled out on the street before he shut the door.

She whirled around to confront Colin. "Now what am I going to do? I doubt he'll come back here after the way you tossed him out, Colin."

"The man insulted you. I can't allow that."

"But I need him to answer my questions."

He shrugged. She threaded her fingers through her hair in an agitated action. She couldn't decide if she was pleased or pricked at Colin. "What did I do with my list?"

"Which list, Princess?" Flannaghan asked.

"The list of questions I was going to ask Neil."

She went hurrying back into the salon, bent down, and found the sheet of paper under the settee.

Flannaghan and Colin watched her. "Princess Alesandra is a firm believer in lists, milord," Flannaghan said.

Colin didn't make any remark on that bit of information. He frowned at Alesandra when she passed him and went up the steps.

"I won't allow you to invite Perry back here, Alesandra," he called out, still burning with irritation over the pompous man's snide remarks.

"I certainly will invite him back," she called over her shoulder. "This is as much my home as it is yours while you're acting as my guardian. I'm determined to find out if Victoria is all right, Colin, and if that means putting up with her horrid brother, then put up with him I will."

Colin turned to his butler. "Don't let him in. Understand?"

"Perfectly, milord. It is our duty to protect our princess from slanderers."

Alesandra had already turned the corner above the stairs and therefore didn't hear Colin's order or Flannaghan's agreement. She was thoroughly weary of men in general and Neil Perry in particular. She decided to put Victoria's brother out of her mind for the time being. Tomorrow would be soon enough to decide what to do next.

Valena was waiting for her mistress in her bedroom. She and Flannaghan had already moved Alesandra's things from Colin's room into the adjoining chamber.

Alesandra sat down on the side of the bed and kicked her shoes off. "It looks as though we're going to have to stay here a few more days, Valena."

"Your trunks arrived, Princess. Shall I begin unpacking?"

"Tomorrow's soon enough. I know it's still early, but I believe I'll go to bed now. You needn't stay to help me."

Valena left her alone. Alesandra took her time getting ready for bed. She felt quite drained from today's meetings. Speaking to so many of her father's friends and hearing the wonderful stories about him made her miss both her father and her mother. Alesandra might have been able to control her mood if Neil hadn't proven to be such a self-serving, cruel-hearted man. She wanted to shout at the man and tell him he should be thankful he had a mother and a sister to love. Perry wouldn't understand, or care, she imagined, for he was like so many other people she'd met who took their families for granted.

Alesandra gave in to self-pity within minutes. She didn't have anyone who truly cared about her. Colin had let it be known she was just a nuisance, and her real guardian, though far more gentle and understanding than his son, probably considered her a nuisance, too.

She wanted her mama. Her memories of family life didn't comfort her now. They made her ache with her loneliness. She went to bed a few minutes later, hid under the covers, and cried herself to sleep. She awakened in the middle of the night, didn't feel any better about herself or her circumstances, and, heaven help her, she started weeping again.

Colin heard her. He was also in bed. He couldn't get to sleep, however. The throbbing in his leg kept him wide awake. Alesandra wasn't making much noise, but Colin was attuned to every sound in the house. He immediately tossed the covers aside and got out of bed. He was halfway across the chamber before he realized he was stark naked. He put on a pair of pants, reached for the doorknob, and then stopped.

He wanted to comfort her, yet at the same time he knew he would probably be embarrassed because he'd heard her crying. The sounds were muffled, indicating to him she was trying to be as quiet as possible. She didn't want to be overheard, and he knew he should respect her privacy.

"Hell," he muttered to himself. He didn't know his own mind anymore. He wasn't usually so indecisive. His instincts were telling him to distance himself from Alesandra. She was a complication he wasn't ready to take on.

He turned around and went back to his own bed. He finally admitted the real truth to himself. He wasn't just protecting Alesandra from embarrassment. No, he was also protecting her from his own lecherous ideas. She was in bed, probably only wearing a thin nightgown, and, damn it all, if he got close, he knew he would touch her.

Colin gritted his teeth and closed his eyes. If the little innocent next door had any idea what he was thinking, she would have her guards doing sentry duty around her bed.

Lord, he wanted her.

*He killed a whore. It had been a mistake. It hadn't been at all satisfying. The rush of absolute power and excitement were missing. It took him days of reflecting upon the problem before he came up with a suitable explanation. The surge came only after a satisfying hunt. The whore had been too easy, and although her screams excited him, it still wasn't the same. No, no, it was the cleverness he had to call upon to lure the bait. It was the seduction of the innocent by the master. Those were the key elements that made all the difference. The whore had been dirty. She didn't deserve to sleep with the others. He tossed her into a ravine and left her for the wild animals.*

*He needed a lady.*

Colin was gone by the time Alesandra came downstairs the following morning. Flannaghan and Raymond sat with her at the dining room table while she sorted through the huge stack of invitations that had arrived that morning. Stefan was sleeping now because he'd taken the night watch. Alesandra didn't believe it was necessary for anyone to stay up all night, but Raymond, the senior of the two guards, wouldn't listen to her. Someone always had to be on the alert in case of trouble, Raymond argued, and since she had placed him in charge, she really should let him do things his way.

"But we are in England now," she reminded the guard again.

"The general isn't to be taken lightly," Raymond countered. "We got here, didn't we? He could have sent men on the next available ship."

Alesandra quit arguing with him then and turned her attention to the mound of invitations.

"It's astonishing to me that so many found out so soon I was in London," she remarked.

"I'm not surprised," Flannaghan replied. "I already heard from Cook who heard from the butcher that you're causing quite a stir. I'm afraid there's a bit of gossip attached to your name because you're staying here, but the fact that you have a lady's maid and two guards with you has taken the sting out of the remarks. There's also a rather amusing bit of talk . . . nonsense really . . ."

Alesandra was in the process of pulling a note out of an envelope. She paused to look up at Flannaghan. "What bit of nonsense?"

"It's believed by some that you and my employer are related," he explained. "They think Colin's your cousin."

"Neil Perry mentioned that," she said. "He also said that there are others who believe Colin's my lover."

Flannaghan was properly appalled. She reached out and

patted his hand. "It's all right. People will believe what they want to believe. Poor Colin. He can barely stand to have me around as it is, and if anyone refers to me as his cousin, heaven only knows what he'll do."

"How can you say such a thing?" Flannaghan asked. "Milord adores having you here."

"I'm impressed, Flannaghan."

"Why is that, Princess?"

"You've just told the most outrageous lie with a straight face."

Flannaghan didn't laugh until she smiled. "Well, he would adore having you here if he wasn't so busy worrying about his ledgers," he remarked.

He was trying to save face, Alesandra supposed. She nodded, pretending agreement, and then turned her attention back to her task. Flannaghan begged to help. She gave him the duty of affixing her seal to the envelopes. Her crest was most unusual. Flannaghan had never seen anything like it. There was a clear outline of a castle and what appeared to be an eagle or falcon atop one turret.

"Does the castle have a name, Princess?" Flannaghan asked, intrigued by the amazing detail.

"It's called Stone Haven. My father and mother were married there."

She answered every question put to her. Flannaghan's jovial mood lightened her own. He was incredulous when he heard she owned not one but two castles, and his expression made her laugh. He really was a delightful man.

They worked together all morning long, but when the bell chimed one o'clock Alesandra went upstairs to change her gown. She told Flannaghan only that she was expecting more company and wanted to look her best.

Flannaghan didn't think the princess needed to change a thing. It simply wasn't possible for her to become any more beautiful than she already was.

Colin came home around seven that evening. He was stiff and irritable from sitting at his desk at the shipping offices for such long hours. He carried his heavy ledgers under his arm.

He found his butler sprawled out on the steps leading upstairs. It was Raymond who opened the front door for him.

Flannaghan looked done in. "What happened to you?" Colin asked.

The butler roused himself from his stupor and stood up. "We had company again today. The princess didn't give me any warning. I'm not faulting her, of course, and she did tell me she was going to have callers, but I didn't realize who, and then he was here with his attendants and I spilled the tea Cook prepared. After he left, a dock worker appeared at the door. I thought he was after begging, but Princess Alesandra heard me tell him to go around to the back door and Cook would give him something to eat. She intervened. Why, she was expecting the man, and do you know, milord, she treated him with the same respect as the other."

"What other?" Colin asked, trying to sort through the servant's bizarre explanation.

"The prince regent."

"He was here? I'll be damned."

Flannaghan sat back down on the steps. "If my uncle Sterns gets wind of my disgrace, he'll box my ears."

"What disgrace?"

"I spilled tea on the prince regent's jacket."

"Good for you," Colin replied. "When I can afford it, you're getting a raise."

Flannaghan smiled. He'd forgotten how much his employer disliked the prince regent. "I was quite rattled by his presence, but Princess Alesandra acted as though nothing out of the ordinary was happening. She was very dignified. The prince regent wasn't his usual pompous self either. He acted like a besotted schoolboy. It was apparent to me he has great affection for the princess."

Alesandra appeared at the landing above. Colin looked up and immediately frowned. A tightness in his chest made him realize he'd quit breathing.

She looked absolutely beautiful. She was dressed in a silver and white gown that shimmered in the light when she moved. The cut of the dress wasn't overly revealing, but there was still a hint of flesh visible at the top of her neckline.

Her hair was pinned up with a thin white ribbon threaded through her curls. Wisps of hair curled at the base of her neck.

She looked breathtakingly beautiful. Every nerve in Colin's body reacted to the sight of her. He wanted to take her into his arms, kiss her, taste her. . . .

"Where the hell do you think you're going?" He snapped out the question in a general's tone of voice. Anger hid his lust—or so he hoped.

Her eyes widened over the hostility in his demand. "To the opera," she answered. "The prince regent insisted I take his box tonight. I'm taking Raymond with me."

"You're staying home, Alesandra," Colin stated.

"Princess, you cannot expect me to go inside the opera and sit near the prince regent," Raymond said, somewhat plaintively for such a large, fearsome man.

"He won't be there, Raymond," she explained.

"I still can't go inside. It wouldn't be proper. I'll wait by the carriage."

"You aren't going anywhere without me," Colin announced. He added a hard glare so she would understand he meant what he said.

Her smile was radiant. He realized then she'd had no intention of dragging Raymond into the opera house. She'd cleverly tricked him into accommodating her.

"Do hurry and change, Colin. We don't want to be late."

"I hate the opera."

He sounded like a little boy complaining about having to eat his vegetables. She didn't have a bit of sympathy for him. She didn't particularly like the opera either, but she wasn't going to admit that fact to him. He'd want to stay home then, and she really couldn't insult the prince regent by not using his box.

"Too bad, Colin. You already gave me your promise to go. Do hurry."

Alesandra lifted the hem of her gown and came down the stairs. Flannaghan watched her with his mouth gaping open. She smiled when she passed him.

"She moves like a princess," Flannaghan whispered to his employer.

Colin smiled. "She is a princess, Flannaghan."

Colin suddenly quit smiling. Alesandra's dress was a little lower on top than he'd realized. Up close he could see the swell of her bosom.

"You're going to have to change your gown before we go anywhere," he announced.

"Why would I want to change?"

He muttered something under his breath. "This gown is too . . . enticing. Do you want every man there boldly staring at you?"

"Do you think they will?"

"Hell, yes."

She smiled. "Good."

"You want to attract their notice?" He sounded incredulous.

She looked exasperated. "Of course I want to attract their notice. I'm trying to find a husband, remember?"

"You're changing your gown."

"I'll keep my cloak on."

"Change."

Flannaghan's neck was beginning to ache from turning his head back and forth during the heated debate.

"You're being ridiculous," she announced. "And acting terribly old-fashioned."

"I'm your guardian. I'll act any damned way I want to act."

"Colin, be reasonable about this. Valena went to a great deal of trouble and time to get all the wrinkles out."

He didn't let her finish. "You're wasting time."

She shook her head at him. She wasn't going to give in, no matter how intimidating his scowl became.

He walked over to her. Before she knew what he was going to do, he grabbed hold of the bodice of her dress and tried to pull the material up to her chin.

"Every time I think your dress needs some adjustment, I'm going to haul it up, just like this, no matter where we are."

"I'll change."

"I thought you might."

As soon as he let go of her, she turned and ran up the steps. "You're a horrible man, Colin."

He didn't mind her insult. He'd gotten his way, and that was all that mattered. He'd be damned if he'd let the unattached predators ogle her.

It didn't take him long to wash and dress in formal attire. He was back downstairs in less than fifteen minutes.

She took much longer. She was coming down the stairs again when Colin sauntered in from the dining room. He was eating a green apple. He stopped when he saw her on the staircase. His gaze lingered on the bodice of her gown for a long minute, then he nodded his approval. He smiled with satisfaction. She thought he might very well be gloating over his victory. It was apparent he found the forest green gown suitable. It wasn't, though. The cut of the bodice was a deep V, but she'd cleverly stuffed a piece of lace down the middle to appease her guardian.

She didn't choose the gown to deliberately provoke Colin. The dress was the only other option left to her. The other gowns were too wrinkled to wear, and Valena had only just finished getting the creases out of this one.

Colin certainly looked dashing. Black suited him. He tugged on his starched white cravat and devoured his apple at the same time.

He still looked incredibly sexy. The fabric of his jacket was stretched tight across his broad shoulders. His pants were indecently snug, and Alesandra couldn't help but notice the bulge of muscle in his thighs.

Colin seemed preoccupied for most of the ride to their destination. Alesandra sat across from him in the small carriage with her hands folded together in her lap. His legs crowded her into one corner, and in the darkness his size was far more intimidating. So was his silence.

"I didn't realize you were friends with the prince regent," he remarked.

"He isn't my friend. I only just met him today."

"Flannaghan told me the prince was taken with you."

She shook her head. "He was taken with what I am, not who I am."

"Meaning?"

She let out a little sigh before answering. "It was an official call, Colin. The prince came because I'm a princess. He doesn't know me personally at all. Now do you understand?"

He nodded. "Most of society will embrace you because of what you are, Alesandra. I'm pleased you understand the shallowness that may exist in the friendships offered to you. It shows you have maturity."

"Maturity? No, it shows cynicism."

He smiled. "That too."

Several minutes passed in silence. Then Colin spoke again. "Did you like him?"

"Who?"

"The prince."

"I don't know him well enough to form an opinion."

"You're hedging, Alesandra. Tell me the truth."

"I was being diplomatic," she replied. "But I'll give you an honest answer. No, I didn't particularly like him. There, are you happy now?"

"Yes. Your answer proves you're a good judge of character."

"Perhaps the prince has a kind heart," she remarked, feeling guilty because she'd admitted she hadn't liked him.

"He doesn't."

"Why don't *you* like him?"

"He broke his word—a promise made to my partner," Colin explained. "The prince regent held a large treasury belonging to Nathan's wife, Sara, and after a time he decided to keep it for himself. It was dishonorable."

"That is shameful," she agreed.

"Why didn't you like him?"

"He seemed . . . full of himself," she admitted.

Colin snorted. "He's full of . . ." He stopped himself from using the crude word he was thinking of and substituted another. "Vinegar."

The carriage came to a rocking stop in front of the Royal Opera House. Alesandra adjusted her white gloves, her attention fully on Colin. "I never would have allowed him entrance into your home if I'd known what he'd done to your partner. I apologize to you, Colin. Your home is your castle, where only friends should be invited."

"You would have refused him?"

She nodded. He winked at her. Her heart immediately started pounding a wild beat. Dear God, he was a charmer.

Raymond had ridden with the driver in front of the carriage. He jumped down from his perch and opened the door for them.

Colin got out first, then turned to assist Alesandra. Her cloak opened when she reached for his hand. The handkerchief she'd stuffed into the bodice shifted, and when she stepped to the pavement, the lace fell out.

He caught it. He took one look at her provocative neckline and started glaring at her.

He was furious with her. She tried to back away from his frown and almost fell over the curb. Colin grabbed her, then turned her around until she was facing the carriage door. He stuffed the bit of lace back into her dress.

She suffered through the humiliation, matching him frown for frown. Their gazes held for a long minute before she finally gave in and turned away.

Colin adjusted her cloak over her shoulders, hauled her into his side, and turned back to the steps. She guessed she should be thankful he hadn't made a scene, and she didn't think anyone had noticed their little confrontation. He had blocked her from the view of the crowd going inside the opera house. Yes, she should have been thankful. She wasn't, though. Colin was acting like an old man.

"You've spent too much time with your ledgers, sir. You really need to get out more often. Then you'd notice my gown isn't at all inappropriate. It's actually quite prim."

She didn't appreciate his snort of disbelief. She felt like

kicking him. "You've taken this duty as guardian to heart, haven't you?"

He kept his arm anchored on her shoulders as they went up the steps. She kept trying to shrug him away from her. Colin was determined to be possessive, however, and she finally gave up.

"Alesandra, my father entrusted me with your care. It doesn't matter if I like this duty or not. I'm your guardian and you'll do as I order."

"It's a pity you aren't more like your father. He's such a sweet, understanding man. You could learn a lesson or two from him."

"When you quit dressing like a trollop, I'll be more understanding," he promised.

Her gasp sounded like a hiccup. "No one has ever dared to call me a trollop."

Colin didn't remark on that outraged statement. He did smile, though.

Neither one said another word to the other for a long, long while. They were escorted to the prince regent's box and took their seats side by side.

The opera house was filled to capacity, but Colin was certain only Alesandra watched the performance. Everyone else watched her.

She pretended not to be aware of their stares. She impressed the hell out of Colin, too. She looked so beautifully composed. Her posture was ramrod straight, and she never once turned her attention from the stage. He could see her hands, however. They were clenched tight in her lap.

He moved a little closer to her. Then he reached over and covered her hands with one of his. She didn't turn her gaze to him, but she latched on to his hand and held tight. They stayed like that through the rest of the performance.

The white starched cravat around his neck was driving him crazy. He wanted to tear the thing off, prop his feet up on the railing overlooking the stage, and close his eyes. Alesandra would probably have heart palpitations if he dared to behave so shamefully. He wouldn't embarrass her, of course, but, God, how he hated all the pretense associated with the ton's affairs.

He hated having to sit in the prince regent's box, too. Nathan would bellow for a week if he found out. His partner disliked their ruler even more than Colin did, for it was his wife who had been cheated out of her inheritance by the not-so-noble prince.

The god-awful opera he was being subjected to didn't improve his cranky disposition. He did close his eyes then, and tried to block out the sounds of screeching coming from the stage.

Alesandra didn't realize until the performance was over that Colin had fallen asleep. She turned to ask him if he had enjoyed the opera as much as she had, but just as she was about to speak, he started to snore. She almost laughed. It took all she had to keep her expression composed. The opera really had been dreadful, and in her heart she wished *she* could have slept through the ordeal. She would never admit such a thing to Colin, however, for the simple reason that she knew he would gloat.

She nudged him hard with her elbow. Colin came awake with a start.

"You really are impossible," she told him in a whisper.

He gave her a sleepy-eyed grin. "I like to think I am."

It simply wasn't possible to offend him. She gave up trying. She stood up, took hold of her cloak, and turned to leave the box. Colin followed her.

There was a crush of people in the foyer below. Most were waiting to get a closer look at her. Alesandra found herself surrounded by gentlemen begging an introduction. She lost Colin in the shuffle, and when she finally located him again, she saw he was surrounded by ladies. One, a gaudy redheaded woman with exposed bosoms down to her knees, was hanging on Colin's arm. The woman kept licking her upper lip, and Alesandra was reminded of a hungry alley cat that had just spotted a bowl of cream.

Colin appeared to be the woman's snack. Alesandra tried to pay attention to what was being said to her by a gentleman who'd introduced himself as the Earl of something or other, but her gaze kept returning to Colin. He looked very happy with all the attention he was getting, and for some strange reason that notice infuriated Alesandra.

It hit her all at once, this unreasonable burst of jealousy. And, Lord, it was the most horrible feeling. She simply couldn't stand to see the woman's hand on Colin's arm.

She was more disgusted with herself than with Colin. Since the moment she'd arrived in England, she'd been trying to behave the way she thought a princess should behave. The mother superior's two sainted words, *dignity* and *decorum* echoed in her mind. Alesandra remembered the nun's warning to avoid spontaneous actions. She'd pointed out over ten examples of trouble that had resulted because of her spur-of-the-moment ideas.

Alesandra let out a sigh. She guessed marching over to Colin's side and ripping that horrible woman's hand off his arm would qualify as a spontaneous action. Further, she knew the gossip tomorrow would make her sorry for her action.

It felt as though the foyer was closing in on her. No one appeared to be in a hurry to leave. More and more people crowded into the tiny area to see who was there and to be seen.

She desperately needed fresh air. She excused herself from the gentleman requesting an audience with her by giving him permission to send her a note, then slowly made her way through the throng of people to the front doors.

She didn't care if Colin followed her or not. She went outside. She paused on the front step, took a deep breath of the not-so-fresh city air, and put on her cloak. Colin's carriage was directly below her. Raymond spotted her right away. He jumped down from his perch, where he'd been waiting with the driver.

Alesandra lifted the hem of her gown and started down the steps. Someone grabbed hold of her arm. She thought it was Colin finally catching up with her. His grip stung. She tried to pull her arm away, then turned to tell him to lessen his hold.

It wasn't Colin. The stranger holding on to her was dressed in black from head to foot. He wore a cap that covered most of his brow. She could barely see his face.

"Let go of me," she commanded.

"You must come home with us now, Princess Alesandra."

A chill settled around her heart. The man had spoken to her in the language of her father's homeland. She understood what was happening then. She tried not to panic. She pulled back and tried to run, but she was captured by another man from behind. He was hurting her with his fierce hold. Alesandra was suddenly too furious to think about the pain. With his friend's assistance, the man started to drag her back toward the side of the building. A third man appeared out of the shadows of the stone columns in front of the opera house and ran down the steps to stop Raymond from interfering. Her guard was charging up the steps to protect her. Raymond landed the first punch, but the man he'd struck only staggered backward. Then he lashed out at her guard with something sharp. Alesandra saw the blood spurting down the side of Raymond's face and started screaming.

A hand clamped down over her mouth, cutting off the sound. She bit her attacker as hard as she could. He let out a howl of pain while he shifted his hold on her.

He was strangling her now. He kept telling her to quit her struggles or he would have to hurt her.

Alesandra was terrified. She couldn't breathe. She kept up her struggle, determined to get away from the horrible men and run to Raymond. She had to help him. He could be bleeding to death, and, dear God, this was all her fault. She should have listened to Raymond when he insisted the general's men would come after her. She should have stayed home . . . she should have . . .

She heard Colin before she saw him. A roar of fury unlike anything she'd ever heard before sounded in the darkness. The man anchoring her from behind was suddenly ripped away from her and tossed headfirst into one of the stone pillars. He collapsed to the ground like a discarded apple core.

Alesandra was coughing and gasping for air. The stranger holding on to her arm tried to pull her in front of him to use as a shield against Colin. He wouldn't allow that. He moved so quickly, Alesandra didn't have time to help. Colin's fist slammed into the man's face. Her attacker's cap went flying in one direction, and he went flying down the steps. He landed with a thud at Raymond's feet. Alesandra's guard was fully occupied circling his adversary, his concentration totally centered on the gleaming knife he held in his hand.

Colin moved in from behind. The man turned to lash out at him. Colin kicked the blade out of his hand, moved forward again, and grabbed hold of his arm. He twisted it into an unnatural position. The bone snapped, and that horrid sound was followed by a scream of pain. Colin was not finished with his victim, however. He shoved him headfirst into the back of the carriage.

Alesandra came running down the steps. She used the handkerchief from the bodice of her gown to stem the flow of blood pouring from the deep cut in Raymond's right cheek.

Colin didn't know if there were others ready to strike or not, and in his mind Alesandra wasn't going to be safe until she was home.

"Get inside the carriage, Alesandra. Now."

His voice was harsh with anger. She thought he was furious with her. She hurried to do as he commanded, but tried to take Raymond with her. She put his arm around her shoulder, braced herself for his weight, and whispered for him to lean on her.

"I'll be all right, Princess," Raymond told her. "Get inside. It isn't safe for you here."

Colin pulled her away from the guard. He half lifted, half tossed her into the carriage, then turned to help Raymond.

If the guard had been in any condition to look after Alesandra, Colin would have stayed behind to get some answers out of the bastards who'd dared to touch her. Raymond had lost quite a bit of blood, however, and now looked close to collapse.

Colin let out a low expletive, then got inside. The driver immediately whistled the horses into a full trot.

Alesandra sat next to the guard. "I don't understand why no one helped us," she whispered. "Couldn't they see we were in trouble?"

"You were the only one outside, Princess," Raymond answered. He slumped into the corner of the carriage. "It happened too fast. Why wasn't your escort with you?"

Raymond turned his head to glare at Colin when he asked his question. The handkerchief he held to his cheek was turning bright red. He adjusted the cloth against the cut, then turned to look at her.

She folded her hands together in her lap and lowered her gaze. "This is all my fault," she said. "I was impatient and there was such a crowd inside. I wanted some fresh air. I should have waited."

"Damn right you should have waited."

"Please don't be angry with me, Colin."

"Where the hell was Hillman?"

"The earl you introduced me to before you left me?"

"I didn't leave you," he muttered. "Hillman was introducing you to some of his friends and I turned my back for one minute to say hello to a couple of business associates. Damn it, Alesandra, if you wanted to leave why didn't you tell Hillman to come and get me?"

"Nothing will be served by raising your voice to me. I accept full responsibility for what happened."

She turned to her guard. "Raymond, can you ever forgive me? I should have stayed home. I put you in danger . . ."

Colin interrupted. "You don't have to hide behind lock and key, Alesandra. You just shouldn't have gone outside without me."

"They would have attacked even if you'd been with me," she countered.

He gave her a speculative look. "Start explaining," he ordered.

"I will explain when you quit shouting at me."

He hadn't been shouting, but she was obviously too upset

to notice. She'd taken her white gloves off. He watched as she folded the pair into a square and turned back to Raymond. She ordered Raymond to use the gloves for his bandage now that the handkerchief was saturated with blood.

"Damn it, Alesandra, you could have been hurt."

"And so could you, Colin," she responded. "Raymond needs a physician."

"I'll send Flannaghan over to fetch Winters as soon as we get home."

"Is Winters your personal physician?"

"Yes. Alesandra, did you know the men who attacked?"

"No," she answered. "At least, not by name. I know where they came from, though."

"They're fanatics," Raymond interjected.

Alesandra couldn't bear to look at Colin's frown. She leaned back against the cushion of the seat and closed her eyes. "The men are from my homeland. They want to take me back."

"For what purpose?"

"To marry their bastard general," Raymond answered. "Begging your pardon, Princess, for using that word in your presence, but Ivan is a bastard to be sure."

Colin had to wait to ask additional questions because they'd reached his town house. He wouldn't let Alesandra leave the safety of the carriage until he had the front door opened and had shouted for Stefan. Stefan came outside to assist Raymond, and Colin took hold of Alesandra.

A good hour was spent seeing to Raymond's care. Colin's physician lived just three blocks away and was thankfully home for the evening. Flannaghan brought him back in Colin's carriage.

Sir Winters was a white-haired man with brown eyes, a gentle voice, and an efficient matter.

He believed thugs were responsible for the attack. No one set him straight on that misconception.

"It isn't safe to go anywhere in London anymore, what with the mob of ruffians roaming the streets. Something has got to be done, and soon, before every decent man and woman is killed."

The physician stood in the center of the foyer, his hand on Raymond's jaw as he studied the damage done to his cheek and lamented the condition of London's streets.

Colin suggested Raymond sit at the dining room table. Flannaghan carried in extra candles so the physician would have enough light.

The cut was cleaned with a foul-smelling liquid, then stitched together with black thread. Raymond never once flinched during the painful ordeal. Alesandra flinched for him. She sat next to the guard, and when Winters applied the needle to his flesh, she reached over and took hold of Raymond's hand.

Colin stood in the doorway, watching. His attention was centered on Alesandra. He could see how upset she was. There were tears in her eyes and her shoulders were shaking. Colin fought the urge to go and comfort her.

Alesandra was such a gentle, compassionate woman, and Colin could well see her vulnerability, too. She was whispering something to the guard but he couldn't make out the words. He walked forward, then came to an abrupt stop when he understood what she was saying.

Alesandra was giving her promise that nothing further would happen to the guard. Ivan, she said, would not make such a terrible husband, after all. She told the guard she'd given the matter considerable consideration and had decided to return to her homeland.

Raymond didn't look too happy with her promises. Colin was furious. "You will not decide anything tonight, Alesandra," he commanded.

She turned to look up at him. The anger in his voice surprised her. Why did he care what she decided?

"Yes, Princess," Raymond said, drawing her attention. "Tomorrow will be soon enough to decide what should be done."

Alesandra pretended agreement. She had already made up her mind, however. She wasn't going to let anyone else get hurt because of her. Until tonight she hadn't realized the lengths the general's supporters would go to in order to accomplish their goal. And if Colin hadn't intervened, Raymond might have been killed.

Colin could have been injured, too. Oh, yes, she had made up her mind on the matter.

Winters finished his work, gave instructions, and then took his leave. Colin poured Raymond a goblet full of brandy. The guard downed the contents in one long swallow.

As soon as Raymond went upstairs to bed, Flannaghan took over his nightly ritual of checking all the locks on the windows and doors to make certain the house was secure.

Alesandra tried to go to her bedroom, but Colin intercepted her just as she was reaching for her doorknob. He took hold of her hand and pulled her along with him back to the study. He didn't say a word to her, just nudged her inside and then pulled the door closed behind him.

The time had come to explain in full her unusual circumstances, she supposed. She walked over to the hearth and stood there warming her hands with the heat of the fire Flannaghan had thoughtfully prepared.

Colin watched her, but he didn't say a word. She finally turned around to look at him. He was leaning against the door with his arms folded across his chest. He wasn't frowning and he didn't look at all angry—just thoughtful.

"I put you in danger tonight," she whispered. "I should have explained everything right away."

She waited for him to agree with that statement of fact. He surprised her by shaking his head. "This is as much my fault as yours, Alesandra. I could have insisted you explain your circumstances. I was too caught up in my own affairs to pay much attention to you. I've been remiss as your guardian. That, however, has changed. You're going to tell me everything, aren't you?"

She gripped her hands together. "None of this is your fault, sir. I didn't believe I would be staying here long enough to bother you with my problems, especially after you explained you had no intention of getting married for a long while. I also believed the general would send an ambassador to request my return. I misjudged, you see. I thought he would be civilized. He isn't. He's obviously determined . . . and desperate."

Tears came into her eyes. She took a deep breath to try to gain control of her emotions. "I'm so sorry for what happened tonight."

Colin took mercy on her. "You weren't responsible."

"They were after me," she argued. "Not Raymond or you."

Colin finally moved. He walked over to the chair behind his desk, sat down, and propped his feet up on the nearby footrest.

"Why does this general want you to come home?"

"It isn't my home," she corrected. "I wasn't even born there. My father was king, you see, until he married my mother. She was English and considered an outsider. Father stepped down so he could marry her and his younger brother, Edward, became ruler. It was all very polite."

Colin didn't remark on her explanation and she didn't have any idea what he was thinking. "Would you like me to continue?" she asked, her worry obvious.

"I want you to explain why the general wants you to come home," he repeated.

"My father was loved by his subjects. They didn't condemn him because he married my mother. In fact, they found it all very romantic. He did give up his kingdom for her, after all, and everyone who met my mother adored her. She was a dear, kindhearted woman."

"Do you resemble your mother in appearance?"

"Yes."

"Then she was also a beautiful woman, wasn't she?"

He had just given her a compliment, but she had difficulty accepting it. Her mother had been so much more than simply beautiful.

"A compliment shouldn't make you frown," Colin remarked.

"My mother was beautiful," she said. "But she also had a pure heart. I wish I was more like her, Colin. My thoughts are rarely pure. I was so angry tonight I wanted to hurt those men."

He found his first smile. "I did hurt them," he reminded her. "Now please continue with your explanation. I'm anxious to hear the rest of this."

"My father's brother died just last year and the country was once again thrown into turmoil. There seems to be a notion held by some that I should come home. The general wants marriage and believes he'll be able to secure the throne if I become his wife."

"Why does he believe that?"

She let out a sigh. "Because I'm the only surviving heir to the throne. Everyone has conveniently forgotten my father abdicated. As I said before, he was well loved by his subjects and that love . . ."

She didn't go on. Colin was intrigued by the faint blush on her cheeks. "And that love what?" he asked.

"Has been transferred to me," she blurted out. "At least, that is what Sir Richards of your War Department explained to me, and all the letters I've received over the years from the loyalists would confirm his supposition."

Colin straightened in his chair. "You know Sir Richards?" he asked.

"Yes," she answered. "He has been quite helpful to me. Why do you look so surprised? Is something wrong? You reacted with quite a startle at the mention of his name."

He shook his head. "How is the head of England's security section involved in this?"

"Then you know Sir Richards too?"

"I work for him."

It was her turn to look startled. And appalled. "But he runs the secret . . . Colin, if you work for him you must be involved in dangerous work. What do your parents think of this double life you lead? Oh, sir, no wonder you have no wish to marry. Your wife would worry all the time. Yes, she would."

Colin regretted telling her the truth. "I used to work for him," he qualified.

She could tell he was lying to her. The proof was in his eyes. They'd gone . . . cold, hard. She decided not to argue with him. If he wanted her to think he wasn't involved with the Security Section, she would pretend to believe him.

"How and why did Sir Richards get involved?"

His irritated tone of voice pulled her back to the primary topic. "He came to see me just the day before your father became ill. He and his associates—or superiors, as he referred to them—wish me to marry General Ivan."

"Then he knows the general?"

She shook her head. "He knows of him," she explained. "Sir Richards considers Ivan the lesser of two evils."

Colin let out a low expletive. She pretended she didn't hear it. "Sir Richards told your father the general would be easier to control. England wants the continuation of imports and the general would certainly look upon your country as a friend if I had been convinced by your leaders to marry Ivan. There is another man eager to snatch the throne and Sir Richards believes he's more ruthless. He also believes he wouldn't cooperate with trade agreements."

"So you're the sacrificial lamb, is that right?"

She didn't answer him.

"What did my father say to Sir Richards?"

She started twisting her hands together. "The director can be very persuasive. Your father listened to his argument and then promised to consider the matter. After Richards left, he decided against the marriage."

"Why?"

She lowered her gaze to her hands, saw how red her skin had become, and immediately relaxed her grip. "I cried," she confessed. "I'm ashamed to admit that, but I did cry. I was very upset. Your mother became furious with your father and I was the cause of a heated argument. That made me feel even more miserable. I felt I was disappointing everyone by being selfish. My only excuse is that my parents had such a happy marriage and I wanted to find that same kind of joy. I didn't believe I would ever find love or happiness married to a man who only wanted me for political gain. I've never met the general, but Raymond and Stefan have told me stories about him. If half of what they said is true, he's a very self-indulgent man."

Alesandra paused to take a deep breath. "Your father has a soft heart. He couldn't stand to see me upset. And he had made a promise to my father to take care of me."

"So he decided you should marry me."

"Yes," she answered. "It was his hope, but he wasn't counting on it. Otherwise your mother would have had your name written down on the invitations. Understand, sir, I was being fanciful when I told your father I wanted to marry for love. I realize that isn't possible now, given the urgency of finding a husband, and so I decided I would consider the marriage a business arrangement. In return for the use of my considerable inheritance, my husband would go his way and I would go mine. I thought I would travel . . . and in time, perhaps, go back to Holy Cross. It was very peaceful there."

"Hell."

She didn't know what to make of that muttered blasphemy. She frowned in reaction and then said, "I also hoped that eventually my husband and I would become friends."

"And lovers?" he asked.

She lifted her shoulders in a shrug. "Anything is possible, Colin, given time and patience. However, I have had time to reevaluate my position. Granted, the gentlemen in England seem to be more civilized, and I had hoped to find one who was at least ethical, but tonight I realized none of it matters anymore. I'm going to cooperate. I'll marry the general. I've caused quite enough trouble. Perhaps in time this man will learn to . . . soften in his attitudes."

Colin snorted. "A snake doesn't ever stop slithering. He won't change, and you aren't going to marry him. Got that?"

She shivered over the harshness in his voice. "I want your agreement, Alesandra."

She wouldn't give it. She kept picturing the blood pouring down Raymond's face. "I won't be the cause of any more . . ."

"Come here."

Alesandra walked over to stand in front of his desk. He motioned her closer with the crook of his finger. She edged her way around the side and stopped when she was just a foot away from him.

"The general would give up his plan and leave me alone if I had a husband . . . wouldn't he?"

The combination of fear and hope in her voice bothered the hell out of him. She was too young to have such worries. Alesandra should be as scatterbrained and as giddy as his younger sisters.

Damn it all, she was in need of a champion. He reached out and took hold of her hands. She realized she was gripping them together again. She tried to relax. She couldn't.

"Marriage to the general is out of the question. Are we agreed on that?"

He squeezed her hands until she nodded. "Good," he remarked then. "Have you left anything out in your explanation?"

"No."

Colin smiled. "No one bucks the head of security," he remarked then, referring to Sir Richards.

"Your father did."

"Yes, he did, didn't he?" He was inordinately pleased with his father. "I'll talk to Richards tomorrow and see if we can't get his support."

"Thank you."

His nod was quick. "Since my family is responsible for you, I'll set up a meeting with my father and my brother as soon as they're feeling well again."

"For what purpose?"

"To figure out what the hell to do with you."

He'd meant the remark as a jest of sorts. She took it to heart. She jerked her hands away from his. His bluntness had offended her. Alesandra had an extremely tender nature. He considered suggesting she learn to toughen her emotional hide, then decided not to offer that advice because she would probably take that as an insult too.

"I will not become a burden."

"I didn't say you were."

"You implied it."

"I don't ever imply. I always tell it the way it is."

She turned and walked toward the door. "I believe it's time to reevaluate."

"You've already done that."

"I'm going to again," she announced.

A wave of nausea caught Colin by surprise. He closed his eyes and took a deep breath. His stomach growled, too, and he assumed his sudden weak condition was due to the fact that he had skipped dinner.

He forced himself to think about her last remark. "What are you going to reevaluate now?"

"Our arrangement," she explained. "It isn't working out. I really believe I should find other lodgings tomorrow."

"Alesandra."

He hadn't raised his voice but the bite was still there in his hard tone. She stopped at the entrance and turned to look at him. She braced herself for his next hurtful bit of honesty.

He felt like hell when he saw the tears in her eyes. "I'm sorry," he muttered. "You aren't a burden. Your current situation, however, is a mess. Wouldn't you agree with that evaluation?" he asked.

"Yes, I would agree."

Colin rubbed his brow in an absentminded action and was surprised to feel the perspiration there. He tugged on his cravat next. Damn, it was hot in the study. The fire from the hearth was putting out more heat than was necessary, he supposed. He thought about taking off his jacket but was too weary to go to the trouble now.

"It's a very serious situation, Colin," she added when he didn't respond to her earlier agreement.

"But it isn't the end of the world, is it? You're looking overwhelmed by it all."

"I am overwhelmed," she cried out. "Raymond was injured tonight. Have you already forgotten? He could have been killed. And you . . . you could have been hurt too."

He was frowning again. She was almost sorry she'd

reminded him of the incident. She decided not to end the evening on such a sour note.

"I've forgotten my manners," she blurted out. "I should say thank you now."

"You should? Why?"

"Because you apologized," she explained. "I know it was difficult for you."

"And how would you know that?"

"Your voice got all gruff, and you were glaring at me. Yes, it was difficult. Yet you did say you were sorry. That makes your apology all the more pleasing to me."

She walked back over to his side. Before she lost her courage, she leaned forward and kissed him on his cheek. "I still prefer your father for my guardian," she told him, hoping to gain a smile. "He's much easier to . . ."

She was searching for the right word. He gave it to her. "Manipulate?"

She laughed. "Yes."

"My four little sisters have worn him down. He's been turned into milk toast by all those women."

Colin let out a weary sigh and rubbed his brow again. He'd developed a pounding headache in the last few minutes, and he could barely concentrate on the topic at hand. "Go to bed, Alesandra. It's late and you've had quite a day."

She started to leave, then paused. "Are you feeling all right? Your face looks terribly pale to me."

"I feel fine," he told her. "Go to bed."

He told the lie easily. He didn't feel at all fine, however. He felt like hell. His insides were on fire. His stomach was reacting as though he'd just swallowed a hot piece of coal. His skin was clammy and hot, and he found himself thanking God he hadn't had much to eat tonight. The mere thought of food made him want to gag.

Colin was certain he would feel better once he had gotten some sleep. At one o'clock in the morning he was wishing he could close his eyes and die.

By three o'clock, he thought he had.

He was burning up with fever, and damn if he hadn't

thrown up at least twenty times the paltry little apple he'd eaten before he left for the opera.

His stomach finally accepted the fact that there wasn't anything more to get rid of and settled down into a tight knot. Colin sprawled out on the bed, face down, with his arms spread wide.

Oh, yes, death would have been a treat.

# Chapter
# 5

She wouldn't let him die. She wouldn't leave him alone either. The minute she was awakened by the sounds of retching coming from Colin's bedroom, she threw off her covers and got out of bed.

Alesandra didn't care about appearances. It didn't matter to her if going into his bedroom would be looked upon as inappropriate behavior; Colin needed her help, and he was going to get it.

By the time she put on her robe and went next door, Colin was back in his bed. He was sprawled out on his stomach on top of the covers. He was stark naked. She tried not to notice. Colin had opened both windows and the room was now so frigid with cold she could see her breath. The drapes billowed out like inflated balloons from the hard, spitting wind and rain coming through the windows.

"Dear God, are you trying to kill yourself?" she asked.

Colin didn't answer her. She hurried over to shut the windows before turning to the bed. Only one side of Colin's face was visible to her, yet that was quite enough for her to surmise from his tortured expression how miserable he was feeling.

It was a struggle, but she finally was able to tug the covers out from under him and then cover him up and properly tuck him in. He told her to leave him the hell alone. She ignored that order. She put the back of her hand to his forehead, felt the heat there, and immediately went to fetch a cold, wet cloth.

Colin was too weak to fight her. She spent the rest of the night with him, mopping his brow every five minutes or so and holding the chamber pot for him just as often. He wasn't able to throw up anything more, for his stomach was empty now, but he still made the most horrible gagging sounds trying.

He wanted water. She wouldn't let him have any. She tried reasoning with him, but he wasn't in the mood to listen to her. Thankfully he was too exhausted to get the water by himself.

"If you swallow anything, it's going to come right back up. I've had this illness, Colin. I know what I'm talking about. Now close your eyes and try to get some rest. You're going to feel better tomorrow."

She wanted to give him a bit of hope, and for that reason she deliberately lied. If Colin followed the same course as everyone else, he was going to be miserable for a good week.

Her prediction proved accurate. He wasn't feeling any better the following day, or the day after that. She personally tended to him. She wouldn't let Flannaghan or Valena into the chamber, fearing they would also catch the illness if they got too close to Colin. Flannaghan tried to argue with her. Colin was his responsibility, after all, and he should be the one to tend to him. It was his noble duty, he explained, to put himself at risk.

Alesandra countered with the explanation that she had already suffered with the illness and was therefore the only one suited to see to Colin's needs. It was highly doubtful she would get sick again. Flannaghan, however, would be taking a much greater gamble, and how would they all ever get along if he became too sick to take care of them?

Flannaghan was finally convinced. He was kept busy with the running of the household, and even took on the added duty of answering all of her correspondence. The town house was off-limits to all callers. The physician, Sir Winters, returned to look at Raymond's injury, and while he was there Alesandra consulted him about Colin's illness. The physician didn't go into Colin's bedroom, for he had no wish to contract the illness, but he left a tonic he thought might settle the patient's irritable stomach and suggested sponge baths to cool the fever.

Colin was a difficult patient. Alesandra tried to follow the physician's advice by giving Colin a sponge bath late that night when his temperature increased. She stroked his chest and arms with the cooling cloth first, then turned to his legs. He seemed to be asleep, but when she touched his scarred leg, he almost came off the bed.

"I would like to die in peace, Alesandra. Now get the hell out of here."

His hoarse bellow didn't affect her, for she was still reeling from the sight of his injured leg. The calf was a mass of scar tissue from the back of his knee to the edge of his heel. Alesandra didn't know how he'd come by the injury, but the agony he must have endured tore at her heart.

She thought it a miracle he could walk at all. Colin jerked the covers over his legs and told her again, though in a much more weary tone of voice, to leave his room.

There were tears in her eyes. She thought he might have seen them. She didn't want him to know the brief glimpse at his leg had caused that reaction. Colin was a proud, unbending man. He didn't want her pity, she knew, and he was obviously prickly about the scar.

Alesandra decided to turn his attention. "Your shouts are most upsetting to me, Colin, and if you continue to give me such harsh commands, I'll probably cry like a child. I won't leave, however, no matter how mean hearted you become. Now kindly give me your leg. I'm going to wash it."

"Alesandra, I swear to God, I'm going to toss you out the window if you don't leave me alone."

"Colin, the sponge bath didn't bother you at all last night. Why are you so irritable now? Is the fever higher tonight?"

"You washed my legs last night?"

"I did," she blatantly lied.

"What the hell else did you wash?"

She knew what he was asking. She tried not to blush when she answered him. "Your arms and chest and legs," she told him. "I left the middle alone. Do quit fighting me, sir," she ordered as she snatched his leg from under the cover.

Colin gave up. He muttered something atrocious under his breath and closed his eyes. Alesandra dipped the cloth into the cold water, then gently washed both legs.

Her composure never faltered, and it was only after she'd covered him up again that she realized he'd been watching her.

"Now then," she said with a sigh. "Don't you feel better?"

His glare was his answer. She stood up and turned away from him so he wouldn't see her smile. She put the bowl of water back on the washstand, then carried a goblet only half filled with water back over to her patient.

She handed him the drink, told him she would leave him alone for a little while, and then tried to do just that. He grabbed hold of her hand and held tight.

"Are you sleepy?" he asked her, his voice still gruff with irritation.

"Not particularly."

"Then stay and talk to me."

He moved his legs out of the way and patted the side of the bed. Alesandra sat down. She folded her hands together in her lap and desperately tried not to stare at his chest.

"Don't you own any nightshirts?" she asked.

"No."

"Cover yourself, Colin," she suggested then. She didn't wait for him to do as she ordered, but saw to the duty herself.

He immediately shoved the quilt back. He sat up, propped his back against the headboard, and let out a loud yawn.

"God, I feel like hell."

"Why do you wear your hair so long? It reaches your shoulders now. It looks quite barbaric," she added with a smile so he wouldn't think she was insulting him. "'Tis the truth, it makes you look like a pirate."

He shrugged. "It's a reminder to me," he said.

"A reminder of what?"

"Being free."

She didn't know what he was talking about, but he didn't look inclined to explain further. He turned the topic then by asking her to catch him up on business matters.

"Did Flannaghan remember to send a note to Borders?"

"Do you mean your associate?"

"Borders isn't an associate. He's retired from the shipping business these days, but he helps out when I need him."

"Yes," she answered. "Flannaghan did send a messenger and Mister Borders is taking care of business. Each evening he sends the daily report, and they're all stacked up on your desk for you to look over when you're feeling better. You also received another letter from your partner," she added with a nod. "I didn't realize the two of you had opened a second office across the sea. You'll soon be worldwide, won't you?"

"Perhaps. Now tell me what you've been doing. You haven't gone out, have you?"

She shook her head. "I've been taking care of you. I did write another note to Victoria's brother begging a second audience. Neil responded with a terse note, denying my request. I do wish you hadn't tossed him out."

"I don't want him coming back here, Alesandra."

She let out a sigh. He gave her a good frown. "You're stirring up unnecessary trouble."

"I promised to be discreet. I'm worried about Victoria," she added with a nod.

"No one else is," he countered.

"Yes, I know," she whispered. "Colin, if you were in trouble, I would do whatever it took to help you."

He was pleased with her fervent promise. "You would?"

She nodded. "We are like family now, aren't we? Your father is my guardian, and I try to think of you as a brother . . ."

"The hell with that."

Her eyes widened. Colin looked furious with her. "You don't want me to think of you as a brother?"

"Damned right I don't."

She looked crushed.

Colin stared at her with an incredulous expression on his face. The fever hadn't diminished his desire for her at all. Hell, he'd have to be dead and buried before he could rid himself of his growing need to touch her.

She didn't have a clue as to her own appeal. She sat so prim and proper next to him, wearing that virginal white gown that wasn't suppose to be the least bit provocative but still damn well was. The dress was buttoned up to her chin. He thought it was extremely sexy. So was her hair. It wasn't bound up behind her head tonight but fell in wild curls around her shoulders. She kept brushing the locks back over her shoulders in a motion he found utterly appealing.

Damned if he would let her think of him as her brother. "Less than a week ago you were thinking of me as your future husband, remember?"

His unreasonable anger fueled her own. "But you declined, remember that?"

"Don't take that tone of voice with me, Alesandra."

"Don't raise your voice to me, Colin."

He let out a long sigh. They were both exhausted, he told himself, and surely that was the reason their tempers were so fragile tonight.

"You're a princess," he said then. "And I'm . . ."

She finished his sentence for him. "A dragon."

"Fine," he snapped. "A dragon then. And princesses don't marry dragons."

"Lord, but you're irritable tonight."

"I'm always irritable."

"Then it's a blessing we aren't going to marry each other. You would make me quite miserable."

Colin yawned again. "Probably," he drawled out.

She stood up. "You need to go to sleep now," she announced. She leaned over him and touched his forehead with her hand. "You've still got a fever, though it isn't as high as last night. Colin, do you dislike women who say I told you so?"

"Hell, yes."

She smiled. "Good. I remember telling you your suspicious nature would get you into trouble, and I was right, wasn't I?"

He didn't answer her. She didn't mind. She was too busy gloating. She turned and walked over to the door connecting the bedrooms. She wasn't quite finished goading him, however. "You just had to find out for yourself that Caine was really sick, and now look at you."

She pulled the door wide. "Good night, dragon."

"Alesandra?"

"Yes?"

"I was wrong."

"You were?" She was thrilled by his admission and waited to hear the rest of his apology. The man wasn't quite an ogre after all. "And?" she prodded when he didn't go on.

"You're still a brat."

Colin's fever continued to plague him for seven long days and nights. He awakened during the eighth night feeling human again and knew the fever was gone. He was surprised to find Alesandra in his bed. She was fully clothed and slept sitting up with her shoulders propped against the headboard. Her hair hung over her face, and she didn't move at all when he got out of bed. Colin washed, changed into a clean pair of britches, and then went back to the bed. He lifted Alesandra into his arms, and even in his weakened condition, it didn't take any effort at all. She was as light as air to him. He smiled when she snuggled up against his shoulder and let out a feminine little sigh. Colin carried her back to her own room, put her in bed, and covered her with a satin quilt.

He stood there staring down at her for a long while. She never opened her eyes. She was clearly exhausted from lack of sleep. He knew she had stayed by his side throughout most of the god-awful ordeal. Alesandra had taken good care of him, and, Lord, he didn't know how he felt about that.

He accepted that he was in her debt, but, damn it all, his feelings went far beyond gratitude. She was beginning to matter to him. As soon as he acknowledged that truth, he tried to think of a way to soften her impact on him. Now wasn't the time to get involved with any woman. Yes, the timing was all wrong, and he sure as certain wasn't going to push his own goals and dreams aside now for any woman.

Alesandra wasn't just any woman, though, and he knew, if he didn't get away from her soon, it would be too late. Hell, it was complicated. His mind was filled with such conflicting emotions. He didn't want her, he told himself again and again, and yet the thought of anyone else having her made his stomach turn.

He wasn't making any sense. Colin finally forced himself to move away from the side of her bed. He went back through his bedroom and continued on into his study. He had at least a month's work piled up now and it would surely take him that long just to transfer all the numbers into the ledgers. Burying himself in his work was just what he needed to take his mind off Alesandra.

Someone had done all the work. Colin was incredulous when he saw the ledgers. The entries were completely up-to-date, ending with today's shipping numbers. He spent an hour double-checking to make certain the totals were accurate, then leaned back in his chair to go through the stack of notes left for him to read.

Caine had obviously taken charge, Colin decided. He would have to remember to thank his brother for his help. It had to have taken him the full week, for there were over fifty pages of transfers added, and Colin hadn't been this current in over a year.

He turned his attention to his messages. Colin worked in his study from dawn until late afternoon. Flannaghan was pleased to see his employer was looking so much better. He carried up a breakfast tray and another tray of food at the noon hour. Colin had bathed and dressed in a white shirt and black britches, and Flannaghan remarked that the color was coming back to his lord's complexion. The servant hovered like a mother hen and soon drove Colin to distraction.

Flannaghan again interrupted him around three that afternoon to give him messages from both his father and his brother.

The note from the Duke of Williamshire was filled with concern for Princess Alesandra's safety. He'd obviously heard about the attack outside the Opera House. He requested a family meeting be set to settle Alesandra's future and asked that Colin let him know the minute he was feeling well enough to bring the princess to their London town house.

Caine's note was similar—confusing, too, for he made no mention of helping with the books. Colin thought Caine was simply being humble.

"It's good news, isn't it?" Flannaghan asked. "Your family has fully recovered. Cook talked to your father's gardener and he said everyone was feeling fit again. Your father has already ordered his town house opened and should be settled in by nightfall. The duchess is with him, but your sisters have been ordered to stay in the country for another week or two. Do you wish for me to send a messenger with the news of your recovery?"

Colin wasn't surprised by his servant's information. The grapevine between the households was always up to the minute with the latest happenings. "My father wants a family council, or did you already find that out from the gardener?" he asked dryly.

Flannaghan nodded. "I had heard, but I wasn't given a specific time."

Colin shook his head in vexation. "Set the meeting for tomorrow afternoon."

"At what time?"

"Two."

"And your brother?" Flannaghan asked. "Should I send a messenger to him as well?"

"Yes," Colin agreed. "I'm certain he'll want to be there."

Flannaghan hurried toward the door to see to his duties. He reached the entrance, then paused again. "Milord, is our home open to visitors yet? Princess Alesandra's suitors have been begging entrance all week."

Colin frowned. "Are you telling me the rakes are already camping out on my doorstep?"

Flannaghan flinched over the outrage in his employer's

voice. "Word has spread like fire that we have a beautiful, unattached princess residing with us."

"Hell."

"Precisely, milord."

"No one is allowed entrance until after the meeting," Colin announced. He smiled then. "You seem as irritated as I am about Alesandra's suitors. Why is that, Flannaghan?"

The servant didn't pretend indifference. "I am as irritated," he confessed. "She belongs to us, Colin," he blurted out, slipping back to their casual relationship of using first names. "And it is our duty to keep those lechers away from her."

Colin nodded agreement. Flannaghan turned the topic just a little then. "What should I do about her father's business associate? Dreyson has sent a note each and every morning begging an audience. He has papers for her signature," he added. "But in one of the notes I chanced to read over Princess Alesandra's shoulder, Dreyson also insisted he had alarming news to give her."

Colin leaned further back in his chair. "How did Alesandra react to this note?"

"She wasn't at all upset," Flannaghan replied. "I questioned her, of course, and asked her if she shouldn't be a little concerned. She said Dreyson's alarm probably had something to do with a market downswing. I didn't know what she was talking about."

"She was talking about financial losses," he explained. "Send a note to Dreyson, too, telling him that he is invited to call on Alesandra at my father's town house. Set the time for three o'clock, Flannaghan. We should be through with family business by then."

The servant still didn't leave. "Was there something more you wanted?"

"Will Princess Alesandra be leaving us?" The worry in the servant's tone was evident.

"There is a good chance she'll move in with my father and mother."

"But, milord . . ."

"My father is her guardian, Flannaghan."

"That may be," the servant countered. "But you're the only one fit enough to watch out for her. Begging your pardon for being so blunt, but your father is getting along in years and your brother has his wife and child to look after. That leaves you, milord. 'Tis the truth, I would be very distressed if anything happened to our princess."

"Nothing's going to happen to her."

The conviction in his employer's voice appeased Flannaghan's worry. Colin was acting like a protector now. He was a possessive man by nature, stubborn, and just a little bit obtuse, in Flannaghan's estimation, because Colin was taking forever to come to the realization that he and Princess Alesandra were meant for each other.

Colin turned his attention back to his ledgers. Flannaghan coughed to let him know he wasn't quite finished bothering him.

"What else is on your mind?"

"I just thought I would mention . . . that is, the incident in front of the Opera . . ."

Colin shut his book. "Yes?" he prodded.

"It's affected her. She hasn't said anything to me, but I know she hasn't gotten over the incident. She's still blaming herself for Raymond's injury."

"That's ridiculous."

Flannaghan nodded. "She keeps apologizing to her guard and this morning, when she came downstairs, I could tell she'd been weeping. I believe you should have a talk with her, milord. A princess should not cry."

Flannaghan sounded like an authority on the topic of royalty. Colin nodded. "All right, I'll have a talk with her later. Now leave me alone. For the first time in months, I'm actually close to being caught up and I want to get today's totals entered. I don't wish to be disturbed until dinner."

Flannaghan didn't mind his employer's gruffness. Colin would take care of the princess, and that was all that really mattered.

The butler's cheerful mood was sorely tested the rest of

the afternoon. He spent most of his time answering the front door and turning away potential suitors. It was a damn nuisance.

At seven o'clock that evening, Sir Richards arrived on their doorstep. He didn't request admission. The head of England's Security Section demanded to be let in.

Flannaghan ushered Sir Richards up the stairs and into Colin's study. The distinguished-looking gray-haired gentleman waited until the butler had taken his leave before speaking to Colin.

"You're looking none the worse for wear," he announced. "I wanted to look in on you to see how you're doing, of course, and also compliment you on a job well done. The Wellingham business could have gotten sticky. You handled it well."

Colin leaned back in his chair. "It did get sticky," he reminded the director.

"Yes, but you handled it with your usual tact."

Colin caught himself before he snorted with laughter. Handled with tact? How like the director to summarize in gentlemen's terms the necessary killing of one of England's enemies.

"Why are you really here, Richards?"

"To compliment you, of course."

Colin did laugh then. Richards smiled. "I could use a spot of brandy," he announced with a wave of his hand in the direction of the side bar against the wall. "Will you join me?"

Colin declined the offer. He started to get up to see to the director's request, but Richards waved him back to his seat. "I can fetch it."

The director poured himself a drink, then went over to sit in the leather-backed chair facing the desk. "Morgan's going to be joining us in just a few minutes. I wanted to talk to you first, however. Another little problem has developed and I thought it might be just the task for Morgan to handle. An opportunity, you see, for him to get his feet wet."

"He's joining the ranks then?"

"He would like to be of service to his country," the director told him. "What do you think of him, Colin? Forget diplomacy and give me your gut reaction to the man."

Colin shrugged. His neck was stiff from leaning over the ledgers for so long and he rolled his shoulders, trying to work the knots out. "I understand he inherited title and land from his father a few years back. He's the Earl of Oakmount now, isn't he?"

"Yes," Sir Richards replied. "But you're only half right. The title and land came from an uncle. Morgan's father ran tail years ago. The boy was shuffled from one relative to another during the growing years. There was talk of illegitimacy and some think that was the reason the father abandoned the boy. Morgan's mother died when he was four or five."

"A difficult childhood," Colin remarked.

The director agreed. "It made him the man he is today. He learned to be clever early on, you see."

"You know more about his background than I do," Colin said. "All I can add is superficial. I've seen him at various functions. He's well liked by the ton."

The director took a long swallow of the brandy before speaking again. "You still haven't given me your opinion," he reminded Colin.

"I'm not hedging," Colin replied. "I honestly don't know him well enough to form an opinion. He seems likable enough. Nathan doesn't particularly like him, though. I do remember him making that remark."

The director smiled. "Your partner doesn't like anyone."

"That's true, he doesn't."

"Did he have specific reasons for disliking Morgan?"

"No. He referred to him as one of the pretty boys. Morgan's a handsome man, or so I'm told by the women."

"Nathan doesn't like him because of his appearance?"

Colin laughed. Sir Richards sounded incredulous. "My partner doesn't like charmers. He says he never knows what they're thinking."

The director filed that information away in the back of his

mind. "Morgan has almost as many contacts as you have, and he would be a tremendous asset to the department. Still, I'm determined to take it slow. I still don't know how he'll handle himself in a crisis. I've invited him here to talk to you, Colin. There's another delicate matter you might want to consider handling for us. If you decide in favor of taking on the assignment, I'd like Morgan to get involved. He could do well to learn from you."

"I'm retired, remember?"

The director smiled. "So am I," he drawled out. "I've been trying to hand the reins over for a good four years now. I'm getting too old for this business."

"You'll never quit."

"And neither will you," Richards predicted. "At least not until your company can survive without your added income. Tell me this, son. Has your partner wondered yet where the additional funds are coming from? I know you didn't want him to know you've started helping the department out again."

Colin stacked his hands behind his neck. "He isn't aware," he explained. "Nathan's been occupied opening the second office. His wife, Sara, is due to have their first baby any day now. I doubt Nathan has had time to notice."

"And when he does notice?"

"I'll tell him the truth."

"We could use Nathan again," the director said.

"That's out of the question. He has a family now."

Sir Richards reluctantly agreed. He turned the topic back to the task he wanted Colin to accept. "About this assignment," he began. "It's no more dangerous than the last, but . . . ah, good evening, Princess Alesandra. It's a pleasure to see you again."

She stood just outside the entrance. Colin wondered how much she had overheard.

She smiled at the director. "It's good to see you again, sir," she replied in a soft whisper. "I hope I haven't intruded. The door was ajar, but if you're in the middle of a conference, I'll come back later."

Sir Richards hastily stood up and walked over to her. He took hold of her hand and bowed low. "You haven't intruded," he assured her. "Come and sit down. I wanted to talk to you before I left."

He latched on to her elbow and ushered her over to a chair. She sat down and smoothed her skirts while she waited for him to take his seat as well.

"I heard about the unfortunate incident outside the Royal Opera House," the director remarked with a frown. He sat down, nodded to Colin, and then turned his attention back to her. "Have you recovered from your upset?"

"There wasn't anything for me to recover from, Sir Richards. My guard was injured. Raymond required eight stitches in all, but they were removed yesterday. He's feeling much better now. Isn't that right, Colin?"

She kept her gaze fully directed on Sir Richards when she included Colin in the conversation. He didn't mind her lack of attention. He was fully occupied trying to hide his amusement. Sir Richards was blushing. Colin couldn't believe it. The hard-nosed, steel-hearted director of covert operations was blushing like a schoolboy.

Alesandra was mesmerizing the man. Colin wondered if she had any idea of her effect or if it was deliberate. Her smile was innocently sweet, her gaze direct, unwavering, and if she started in batting her eyelashes, then Colin would know the seduction wasn't quite so innocent after all.

"Have you had an opportunity to look into the other matter we discussed?" she asked. "I realize it was bold of me to ask anything of such an important man, Sir Richards, and I want you to know how grateful I am for your offer to send someone to Gretna Green."

"I've already taken care of that duty," the director replied. "My man, Simpson, only just returned last evening. You were correct, Princess. There isn't a record with either Robert Elliott or his rival, David Laing."

"I knew it," Alesandra cried out. She clasped her hands together as though in prayer and turned to frown at Colin. "Didn't I tell you so?"

Her enthusiasm made him smile. "Tell me what?"

"That Lady Victoria wouldn't elope. Your director has just confirmed my suspicions."

"Now, Princess, it's still a possibility—remote, of course —that she did marry there. Both Elliott and Laing keep accurate records so each can boast the number of weddings performed. It's a competitive thing, you see. However, they aren't the only men in Gretna Green who can marry a couple. Some less reputable gents just don't bother with records. They would fill out the certificate and hand it over to the husband. So you see, my dear, she still could have eloped after all."

"She didn't."

Alesandra was emphatic in that belief. Colin shook his head. "She's stirring up a hornet's nest, Richards. I've told her to leave it alone but she won't listen to me."

She frowned at Colin. "I am not stirring anything up."

"Yes, you are," Colin replied. "You're going to cause Victoria's family additional heartache if you pester them with questions."

His criticism stung. She bowed her head. "You must have a low opinion of me if you believe I would deliberately set out to hurt anyone."

"You didn't have to be so harsh with her, son."

Colin was exasperated. "I wasn't being harsh, just honest."

Sir Richards shook his head. Alesandra smiled at the director. She was pleased he'd taken her side.

"If he would only listen to my reasons for being worried, Sir Richards, he wouldn't be so quick to call my concern interference."

The director glared at Colin. "You wouldn't listen to her reasons? She makes a sound argument, Colin. You shouldn't judge without knowing all the facts."

"Thank you, Sir Richards." Colin snorted.

Alesandra decided to ignore the rude man. "What is our next step in this investigation?" she asked the director.

Sir Richards looked a bit confused. "Investigation? I hadn't thought of the problem in that light. . . ."

"You said you would help me," she reminded the director. "You mustn't become discouraged so quickly."

Sir Richards looked to Colin for assistance. Colin grinned.

"It isn't a matter of giving up," Sir Richards said. "I'm just not certain what it is I'm investigating. It's a plain fact your friend did run off with someone and I believe Colin's correct when he suggests you let the matter go."

"Why is it a plain fact?"

"Victoria left a note," Sir Richards explained.

She shook her head. "Anyone could have written a note."

"Yes, but . . ."

"I had so hoped you would help me, Sir Richards," she interrupted. Her tone of voice sounded forlorn. "You were my last hope. Victoria could be in danger and she only has you and me to help her. If anyone can ferret out the truth, it's you. You're so intelligent and clever."

Sir Richards puffed up like a rooster. Colin had to shake his head. One compliment had turned the man into mush.

"Will you be satisfied if I can find a record of the marriage?"

"You won't find one."

"But if I do . . ."

"I'll let the matter rest."

Sir Richards nodded. "Very well," he agreed. "I'll start with her family. I'll send a man around tomorrow to talk to the brother. One way or another, I'll find out what happened."

Her smile was radiant. "Thank you so much," she whispered. "I should warn you, though. I sent a note to Victoria's brother and he refused to grant me another audience. Colin, you see, was rude to him and he obviously hasn't forgiven him."

"He won't refuse me," Sir Richards announced with a hard nod.

Colin had heard enough of what he considered a ridiculous topic. He didn't like the idea that the director of England's Security Section was lowering himself to snoop into another family's private affairs.

He was about to change the subject when Sir Richards's next remark caught his attention. "Princess Alesandra, after the cooperation you've given, looking into this delicate matter is the very least I can do for you. Rest easy, my dear. I'll have some answers for you before you leave England."

Colin leaned forward. "Back up, Richards," he demanded, his voice hard. "Exactly how has Alesandra cooperated?"

The director looked surprised by the question. "She didn't explain to you . . ."

"I didn't believe it was necessary," Alesandra blurted out. She hastily stood up. "If you'll excuse me now, I'll leave you two gentlemen alone to discuss your business."

"Alesandra, sit down."

Colin's tone suggested she not argue with him. She let out a little sigh and did as he ordered. She refused to look at him, however, and kept her gaze directed on her lap. She wanted to run and hide rather than talk about her decision, but that would be cowardly and irresponsible, and Colin deserved to know what had been decided.

Dignity and decorum, she thought to herself. Colin would never know how upset she was, and there was a bit of victory in that, wasn't there?

"Explain to me why Richards is so pleased with your cooperation."

"I've decided to return to my father's homeland," she explained in a bare whisper. "I'm going to marry the general. Your father has given his approval."

Colin didn't say anything for a long while. He stared at Alesandra. She stared at her lap.

"All of this was decided while I was sick?"

"Yes."

"Look at me," he commanded.

She was close to bursting into tears. She took a deep breath and finally turned to look at him.

Colin knew she was upset. She was twisting her hands together and trying not to cry.

"She wasn't coerced," Sir Richards interjected.

"The hell she wasn't."

"It was my decision," she insisted.

Colin shook his head. "Richards, nothing has been decided. Understand? Alesandra is still reacting to the incident last week. Her guard was injured and she feels responsible."

"I am responsible," she cried out.

"No," he countered, his voice emphatic. "You were frightened."

"Does it matter what my reasons were?"

"Hell, yes, it matters," he snapped. He turned his attention back to the director. "Alesandra has obviously forgotten her promise to me last week."

"Colin . . ."

"Be silent."

Her eyes widened in disbelief. "Be silent? This is my future under discussion, not yours."

"I'm your guardian," he countered. "I decide your future. You seem to have forgotten that fact."

His scowl was as hot as the fire from a dragon's nostrils. She decided not to argue with him. He wasn't being at all reasonable, and if he didn't quit glaring at her she was definitely going to get up and leave the room.

Colin turned his attention back to the director. "Alesandra and I talked about this problem last week," he explained. "We decided she wouldn't marry the general. You can tell your associates in finance the deal's off."

Colin was so furious he barely noticed the director's nod of agreement as he continued on. "She isn't going to marry him. The general sounds like a real sweetheart, doesn't he? He sent a gang of cutthroats to kidnap his bride for him. A hell of a courtship, wouldn't you say? How I wish he'd come to England. I'd like to have a few minutes alone with the bastard."

Alesandra couldn't understand why Colin was getting so worked up. She had never seen him this angry. She was too astonished to be frightened. She didn't know what to say or do to calm him.

"He won't give up, Colin," she whispered, grimacing over the shiver in her voice. "He'll send others."

"That's my problem, not yours."

"It is?"

The fear he glimpsed in her eyes took away some of his anger. He didn't want her to be afraid of him. He deliberately softened his voice when he answered her. "Yes, it is."

They stared at each other a long minute. The tenderness in his expression made her want to weep with relief. He wasn't going to let her leave England.

She had to force herself to turn her gaze away from him so he wouldn't see the tears in her eyes. She stared at her lap, took a deep breath in an attempt to control her emotions, and then said, "I was trying to be noble. I didn't want anyone else to get hurt and Sir Richards said there was a chance for better trade agreements . . ."

"My associates believe the general would cooperate," Sir Richards interjected. "I personally don't hold with that nonsense. I'm of the same mind as Colin," he added with a nod. "The general isn't a man to be trusted. So you see, my dear, you don't have to be noble."

"And if Colin gets hurt?" she blurted out.

Both Sir Richards and Colin were astonished by that question. The fear was back in Alesandra's expression. Colin leaned back in his chair and stared at her. She wasn't afraid for her own safety; no, she was worried about him. He probably should have been irritated with her. He could take care of himself, and it was a bit insulting to know she was worried about him.

It was damned flattering, too.

Sir Richards raised an eyebrow and looked at Colin, waiting for him to answer her.

"I can take care of myself," Colin said. "I don't want you to worry, understand?"

"Yes, Colin."

Her immediate agreement pleased him. "Leave us now, Alesandra. Richards and I have other matters to discuss."

She couldn't get out of the room fast enough. She didn't even say good-bye to the director. Her conduct was most unladylike, but she didn't care. She was shaking so violently she could barely get the door closed behind her.

Relief made her knees weak. She sagged against the wall and closed her eyes. A tear slipped down her cheek. She took a deep breath in an attempt to calm herself.

She wasn't going to have to be noble and marry that horrible man after all. Colin had taken the decision out of her hands and she was so grateful she didn't mind at all that he'd been so angry. For some reason she couldn't define, Colin had decided to take the duty of guardian to heart. He had acted like a protector, and Alesandra was so thankful to have someone on her side she said a prayer of thanksgiving.

"Princess Alesandra, are you all right?"

She jumped a good foot. Then she burst into laughter. Flannaghan and another man she'd never met before stood just a few feet away from her. She'd not even heard their approach.

She could feel herself blushing. The stranger standing just behind the butler was smiling at her. She decided he probably thought she'd lost her mind. Alesandra moved away from the wall, forced herself to quit laughing, and then said, "I'm quite all right."

"What were you doing?"

"Reflecting," she replied. And praying, she silently added. Flannaghan didn't know what she meant by that remark. He continued to stare at her with a perplexed look on his face. She turned to their guest. "Good evening, sir."

The butler finally remembered his manners. "Princess Alesandra, may I present Morgan Atkins, the Earl of Oakmount."

Alesandra smiled in greeting. "It is a pleasure to meet you."

He moved forward and took hold of her hand. "The pleasure is all mine, Princess. I've been most eager to meet you."

"You have?"

He smiled over the surprise in her eyes. "Yes, I have," he assured her. "You're the talk of London, but I imagine you realize that."

She shook her head. "No, I didn't realize," she admitted.

"The prince regent has been singing your praises," Mor-

103

gan explained. "You mustn't frown, Princess. I've only heard wonderful things about you."

"What wonderful things?" Flannaghan dared to ask.

Morgan didn't take his gaze away from Alesandra when he answered the butler. "I was told she was very beautiful and now I know that story is true. She is beautiful—exquisite, in fact."

She was embarrassed by his flattery. She tried to pull her hand away from his, but he wouldn't let go.

"You have a delightful blush, Princess," he told her. He moved closer, and in the candlelight she could see the handsome silver threads streaking his dark brown hair. His eyes, a deep black brown color, sparkled with his smile. Morgan wasn't much taller than Flannaghan, but he seemed to overwhelm the butler. The aura of power surrounding him was probably due to his important position in society, she guessed. His title allowed him to be arrogant and self-assured.

The man was a charmer, however, who understood his own appeal. He knew he was making her uncomfortable under his close scrutiny, too.

"Are you enjoying your stay in England?" he asked.

"Yes, thank you."

Colin opened the door just as Morgan was asking Alesandra if he might be permitted to call on her the following afternoon. He immediately noticed Alesandra's blush. He noticed Morgan was holding her hand, too.

He reacted before he could stop himself. He reached out, grabbed hold of Alesandra's arm, and jerked her into his side. Then he draped his arm around her shoulders in an action she found terribly possessive and frowned at their guest.

"Alesandra's going to be busy tomorrow," he announced. "Go on inside, Morgan. The director's waiting to talk to you."

Morgan didn't seem to notice the irritation in Colin's tone of voice, or if he did notice, he chose to ignore it. He nodded his agreement, then turned his attention back to her.

"With your permission, Princess, I'll continue to try to convince your cousin to let me call on you."

As soon as she nodded agreement, he bowed to her and walked into the study.

"Do quit squeezing me, Cousin," Alesandra whispered.

He heard the laughter in her voice and looked down at her. "Where the hell did he get that idea? Did you tell him I was your cousin?"

"No, of course I didn't," she replied. "Will you unhand me now? I have to go back to my room to fetch my notecard."

He wouldn't let go of her. "Alesandra, why are you so damned happy?"

"I'm happy because it appears as though I won't have to marry the general," she said. She squirmed her way out of his grasp and went hurrying down the hallway. "And," she called over her shoulder, "I have a new name to put on my list."

As she ran down the hall, Morgan stepped out of the study and watched her—a devil-may-care smile upon his lips— until Colin's curt reminder called him back into the study.

*All married women were unhappy creatures. The bitches all felt neglected by their husbands. They whined and complained, and nothing ever pleased them. Oh, he'd watched, he'd observed. The husbands usually ignored their wives, too, but he didn't fault them. Everyone knew mistresses were reserved for affection and attention; wives were simply necessary leeches to be used for the reproduction of heirs. One put up with a wife when one had to, rutted with her as often as necessary until she was carrying one's child, and then forgot about her.*

*He had deliberately ignored married women because he believed the hunt wouldn't amount to much. There wouldn't be any satisfaction gained in chasing a dog who wouldn't run. Still, this one intrigued him. She looked so miserable. He'd watched her for over an hour now. She was clinging to her husband's arm, and trying every now and then to say or do something to draw his attention. It was wasted effort. The gallant husband was thoroughly occupied talking to his friends from the clubs. He wasn't giving his pretty little wife any attention.*

*The poor little chit. It was obvious to anyone watching she loved the man. She was pitifully unhappy. He was about to change all that. He smiled then, his mind made up. The hunt was on again. Soon, very soon, he would put his new pet out of her misery.*

# Chapter
# 6

Colin stayed in conference with Sir Richards and Morgan for several hours. Alesandra ate her supper alone in the dining room. She stayed downstairs as long as she could manage without falling asleep, hoping Colin would join her. She wanted to thank him for showing such an interest in her future and ask him a few questions about the Earl of Oakmount.

She gave up the wait around midnight and went up to bed. Valena knocked on her door fifteen minutes later.

"You are requested to be ready to go out tomorrow morning, Princess. You must be ready to leave at ten o'clock."

Alesandra got into her bed and pulled the covers up. "Did Colin explain where we're going?"

The lady's maid nodded. "To Sir Richards's home," she answered. "On Bowers Street at number twelve."

Alesandra smiled. "He gave you the address?"

"Yes, Princess. He was very thorough in his instructions to me. He wanted me to tell you he doesn't wish to be kept waiting," she said with a frown. "There was something more he wanted me to . . . oh, yes, now I remember. The meeting scheduled for the afternoon with the Duke and Duchess of Williamshire has been canceled."

"Did Colin tell you why it was canceled?"

"No, Princess, he didn't."

Valena let out a dramatic yawn and immediately begged her mistress's pardon. "I'm very weary tonight," she whispered.

"Of course you're weary," Alesandra said. "It's quite late and you've put in a full day's work, Valena. Go to bed now. Sleep well," she called out when the maid went hurrying out the doorway.

Alesandra fell asleep a few minutes later. She was so exhausted from the long week of taking care of Colin, she slept the night through. She awakened a little after eight the next morning and hurried to get ready. She wore a pale pink walking dress. Colin would approve of the garment for the square-cut neckline was very prim and proper.

Alesandra was downstairs a good twenty minutes before they were scheduled to leave. Colin didn't join her until a few minutes after ten. As soon as she spotted him coming down the stairs, she called out to him. "We're already late, Colin. Do hurry."

"There's been a change in plans, Alesandra," Colin explained. He winked at her when he passed her on his way into the dining room.

She chased after him. "What change in plans?"

"The meeting's been canceled."

"The meeting with Sir Richards or the meeting this afternoon? Valena said . . ."

Colin pulled the chair out and motioned for her to sit down at the dining room table. "Both meetings were canceled," he said.

"Would you care for chocolate or hot tea, Princess?" Flannaghan called out from the entrance.

"Tea, thank you. Colin, how did you find out the meeting was canceled? I've been waiting in the foyer and no messenger came to the door."

Colin didn't answer her. He sat down, picked up the newspaper, and started reading. Flannaghan appeared at his side with a basket of biscuits, which he placed in front of him.

Alesandra was both irritated and confused. "Exactly why did Sir Richards want a meeting? We both spoke to him last evening."

"Eat your breakfast, Alesandra."

"You aren't going to explain, are you?"

"No."

"Colin, it's impolite to be rude first thing in the morning."

He lowered the paper to grin at her. She realized then her statement had been foolish. "I mean to say, it's always impolite to be rude."

He disappeared behind his paper again. She drummed her fingertips on the tabletop. Raymond walked into the dining room then. Alesandra immediately motioned him to her side. "Did a messenger . . ."

Colin interrupted her. "Alesandra, are you challenging my word?"

"No," she answered. "I'm just trying to understand. Will you quit hiding behind that paper?"

"Are you always in such a foul mood in the morning?"

Alesandra gave up trying to have a decent conversation with the man. She ate half a biscuit and then excused herself from the table. Raymond gave her a sympathetic look when she walked past him.

Alesandra went back upstairs and worked on her correspondence the rest of the morning. She wrote a long letter to the mother superior, telling her all about her journey to England. She described her guardian and his family, and spent three full pages explaining how she had ended up living with Colin.

She was sealing the envelope closed when Stefan knocked on the door. "You're wanted downstairs, Princess Alesandra."

"Do we have company, Stefan?"

The guard shook his head. "We're going out. You'll need your cloak. The wind's up today."

"Where are we going?"

"To a meeting, Princess."

"On again, off again, on again," she remarked.

"Begging your pardon, Princess?"

Alesandra closed the lid to the inkwell, straightened the desk, and then stood up. "I was just complaining to myself," she admitted with a smile. "Is this meeting with Colin's father or with Sir Richards?"

"I'm not certain," Stefan admitted. "But Colin's waiting in the foyer and he seems impatient to get going."

Alesandra promised the guard she would be right down. Stefan bowed to her and then left the room. She hurried to brush her hair, then went to the wardrobe to fetch her cloak. She was walking out the doorway when she remembered her list. If they were going to the Duke of Williamshire's town house, she would certainly need the notecard, she decided, so that she could go over the names with her guardian and his wife. She hurried back over to the desk to get the list and tucked it into the pocket of her cloak.

Colin was waiting in the foyer. She paused at the landing to put her cloak over her arm.

"Colin? Are we going to see your father or Sir Richards?"

He didn't answer her. She hurried down the steps and then repeated her question.

"We're going to see Sir Richards," he explained.

"Why does he want to see us again so soon? He was just here last evening," she reminded him.

"He has his reasons."

Valena was standing with Stefan and Raymond near the entrance to the salon. She hurried forward to assist her mistress with her cloak.

Colin beat her to the task. He put the cloak around Alesandra's shoulders, took hold of her hand, and then walked outside, dragging her behind him. She had to run to keep up with his long-legged stride.

Raymond and Stefan followed behind. The two guards climbed up the rack to sit with the driver. Colin and Alesandra sat across from each other inside the carriage.

He locked the doors, then leaned back against the cushions and smiled at her.

"Why are you frowning?" he asked.

"Why are you acting so peculiar?"

"I don't like surprises."

"Do you see? That was a peculiar answer."

Colin stretched out his long legs. She adjusted her skirts and moved closer to the corner to give him more room.

"Do you know what Sir Richards wants to talk to us about?" she asked.

"We aren't going to see him," Colin explained.

"But you said . . ."

"I lied."

Her gasp made him smile. "You lied to me?"

She looked incredulous. He slowly nodded. "Yes, I lied to you."

"Why?"

Her outrage made him want to laugh. She was such a delight when she was riled. And, Lord, she was certainly riled now. Her cheeks were flushed with a blush, and if her shoulders got any straighter, he thought, her spine might snap.

"I'll explain later," he told her. "Quit your frown, brat. It's too fine a day to get upset."

She finally noticed how cheerful he was. "Why are you so happy?"

He shrugged his answer. She let out a sigh. The man was deliberately trying to confuse her, she decided. "Exactly where are we going, Colin?"

"To a meeting with the family to decide what to do . . ."

She finished his explanation for him. "With me?"

He nodded. Alesandra lowered her gaze to her lap, but not before Colin saw her expression. She looked crushed. Her feelings had been hurt, he knew, but he didn't know what he'd said to cause that reaction.

His voice was gruff when he said, "Now what's the matter with you?"

"Nothing's the matter."

"Don't lie to me."

"You lied to me."

"I said I'd explain later," he countered. He tried to keep the irritation out of his voice when he added, "Now explain why you're looking ready to weep."

"I'll explain later."

Colin leaned forward. He grabbed hold of her chin and forced her to look at him. "Don't turn my words back on me," he ordered.

She pushed his hand away. "Very well," she announced. "I was a little upset when I realized why you're so happy."

"Make sense, damn it."

The carriage came to a stop in front of the Duke of Williamshire's town house. Colin unlatched the door but kept his gaze on her. "Well?" he demanded.

She adjusted her cloak around her shoulders. "It makes perfect sense to me," she told him with a nod.

Raymond opened the door and held his hand out to assist her. She immediately stepped outside, then turned to frown at Colin. "You're happy because you're finally getting rid of me."

He opened his mouth to argue with her. She raised her hand in an unspoken command to keep silent. "You needn't worry, sir. I'm over my upset. Shall we go inside now?"

She was trying to be dignified. Colin wouldn't let her. He started laughing. She turned and hurried up the steps. Raymond and Stefan flanked her sides.

"You still look upset, brat."

The door was opened by the butler just as she whirled around to tell Colin what she thought of that rude remark. "If you call me a brat again, I swear I'll do something most undignified. I am not upset," she added in a voice that mocked that lie. "I just thought you and I had become friends. Yes, I did. You were becoming like a cousin to me and I . . ."

Colin leaned down until he was just an inch or so from her face. "I'm not your cousin," he snapped.

Colin's brother, Caine, took over the butler's duty and stood in the doorway, waiting for someone to notice him. He could only see the back of Princess Alesandra. She was a little thing and, he judged, quite courageous. Colin was towering over her, giving her his best glare, but she wasn't cowering away. She didn't seem to be at all intimidated.

"Everyone believes we're cousins," she snapped.

"I don't give a damn what everyone else thinks."

She took a deep breath. "This conversation is ridiculous. If you don't wish to be related to me, that's just fine."

"I'm not related to you."

"You don't have to shout, Colin."

"You're making me crazed, Alesandra."

"Good afternoon."

Caine fairly bellowed his greeting so he'd be heard. Alesandra was so startled by the interruption, she grabbed hold of Colin.

She was quick to recover. She pushed herself out of his arms and turned around. She tried to force a serene, dignified expression. The incredibly handsome man standing in the doorway had to be Colin's brother. Their smiles were almost identical. Caine's hair was a bit lighter in shade, however, and his eyes were an altogether different color. They were gray, and in her estimation not nearly as attractive as Colin's more-green-than-hazel color.

Alesandra tried to curtsy. Colin wouldn't let her. He grabbed hold of her arm and nudged her through the opening.

She pinched him to make him let go of her. A tug of war resulted when Colin tried to take her cloak. She kept slapping his hand away so she could retrieve her notecard from the pocket of the garment.

Caine stood behind his brother. His hands were clasped behind his back and he was desperately trying not to laugh. He hadn't seen his brother this rattled in a good long while.

Alesandra finally pulled the notecard free. "Now you may take my cloak, thank you."

Colin rolled his eyes heavenward. He tossed her cloak in Caine's direction. His brother caught the garment in midair just as Colin spotted the notecard clutched in Alesandra's hand. "Why in God's name did you bring that thing along?"

"I'm going to need it," she explained. "I simply don't understand your aversion to this list, Colin. Your hostility is most unreasonable."

She turned her attention to his brother. "You'll have to excuse your brother's rudeness. He's been ill."

Caine smiled. Colin shook his head. "You don't have to

make excuses for me," he stated. "Caine, this is the woman you've been referring to as The Plague. Alesandra, meet my brother."

She again tried to curtsy and Colin again ruined it. She was just leaning forward to catch hold of her gown when Colin grabbed hold of her hand and started dragging her into the salon.

"Where's your wife, Caine?" Colin called over his shoulder.

"Upstairs with Mother," he answered.

Alesandra was tugging on Colin's hand, trying to get loose. "Why don't you just toss me on a chair and leave. You're obviously in a hurry to get rid of me."

"Which chair do you prefer?"

He finally let go of her. She took a step back and immediately bumped into Caine. She turned around, begged his forgiveness for her clumsiness, and then asked where his father was. She really wanted to speak to him as soon as possible, she explained.

Because she was looking so serious and worried, Caine didn't dare smile. Princess Alesandra was a pretty thing, he thought to himself. Her eyes were a brilliant shade of blue and the freckles on the bridge of her nose reminded him of his wife, Jade. She was actually very beautiful, he realized.

"Jenkins went upstairs to tell my father you're here, Princess Alesandra. Why don't you make yourself comfortable while you wait?"

She thought that was a splendid idea. Caine had obviously been given all the manners in the family. He was very solicitous and polite. It was a nice change from his brother.

Colin stood near the fireplace watching her. She ignored him. She hadn't paid any attention to the exterior of her guardian's town house, but she imagined it was just as grand as the interior. The salon was at least four times the size of Colin's. There were three settees placed in a half circle around the ivory-colored marble hearth. It was a lovely room filled with treasures the Duke of Williamshire had collected from around the world. Her gaze scanned the room, then came to rest on the gleaming object in the center of the mantel. She let out a gasp of pleasure. The replica in gold of her father's castle hadn't been misplaced after all. The reproduction of her childhood home was the size of a small brandy decanter and was exact in every detail to the real castle.

The look of joy on Alesandra's face took Colin's breath away. "Alesandra?" he asked, wondering what had caused that reaction.

She turned to smile at him. Then she hurried over to the mantel. Her hand trembled when she reached up and gently touched the side of one golden turret. "This is a replica of my home, Colin. It's called Stone Haven. I lived there with my mother and father."

"I thought your father gave up his kingdom when he married your mother," Colin remarked.

She nodded. "Yes, he did. He purchased Stone Haven before he married her. The general can't touch it, either. It's located in Austria and he won't have any jurisdiction there, even if he is able to take over the throne. The castle will continue to be safe."

"Who owns it now?" Caine asked.

She didn't answer him. He assumed she hadn't heard his question. He was as intrigued by the castle as Colin appeared to be. The two brothers flanked Alesandra's sides as they stared at the reproduction. "The detail is quite impressive," Caine remarked.

"My father gave it as a gift to your father," she explained. "He was playing a bit of trickery—good-hearted, of course—and I looked for the castle when I was staying at his country home, but I couldn't find it. I thought it had been lost. It pleases me to see it has a place of honor."

Colin was about to ask her what she'd meant by her remark that trickery had been involved when they were interrupted.

"Of course it has a place of honor," the Duke of Williamshire called out from the entrance. "Your father was my friend, Alesandra."

She turned at the sound of her guardian's voice and smiled in greeting. The Duke of Williamshire was a distinguished-looking man with silver-tipped hair and dark gray eyes. The sons had gotten their good looks from him, of course, and their height as well.

"Good afternoon, Father," Colin called out.

His father returned the greeting, then walked into the salon. He stopped in the center and opened his arms to Alesandra.

She didn't hesitate. She ran to him and threw herself into his arms. He hugged her tight and kissed the top of her head.

Colin and Caine shared a look of disbelief. They were astonished by their father's show of affection to his ward. The elderly man was usually very reserved, but he was treating Alesandra as though she were his long-lost daughter.

"Has Colin been treating you well?"

"Yes, Uncle Henry."

"Uncle Henry?" Caine and Colin repeated the name at the same time.

Alesandra pulled away from her guardian and turned to glare at Colin. "Uncle Henry doesn't mind being related to me."

"But he isn't related to you," Colin stubbornly reminded her.

His father smiled. "I've asked her to call me Uncle," he explained. "Alesandra's part of our family now, son."

He turned to his ward then. "Sit down and we'll talk about this marriage business."

She hurried to do as he requested. She spotted her notecard on the floor and immediately went to fetch it. Colin waited until she was settled in the center of the brocaded settee and then went over and sat down next to her.

His bulk crowded her into the corner. Alesandra nudged his hard thigh away so she could collect her skirts from underneath him. "There are plenty of other seats available," she whispered so her Uncle Henry wouldn't hear her criticizing his son. "Do sit somewhere else, Cousin."

"If you call me cousin one more time I swear I'm going to

throttle you," Colin threatened in a low growl. "And quit squirming."

"You're crowding her, son. Move over."

Colin didn't budge. His father frowned, then took his seat next to Caine on the larger settee facing Alesandra.

"How have you two been getting along?" his father asked.

"Colin was sick all week," Alesandra announced. "Am I moving in with you today, Uncle?"

"No." Colin's denial was abrupt—harsh, too.

His father frowned at his son before turning his gaze back to Alesandra. "Would you like to move in here?" he asked.

"I thought Colin wanted me to," she answered. Her confusion was apparent in her expression. "It seemed an imposition, having to look out for me. He's been acting very irritable today. I believe the cause is anxiety."

Colin rolled his eyes heavenward. "Let's get back to the main topic," he muttered.

His father ignored that command. "Colin's anxious?" he asked Alesandra.

"Yes, Uncle," she answered. She folded her hands together in her lap while she added, "He's anxious to get rid of me. So you can understand my confusion, can't you? A few minutes ago he was ready to toss me on the settee and leave, and now he's telling you I should stay with him."

"That is a contradiction," Caine interjected.

Colin leaned forward. He braced his elbows on his knees and stared at his father. "I don't believe it's a good idea to have her move anywhere just now. There was an incident outside the Opera House," he added with a nod.

Alesandra interrupted him by nudging him in his side. He turned back to look at her.

"You don't need to go into that," she whispered. "You'll only worry him."

"He needs to be worried," Colin told her. "If he's going to take over the responsibility of looking out for you, he'll have to understand what he's up against."

Colin didn't give her time to argue with him, but turned back to his father. He quickly explained what had happened, added a few pertinent details he'd gathered from his talk with Sir Richards, and ended with his opinion that the threats weren't going to stop until Alesandra was married.

"Or until the general has either won or lost his campaign for the throne," Caine interjected.

"Hell, that could take a year," Colin predicted with a scowl.

"Perhaps," his brother agreed. He turned to his father then and said, "I think Colin's right. Alesandra should continue to stay with him. He's more experienced in these matters and it would be less dangerous for you and Mother."

"Nonsense," his father countered. "I know a thing or two about protecting my family. I can handle any danger that comes my way. The gossip, however, is something we must address. Now that your mother and I are feeling fit again, Alesandra will have to move in with us. It isn't acceptable for an unattached man and woman to live together."

"It was the thing last week," Caine reminded his father.

"Because of our illness," his father replied. "Surely people will understand."

Colin was incredulous. He didn't know what to say to his father's naive belief. He turned to his brother for help in arguing his point against Alesandra moving and saw that Caine was just as incredulous.

"Have you heard any gossip?" his father asked Caine, frowning now over that worry.

Caine shook his head. Colin tried to hold on to his patience. "Father, gossip isn't the important issue here," he said. "You cannot equate the danger you would be placing your family in with a few whispered remarks. Of course people are talking. Alesandra and I don't care."

"I won't let you argue me out of my decision," his father stubbornly insisted. "You insult me if you believe I can't look out for my ward. I've taken care of a wife and six children all these years without a problem and I'm not about to stop now."

"But no one has wanted to kidnap Mother or . . ." Caine began.

"Enough," his father ordered. "The topic is closed." He softened his tone when he added, "Your mother was right when she said Alesandra should get married as soon as possible. That would put an end to all this nonsense."

Colin looked at Caine. "She has this damned list."

"I gave her that list, son."

Colin didn't know what to say to that.

"A list of what?" Caine asked.

"Must you explain to Caine?" she whispered. Her cheeks were turning pink with embarrassment. "He's already married."

"I know he's married," Colin replied with a grin.

Caine pretended he hadn't heard Alesandra's protest. "A list of what?" he asked his brother again.

"Men," Colin answered. "She and Father have made a list of suitable men to marry."

Caine didn't show any outward reaction to that explanation. He could tell from Alesandra's expression she was uncomfortable with the topic they were discussing. He decided to try to make her feel more at ease. "That sounds reasonable to me," he announced.

"Reasonable? It's barbaric," Colin told him.

Caine couldn't suppress his grin.

"This isn't amusing," Colin snapped.

"No," Caine agreed. "It isn't amusing."

"It's most serious, sir," Alesandra interjected with a nod.

Caine sat up a little straighter. "So the purpose of this meeting is to select a husband from the list? Have I got it straight in my mind?"

"Yes," Alesandra answered. "I wanted to interview the candidates last week, but Colin became ill and I was occupied nursing him back to health."

"You nursed him?" Caine asked with a smile.

She nodded. "Night and day," she said. "He needed me."

Colin was exasperated. "I did not need you."

She took exception to his gruff tone of voice. She leaned back against the settee. "You're a very unappreciative man," she whispered.

Colin ignored her remark. He nodded to Caine. "That reminds me," he said. "I wanted to thank you for your help. The ledgers haven't looked so organized in over a year."

"What ledgers?"

"The shipping ledgers," Colin explained. "I appreciated your help."

Caine shook his head. Alesandra nudged Colin to get his attention. "Couldn't we get back to the topic at hand? I would like to get this settled as soon as possible."

"I didn't touch your ledgers," Caine told his brother.

"Then who . . . ?"

No one said a word for a long minute. Alesandra turned her attention to straightening the folds in her gown. Colin slowly turned to look at her.

"Did you hire Dreyson or someone else to work on my books?"

"Of course not. Your books are private. I wouldn't let an outsider look at them. Besides, no one was admitted while you were sick."

"Then who the hell did the work?"

"I did."

He shook his head. She nodded. "Don't jest with me, Alesandra. I'm not in the mood for it."

"I'm not jesting. I did do the work. I organized all of your logs, too, and filed them away."

"Who helped you?"

She was highly insulted by that question. "No one helped me. I'm very good with figures," she told him. "You have my permission to write to Mother Superior if you don't believe me. I made a second set of books for her so the banker would give her . . . Oh, dear, I probably shouldn't have mentioned that. Mother Superior called it a sin, but I didn't believe it was. It wasn't larceny, either. I only changed the numbers so she could get the loan."

Colin had an astonished expression on his face. She guessed he found her confession shameful. She quit trying to explain herself and took a deep breath. "As for your ledgers," she continued. "Transferring numbers and totaling your columns didn't require special training. It wasn't difficult, just tedius."

"And the percentages?" Colin asked, still not certain he believed her.

She shrugged. "Anyone with half a mind could figure out percentages."

He shook his head. "But you're a woman . . ."

He was going to add that he couldn't imagine where she'd gotten the training for book work, but she wouldn't let him finish.

"I knew that would come up," she cried out. "Just because I'm a woman, you assume I couldn't possibly understand anything but the latest fashions, isn't that right? Well, sir, you're in for a surprise. I don't give a twit about fashions."

Colin had never seen her this riled. Her eyes had turned into blue fire. He thought he might like to strangle her. But he'd kiss her first, he decided.

Caine came to her rescue. "And did the mother superior get her loan, Alesandra?"

"Yes, she did," Alesandra answered, her voice tinged with pride. "Mother didn't know the banker was looking at the second set of books, of course, or her vows would have forced her to confess. The nuns all follow very strict rules. She didn't find out until it was too late. She'd already spent the money on a new chapel. So it all worked out quite nicely."

Colin let out a snort. "I'll wager she was sorry to see you leave," he said dryly.

"Shall we get back to our reason for being here?" Caine suggested. He stood up and walked over to Alesandra. "May I have a look at your list, please?"

"Yes, of course."

Caine took the notecard and went back to his seat. "It isn't complete," Alesandra explained. "There are ten names on the list now, but if you want to add another one or two, please do so."

"I believe we should go ahead and start without Gweneth," her guardian announced. "Caine, read the first name and we'll put the man under discussion."

Caine unfolded the sheet of paper, scanned the contents, and then looked at his brother.

"Get started, son," his father insisted.

"The first name on the list is Colin," Caine announced, his gaze directed on his brother.

"Yes, but I've scratched him off," Alesandra explained. "Do you see the line through his name? Please go on to the names I haven't scratched through."

"Hold on," Caine said. "I want to know why he was marked off, Alesandra. Did you put his name on the list or did my father suggest Colin?"

"I gave her his name," his father answered. "She hadn't even met Colin when we started the list. I believed it would be a sound match, but now I can see it wouldn't wash. They aren't suitable for each other."

Caine was of the opposite opinion. The sparks flying between Alesandra and Colin were close to igniting, and each was desperately trying not to acknowledge the reason behind his or her frustration.

"How did you come to the conclusion they weren't suited?" Caine asked his father.

"Just look at the two of them together, son. It's plain for anyone to see. Alesandra's looking terribly uncomfortable and Colin hasn't quit frowning since he sat down. It's apparent they don't get along. And that, you see, is an important ingredient for a sound marriage."

"Could we get on with it, Caine?" asked Colin.

"Colin, do you have to be so irritable?" Alesandra asked.

He didn't answer her. She turned her attention to Caine. "He's been ill," she reminded his brother, using that as her excuse for Colin's surly mood.

"It's this topic," his father interjected with a frown in Colin's direction.

"If Colin agreed to marry you, Alesandra, would you have him?" Caine wanted to know.

"He has already declined," Alesandra explained. "And he wouldn't be acceptable anyway."

"Why not?" Caine asked.

"Will you let it go?" Colin demanded.

Caine ignored his brother's protest. So did Alesandra. She frowned while she thought about her answer. She didn't want to confuse Caine but she didn't want to have to go into a lengthy explanation either. "He isn't acceptable because he wouldn't touch my inheritance."

"Damned right I wouldn't touch it."

"There, do you understand now?"

Caine didn't understand anything. The look on his brother's face told him not to prod further, however. Colin looked ready to grab somebody's throat and Caine didn't want to be his victim.

"Isn't there a better way to handle this situation?" Caine asked then. "Alesandra should be allowed to take her time . . ."

"But there isn't time," his father interjected.

"I do thank you for your concern, Caine," Alesandra added.

"Go ahead, son. Read the second name on the list."

Caine gave up. The second name had also been crossed through. Caine moved to the third name. "Horton," he read. "The Earl of Wheaton."

"I met him once," his father announced. "He seemed like a decent chap to me."

Caine was nodding agreement when Colin started shaking his head. "What's wrong with him, Colin?" his brother asked.

"He's a drunk. He won't do."

"He's a drunk?" his father asked. "I never realized that about Horton. Cross him off, Caine," he added with a scowl. "I won't have her wed to a drunk."

"Thank you, Uncle Henry."

Colin could feel himself getting ready to explode. It took all he had to keep his temper under control. In truth, he didn't understand why he was so agitated. He had made the decision not to marry Alesandra, but, damn it all, the thought of anyone else touching her didn't sit well with him.

As though it were the most natural thing in the world to do, Colin leaned back against the cushions and put his arm around Alesandra's shoulders. She instinctively moved closer to him. He could feel her trembling, knew then she hated having to go through this ordeal as much as he did.

Caine was right. There had to be a better way.

His brother drew his attention when he read the next name. "Kingsford, the Earl of Lockwood."

"Gweneth suggested Kingsford," his father announced. "She was taken with his polite ways."

Colin shook his head. "He might be polite, but he's also got a reputation for his sadistic pleasures."

"Good God," his father muttered. "Sadistic pleasures, you say? Mark him off, Caine."

"Yes, Father," Caine agreed. He read the next name. "Williams, the Marquess of Coringham."

"I suggested him," his father explained. His voice reeked with fresh enthusiasm. "He's a fine fellow. I've known the family for years. Comes from good blood, Harry does."

Caine was having difficulty maintaining his serious expression. Colin was already shaking his head.

"Harry's a womanizer," Colin announced.

"I never realized that about Harry," his father muttered. "Gweneth and I need to get out more often. I'd pick up on these things if we mingled more with society. All right, then, he won't do. We aren't marrying her to a future adulterer."

Caine stared at Colin when he called out the next name on the list. "Johnson, the Earl of Wentzhill."

He hadn't gotten the man's full title out of his mouth before Colin started shaking his head.

And so it continued. Colin found something wrong with every man mentioned. By the time Caine had gotten to the last name on the list, the Duke of Williamshire was slumped in the corner of the settee, his hand to his forehead, looking thoroughly defeated. Caine could barely contain his amusement. His brother was having difficulty coming up with a suitable vice after Caine had read the last name, Morgan Atkins, the Earl of Oakmount, and Caine was dying to hear what he had to say about him.

"I've met Morgan," Alesandra announced. "He came to Colin's house to discuss a business matter. He seemed very nice."

Alesandra's voice lacked conviction. She was having trouble hiding her unhappiness now. She hated what was happening. She felt out of control of her future and her destiny. Just as horrible to her, she was beginning to feel like a charity case.

"I can't give you an opinion of Morgan," Caine remarked. "I've never met him."

"I've met him," his father said. "I liked him well enough. Perhaps we could invite him over for . . . Why in God's name are you shaking your head now, Colin?"

"Yes, brother," Caine interjected. "What's wrong with Morgan?"

Colin let out a sigh. He was having difficulty finding anything wrong with the man. Caine wasn't helping him concentrate. He started laughing.

"This isn't amusing," Colin snapped.

"Yes, it is," Caine contradicted. "Let's see now," he drawled out. "So far we've discarded nine possible candidates because of drunkenness, averice, gluttony, jealousy, perversion, greed, lust, and so on, and I'd really love to hear your reason for finding Morgan unsuitable. I believe you've used up all the seven deadly sins, Colin."

"What are you suggesting, Caine?" Colin demanded.

"You don't like any of them."

"Damned right I don't. I'm thinking of Alesandra's happiness. She's a princess. She deserves better."

That last remark told Caine everything he needed to know. He now understood why Colin was in such a foul mood. It was obvious to Caine that his brother wanted Alesandra, but in his mind he had decided he wasn't worthy enough. Oh, yes, that was it, Caine decided. Colin was the second son and therefore hadn't inherited land or title. His obsession with building an empire was all part of his quest to achieve recognition on his own. Caine was proud that his brother was an independent man, but, damn it all, that pride would force him to let Alesandra slip away.

Unless he was forced into marriage, of course.

"But what about Morgan?" his father asked again. "What's wrong with him?"

"Nothing," Colin snapped.

His father was beginning to smile when Colin added, "If Alesandra doesn't mind bowlegged children."

"For the love of . . ." His father slumped back against the cushions in defeat.

"Is Morgan bowlegged?" Caine asked Alesandra. He was feeling quite proud of himself. He'd been able to ask that question without even cracking a smile.

"I must confess I didn't notice his legs, but if Colin says he's bowlegged, then he must be. Will I have to have children?"

"Yes," Colin told her.

"He won't do then. I don't wish to have bowlegged children."

She turned to look up at Colin. "Is it a painful condition?" she asked him in a whisper.

"Yes," Colin lied.

The discussion continued for another hour. Caine and his father both took turns tossing out names of possible husbands and Colin found something wrong with every one of them.

Caine was thoroughly enjoying himself. He pulled the footrest over, stretched out, and propped his feet up so that he'd be more comfortable.

Colin was becoming more and more agitated. He'd removed his arm from Alesandra's shoulders and was now leaning forward with his elbows on his knees while he waited for his father to think of another candidate.

The longer the talk continued, the more upset Alesandra became. She hid behind her mask of serenity, but her hands were clutched into fists in her lap.

Just when she thought she couldn't stand to hear another name offered, Colin leaned back and covered her hands with one of his.

She didn't want his comfort, yet she clung to his hand.

"Alesandra, what do you want to do?"

Caine asked her that question. She was too embarrassed to tell him the truth, to admit that more than anything she wished she could marry a man she loved. She wanted the kind of marriage her parents had had, but that wasn't possible.

"I thought I wanted to become a nun, but Mother Superior wouldn't let me."

There were tears in her eyes and for that reason no one laughed. "And why wouldn't she let you?" Caine asked.

"I'm not Catholic," Alesandra explained. "It's an important requirement."

He did smile then. He simply couldn't help it. "You wouldn't have been happy as a nun," he predicted.

She wasn't particularly happy now, but she didn't believe it would be polite to mention that.

"Alesandra, why don't you go and find Gweneth," her guardian suggested. "You haven't met Jade yet, now have you? Go and introduce yourself to Caine's lovely wife."

She acted as though she'd just been given a reprieve. The look of relief on her face was there for all of them to see.

Alesandra had stood up before she realized she hadn't let go of Colin's hand yet. She quickly pulled away, and then left the room.

The three men stood up until she'd left the salon, then resumed their seats. Colin dragged the footrest over, propped his feet up, and leaned back.

"This is damned difficult for her," he muttered.

"Yes," his father agreed. "I wish there was time for her to adjust to her circumstances, but there isn't, Colin."

Caine decided to turn the topic. "I'm curious, Father," he remarked. "How did you meet Alesandra's father?"

"It was at Ashford's annual bash," his father explained. "Nathaniel and I took to one another right away. He was quite a man," he added with a nod.

"And so are you to take on responsibility for his daughter," Colin remarked.

His father's expression underwent a dramatic change. He looked terribly sad now. "No, you've got it all wrong," he said. "There is something neither one of you knows and I imagine now is the time for me to confess my sins. You're going to find out sooner or later."

The seriousness in their father's voice told both sons the matter was of grave importance. They gave him their full attention and waited for him to compose his thoughts.

Long minutes passed before he spoke again. "I got into trouble just after your mother died, Caine," he explained. "I hadn't met Gweneth yet and I had started drinking—quite heavily, as a matter of fact."

"You? But you never drink," Colin argued.

"I don't drink now," his father agreed. "I did back then. I gambled too. The debts, they piled up, of course, and I kept fooling myself into believing I would win back enough to cover my losses."

Colin and Caine were too astonished to say anything. They stared at their father as though he'd suddenly turned into a complete stranger.

"This is a difficult confession for me to make," he continued. "No father likes parading his sins in front of his sons."

"The past is over," Colin told him. "Let it go."

His father shook his head. "It isn't as simple as all that," he explained. "I want you to understand. I was almost ruined, you see, and would have been if it hadn't been for Alesandra's father. Everything I'd inherited and worked so hard to build was in the hands of the moneylenders as collateral against the loans. Yes, I would have been ruined."

"What happened then?" Caine asked when his father didn't continue.

"Nathaniel came to my rescue. I was at White's one minute and the next I remember I was back home. I was told I blacked out at the tables from too much drink. When I next opened my eyes, Nathaniel was standing over me, and, Lord, was he angry. I was so hung over all I wanted was to be left alone. He wouldn't leave, however. He threatened me, too."

"What was his threat?" Caine asked. He was so surprised by his father's confession he leaned forward and clasped his hands together in expectation.

"He told me you were downstairs," his father said. "You

were so young and impressionable and Nathaniel threatened to bring you up so you could see what your father had become. Needless to say, the threat sobered me up. I would rather have died than let you see me in such a humiliating condition."

No one said a word for several minutes. Caine didn't have any memory of his father's drinking days. "How old was I?" he asked.

"Almost five."

"If I was that young, I probably wouldn't have remembered if I had seen you drunk," he remarked.

"Nathaniel knew how much I loved you," his father said. "Oh, he was clever, all right. It was my darkest hour, my turning point as well."

"What was done about the debts?" Colin asked.

His father smiled. How like Colin to be the one to ask that question. His younger son was the most practical member of the family—the most disciplined, too.

"Nathaniel went to all the moneylenders. He purchased the notes. In less than one day, I was completely out of debt. He tried to give me the notes, but I refused his charity. I wouldn't let him tear them up either. I wanted him to hold on to them until I could repay. I even insisted he add interest."

"And has the debt been repaid?" Caine asked.

"No, it hasn't. Nathaniel took his wife back to Stone Haven. He gave me that beautiful treasure before he left," he said with a nod toward the castle perched on the mantel. "Imagine that, giving me a gift after all he'd done. We kept current through letters, of course, and the next time he and his wife came to England, they had Alesandra with them. I tried to give him half of what I owed, but he wouldn't take it. It was damned awkward. Because he had acted so honorably with me, I couldn't ask him where the notes were. He died the following winter. Lord, I still mourn his passing. He was my dearest friend."

Both sons agreed. Nathaniel had been a good friend.

"Who holds the notes now?" Caine asked.

"That's the dilemma, son. I don't know."

"Have you asked Alesandra?" Colin wanted to know.

"No," his father answered. "I doubt she knows anything about the transaction. As her guardian, I have access to some of her accounts. Dreyson, her agent, takes care of investments, but I don't believe he knows anything about the notes either."

"Would you be able to repay the full amount if the notes and interest were called today?" Caine asked.

"Not all of it," his father replied. "But I'm in a strong financial position now. If the notes were called, I could borrow what I need. I don't want to give either one of you the impression I'm worried. Nathaniel was a methodical, careful man. He put the notes in a safe place. I'm just curious to know where they are."

"I'm curious, too," Caine agreed.

"The purpose of my confession is twofold," their father continued. "First, I want both of you to know the kind of man Alesandra's father was, and to understand the debt I owe him. Second, I want you to understand how I feel about his daughter. She's all alone in this world now and it is my duty to see she's protected from harm."

"It is our duty as well," Caine interjected.

Colin nodded agreement. The three men lapsed into silence again, each caught up in his own thoughts.

Colin tried to consider all the ramifications.

He had nothing to offer her. He had an empire to build, damn it, and there simply wasn't room or time for a wife.

She would drive him to distraction.

But there was the debt to be repaid, and all three of them were bound by honor to look out for Princess Alesandra.

His father was too old to take on the duty of keeping her safe. He didn't have the experience dealing with bastards either, Colin decided.

And then there was Caine. His older brother was busy running his own estates. He was married, too, and had his own family to consider.

There was only one son left.

Colin glanced up and noticed both his father and his brother were staring at him. He let out a loud sigh. They had known all along, of course, and were only waiting for him to come to the same conclusion.

"Hell, I'm going to have to marry her, aren't I?"

# Chapter
# 7

Colin's father wanted to be the one to break the good news to Alesandra. Colin wouldn't let him. He thought he should be the one to tell her what had been decided.

"May I offer a word of advice, brother?" Caine asked.

He waited for Colin's nod, then said, "I don't believe you should tell her anything . . ."

His father wouldn't let him finish. "She'll have to know, Caine."

His son smiled. "Yes, of course she'll have to know," he agreed. "However, from my rather limited experience with women I've still been able to surmise that they don't like being told anything. Colin should ask her to marry him."

"Do it at the dinner table then," his father suggested.

Colin smiled. "I'll decide when and where," he announced.

"Will you promise me you'll have it settled before the night is over?" his father demanded. "I can't say a word until you've asked. And Gweneth will have to start work on the arrangements."

"Mother has already seen to everything," Colin replied.

His father stood up and rubbed his hands together. "I can't tell you how pleased I am, and I'm certain Alesandra's going to be thrilled."

Because his father was looking so proud of himself, neither Colin nor Caine reminded him that less than an hour ago he'd been against a marriage between his ward and his son. He'd believed they were completely unsuited to each other.

Caine wanted to have a private discussion with Colin but their mother came hurrying into the salon then, demanding everyone's attention.

The Duchess of Williamshire was a petite woman with blond curls and hazel-colored eyes. Her husband and sons towered over her. The years had been very kind to the lovely woman. She had very few wrinkles and only a hint of gray in her hair.

Gweneth was actually Caine's stepmother, but no one paid any attention to that distinction. She treated him as one of her own, and Caine had long ago accepted her as his mother.

"Jade and Alesandra will be down in just a moment. Do come into the dining room. Supper will get cold. Boys, give your mother a kiss. Heavens, you've lost some weight, Caine, haven't you? Colin, dear, how is your leg? Is it paining you?"

Her sons understood that their mother didn't really expect answers to her questions. They understood she liked to coddle, too, and put up with the show of motherly concern without even a hint of a reminder that they were both fully grown men now.

Gweneth was the only one who dared inquire about Colin's leg. Everyone else understood they were to ignore the affliction.

"Caine, Princess Alesandra is the most delightful young woman."

His wife made that remark as she came strolling into the salon. She paused on her way to her husband's side to give his father a kiss in greeting, then stopped again to kiss Colin on his cheek.

"Are you enchanted by Alesandra, Dolphin?" she asked Colin, using the nickname he'd earned from his days on the seas.

"Where is she?" Colin asked.

"In your father's library," Jade answered. Her green eyes sparkled with amusement. "She caught sight of all his books and almost swooned with joy. When I left her, she was looking through his journal on the latest shipping innovations."

Gweneth immediately turned to the butler and requested that he go upstairs and tell Alesandra dinner was waiting.

Jade linked her arm through her husband's. She was dying to ask him what had been decided at the family conference, but couldn't because Colin and their parents were standing so close.

Caine brushed his wife's deep red hair back over her shoulder and leaned down to kiss her.

"I believe we should go on in," Gweneth announced. She took her husband's arm and walked by his side out of the salon. Colin followed until Caine called out to him. "I want to talk to you in private later," he requested.

"There isn't anything to talk about," Colin countered. He could tell from his brother's expression he wanted to discuss Alesandra again.

"I believe there is," Caine countered.

"Do forgive me for interrupting," Jade said then. "But I've just come up with a wonderful suggestion for a suitable husband. Have you considered Johnson? You remember him, Colin. He's Lyon's good friend," she reminded her brother-in-law.

"I remember him," Colin agreed.

"And?" Jade prodded when he didn't continue.

"I can tell you right now he won't do," Caine drawled out.

"Why not?" Jade asked. "I like him."

"So do I," Caine agreed. "But Colin will find something wrong with him. Besides, the matter has already been settled."

Caine shook his head at his wife when she started to protest, added a wink so her feelings wouldn't be injured, and then whispered, "Later," to let her know he would explain everything when they were alone.

Colin turned around and walked out of the salon. He

didn't go into the dining room however, but started up the steps.

"Go ahead without us," he called down to Caine. "I must speak to Alesandra for a few minutes."

Colin didn't think it would take him any time at all to explain to Alesandra he was going to marry her. No, that announcement wouldn't take more than a minute. The rest of the time would be spent on expectations. His.

The library was down at the end of the long corridor. Alesandra was standing in front of the window, looking out. She held a thick book in her hands. She turned when Colin walked inside.

He shut the door behind him and then leaned against it. He frowned at her. She smiled at him.

"You are finished with your conference?" she asked.

"Yes."

"I see," she whispered when he didn't continue. She walked over to the desk and put the book down on the ink blotter. "What was decided?" she asked then, trying desperately to sound only mildly interested.

He started to tell her he was going to marry her, then took Caine's advice and put the decision into a question.

"Will you marry me, Alesandra?"

"No," she answered in a whisper. "But I do thank you for offering."

"After the wedding, you and I . . . what do you mean, no? I'm going to marry you, Alesandra. It's all been decided."

"No, you aren't going to marry me," she countered. "Quit frowning, Colin. You're off the hook. You asked and I turned you down. You can start breathing again."

"Alesandra . . ." he began in a warning tone of voice she completely ignored.

"I know exactly what happened downstairs after I left," she boasted. "Your father cleverly manipulated you into agreeing to have me. He told you about the gift my father gave him, didn't he?"

Colin smiled. Alesandra was really very astute. "Yes," he answered. "It wasn't a gift, however. It was a loan."

135

He moved away from the door and walked toward her. She immediately started backing away.

"It was a loan only in your father's eyes," she argued.

He shook his head. "Forget the loan," he ordered. "And start making sense. You need to get married, damn it, and I've agreed to become your husband. Why are you being so difficult?"

"Because you don't love me."

She'd blurted out that truth before she could stop herself. Colin looked astonished. She was so embarrassed now she wished she could open the window and leap out. That ridiculous notion made her want to scream. She really needed to get a better hold on her emotions, she told herself.

"What does love have to do with anything? Do you honestly believe any of the men on your list would love you? Hell, whomever you chose wouldn't even know you well enough to form an opinion . . ."

She interrupted him. "No, of course he wouldn't love me. I wouldn't want him to. It was going to be a purely financial arrangement. You, however, have made it perfectly clear you won't touch my funds. You told me you were determined to make it on your own, remember?"

"I remember."

"And have you changed your mind in the last five minutes?"

"No."

"There, do you finally understand? Since you have nothing to gain from marrying me, and since you don't love me, which would be the only other reason for marriage, then there really isn't any point to your noble sacrifice."

Colin leaned on the edge of the desk and stared at her. "Let me get this straight," he muttered. "You actually believed you could buy a husband?"

"Of course," she cried out in exasperation. "Women do it all the time."

"You aren't buying me."

He sounded furious. She let out a sigh and tried to hold on to her patience. "I know I'm not buying you," she agreed.

"And that puts me in a weaker bargaining position. I can't allow that."

Colin felt like shaking some sense into her. "We're talking about marriage, not contracts for hire," he snapped. "Were you planning to sleep with your husband? What about children, Alesandra?"

He was asking her questions she didn't want to answer. "Perhaps . . . in time. Oh, I don't know," she whispered. "It doesn't concern you."

Colin suddenly moved. Before Alesandra had time to guess his intent, he pulled her into his arms.

He held her around her waist with one arm and forced her chin up with his other hand so she would look at him.

He thought he might want to shout at her, but then he saw the tears in her eyes and he forgot all about arguing with her.

"I'm going to be touching you all the time," he announced in a gruff whisper.

"Why?"

He took exception to the fact that she looked so surprised. "Call it a benefit," he drawled out.

He probably would have only given her a chaste kiss to seal his commitment to wed her, but she goaded his temper again when she whispered her denial.

"Yes," he whispered back just seconds before his mouth descended to hers. The kiss was meant to gain her submission. It was hard, demanding, thorough. He felt her try to pull away with the first touch of his mouth on hers, but he ignored her struggle to get free by tightening his hold on her. He forced her mouth open by applying pressure on her chin with his hand, and then his tongue swept inside to rid her of her resistance.

The kiss wasn't at all gentle. But, Lord, it was hot. Alesandra didn't know if she struggled or not. She was having trouble thinking at all. Colin's mouth was so wonderfully thorough, she never wanted him to stop. Alesandra had never been kissed before and had therefore never experienced passion. She was overwhelmed by it now. Colin was certainly experienced, though. His mouth slanted over hers again and again while his tongue rubbed against hers in intimate love play.

Colin realized he should stop when he heard her sexy little whimper. He growled low in his throat and kissed her again. Damn, he wanted her. His hand brushed against the swell of her breast and the heat and fullness he felt under his hand through the material of her gown made him ache to make love to her.

He forced himself to pull away from her. Alesandra collapsed against him. She didn't realize she had her arms around his waist until he told her to let go.

She was so confused by what had just happened to her, she didn't know what to say or do. She tried to back away from him, but she was trembling so much she could barely get her legs to support her.

He knew he'd rattled her. The grin on his face was extremely telling—arrogant, too.

"That was my first kiss," she stammered out as an excuse for her sorry condition.

Colin couldn't resist. He pulled her back into his arms and kissed her again. "And that was your second," he whispered.

"Begging your pardon," Jenkins called out from the doorway. "The duchess is most insistent you join her in the dining room."

Alesandra jerked away from Colin. She acted as though she'd just been scorched by the sun. Her cheeks turned pink with embarrassment. She peeked around Colin to look at the butler. He smiled at her.

"We're coming, Jenkins," Colin called out. He kept his gaze on Alesandra, smiling over her embarrassment.

She tried to skirt her way around him. He took hold of her hand and wouldn't let go. "I'll make the announcement during dinner," he told her as he pulled her through the doorway.

"No," she countered. "Colin, your kisses haven't changed anything. I'm not going to marry you and ruin all your carefully laid plans."

"Alesandra, I always win. Understand me?"

She let out an unladylike snort. He squeezed her hand and started down the steps. She had to run to keep up with him.

"I dislike arrogant, think-they're-always-right men," she muttered.

"I do too," he agreed.

"I was referring to you." Lord, she felt like screaming. "I'm not marrying you."

"We'll see."

He wasn't going to give up. The man was sinfully stubborn. But then so was she, she reminded herself. Her guardian had given her his word she could choose her own husband and Colin's intimidating tactics didn't matter.

Dinner was a nerve-racking affair. Alesandra's stomach was tied in knots and she could barely swallow anything. She should have been hungry, but she wasn't. She kept waiting for Colin to say something, and was praying at the same time that he wouldn't open his mouth.

Jade drew her into conversation. "I understand the prince regent called on you," she remarked.

"Yes," Alesandra answered. "I wouldn't have allowed him entrance into Colin's home if I'd known he'd cheated Colin's partner out of an inheritance, however."

Jade smiled. "His partner is my brother," she said. She turned to the duchess to explain what they'd been talking about. "The prince regent was holding my brother's wife's inheritance while the fighting was going on between the families, but once it was all resolved, he decided to keep the gift for himself. It was a sizable sum."

"You really wouldn't have let the prince regent in?" Caine asked.

"No, I wouldn't have," Alesandra said again. "Why do you look so surprised? Colin's home is his castle. Only friends should be allowed inside."

Alesandra turned her attention to Jade and therefore missed the grin the two brothers shared.

"Do you happen to know a lady named Victoria Perry?" she asked.

Jade shook her head. "The name isn't familiar to me. Why do you ask?"

"I'm worried about her," Alesandra confessed. She explained how she'd met Victoria and what she had learned since she'd last received a letter from her.

"My dear, I don't believe it's a good idea to pursue this further," the duchess announced. "Her mother must be heartbroken. It's cruel to dredge it all up again."

"Colin said the very same thing to me," Alesandra said. "Perhaps you are right. I should let the matter rest. I wish I could quit worrying about her."

The duchess turned the conversation then to the topic of her eldest daughter. This was Catherine's year for coming out and she was full of plans for her first ball.

Caine didn't say a word throughout the rest of the meal. He kept his gaze on his brother.

Colin wasn't giving anything away. His expression could have been carved in stone.

Alesandra actually began to relax a little when dessert was served and Colin still hadn't brought up the topic of marriage. She thought he'd probably had enough time to think the matter through. Yes, he'd come to his senses.

"Have you had time to talk to Alesandra, son?" the Duke of Williamshire asked.

"Yes," Colin replied. "We've decided . . ."

"Not to marry," she blurted out.

"What's this? Colin, I thought it had all been decided," his father protested.

"It has been decided," Colin agreed. He reached over and covered Alesandra's hand with his. "We're getting married. Alesandra has agreed to become my wife."

She started shaking her head in denial but no one seemed to be paying any attention to her.

"Congratulations," her guardian announced. "Gweneth, this calls for a toast."

"Don't you think Alesandra should agree first?" Jade asked just as her father-in-law started to stand up with his water glass in hand.

He sat back down. "Yes, of course," he replied.

"She'll marry me," Colin said, his voice hard, unbending.

She turned to him. "I won't let you make this noble sacrifice. You don't want to get married for another five years, remember? What about your schedule?"

She didn't wait for Colin to answer her question but turned her attention back to Uncle Henry. "I don't want to marry him, Uncle, and you did promise me I could choose."

Her guardian slowly nodded. "I did agree to let you select your husband. Was there a specific reason why you refused Colin?"

"He won't agree to a financial arrangement," she explained. "He wants other benefits."

"Benefits?" Caine asked, his curiosity pricked. "Such as?"

She started blushing. She looked at Colin, hoping he'd explain. He shook his head at her. "You started this, you finish it," he ordered.

The sparkle in his eyes indicated his amusement. She straightened her shoulders. "Very well," she announced. She couldn't quite look at Caine when she gave him her answer, however, and stared at the wall behind him. "Colin would demand . . . intimacy."

No one knew what to say to that confession. Her guardian looked thoroughly confused. He started to open his mouth to say something, then changed his mind.

"Aren't most marriages intimate?" Caine asked. "You are referring to the marriage bed, aren't you, Alesandra?"

"Yes."

"And?" he prodded.

"My marriage will not be intimate," she announced, her voice emphatic. She tried to change the subject by adding, "Colin didn't want to marry me until after he'd talked to his father. Now he's feeling honor bound. Clearly, he's marrying me out of duty."

Her guardian let out a sigh. "I did give you my word," he admitted. "If you don't want to marry Colin, I won't force you."

The duchess was fanning herself with her napkin. "Jade, dear, I believe you should be the one to have a private talk with Alesandra. You're younger and not as set in your ways as I am, and it should be a woman to discuss this topic I have in mind. Alesandra seems to harbor some fears about the . . . marriage bed . . . and I don't feel qualified to explain . . . that is . . ."

She couldn't finish her request. The duchess was violently fanning herself now and her face looked like it was on fire.

"Mother, you've had children. I believe that makes you very qualified," Colin told her.

Jade poked her husband in his side in a bid to get him to quit laughing.

"I believe Morgan Atkins will be suitable," Alesandra blurted out. "If he needs my inheritance, he'll agree to my terms, and I don't mind bowlegged children. No, I don't mind at all."

"If you aren't going to be intimate with your husband, how the hell are you going to have children?" Colin asked.

"I was thinking into the future," Alesandra stammered. She realized the contradictions in her argument but couldn't seem to think of a way to straighten it all out. Why would she want to be intimate with a man she didn't know? The very thought made her stomach twist.

"Jade, I believe you should have that talk with Alesandra directly after dinner," the duchess interjected.

"Yes, Mother," Jade agreed.

"Has anyone ever discussed the facts of marriage to you?" Caine asked.

Alesandra's blush was hot enough to scorch the tablecloth. "Yes, of course. Mother Superior told me everything I need to know. Could we please change this topic now?"

Her guardian took mercy on her. "So it's Morgan you've chosen?" he asked. He waited for her nod, then continued. "Very well. We'll invite him over for supper and take his measure."

"I'll want to talk to him too," Colin announced. "He'll need to know, of course."

"Know what?" his father inquired.

Caine was already grinning. He knew his brother was up

to something, but he couldn't imagine what it was. Only one thing was certain in Caine's mind. Colin had made the decision to marry Alesandra, and he wasn't going to let her get away now.

"Yes, son," his mother said. "What is it Morgan needs to know?"

"That Alesandra and I slept together."

The duchess dropped her napkin and let out a little screech. Jade's mouth dropped open. Caine started laughing. The Duke of Williamshire had just taken a swallow of water when Colin made his announcement. He started choking.

Alesandra closed her eyes and fought the urge to scream.

"You slept with her?" his father demanded in a strangled roar.

"Yes, sir," Colin answered. His voice was very pleasant, cheerful in fact. He seemed completely unaffected by his father's wrath. "Several times in fact."

"How could you deliberately . . ." Alesandra couldn't go on. She was so mortified, she couldn't seem to catch a thought long enough to speak it.

"How could I lie?" Colin asked her. "You know better. I never lie. We did sleep together, didn't we?"

Everyone was staring at her now, waiting for her denial.

"Yes," she whispered. "But we . . ."

"For the love of God," her guardian shouted.

"Henry, calm yourself. You're going to make yourself ill," his wife advised when she saw how mottled his complexion was becoming. The duchess was once again frantically fanning herself with her napkin in an effort to remain composed.

Colin leaned back in his chair and let the sparks fly around him. He looked bored. Caine was thoroughly enjoying himself. Jade kept trying to make her husband take the matter more seriously by poking him in his ribs.

"Colin, have you nothing to say to straighten out this misconception?" Alesandra demanded in a near shout so she would be heard above Caine's laughter.

"Yes," Colin answered.

She sagged with relief and gratitude. The feeling was short-lived, however.

"If Morgan still wants you after I've explained how we spent the last week, he's a better man than I am."

"You don't have to tell him anything." Alesandra tried to control the anger in her voice. She didn't want to lose her dignity, but, Lord, Colin was making that difficult. Her composure was in shreds and her throat was aching with the need to shout.

"Oh, but I do have to explain the situation to Morgan," Colin said. "It's the only honorable thing to do. Isn't that right, Caine?"

"Absolutely right," Caine agreed. "It's the only honorable thing to do."

Caine turned to his wife then. "Sweetheart, I don't believe you'll need to have that private talk about the marriage bed with Alesandra after all."

Alesandra glared at Caine for that comment, because she could tell from his grin he was jesting.

"Dear God, what must Nathaniel be thinking? He's looking down from heaven and probably shaking his head in regret for leaving his daughter in my hands."

"Uncle Henry, my father wouldn't have any regrets," Alesandra announced. She was so furious with Colin for getting his own papa upset her voice crackled with tension. "Nothing sinful happened. I did go into his room and I did sleep with him, but only because he was so demanding and I became so weary . . ."

The Duke of Williamshire covered his forehead with his hands and let out a low groan. Alesandra knew she was making a mess out of her explanation and tried to start over. "I kept my clothes on," she blurted out. "And he . . ."

She was going to explain that Colin had been ill and had needed her help, but she was interrupted before she could finish.

"I wasn't wearing anything," Colin cheerfully informed his family.

144

"That's it," his father bellowed. His fist came down hard on the tabletop. The crystal goblets clattered together in reaction.

Alesandra jumped, then turned to glare at Colin. She'd never been this angry in all her life. Colin had deliberately twisted the truth to his advantage and now her guardian thought she was a trollop. She decided she wasn't going to sit there another second. She threw her napkin on the table and tried to leave. Colin caught her before she'd even pushed her chair back. He put his arm around her shoulders and hauled her into his side.

"You two are going to be married in exactly three days' time. Caine, you see to the special license. Colin, you keep silent about what happened. I won't have Alesandra's reputation in tatters because of your lust."

"Three days, Henry?" Gweneth asked. "The church is reserved for the Saturday after next. Couldn't you reconsider?"

Her husband shook his head. "Three days," he repeated. He noticed Colin had his arm around Alesandra's shoulders and added, "He can't keep his hands off her as it is."

"But, Henry . . ." his wife pleaded.

"My mind's set, Gweneth. You may invite a few close friends if you're wanting to, but that is the only concession I'll allow."

"No, Father," Colin said. "I don't want the news of the marriage to get out until it's over. It's safer for Alesandra that way."

His father nodded. "I'd forgotten," he admitted. "Yes, it would be safer. All right then, only the immediate family will be here."

He turned his full attention to Alesandra. "I want your agreement to wed Colin," he commanded. "And I want it now."

"Do you agree?" Colin asked.

He'd won and he knew it. She slowly nodded. Colin leaned down and kissed her. She was so startled by the show of affection she didn't pull away.

"That's quite enough of that," Henry snapped. "You won't be touching her again until you're married."

Alesandra turned to Colin. "You're going to regret marrying me."

He didn't seem overly worried about that possibility. He wouldn't have winked at her if he'd really been concerned.

Jenkins appeared in the doorway. "Begging your pardon, your grace, but we have a visitor at the door. Sir Richards is requesting an immediate audience with your son, Colin."

"Show him into the salon, Jenkins," Colin called out.

"Why would the director of security be wanting to see you?" his father demanded to know. "You told me you'd quit the department."

The worry in his voice confused Alesandra. She started to ask her guardian why he was so concerned, but just as she opened her mouth to say something, Colin tightened his hold on her shoulders. She turned to look at him. His expression didn't give anything away and she knew no one else at the table realized he was silently ordering her to remain quiet.

"After what happened to your leg, I can't imagine why you would continue working for the director," his mother interjected.

Colin tried to hold on to his patience. "The director had nothing to do with my injury."

"It was a long time ago," Jade reminded the duchess.

"By God, he's finished with that cloak-and-dagger business," his father announced.

Caine leaned forward, drawing Colin's attention. "Why exactly is Richards here?" he asked.

"I requested his help," Colin answered. "And he was also going to gather some information for me."

"Regarding?" Caine asked.

"Alesandra."

Their father looked relieved. "Well, then, that's quite all right. Yes, Richards is just the man to ask about the general. Shall we go into the salon and hear what he has to tell us?"

"We aren't going to be left out, Henry," his wife announced. She stood up to face her husband. "Come along, Jade. You, too, Alesandra. If the matter concerns one of us, it concerns all of us. Isn't that right, Henry?" Then she and the others left the room.

Colin let go of Alesandra. She stood up when he did. She caught hold of his hand before he could leave.

"Your father now believes I'm a trollop," she whispered. "I would appreciate it if you would set him straight."

Colin leaned down close to her ear. "I'll explain everything after we're married."

His warm breath sent a shiver of pleasure down her neck, making it difficult for her to concentrate. Up until an hour ago, when Colin had kissed her so passionately, she'd been desperately trying to think of him as a friend . . . or a cousin. She'd been lying to herself, of course, but, damn it all, it was working. Colin had turned the tables on her, though, when he'd touched her. Now, just standing so close to him made her heartbeat race. He smelled so wonderful, so masculine, and . . . Oh, Lord, she really needed to get hold of her thoughts.

"You're a scoundrel, Colin."

"I like to think I am."

She gave up trying to make him angry. "Why don't you want your family to know you're working for . . ."

He wouldn't let her finish. His mouth covered hers in a quick, hard kiss. She let out a little sigh when he pulled back, then repeated her question. He kissed her again.

She finally got his message and quit her questions. "Will you explain after we're married?"

"Yes."

Jade walked back into the dining room. "Colin, I would like to speak to Alesandra in private. We'll be along in a minute."

Alesandra waited until Colin had left the dining room, then went around the table to stand next to Jade.

"Do you really dislike the idea of marrying Colin?"

"No," Alesandra answered. "And that, you see, is the problem."

"How is it a problem?"

"Colin's being forced into marrying me. He's acting out of duty. I can't control that."

"I don't understand," Jade remarked.

Alesandra brushed her hair back over her shoulder in a nervous gesture. "I wanted to control the situation," she whispered. When it first became apparent I would have to get married, I was very angry inside. I felt so . . . powerless. It didn't seem fair. I finally came to terms with my circumstances, however, as soon as I began to think of the marriage as a business transaction and not a personal relationship. I decided that if I chose my husband and set my own terms, then it wouldn't matter if he loved me or not. It would be a business arrangement, nothing more."

"Colin won't agree to your terms, though, will he? I'm not surprised," Jade remarked. "He's an independent man. He's proud of the fact that he's making it on his own, without help from family or friends. He isn't going to be easy to control, but in time I believe you'll be happy about that. Have some faith in him, Alesandra. He'll take care of you."

Yes, Alesandra thought to herself. Colin would take care of her.

And she would become a burden to him.

He wasn't interested in her inheritance and in fact had made it perfectly clear he wouldn't touch it.

He wasn't impressed with her title, either. Being married to a princess was going to be a nuisance because he would have to suffer going to several important functions during the year. He'd have to mingle with the prince regent, and, Lord, she knew he'd hate that.

Colin had rejected everything she had to offer.

No, it wasn't a fair exchange.

# Chapter
# 8

Sir Richards had just finished greeting everyone when Jade and Alesandra walked into the salon. The director turned to both ladies. He knew Jade, and after telling her how wonderful it was to see her again, he turned his full attention to Alesandra.

"Henry told me the good news. Congratulations, Princess. You've chosen a fine man."

Alesandra forced a smile. She thanked the director, agreed Colin was indeed a fine man, and asked him if he would be attending the wedding.

"Yes," Sir Richards replied. "I wouldn't miss it. It's a pity it has to be kept a secret, but you understand well enough the reasons. Come and sit down now. I've some information you'll be interested in hearing."

Sir Richards ushered her over to one of the settees. Jade and Caine were seated across from her, and the duke and duchess took the third settee.

Colin stood alone in front of the hearth. He wasn't paying any attention to the director or his family. His back was turned to the gathering and he was intently studying the miniature on the mantel. Alesandra watched Colin as he lifted the castle to get a better look at it. The expression on

Colin's face was masked, and she wondered what he was thinking.

The duchess was explaining her plans for the wedding. She was determined to make the intimate affair as lovely as possible. She was interrupted by her husband when he called out to Colin.

"Be careful with that, son. It's priceless to me."

Colin nodded but he didn't turn around. He had just noticed the tiny drawbridge latched with a delicate-looking chain. "This really is a piece of workmanship," he remarked as he gently pried the drawbridge away from the hook. The door immediately dropped down. Colin lifted the castle higher so that he could look inside.

Alesandra saw the surprised look in his eyes. He smiled, too. She smiled in reaction. He had just figured out the bit of trickery her father had played on his friend so many years ago.

Colin turned to Caine and motioned to him with a quick tilt of his head. Caine stood up and walked over to the mantel. Colin didn't say a word to his brother. He simply handed him the castle, then turned and walked over to sit next to Alesandra.

The duchess had only just warmed to her topic of the wedding plans. Both her husband and the director were patiently listening to her.

Caine suddenly let out a hoot of laughter. He drew everyone's attention, of course.

Caine turned to Alesandra. "Did you know about this?"

She nodded. "My mother told me the story."

"Later, when you're alone with Father, would you show him?" Caine asked.

"Yes, of course."

"Put that down," his father ordered. "It makes me nervous to see it handled. Do you have any idea of its value, Caine?"

His son laughed. "Yes, father, I understand its value." He closed the drawbridge and put the castle back where it belonged.

"Mother, I don't believe Sir Richards is interested in your

plans for the wedding," Colin said. "He's been polite long enough. Let him get to his reason for calling."

Gweneth turned to the director. "Were you just being polite?"

"Of course he was, Gweneth," her husband told her. He softened his bluntness by patting his wife's hand.

Caine had returned to his seat next to his wife. He put his arm around her shoulders and pulled her close to his side.

Alesandra noticed that both her guardian and his eldest son were very open in showing their affection for their wives. Caine was stroking his wife's arm in an absent-minded way and her uncle Henry hadn't let go of his wife's hand. Alesandra envied the loving couples. She knew it had been a true love match between her guardian and his wife, and from the way Jade and Caine looked at each other, she assumed they had also fallen in love before they were married.

She and Colin were another matter altogether. She wondered if he realized what he was giving up to marry her and almost asked him that question then and there.

Sir Richards saved her from embarrassing herself when he took the floor. "Colin asked me to assist him with a little experiment. He had reason to believe the lady's maid, Valena, was in a league with the ruffians trying to snatch the princess."

Alesandra was stunned by the director's explanation. She turned to Colin. "What reason would you have to distrust that sweet . . ."

He interrupted her. "Let him finish, Alesandra."

"Colin was correct," Sir Richards announced. He smiled at his host. "Both your sons have the best instincts I've ever come across in all my days working for the department."

Henry beamed with pleasure. "It's a trait I like to think they inherited from me," he remarked.

"Yes," Gweneth agreed. Her loyalty to her husband was absolute. "Henry's always been as cunning as a lion."

Colin tried not to smile. He believed his father was more like a lamb than a lion, but he didn't see that as a flaw. In truth, he envied his innocence. He'd lost his own years ago.

His father was a rare man indeed. He seemed to be immune to the darker side of life. Having heard his father's confession of the dark period he went through when he was a younger man made him all the more remarkable. The experience hadn't made him cynical. He wore his heart on his sleeve most of the time, and Colin knew that if there was any softness at all left in his own nature, it had come from his father.

"Now, then, as I was saying," the director continued. "Colin told the maid to inform the princess that there would be a meeting at my town house. He set the time for ten the following morning. Valena slipped out during the night to tell her companions. Colin had one of Alesandra's guards follow her. Right as rain the following morning, there they were, four in all, hiding in wait near my home to nab the princess."

"So there were four in all?" Colin asked. He wasn't at all surprised by the news. Alesandra was speechless. She had always believed she was a good judge of character but now admitted she'd certainly been off the mark with Valena. Alesandra's thoughts immediately turned to Victoria and she wondered if she'd been wrong about her, too.

"Good heavens, I hired Valena," the duchess blurted out. "She came to me and I should have thought that odd, but I was so pleased with her because she was born near Alesandra's father's home. I thought it would make our ward feel more comfortable to have a reminder of her past. Valena spoke the language, you see. I looked into her references, Henry. Yes, I did, but now I realize I should have been more thorough."

"No one's blaming you, Mother," Colin told her.

"Why didn't you tell me about your suspicions?" Alesandra asked Colin.

He was surprised by the question. "Because it was my problem to solve, not yours."

He looked like he believed what he'd just told her. Alesandra didn't know how to respond to that arrogant belief. "But how did you know? What made you suspicious?"

"The latch on one of the windows was unlocked an hour after Raymond had checked," he explained. "And someone had to alert the men that we would be attending the opera."

"The prince regent could have mentioned it to . . ."

Colin cut her off. "Yes, he could have," he agreed. "But he wouldn't have unlocked the window."

"Did you catch all of them?" Henry asked the director then.

"Yes, we did," Richards answered. "They're safely tucked away."

"I'll talk to them first thing tomorrow," Colin announced.

"May I go with you?" Alesandra asked.

"No."

Colin's voice suggested she not argue. His father supported his son's decision, too. "It's out of the question, Alesandra."

The discussion was over. Sir Richards took his leave a few minutes later. Colin accompanied the director to the door. Jade and Caine said their farewells at the same time. Both the duke and duchess walked to the door with them. Alesandra stood by the hearth, watching the way the family members talked and laughed with one another, and the sudden yearning to be a part of the loving, close-knit family fairly overwhelmed her. She shook her head against the possibility. Colin wasn't marrying her because he loved her. She mustn't forget that, she told herself.

The door closed behind Jade and Caine, and she realized then that Colin had already taken his leave.

He hadn't even bothered to say good-bye. Alesandra was so hurt by his rudeness, she turned around to stare at the mantel so her guardian wouldn't see the tears in her eyes.

*Dignity and decorum,* she silently chanted to herself. She would get through the wedding with her cloak of serenity tightly wrapped around her. If Colin was determined to be stupidly noble, then so be it.

The castle caught her attention and the anger she was trying to stir up over Colin's high-handed methods in gaining her agreement was all but forgotten. A wave of homesickness for her mother and father made her ache inside.

Dear God, she was miserable. She never should have left the convent—she realized that mistake now. She'd been safe there, and the memories of her mother were somehow far more comforting.

Alesandra took a deep breath in an attempt to stop the panic she could feel catching hold. She understood why she was so afraid. God help her, she was falling in love with the Dragon.

It was unacceptable to her. Colin would never know how she felt about him. She wasn't about to end up like a vine of ivy clinging to a man who didn't love her. She wouldn't hover, either, no matter how much she wanted to, and she would force herself to think of the marriage as nothing but an arrangement. Colin had his reasons for marrying her, foolish though they were, and in return for his name and protection she would leave him to his own agenda. She wouldn't interfere in any way with his schedule, and in return for her consideration he would leave her alone to follow her own destiny.

Alesandra mopped the tears from her eyes. She was feeling better now that she'd come up with a viable plan of action. She would request an audience with Colin tomorrow and tell him how she had worked it all out in her mind.

She would even allow for negotiating, but only on minor points, of course.

"Alesandra, your guards will bring your things over in just a little while."

Her guardian made that announcement as he walked back into the salon. She turned to thank him. Uncle Henry frowned when he saw the tears in her eyes.

"What's this?" he demanded. "Are you so unhappy over my choice for your husband that you . . ."

She shook her head. "I was looking at the castle and it made me a bit homesick."

He looked relieved. He walked over to stand next to her. "I believe I'll take that back to our country house. I don't like seeing it touched. Colin and Caine couldn't keep their hands off it, could they?" he added with a grin. "They can both be like bulls in a pen at times. I wouldn't want this treasure broken."

He turned to look at the miniature. "Do you know the story behind this gift?" he asked.

"My mother told me Father gave it to you," Alesandra answered.

"The castle was a gift," Uncle Henry explained. "But I was asking you if you'd been told about the loan your father gave me? You have every right to hear it, and to know how your father came to my aid."

His voice had gotten gruff with emotion. Alesandra shook her head. "It wasn't a loan, Uncle, and, yes, I did know what happened. Mother told me the story because she thought it clever and amusing the way he tricked you."

"Nathaniel tricked me? How?"

Alesandra turned and lifted the castle from the mantel, nodding when her guardian instinctively warned her to be careful. While he watched, she pried the drawbridge away from the latch, then handed the castle to him.

"They've been inside all the while," she explained, her voice a gentle whisper. "Have a look, Uncle Henry. The notes are there."

He couldn't seem to comprehend what she was telling him. He stared at her with a look of astonishment on his face.

"All these years . . ." His voice cracked with tension and his eyes turned quite misty.

"Father liked to get his way," Alesandra explained. "He insisted it was a gift and you insisted it was a loan. Mother told me you demanded notes be signed and father accommodated you. But he had the last laugh, Uncle, when he gave you the castle as a gift."

"With the notes."

She put her hand on his arm. "You hold the notes," she said. "And you must therefore accept that the debt has been repaid."

Her guardian held the castle up and looked inside. He spotted the folded pieces of paper immediately. "The debt will be repaid when you marry my son," he said.

He didn't have any idea how his words affected her. His attention was on the castle now, and he therefore missed the look on her face.

She turned around and walked out of the salon. She passed Aunt Gweneth in the foyer but didn't trust her voice enough to speak.

Gweneth hurried into the salon just as Alesandra ran up the steps. "Henry, what did you say to that child?" she demanded.

Henry motioned her over to his side. "Alesandra's fine, Gweneth. She's just feeling a little homesick, that's all. Let her have a few minutes alone. Look at this," he ordered then, his concentration turned back to the notes hidden inside the treasure.

Alesandra was forgotten for the moment. She was thankful no one followed her up the stairs. She went into her uncle Henry's study, closed the door behind her, and promptly burst into tears. She cried for at least twenty minutes and all because she was feeling so horribly sorry for herself. She knew she was being childish—pitiful, too—but she didn't care.

She didn't feel any better when she'd finished weeping. Her nerves were still frazzled with worry and confusion.

Dreyson arrived on the doorstep an hour later. She signed the papers he'd prepared and then listened to his long explanation regarding the transfer of her funds from her father's homeland to the Bank of England. The agent Dreyson had hired to make the transaction was having difficulty getting the money released, but Dreyson assured her it wasn't anything to worry about. It would just take time and patience.

Alesandra could barely concentrate on financial matters. She went to bed early that night and prayed for strength to get through the next three days.

Time didn't drag, however. Aunt Gweneth kept her busy with the preparations for the wedding. Unbeknownst to her

husband or her family, Gweneth invited a few close friends
to join in the celebration—thirty-eight, in fact—and there
was so much to be done before the wedding she could barely
keep up with her lists of duties. There were fresh flowers to
be ordered for the tables inside, food to be prepared for the
formal sit-down dinner she planned on serving everyone,
and a gown to be sewn by the sour-dispositioned but
incredibly creative Millicent Norton. The dressmaker and
her three assistants had taken over one of the larger rooms
on the third floor and were working around the clock with
their needles and threads on the yards and yards of im-
ported lace Millicent Norton had been hoarding for just
such an occasion.

When Alesandra wasn't needed for fittings, she worked on
the task Gweneth had assigned her—writing out the an-
nouncements. There were over two hundred names on her
list. The envelopes had to be addressed too, of course, and
Gweneth insisted they be ready to be sent out by messenger
as soon as Colin and Alesandra were married.

Alesandra didn't understand the need for all the fuss. She
believed only the immediate family, the minister, and Sir
Richards would be attending. She asked her aunt why she
was going to all the trouble and was told that it was the very
least she could do to repay the goodness Alesandra's father
had shown her family.

The day of the wedding finally arrived. The weather
proved accommodating, much to Gweneth's delight. The
garden could be used after all. The sun was bright and the
temperature quite warm for spring. The guests wouldn't
even need to wear cloaks, the duchess decided. She ordered
the French doors opened and put the servants to work
sweeping the stones clean.

The ceremony was scheduled for four o'clock in the
afternoon. The flowers began arriving at noon. The parade
of messengers seemed endless. Alesandra stayed in the
dining room and out of everyone's way. Her Aunt Gweneth
had really gone all out, she decided when she saw two huge
vases of flowers being carried upstairs. She imagined the
library was also going to be decorated. Perhaps Gweneth

thought her husband might decide to entertain Sir Richards in the library.

Alesandra was just about to go up to her room to get ready for the ceremony, but she was waylaid from that duty when Colin's sisters arrived. The youngest, Marian Rose, was only ten years old, and so thrilled to be included in the party she could barely stand still. Marian had been a happy surprise to her parents for, almost four years after their third daughter had been born, they had believed Gweneth's childbearing years were over. The youngest was doted upon by her parents and her older brothers, of course, but she was kept from being completely spoiled by her sisters. Alison was fourteen years old, Jennifer was fifteen, and Catherine had just turned sixteen.

Alesandra liked all of Colin's sisters, but her favorite was Catherine. She was careful not to let the others know how she felt, fearing she would cause hurt feelings.

Catherine was such a delight. She was the complete opposite of Alesandra, and perhaps that was the reason she liked her so much. She admitted she envied Colin's sister. Catherine was outrageously outspoken. One never had to guess what she might be thinking. She told her every thought. She was very dramatic, too, and was constantly getting into mischief with her dearest friend, Lady Michelle Marie. Catherine never worried about restraint. Alesandra doubted she fully understood what dignity and decorum were, and she was the most wonderfully honest person Alesandra had ever known.

She was becoming a very pretty young lady, too. Catherine had dark blond hair and hazel-colored eyes. She was taller than Alesandra by a good two inches.

None of Colin's sisters had been given the reason why they were being called to London, and when their mother gathered them together and explained about the wedding, Catherine was the first to screech with delight. She threw herself into Alesandra's arms and hugged her tight.

"Michelle Marie will probably try to kill you for ruining her plans," she cheerfully informed Alesandra. "She thinks she's going to marry Colin. She's planned it for years and years."

Gweneth shook her head in exasperation. "Colin's never even met your friend. Why in heaven's name would she believe he would marry her? She's your age, Catherine, and Colin's much too old for her. Why, he's almost twice her age."

Alison and Jennifer rushed forward to hug Alesandra, too. All three sisters clung to her and it was all Alesandra could do to keep her balance. They were all talking at once, of course. It was chaotic, and a little overwhelming for Alesandra.

There wasn't room for Marian Rose. She hung back, but not for long. She stomped her foot in a bid to get attention, and when that didn't work, she let out a bloodcurdling scream. Everyone immediately turned to see what was wrong, and Marian Rose used that opportunity to hurl herself at Alesandra.

Raymond and Stefan heard the scream and came running. Gweneth apologized for her daughter's behavior, told Marian Rose to hush, and then put the guards to work carrying up the extra crates of wineglasses from the cellar.

Raymond motioned to Alesandra. She excused herself from Colin's family and went over to him.

"The duchess keeps opening the French doors, Princess. We keep closing them. It isn't safe to have the back of the house unlocked. Could you please talk to her? Colin's going to be furious when he gets here and sees all the doors and windows open."

"I'll try to talk to her," Alesandra promised. "I doubt she'll listen. I guess we're going to have to have faith it will all go well. Just a few more hours and the worry will be over."

Raymond bowed to the princess. He wasn't about to sit back and hope things would go well. Both he and Stefan were ready to pull their hair out over the number of strangers stomping into the town house with flowers and trays and gifts. It had been almost impossible to keep count of who everyone was. Raymond went into the kitchen. He grabbed hold of a servant and ordered him to take a message to Colin. The duchess wouldn't listen to a guard, but she would certainly listen to her son.

Raymond didn't stop there. He went upstairs next to look for the Duke of Williamshire and alert him to the possible danger.

The time got away from Alesandra. Millicent Norton and her assistants came downstairs and waylaid her just as she was about to go up. The dressmaker explained that the wedding gown was hanging in front of the wardrobe in Alesandra's bedroom and that it was without a doubt the most exquisite dress she'd ever created. Alesandra was in full agreement. She spent a long while complimenting the dressmaker and longer still promising to take every care when she put on the delicate gown.

Gweneth came rushing into the foyer just as Millicent and her assistants left. "Good heavens, Alesandra. It's already three and you haven't begun to get ready. Have you had your bath yet?"

"Yes, Aunt."

"The girls are getting ready now," Gweneth told her. She took hold of Alesandra's hand and started up the steps. "Janet will be in to help you just as soon as she finishes braiding Marian Rose's hair. Is your stomach full of butterflies, Alesandra? I know you must be excited. You mustn't worry though. Everything's ready. It's going to be a beautiful wedding. Hurry now or you'll miss it."

The duchess laughed over her own jest. She gave Alesandra's hand an affectionate squeeze when she reached her bed chamber, then opened the door and went inside. Alesandra could hear Marian Rose begging the maid to let her hair loose and then Gweneth's command to sit still.

Alesandra's bedroom was the last along the corridor. She opened the door and went inside. She was in such a hurry now, she didn't pay attention to anything but getting out of her dress. The buttons were in the front, and she had them undone before she'd even pushed the door shut behind her. She stripped out of her clothes, washed from top to bottom again, and then put on her white cotton robe. She was just securing the belt around her waist when the door opened behind her. Alesandra assumed it was the maid coming in to assist her. She started to turn around, but was suddenly grabbed from behind. A hand clamped down over her mouth to silence the instinctive scream already gathering in her throat.

She heard the sound of the door being bolted and knew then that there were at least two men in the room with her.

It took all of her determination to remain calm. She forced herself not to struggle. She was terrified inside, but she wasn't going to let that interfere with her ability to think. She could become hysterical later, after she'd gotten away from the horrible men.

She would have to be patient, she told herself, and wait for her opportunity to get free. She wouldn't scream, no matter how strong the urge became. Colin's sisters would come running and, dear God, she didn't want any of them to get hurt.

Alesandra calmed down as soon as she settled on a plan of action. She would cooperate until she was well away from the town house. It would be safer for the family that way. Then she would fight, scream, and bite, to make them sorry they'd dared to touch her.

A knock sounded at the door. The infidel behind her tightened his hold. He ordered her in a whisper to tell whoever it was begging entrance to go away.

She nodded agreement before he removed his hand from her mouth. The second man unbolted the door. Alesandra got a good look at his face. He was a dark-haired man with heavy eyebrows and oily skin. The sinister expression on his face made her shiver with fear. From the look of him, she knew he wouldn't suffer any remorse about hurting anyone.

The man behind her waved a knife in front of her face and told her that if she called out a warning he would kill her.

She wasn't worried about that possibility, for she knew he was bluffing. The general needed a live bride, not a dead one. She thought about telling the horrid man she wasn't afraid about her own safety, then changed her mind. It would be more cunning not to argue. If they believed she was going to cooperate, they might let their guard down just a little.

Alesandra was allowed to open the door a few inches. Jade stood in the hallway, smiling at her.

"Goodness, Alesandra, you're not even dressed. Would you like me to help you?"

Alesandra shook her head. "I don't need any help, Catherine, but I thank you for offering. Why don't you go back downstairs and wait with your husband? I'm sure your Henry would like you to stand by his side while he greets the guests."

Jade's expression didn't change. She kept right on smiling until the door closed again. She heard the sound of the bolt sliding into place as she turned and ran down the hallway.

Colin had just walked into the foyer when Jade reached the landing above. Marian Rose came running in from the salon and threw herself at her older brother. He lifted her up, kissed her on the cheek, and then bent down to take Caine's daughter, Olivia, into his other arm. The four-year-old gave her uncle a wet kiss.

Jade came rushing down the stairs. Caine caught her at the bottom. "Slow down, sweetheart. You're going to break . . ."

The fear he saw in her eyes stopped him cold. "What's wrong?" he demanded.

"Alesandra called me Catherine."

Colin heard his sister-in-law's worried remark. He put the little girls down and walked forward. He noticed then that the French doors leading to the garden were wide open and scowled in reaction. Didn't his parents understand the need for caution?

"She was just confused," Caine suggested to his wife. "It's her wedding day and she's bound to be a little nervous."

Jade shook her head. She turned to explain to Colin. "Alesandra told me to go downstairs and stand with my husband, Henry. Someone's in that room with her. I'm sure of it. She was trying to warn me."

Colin was already moving toward the steps. "Have Raymond and Stefan stand guard below Alesandra's window outside," he ordered. "Caine, you take the back steps. They'll probably try to take her out that way."

He'd reached the landing before he'd finished his instructions, passed his mother and father as they started down the staircase, and continued on down the corridor.

He was deadly calm about what he was going to do. Rage burned inside him, but he wouldn't let that emotion overwhelm his judgment. Only after Alesandra was safe would he unleash his fury.

He reached her bedroom, quietly tested the door to make certain it was locked, then slammed his shoulder against the wood with all his might. The door splintered off its hinges, the bolt snapped, and what was left of the door flew into the bedroom.

Alesandra tried to shout a warning to Colin but she was silenced by her captor's hand over her mouth again.

The second man charged Colin with his knife in his hand. Colin moved so swiftly, his enemy didn't understand until it was too late that his knife had been snatched away. Colin didn't let go of his hand, however. He twisted it behind his back, then upward, until the shoulder bone had popped out of its socket. The man howled with pain. Colin didn't show him any mercy. He threw him headfirst into the wall next to the doorway.

Fury gave him the strength of four men. He was almost blind with his anger now, for Alesandra looked so damned frightened and the bastard had his hands all over her. The robe she wore had opened enough for him to realize she wasn't wearing anything underneath.

"Get your hands off my bride."

Colin roared that command and started forward. Alesandra's captor knew he was trapped. He waited until Colin was almost upon him, then threw Alesandra forward and tried to run out of the room.

In one quick motion Colin tossed Alesandra onto the bed and out of harm's way, then turned and grabbed her captor by his neck.

He thought about breaking the son-of-a-bitch's neck then and there, but Alesandra was watching him and, damn it all, he didn't want her any more frightened than she already was.

"There's a quicker way out than taking the steps," he announced.

Because his voice had sounded so calm and reasonable, Alesandra wasn't at all prepared for his next action. Colin literally picked up the man by the seat of his britches and threw him headfirst out the window.

It wasn't open. Glass sprayed the walls and floor, and a few of the wooden panes that weren't imbedded in the man's shoulders fell to the ledge.

Colin didn't even look winded. He muttered, "Hell," when he noticed the dust on his trousers, let out a sigh, and then turned back to her.

Alesandra didn't know what to think. Colin had been quite terrifying just a minute before, and now he was acting like nothing out of the ordinary had taken place.

Didn't he realize that he might have killed that man? Or did he realize and simply not care?

Alesandra was determined to find out for herself. She jumped off the bed and went running toward the window. Colin intercepted her before she could step on the broken glass with her bare feet. He dragged her back toward the bed, then roughly pulled her into his arms.

"Dear God, Colin, do you think you killed him?"

The raw fear in her voice made him regret the fact that she had witnessed the fight. She was too young and innocent to understand that some men were really better off in hell. The way she trembled in his arms told him she was afraid of him.

"No, I didn't kill him," he told her, his voice a gruff whisper. "I'm sure Raymond caught him."

Colin was proud of himself. He'd told the outrageous lie without laughing.

She couldn't believe he would think she would believe such nonsense. She could feel him shaking, knew he was still reacting to the upsetting fight, and decided to placate him.

"If you say so," she agreed. She let out a pent-up sigh and relaxed against him. "You forgot to open the window, didn't you?"

"Yes," he lied. "I forgot."

She peeked up to look over his shoulder. "You're certain Raymond caught him?"

He didn't hear the amusement in her voice. "Absolutely certain."

He tightened his hold on her and leaned down to kiss the top of her head.

"Did they hurt you?" he asked, his voice harsh with worry over that possibility.

She found comfort in his concern. "No," she whispered against his chest.

She caught a movement out of the corner of her eye and looked around Colin again. "The other one's crawling away."

"Caine's waiting for him," he answered. He leaned down to kiss her again. She turned her face up at the same time. The temptation was too great to resist. His mouth covered hers in a gentle caress, but it wasn't enough for him. He deepened the kiss, pleased he didn't have to force her mouth open for him. His tongue swept inside to mate with hers and a low, primitive growl sounded in the back of his throat.

The kiss consumed her. Because she was so inexperienced, she couldn't control her response to his magical touch. She couldn't get enough of the taste of him either, and, dear God, his scent—so clean, so wonderfully masculine—was extremely arousing.

Her uninhibited response was almost shattering to his own control. Colin knew it was time to stop. He tried to pull back, but Alesandra wouldn't cooperate with his noble plan. She wound her arms around his neck and tugged on his hair to get him to deepen the kiss again.

He let her have her way. She sighed into his mouth seconds before her tongue timidly rubbed against his. Colin felt his discipline slipping away. His mouth slanted over hers again and again with hard demand.

"Is everything . . . for the love of . . . save that for after the ceremony, Colin."

Caine's voice cut through the passionate haze surrounding Colin and Alesandra. He slowly pulled back. She took a little longer to recover her wits. Colin had to help her take her hands away from the back of his neck. He tightened the belt on her robe, too. She didn't take over the task, but watched as he adjusted her robe to hide every inch of her neck.

"You should get dressed now," he suggested in a whisper, smiling over the look of bemusement on her face. She still hadn't recovered from his touch, and that fact pleased the hell out of him.

"Didn't you hear me?" he asked when she didn't move.

She knew she had to get hold of herself. She took a step back, away from the cause of her befuddled condition. "Yes, I should get dressed," she agreed with a nod. She immediately contradicted herself by shaking her head. "I can't get dressed. They . . ."

"I'll be happy to help you," Jade volunteered. Colin's sister-in-law was frowning with worry and sympathy. "It won't take any time at all," she promised.

Alesandra turned and forced a smile. She was surprised to find both Caine and Jade standing only a few feet away. She hadn't heard either one of them come into the room.

Colin's kiss had blocked out the world, she decided, and, Lord, had they seen the way she'd been clinging to him? She blushed just thinking about that possibility.

She was suddenly so rattled she couldn't seem to think. There was something she wanted to say, but she couldn't remember what it was. She threaded her fingers through her hair in an absentminded gesture. The robe parted just a little with her movement. Colin immediately stepped forward to tug it back into place. He was acting like a possessive husband now. She might have thought that was an endearing action if he hadn't started frowning at her.

"You shouldn't be entertaining in your robe," he told her. "Didn't the nuns teach you anything?"

He wasn't jesting. She slapped his hand away from her throat and backed up another space. "Did you catch the man crawling down the steps?" she asked Caine.

"Yes."

"Good," she whispered. "They came in with the flowers," she added with a nod. "I should have realized . . . when they carried the vases upstairs, but I . . ."

Everyone waited for her to finish her explanation. After a minute or two they realized she wasn't going to say anything more.

"What happened to the other one?" Caine asked.

"Colin threw him out the window."

"Raymond caught him," Colin said.

Caine almost laughed until his brother tilted his head toward Alesandra. He immediately nodded agreement over the ridiculous lie. "That's good to know."

"Could there be more waiting in one of the other rooms?" Alesandra asked.

Colin answered her. "No."

"Your guards have made a thorough check of the house." Caine made that comment in an attempt to ease her fear. "There aren't any others."

Jade drew her husband's attention when she let out a little gasp. He turned to her and saw the tears in her eyes. "What is it, sweetheart?" he asked in a whisper.

Jade pointed to the floor in front of the wardrobe. Caine turned, saw the wedding gown, and let out a low expletive.

Alesandra wasn't paying any attention to anyone but Colin. She'd only just decided that there was something different about him, but she couldn't seem to put her finger on what that might be.

"We're getting married in ten minutes, Alesandra. If you're still wearing that robe, you'll be wed in it. Caine, change jackets with me. I tore mine."

"I don't think it's a good idea to get married today," Alesandra whispered.

"Ten minutes," Colin repeated.

The set of his jaw told her he wasn't going to listen to reason. She still gave it one last try. "No," she announced, her expression mutinous.

He leaned down until he was just inches from her face. "Yes."

She let out a sigh. Then she nodded. Colin was so pleased she had finally decided to cooperate, he gave her a hard kiss. Then he turned and walked toward the doorway.

"They destroyed her wedding dress, Colin."

Jade gave him that news. Alesandra burst into tears. Everyone believed she was upset about the dress, of course, but that wasn't the real reason she was so distraught. She had just noticed what was different about Colin.

"You cut your hair."

The fury in her voice stunned Colin. He turned around, saw the tears streaming down her face, and immediately wanted to comfort her. As soon as he started toward her, she started backing away. He stopped so she would stand still. He didn't want her to accidentally step on a piece of glass. He didn't want her to panic, either, and she appeared ready to do just that.

Alesandra had gone through a hell of an ordeal and that, added to the usual wedding day jitters he assumed most brides experienced, was making her act unreasonable now.

Colin knew he would never get her downstairs and married until he helped her calm down first. He decided that if she wanted to talk about his hair now instead of focusing on the real issue upsetting her, he would let her.

"Yes," he said, his voice as soothing as he could manage. "I cut my hair. Does that displease you?"

She nodded. "Oh, yes, it does displease me," she said, her voice shaking with her anger. "As a matter of fact, it makes me furious."

She could tell from his expression he didn't understand why she was so angry with him. He obviously didn't remember what he'd told her when she'd asked him why he wore his hair so long.

Freedom. Yes, that's what he'd told her. She remembered every word of his explanation. The shoulder-length hair reminded him that he was a free man.

Alesandra turned her attention to his feet. "Why aren't you wearing shackles, Colin?"

"What are you talking about?" Colin hadn't been able to keep his exasperation out of his voice.

"She's upset about the dress," Caine decided.

"Do stay out of this," Alesandra ordered.

Caine raised an eyebrow over that command. Alesandra was acting very like a princess now, and she was treating Caine like one of her subjects. He didn't dare smile, fearing his amusement would push her temper right over the edge. She looked furious, and miserable.

"Oh, Lord, look what you've made me do," she told Colin. She folded her arms in front of her and glared at him before turning to his brother. "Pray forgive me for snapping at you. I don't usually let anyone notice when I'm upset, but that man makes me forget Mother Superior's golden rules. I wouldn't be in such a state if he hadn't cut his hair."

"That man?" Caine repeated with a grin.

"What golden rules?" Jade asked, curious over that remark.

"Isn't the wedding dress the reason you're so upset?"

"Dignity and decorum," Alesandra explained to Jade before turning back to Colin. "No, it isn't really the dress," she announced. She took a deep breath and ordered herself to calm down. Colin couldn't help being such an insensitive clout, she supposed, and he was giving up his freedom. "Oh, never mind. Yes, of course I'm upset about the dress. Your mother's going to be most upset. She paid a fortune for that lace. It will break her heart if she finds out it was destroyed."

"Then you're worried about my mother's feelings?" Colin asked, trying to get to the heart of the issue.

"Didn't I just say I was? Colin, how can you smile at a time like this? I don't have anything to wear."

"Surely . . ."

She wouldn't let him finish. "Promise me you won't tell your mother," Alesandra demanded. "I want your word, Colin. It would ruin her wedding if she finds out."

"It's your wedding, Alesandra, not hers."

She didn't want to listen to reason. "Promise me."

Colin let out a sigh. "I won't tell her." He didn't add that his mother was damn well going to notice Alesandra wasn't wearing the gown. She was still too rattled to think about that, and he wasn't going to remind her.

She made Jade and Caine promise, too. Everyone's quick agreement calmed Alesandra. Colin had to shake his head over her bizarre behavior. He grabbed her by her shoulders, pulled her close, and kissed her. Then he let go of her and walked out of the room. His brother followed him.

"She seems a little nervous, doesn't she?" Colin remarked to Caine.

His brother burst into laughter. "I can't imagine why," he replied dryly. "Your bride has been mauled, nearly kidnapped by two of the ugliest bastards I've ever laid eyes on, and certainly terrorized. She has also made it perfectly clear she doesn't want to marry you, and her wedding dress was torn into shreds. No, I can't imagine why she would be nervous."

Colin's shoulders slumped. "It has been a difficult day," he muttered.

"It can only get better," Caine predicted. He hoped to God he was right.

Neither brother said another word until they reached the foyer. They exchanged jackets on the way down the stairs. The fit was almost exact, for Colin had filled out through his shoulders over the past few years and was now every bit as muscular as his brother.

Colin noticed the crowd gathered in the salon, started to go inside, then suddenly stopped and turned to Caine.

"You're wrong."

"It won't get better?"

Colin shook his head. "You said Alesandra didn't want to marry me. You're wrong. She does."

Caine smiled. "So you realize she's in love with you?"

He'd made that remark as a statement of fact, but Colin treated it as though it were a question. "No, she doesn't love me yet, but she will. In five years, after I've made my fortune, then she'll realize she didn't make a mistake."

Caine couldn't believe his brother could be so obtuse. "She already has a fortune, Colin. She needs . . ."

"To get married," Colin finished for him. "What are all those people doing here?"

The switch in topics was deliberate, of course. Colin

didn't want to get into a heated discussion about Alesandra's motives now. He didn't particularly want to think about his own reasons for marrying her, either.

The ceremony took place an hour later. Colin stood with his brother in front of the minister. The wait for his bride was taking its toll on him, and it was a struggle to hold on to his composure. His own agitation was appalling to him, for he liked to believe that he was a man who was always in control. Nothing ever rattled him, he reminded himself. Hell, he admitted with a sigh, he was rattled now, and the feeling was so foreign to his nature he didn't know how to fight it. He blamed his lack of discipline on Alesandra. Until the day she came into his life, the mere idea of marrying made him blanch. Now, however, his agitation was for the opposite reason. He wanted to get the deed done before anything else could go wrong.

He could still lose her.

"For the love of God, Colin. This is a wedding, not a burial. Quit scowling."

Colin wasn't in the mood to accommodate his brother. His mind was occupied thinking about all the things that could still go wrong.

And then the Duke of Williamshire escorted Alesandra into the salon. She held on to his father, but Colin didn't give him any notice. His gaze was centered on his bride. The closer she came, the more his composure returned. A feeling of contentment rid him of his need to worry, and by the time she reached his side he wasn't scowling at all.

She was going to belong to him.

Alesandra was so nervous she was shaking. She wore an ivory-colored satin gown. The cut was simple, yet elegant. The neckline wasn't overly revealing, but it was still provocative. Alesandra wasn't wearing any jewels. She didn't carry flowers in her hands, and her hair wasn't confined with pins. The dark curls that gently swayed around her shoulders when she moved were all the adornment she needed.

Dear God, she pleased him. He smiled over her shyness. She wouldn't look at him, but kept her gaze downcast, even when her guardian kissed her cheek. She didn't want to let go of him, either. He had to pry her hand away and place it on Colin's arm.

The crowd of family and friends gathered around them. Alesandra almost bolted then and there. She felt trapped, overwhelmed, and terrified that both she and Colin were making a mistake. Her trembling increased until she could barely stand still, and she couldn't seem to catch a proper breath. Then Colin took her hand in his and tightened his hold on her. Odd, but his touch made her trembling ease a little.

Caine's four-year-old daughter helped Alesandra get rid of the rest of her fear. The little girl couldn't see what was going on and squirmed her way through the crowd to stand next to Alesandra. She pretended she didn't see her mother frantically shaking her head at her and reached up to take hold of Alesandra's hand.

The minister had just opened his book of prayers when he happened to glance down and see the child. He immediately coughed to cover his amusement.

Alesandra wasn't as disciplined. She took one look at the dark-haired, green-eyed imp and burst into laughter. Olivia had obviously been having the time of her life and whoever was suppose to be watching her hadn't done his duty. The child was a disaster. The lower part of her skirt was smudged with dirt, indicating she'd spent some of her time running in the garden, and there was another spot the color of the red punch the duchess planned to serve after the ceremony, indicating she'd gotten into the kitchen too. The sash was hanging down around her hips, but what made Alesandra completely lose her composure was Olivia's fat pink bow. It was precariously perched over her right eye, and while she smiled up at Alesandra, she kept trying to bat the thing back on top of her head.

Jade was probably having heart palpitations over Olivia's appearance. Caine bent down and tried to reach behind both Colin and Alesandra to grab hold of his daughter. She wiggled back and giggled with delight.

Alesandra took charge. She couldn't do anything about the smudges on Olivia's dress, but she could straighten her appearance. She pulled away from Colin's hold, retied Olivia's sash, then repinned the bow on top of her head. Olivia suffered through the minute of fussing, and when Alesandra finished, she took hold of her hand again.

She straightened back up and turned to the minister. She still wouldn't look at Colin, but she reached over and brushed her fingers against his. He took the hint and held her hand again.

She was in control now. Her voice barely shivered when she answered the minister's questions. She noticed that as soon as she agreed to become Colin's wife, he visibly relaxed. She looked up at him then and found him smiling at her. The sparkle in his eyes made her heart pound a bit quicker.

It was finally over. Colin gently turned her to face him and leaned down to kiss her. Everyone cheered, and Colin had only just brushed his mouth over hers when he was pounded on his back and pulled away to be congratulated.

He took Alesandra with him. He wasn't going to let her out of his sight . . . or his touch. He put his arm around her waist and pulled her up against his side.

Alesandra didn't remember much of the celebration that followed the ceremony. She felt as though she were walking around in a fog. Toasts were given before, during, and after the supper, but she couldn't remember anything that was said. She was surrounded by Colin's family and friends, and their immediate acceptance of her was both pleasing and overwhelming.

Sir Richards insisted on having a word with Colin and his brother in the library, but Colin kept putting him off. The director wouldn't be denied, however, and finally, after Alesandra promised to stay within sight of her guards, Colin agreed. He and Caine followed the director up the stairs. They had their conference and were back downstairs less than fifteen minutes later.

Colin found his bride in the salon. She was trying to listen to three different conversations at the same time. Marian Rose was demanding permission to go home with her, Catherine was asking her when she would see her again, and

Colin's father was telling anyone who would listen an amusing childhood story involving his sons.

Alesandra looked overwhelmed by it all. Colin decided it was time to take her home. She didn't argue with his decision and, in fact, seemed relieved.

It took twenty minutes to say thank you and farewell, and just when Colin's patience was all used up, they were in the carriage and on their way back to his town house.

The silence inside the carriage was a stark contrast to the chaos they'd just left. Colin stretched out his long legs, closed his eyes, and grinned.

He was thinking about the wedding night.

Alesandra sat across from him. Her posture was rigid and her hands were tightly folded together in her lap.

She was also thinking about their wedding night.

Colin opened his eyes and saw her frown. He noticed she was wringing her hands together, too.

"Is something wrong?" he asked, already guessing what that might be.

"Tonight . . ."

"Yes?"

"Are you going to insist I share your bed?"

"Yes."

Her shoulders slumped. The color left her face and, damn, she looked forlorn. He almost laughed. He caught himself in time, and he felt like a cad for finding any amusement at all in her distress. She was innocent, obviously frightened of the unknown, and it was his duty to help her get over her fear, not increase it.

He leaned forward and captured her hands in his. "It's going to be all right," he told her, his voice a husky whisper.

The look she gave him told him she didn't believe him. "Then you aren't interested in renegotiating?"

"Renegotiating what?"

"Your benefits."

He slowly shook his head. She pulled her hands away from him. "Alesandra, everything will be fine," he told her again.

"So you say," she countered in a bare whisper. "But I don't have any information to prove you're right. Do you happen to have any material on the subject I could read before going to bed?"

He leaned back, propped his leg against the opposite seat, and stared at her. To his credit, he didn't smile. "What kind of material?"

"I thought you might have a manual . . . or something," she explained. She was trying to stop herself from twisting her hands together so he wouldn't notice how nervous she was. "Just something that would explain what's going to happen," she added with a deliberate shrug. "I'm only mildly curious, you understand."

He understood she was completely terrified. He nodded so she would think he believed her lie, then asked in a casual tone of voice, "Didn't you say that the mother superior told you everything you needed to know?"

She didn't answer him for a long while. Colin patiently waited. Alesandra turned to look out the window. It was dark outside, but the moon was bright enough for her to recognize the street they were on and to realize they were almost home. She wasn't going to panic, she told herself. She was a fully grown woman and it was ridiculous to get so upset.

"Alesandra, answer me," Colin ordered.

She tried to hide her embarrassment and sound nonchalant when she finally explained. "Mother Superior did have a private talk with me, but now I realize she didn't give me sufficient information."

"Exactly what did she tell you?"

She didn't want to continue with this topic and was sorry she'd ever brought it up. "Oh, this and that," she whispered with a shrug.

Colin wouldn't let it go. "Exactly what this and that?"

The carriage came to a stop in front of his town house. She all but lunged for the latch. Colin grabbed her hand and held it. "You haven't answered me yet," he reminded her.

She stared at his hand on top of hers. It was at least twice the size of her own and, dear God, why hadn't she paid attention to his size before? She hadn't thought she'd be sharing his bed, she reminded herself. At least not for years and years, until she'd grown comfortable with the idea . . . and, Lord, how naive that ignorant belief was. Alesandra suddenly felt like a complete fool.

She really should have insisted on becoming a nun after all, she decided.

"Mother Superior said I wasn't suited for the holy order." She blurted that thought aloud, then let out a sigh. "I'm not humble enough. She told me so."

She was deliberately trying to turn the topic. Colin knew exactly what she was up to, of course. "And what did she tell you about the marriage bed?"

She turned her gaze back to his hand when she finally answered. "She said that a woman's body is like a temple. There, I've told it. Now will you let go of me? I wish to get out."

"Not yet," he countered. The tenderness in his voice cut through some of her embarrassment.

"You're going to make me tell it all, aren't you?"

He smiled over the disgruntled look on her face. "Yes," he agreed. "I'm going to make you tell it all."

"Colin, you probably haven't noticed, but this topic embarrasses me."

"I noticed."

She heard the thread of amusement in his voice but refused to look up at him, for she knew that if she saw him smiling, she would probably start in screaming.

"Are you embarrassed?" she asked.

"No."

She tried to pull her hand away from his again. He held tight. Lord, he was stubborn. She knew he wasn't going to let her out of the carriage until she explained.

"Men will want to worship there," she blurted out.

"Where?" he asked, his confusion obvious.

"At the temple," she told him in a near shout.

He didn't laugh. He let go of her hand and leaned back. His leg effectively blocked her exit in the event she still wanted to bolt. "I see," he replied. He kept his voice as neutral as possible, hoping his casual attitude would ease her distress.

The color had come back into her face with a vengeance. She looked like she was suffering from sunburn now. Colin found her innocence incredibly pleasing.

"What else did she tell you?" he asked.

"I mustn't let them."

"Worship?"

She nodded. "I mustn't let anyone touch me until I married. Then Mother Superior assured me it was all right because the result of the union was worthy and noble."

She glanced up to see how he was reacting to her explanation, noticed his incredulous expression, and thought he didn't quite understand. "A child is the worthy result."

"I gathered as much."

Alesandra sat back and turned her attention to straightening the folds in her gown. A long minute passed in silence before Colin spoke again. "She left out a few details, didn't she?"

"Yes," Alesandra whispered. She was relieved Colin finally understood her lack of knowledge. "If there was a book or a manual I could read . . ."

"I don't have anything on the topic in my study," he told her. "I don't even know if there is such a thing in print."

"But surely . . ."

"Oh, there are books around, but not the kind I would ever allow you to read," he said with a nod. "They aren't sold on the open market, either."

Colin reached over, flipped the latch up, and pushed the door open. He kept his gaze on his blushing bride all the while.

"What do you suggest I do?"

She asked her lap that question. He nudged her chin up and forced her to look at him. Her blue eyes were cloudy with worry. "I suggest you trust me."

It sounded more like an order than a suggestion to her. She decided she was going to have to trust him, however, for the simple reason that she didn't have any other options available to her. She gave him a quick nod. "All right then. I'll trust you."

Her immediate agreement pleased him. Colin understood why she wanted to know beforehand exactly what was going to happen. It was a way for Alesandra to gain control. The more she knew, the less afraid she would be.

It was usual and customary for a young lady to get the needed information from her mother, of course. At least, Colin thought that was how it worked. He assumed his mother had spoken to his sister Catherine about the marriage act. Regardless, Alesandra's mother had died before her daughter was old enough to need such knowledge.

And so one of the nuns had tried to take over the duty. "Exactly how old is this mother superior?" he asked.

"She looks eighty, but I imagine she's probably younger," Alesandra replied. "I never dared ask her. Why do you ask?"

"Never mind," he said. He turned the topic back to her worry. "Alesandra, I'm going to explain everything you need to know."

The tenderness in his voice felt like a soothing stroke against her cheek. "You will?"

"Yes," he promised almost absentmindedly. His mind was occupied trying to picture the ancient nun explaining the facts of life to Alesandra, using such descriptive words as *temple* and *worship*. Lord, he wished he'd been there to hear the private discussion.

Alesandra saw the sparkle in Colin's eyes and immediately jumped to the conclusion that her naïveté amused him.

"I'm sorry I'm acting so . . . inexperienced."

"You are inexperienced," he gently reminded her.

"Yes, and I'm sorry."

Colin laughed. "I'm not," he told her.

"You'll really answer all my questions?" she asked, still not certain she believed him. "You won't leave anything out? I don't like surprises."

"I won't leave anything out."

She let out a sigh. She quit twisting the wrinkles in her gown, too. Colin's promise had just helped her regain control of her fear. She didn't even mind that he found her embarrassment amusing. He was going to give her the necessary information and that was all that counted. Her relief made her weak with gratitude.

"Well, then, it's going to be all right," she announced. "Shouldn't we get out of the carriage now?"

Colin agreed. He jumped out first, then turned to assist Alesandra. Both the guards were frowning with obvious concern for their princess. They wanted her under lock and key.

Flannaghan hovered in the doorway, waiting to greet his new mistress. He took her cloak from her, draped it over his arm, and then gave her his heartfelt congratulations.

"If you would like to go upstairs now I'll prepare your bathwater, Princess," he suggested.

The idea of a long hot bath after the stress-filled day appealed to her. It would be her second today, but Mother Superior had told her that cleanliness was next to godliness, so she didn't feel at all decadent.

"Colin's going to have a talk with me in the study," she told Flannaghan. "I'll have my bath after."

"Have your bath first," Colin suggested. "I have some papers to look over."

It was a lie, of course. Colin didn't have any intention of working on his wedding night, but he thought a bath might help relax Alesandra, and she looked in need of the diversion.

It had been one hell of a wedding day for her, and even though she appeared to be a little less worried and a little more in control of her emotions now, he knew her nerves were still frayed.

"As you wish," Alesandra agreed. She turned to follow the butler up the steps. Colin was right behind her.

"Was it a beautiful wedding?" Flannaghan asked.

"Oh, yes," Alesandra answered, her voice filled with enthusiasm. "Everything went quite well. Didn't it, Colin?"

"You were almost kidnapped," he reminded her.

"Yes, but other than that, it was wonderful, wasn't it?"

"And terrorized."

"Yes, but . . ."

"They destroyed your wedding dress."

She stopped on the top step and whirled around to glare at him. She obviously didn't want to be reminded of those incidents.

"Every bride wishes to believe her wedding was perfect," she announced.

He winked at her. "Then it was perfect," he announced.

She smiled, satisfied.

Flannaghan waited until he and Alesandra were alone in her bedroom to nag the details out of her. Raymond and Stefan carried in additional buckets of hot, steaming water to fill the oval tub. The butler had thoughtfully unpacked her clothes and had placed a white gown and wrapper on her bed.

She took her time in the bath. The hot water relaxed her and helped ease the tension out of her shoulders. She washed her hair with the rose-scented soap, then sat by the hearth to dry it. Alesandra didn't worry about hurrying because she knew Colin was busy working and had probably already lost track of the time.

At least an hour had passed before she decided to interrupt him. Her hair was completely dry, but after she put on her robe, she took another ten minutes or so brushing the curls again. She was yawning every other minute. The hot bath, added to the heat radiating from the fire in the hearth, made her drowsy, and she didn't want to fall asleep during Colin's explanation.

She went down the hallway to the study. She knocked on the door, then walked inside. Colin wasn't at his desk. Alesandra wasn't certain if he'd gone into his bedroom or downstairs. She decided to wait in the study for him, assuming he would want to have his talk with her there, and went over to the desk to collect a sheet of paper. She was just reaching for the pen and inkwell when Colin appeared in the doorway to his bedroom.

The sight of him took her breath away. Colin had obviously just had a bath too, for his hair was still damp. He wasn't dressed, but wore only a pair of black pants. They weren't buttoned.

He had a powerful build. His skin was beautifully bronzed and the bulge of sinewy strength hiding under the sleek exterior reminded her of a panther. The roped muscles rolled ever so slightly when he moved. His chest was covered with a thick mat of dark curly hair that tapered to a **V** at his waist.

She didn't look any lower.

Colin leaned against the doorframe, folded his arms across his chest, and smiled at her. A faint blush stained her cheeks. She was folding and refolding the sheet of paper in her hands and desperately trying to act nonchalant, and he knew he was going to have to take it slow and easy with her in order to help her keep her fear at bay. It was going to be a difficult undertaking, because Colin had never taken a virgin to his bed before and the sight of Alesandra in her white gown and robe was already sending heat coursing through his body. He was getting aroused just looking at her. His gaze was centered on her mouth and he was thinking what he would like her to do to him with those sweet, full, pouting lips.

"Colin, what are you thinking?"

He didn't believe it would be a good idea to tell her the truth. "I was wondering what you're doing with that paper," he lied instead.

Her concentration had become so scattered from her nervousness she had to look down at her hands before she understood what he was asking her. "Notes," she blurted out with a quick nod.

He raised an eyebrow. "Notes?"

"Yes. I thought I would take notes during your explanation so I won't forget anything important. Is that all right, Colin?"

The worry in her voice cut through his amusement. "How very organized of you," he said.

She smiled. "Thank you. My father was the first to teach me how important it is to be organized. Then Mother Superior took over my training."

Dear God, she wished she could quit rambling.

"How old were you when your father died?"

"Eleven."

"Yet you remember . . ."

"Oh, yes, I remember everything he taught me," she replied. "It was my way of pleasing him, Colin, and I thoroughly enjoyed the time we spent together. It made him happy to talk about his business transactions and it made me happy to be included."

She'd turned the sheet of paper into a wrinkled ball. Colin doubted she was aware of what she'd just done. "I'll only write down key words," she promised.

He slowly shook his head. "You won't need to take notes," he assured her. "You're going to remember everything I tell you."

He was feeling damn proud of himself. The urge to laugh had almost overwhelmed him, but he'd been able to contain himself.

"All right then." She turned back to the desk, started to put the sheet of paper back, and only then realized the mess she'd made. She tossed it into the trash basket, then turned back to stare at him.

The warm glint in his eyes made her shiver with pleasure and that wonderful lopsided grin of his made her heartbeat become quite frantic. She took a deep breath and ordered herself to calm down.

Dear God, he was beautiful. Without realizing what she was doing, she blurted that thought aloud.

He laughed in reaction to her praise. His amusement didn't upset her, though, and she found herself smiling back. "For a dragon," she teased.

The way he was looking at her made her feel as though butterflies were gathering inside her stomach. She needed to give her hands something to do, she decided, and immediately folded them together. "Are we going to have our talk now?"

"First things first," he announced. "I just realized I didn't give you a proper wedding kiss."

"You didn't?"

He shook his head. Then he crooked his finger at her. She

slowly walked across the room to stand directly in front of him.

"Are you going to kiss me now?" she asked, her voice a breathless whisper.

"Yeah."

He'd drawled out that admission. He slowly unfolded himself from the doorway to tower over her. She took an instinctive step back. She immediately stopped herself. She wasn't afraid of Colin, she reminded herself, and she really did want him to kiss her. She moved forward again. "I like the way you kiss me," she whispered.

"I know."

His grin was arrogant. He knew she was nervous, too. She didn't have any doubt about that. And he was enjoying her embarrassment, too.

"How do you know?" she asked, thinking to give him some clever reply once he answered.

"The way you respond to me tells me you like me to touch you."

She couldn't think of anything clever to say to that fact. In truth she was having trouble holding on to any thought. Colin was fully responsible for her condition, of course. The warmth in his gaze was making her stomach quiver.

She felt his hands on her waist, looked down, and watched him untie the belt to her robe. She tried to stop him, but before she'd even placed her hands on top of his, he was easing her robe off her shoulders.

"Why did you do that?"

"You look warm."

"Oh."

The robe dropped to the floor. Her gown was transparent enough for him to see the soft curves of her body. She tried to pull the folds of the garment close around the front of her. Colin didn't give her time to shield herself. He pulled her tight against him. "Put your arms around me, Alesandra. Hold me while I kiss you."

She wound her arms around his neck just as he leaned down and began to nibble on her lips. His tongue traced the inside of her lower lip, sending shivers down her spine. She tightened her hold and leaned up on tiptoes to try to deepen the kiss. Her breasts rubbed against his chest and she let out a broken sigh over the strange feeling of his skin against her. Her breasts suddenly felt heavy, tight, and her nipples hardened. It wasn't an unpleasant feeling, just strange and wonderful. She deliberately rubbed against him again, but ever so slightly so he wouldn't know what she was doing. She didn't want him to think she was bold. She wanted to be bold, though, for the heat from his hard body affected her like an aphrodisiac and she couldn't seem to get close enough to him.

He was driving her crazy teasing her lips with his tongue, his teeth. She couldn't put up with the gentle torment long. She tugged impatiently on his hair, telling him without words that she wanted more.

His mouth finally settled on top of hers in a gentle caress and his tongue eased inside to stroke hers. He acted as though he had all the time in the world. He was slow, deliberate, exerting only scant pressure as he nudged the fires of passion inside her.

Her soft moan told him how much she liked what he was doing to her. He pulled back, saw the passion in her eyes, knew it was mirrored in his own, and let out a low groan of his own. "So sweet," he whispered against her mouth. "Open up for me," he commanded in a rough whisper.

He didn't give her time to comply with that order but used his thumb to force her chin down. His tongue thrust inside, then retreated before penetrating again. She went all soft and willing on him, and that innocent response made him forget about going slow. He was suddenly so hungry for her he couldn't control his pace. His mouth became hard, demanding. The love play between their tongues—his bold, hers timid—made both of them shake with desire. She was too overwhelmed by the fire Colin was spreading inside her to be afraid of what was to come. She couldn't think, only react. She moved against him restlessly, unaware of what she was doing now, or what she was doing to him. Her fingers threaded through his hair, and his control almost snapped when she began to whimper and move so enticingly against his hard arousal. The kiss turned carnal, ravenous. Passion ignited into raw desire as his mouth slanted over hers with primal ownership. His hunger stroked her own.

The kiss seemed unending and yet over all too soon. When Colin pulled back, her mouth was rosy and wet from his touch. The taste of her was on his mouth now, but it wasn't enough for him.

She collapsed against his chest and tucked her face under his chin. Her breathing was choppy against his collarbone.

Colin lifted her into his arms and carried her into his room. He gently placed her in the center of his bed and then stood by the side, staring down at her. His hot gaze warmed her and made her shiver at the same time.

She felt drowsy from his kisses. Her mind cleared when he hooked his thumbs into the waistband of his pants and began to pull them off. She closed her eyes and tried to turn away from him. Colin was quicker than she was, however. He'd stripped out of his pants and joined her in the bed before she'd even made it to the other side.

He caught her by her nightgown. The fabric ripped when he pulled her back to him. She only had enough time to gasp before the gown was completely discarded and Colin was covering her with his body.

She became as rigid as a board. He gently pried her legs apart with his knee and then completely stretched out on top of her just the way he'd fantasized in his dreams since the moment he met her. His hard arousal pressed against the soft curls at the junction of her thighs, and it felt so damn good to him he let out a low growl of satisfaction.

Reality was better than fantasy, however, for he hadn't been able to imagine how incredibly soft and smooth her skin would feel against him. Her breasts were much fuller than he'd fantasized, and he hadn't been able to capture the intensity of his reaction to having her trembling underneath him. It was as close to heaven as he thought he'd ever be.

"Colin, shouldn't we have our talk now?"

He leaned up on his elbows to look at her. Worry was evident in her eyes; victory was evident in his.

"Absolutely." He cupped the sides of her face to hold her still, then kissed her long and hard.

He made her shiver with desire. She couldn't resist putting her arms around his waist to draw more of his warmth. Her toes curled against his legs and it suddenly wasn't enough to simply hold on to him. She needed to touch him, stroke him. Her hands moved up his back, then down the sides of his arms.

Her touch was as light as a butterfly's wings against his skin and yet it was the most erotic caress he'd ever received. He turned his attention to her neck. She turned her head ever so slightly to give him better access. His teeth gently tugged on her earlobe, sending jolts of pleasure cascading all the way down to her toes, and, dear God, his tongue was making it impossible to think.

She started moving with silent demand for more. Colin shifted his position and kissed a line down her throat. He moved lower and kissed the valley between her breasts. She smelled like roses and woman. It was a heady combination. Colin inhaled her sweet scent, then used his tongue to taste her.

He was taking entirely too many liberties with her body. She thought she would die if he stopped. His hands cupped her breasts and they immediately began to ache for more. She didn't understand the frustration building inside her. She felt as though she was made of seams and they were all splitting apart on her. Then Colin's tongue brushed across her nipple. She almost came off the bed. She cried out in fear and pleasure. The feeling was almost too intense to endure, yet it was exquisitely wonderful, too. Her hands dropped back to her sides and she grabbed fistfuls of the sheets in an attempt to anchor herself against the storm of emotions flooding her.

"Colin!"

His name came out with a sob and she began to writhe against him when he took her nipple into his mouth and began to suckle. He was driving her beyond control. His hands stroked her everywhere. She drew a deep, ragged breath and began to whimper. His mouth captured hers again just as his hand slid into the soft curls shielding her virginity. She tried to stop him, but he wouldn't be denied. His fingers slowly penetrated the tight, slick opening, then withdrew. The pad of his thumb rubbed against the very spot he knew would drive her wild.

He made love to her with his fingers until she was mindless to everything but finding fulfillment. Colin had never had a woman respond to him with such honesty. It made it impossible for him to hold on to his own discipline.

"Baby, you're so tight," he whispered, his own voice a harsh whisper.

She could barely concentrate on what he was telling her. "You're making me ache. Please . . ."

She didn't know what she wanted from him, only knew she would go mad if he didn't do something to ease the sweet torment.

He hoped to God she was ready for him. He pulled her hands away from the sheets and wrapped them around his neck. His knee nudged her thighs wider and then his hands slid under her hips to hold her close. The tip of his arousal was surrounded by her liquid heat. He slowly pressed inside her, paused when he felt the barrier of her virginity, and then tried to gently push past the obstacle. The barrier wouldn't give. Colin's jaw was clenched tight and his breathing was as ragged as though he'd just run a mile, for the pleasure was already so intense he could barely hold on to what little control he had left. He knew he was hurting her. She cried out against his mouth and tried to push him away at the same time.

He soothed her with honeyed words. "Sweetheart, it's going to be all right. The pain won't last long. Hold on to me. Oh, baby, don't move like that . . . not yet."

Trying to be gentle was only prolonging the pain for her . . . and it was killing him. His forehead was covered with perspiration and he knew he would go completely out of his mind if he didn't bury himself deep inside her.

He shifted his hold on her, lifted her hips, then thrust deep with one powerful surge. She cried out, her pain as intense now as his pleasure, and tried to push away from him again. His weight wouldn't allow any movement. His possession was complete and, dear God, she fit him like a second skin. He fought the urge to partially withdraw and then thrust back into her, for he wanted to give her time to adjust to him. Her nails scored his shoulderblades and he knew she was trying to get him to let her go. Colin tried to capture her mouth for another searing kiss, but she turned her head away from him. He kissed her ear instead, then her cheek, trying his damnedest to hold on to the remnants of his control long enough to rekindle the passion inside her. Tears streamed down her face and she let out a little broken sob.

"Sweetheart, don't cry. I'm sorry. God, I had to hurt you. It's going to get better in just a few minutes. You feel so damned good. Hold me, baby. Hold me."

The worry in his voice soothed her far more than his words. Pleasure warred with pain. She was so confused by the conflicting feelings, she didn't know what to do. She wanted him to stop and yet she wanted him to stay joined with her too. His breath was hot against her ear. Harsh, too. The sound excited her. She didn't understand what was happening to her. Her body was demanding release, but release from what? She didn't know. The urge to move was suddenly there, and every nerve inside her clamored in anticipation.

"I want to move." Her voice was a bare whisper of confusion.

Colin leaned up on his elbows to look at her. Her eyes shimmered with passion, but more important to him, she'd quit crying.

"I want to move, too. I want to pull out, then sink deep inside you again."

His voice was rough with emotion. She instinctively squeezed him tight. She decided to test just to make certain it really had gotten better. She'd felt as though he'd torn her apart a minute ago, but now the throbbing wasn't as intense, and when she moved restlessly against him, pain didn't result. The touch of splendor caught her by surprise.

"It's starting to feel . . . nice."

It was all the permission he needed. His control snapped. His mouth covered hers in a ravenous kiss. The hunger inside him raged out of control. He slowly withdrew from her, then thrust deep inside. The mating ritual consumed him, and when she tightened around him again and lifted her hips up to meet his thrusts, he buried his face against the side of her neck and let out a raw groan. The pressure building inside him was excruciatingly beautiful. Colin had never experienced anything like this before. Alesandra was like fire in his arms, and her wild, uninhibited response shook him to his very soul. She held nothing back, and that selfless act forced him to do the same. The bed squeaked in protest as he thrust inside her again and again. He was mindless to everything but giving both of them fulfillment.

It came upon them in a rush. She found her release first and when she instinctively squeezed him tight and arched against him, he gave in to his own orgasm.

It took her a long while to come back to reality. She clung to her husband and let the waves of blissful surrender wash over her. A part of her mind understood that as long as she was holding Colin, she was safe. She didn't have to worry about control. He would take care of her. Alesandra closed her eyes and let the wonder of their lovemaking consume her every thought.

She had never felt this safe, this free.

Colin was experiencing the opposite reaction. He was shaken by what had just happened to him, for he'd never allowed himself to completely abandon his control. Never. It scared the hell out of him. Her silky thighs had squeezed every thought out of his mind. She was the innocent, he experienced, and yet she'd been able to strip him of all his defenses. He hadn't been able to hold a part of himself back and toward the end, when they were both reaching for their fulfillment, he had been as much at her mercy as she at his—and, God help him, it had never been this good before. It scared the hell out of him.

For the first time in his life he felt vulnerable, trapped.

They were still joined together. Colin slowly withdrew before the feel of her made him hard again. He gritted his teeth against the pleasure that movement caused. He didn't have the strength to move away from her yet, but he knew his weight was probably crushing her. Her arms were wrapped around his neck. He reached up and gently pulled them away. He leaned down to kiss the base of her throat, felt her frantic heartbeat, and found arrogant male satisfaction then, for he realized she hadn't completely recovered either.

A minute later he rolled onto his back, away from her. He took a deep, shuddering breath and closed his eyes. The scent of their lovemaking permeated the air around them. The taste of her was still in his mouth and, God help him, he could feel himself getting hard again.

Alesandra finally roused herself from her thoughts and turned to him. She propped herself up on one elbow to look at him.

His scowl stunned her. "Colin?" she whispered. "Are you all right?"

He turned his head to look at her. Within a bare second, his expression changed. Colin wasn't about to let her see his vulnerability. He smiled at her and then reached over to brush the back of his hand against the side of her face. She leaned into his caress.

"I'm supposed to ask you if *you're* all right," he explained.

She looked more than all right to him. Her eyes were still shimmering with passion, her mouth looked swollen from his kisses, her hair was draped over one shoulder, and Colin thought she was the sexiest woman in the world.

"I hurt you, didn't I?"

She slowly nodded. She noticed he didn't seem overly worried about that fact. "I was . . ."

"Hot?"

She blushed. He laughed. Then he pulled her into his arms and let her hide her face against his chest. "It's a little late to become embarrassed, isn't it? Or have you forgotten how wild you were a few minutes ago?"

She hadn't forgotten. She blushed to the roots of her hair just thinking about her wanton reaction. His chest rumbled with amusement. She didn't mind that he was laughing at her. The most wonderful thing in the world had just happened to her and she wasn't going to let anything ruin it. A warm glow still surrounded her, making her feel both blissful and sleepy.

"I wasn't very dignified, was I?"

"Do you mean you weren't dignified when you begged me not to stop?"

He rubbed her backside in a lazy fashion while he waited for her answer.

"I did do that, didn't I?"

The wonder in her voice made him smile. "Yes," he drawled out. "You did."

She sighed. "It was nice, wasn't it?"

He laughed. "It was a whole lot better than nice."

Long minutes passed in silence. He broke the peaceful interlude when he let out a loud yawn.

"Colin? Did I . . . was I . . ."

She couldn't seem to finish her question. Her own vulnerability made her too timid to find out if she had been satisfactory.

He knew what she needed from him now. "Alesandra?"

The way he whispered her name felt like a caress. "Yes?"

"You were perfect."

"It's good of you to say so."

She relaxed against him and closed her eyes. The sound of his heartbeat mingled with his soft laughter soothed her. His one hand stroked her back and his other gently rubbed her neck. She was just drifting off to sleep when he called her name again.

"Hmm?"

"Would you like me to begin explaining now?"

He waited several minutes before he realized she'd fallen asleep. His fingers threaded through her hair and he shifted positions just a little so he could kiss the top of her head. "A woman's body is like a temple," he whispered.

He didn't expect an answer and didn't get one. He pulled the covers up, wrapped his arms around his bride, and closed his eyes.

His last thought before he drifted off to sleep made him

smile. The nun really had been right when she'd told Alesandra men would want to worship.

He sure as certain had.


*He was neither mad nor out of control. He still had a conscience. He simply chose not to listen to it. Yes, he knew what he was doing was wrong. It still mattered to him, or at least it had mattered that first time. She had rejected him and had deserved to die. Rage had guided his hands, his dagger. He'd only wanted to kill her. He hadn't expected the rush, hadn't known how powerful he would feel, how invincible.*

*He could stop. He raised his glass and took a long drink. He would stop, he vowed.*

*His scarred boots were in the corner. He stared at them a long minute before making up his mind to throw them away tomorrow. There were flowers on the table . . . waiting . . . ready . . . taunting him.*

*He hurled the glass at the hearth. Glass splintered to the ground. He reached for the bottle while he chanted his promise.*

*He would stop.*

# Chapter
# 9

Alesandra awoke late the next morning. Colin had already left the bedroom. It was just as well because she didn't want him to see her pitiful condition. She was so stiff and sore, she groaned like an old woman when she got out of bed. And no wonder, she thought to herself when she saw the stains of blood on the sheets. No one had warned her that making love would cause her to bleed. She frowned with worry and irritation then, for it was a fact that no one had told her anything. Was it a usual occurrence to bleed? What if it wasn't usual at all? What if Colin had accidentally torn something that couldn't be repaired?

She tried not to panic and succeeded until she bathed. The tenderness and the additional blood on the washcloth frightened her, though. She was embarrassed, too. She didn't want Flannaghan to see the stains when he changed the sheets, so she stripped the bed herself.

Alesandra continued to fret while she dressed. She put on a pale blue dress and matching soft leather shoes. The gown had a white border along the square neckline and around the cuffs of the long sleeves. It was a very feminine dress and one of Alesandra's favorites. She brushed her hair until it crackled with curl, then went in search of her husband.

Their first encounter in the light of day after the intimacy they had shared the night before was going to be awkward for her and she wanted to get it over with as soon as possible. If she tried, she was certain she would be able to hide her embarrassment.

Colin was sitting at his desk in the study. The door facing the corridor was open. She stood in the entrance, debating whether she should interrupt him or not. He must have felt her gaze on him, however, because he suddenly looked up. He was still frowning with concentration over the letter he was reading, but his expression quickly changed. Tenderness came into his eyes when he smiled at her.

She thought she might have smiled back. She couldn't be certain. Dear Lord, was she ever going to become accustomed to having him around? He was such a handsome man. His shoulders seemed wider to her today, his hair appeared darker, his skin more bronzed. The white shirt he wore accentuated his appeal. It was a stark contrast to his coloring. Her gaze turned to his mouth and she was suddenly flooded with memories of how it had felt to be kissed by him . . . everywhere.

Alesandra hastily lowered her gaze to his chin. She wasn't about to let him know how embarrassed she was feeling. She would be dignified and sophisticated.

"Good morning, Colin." Her voice croaked like a frog. Her face felt as though it was on fire. Retreat seemed the only choice. She would try to face him later, when she was more in control. "I can see you're busy," she told him in a rush as she backed away. "I'll go on downstairs."

She turned and started to walk away. "Alesandra."

"Yes?"

"Come here."

She walked back to the entrance. Colin leaned back in his chair and crooked his finger at her. She straightened her shoulders, forced a smile, and walked inside. She stopped when she reached his desk. That wasn't good enough for him. He motioned her over to his side. She maintained her nonchalant attitude as she circled the desk. Colin was never going to know how awkward she was feeling.

He looked at her for a long minute. "Are you going to tell me what's the matter with you?"

Her shoulders slumped a little. "You're a difficult man to fool," she remarked.

He frowned. "Since you're never going to try to fool me, that fact isn't significant, is it?"

"No."

He waited another minute or two, and when she didn't explain, he asked her again. "Tell me what's bothering you."

She turned her gaze to the floor. "This is . . . awkward for me, seeing you after . . ."

"After what?"

"Last night."

A faint blush turned her cheeks pink. Colin found her reaction delightful—arousing, too. He pulled her onto his lap, then nudged her chin up and smiled at her. "And?" he prodded.

"In the light of day, the memory of what we did together makes me feel a little embarrassed."

"The memory makes me want you again."

Her eyes widened over his gruff confession. "But you can't."

"Sure I can," he told her cheerfully.

She shook her head. "I can't," she whispered.

He frowned. "Why can't you?"

Her blush felt as though it was burning her skin. "Isn't it enough that I tell you I can't?"

"Hell, no, it isn't enough."

She turned her gaze to her lap. "You're making this difficult," she remarked. "If my mother was here I could talk to her, but . . ."

She didn't continue. The sadness in her voice made him forget his irritation. She was worrying about something and he was determined to find out what it was. "You can talk to me," he said. "I'm your husband, remember? We shouldn't have any secrets between us. You liked making love," he added with a nod.

He sounded terribly arrogant to her. "Perhaps," she replied, just to prick his temper.

He let her see his exasperation. "Perhaps? You came apart in my arms," he whispered. The memory made his own voice harsh. "Have you forgotten so soon?"

"No. I haven't forgotten. Colin, you hurt me."

She blurted out that truth and waited for him to apologize. She would tell him about her injury then and he would understand why he couldn't touch her again.

"Baby, I know I hurt you."

The heat in his voice, so rough, so masculine, made her shiver. She shifted in his lap. He immediately grabbed hold of her hips to hold her still. She didn't have any idea what the conversation was doing to him, of course—having her sweet bottom rubbing so intimately against him made him hard with desire.

Alesandra wasn't embarrassed any longer. She was irritated because she had just realized her husband was callous in his attitudes. He didn't seem at all contrite.

The disgruntled look on her face made him smile. "Sweetheart," he began, his voice soothing now. "It won't hurt like that again."

She shook her head. She wouldn't look into his eyes and turned her gaze to his chin. "You don't understand," she whispered. "Something . . . happened."

"What happened?" he asked, holding on to his patience.

"I bled. It was on the sheets and I . . . ."

He finally understood. Colin wrapped his arms around her and pulled her against his chest. He had two purposes in mind. One, he wanted to hold her, and two, he didn't want her to see his smile. She might think he was laughing at her.

She didn't want his embrace at all, but he was much stronger than she was and much more determined. He was going to soothe her whether she wanted him to or not. When she finally gave in and relaxed against him, he let out a sigh and rubbed his chin against the top of her head. "And you thought something was wrong, didn't you? I should have explained. I'm sorry. You've been worrying for no reason."

The tenderness in his voice calmed her fear just a little. She still wasn't certain she believed him, though. "Are you telling me I was supposed to bleed?"

She sounded suspicious—and appalled at the very idea. Colin didn't laugh. "Yes," he announced. "You were supposed to bleed."

"But that's . . . barbaric."

He disagreed with that opinion. He told her he found it both pleasing and arousing, and she immediately announced that he was barbaric, too.

Alesandra had lived in a cocoon with the nuns. She'd arrived as a little girl and left as a woman. She hadn't been allowed to talk to anyone about the changes taking place in her body or talk about the feelings those changes evoked, and Colin counted himself blessed because her sensuality hadn't been destroyed or marred. The mother superior might not have wanted to talk about sex, but she hadn't filled Alesandra's head with a lot of frightening nonsense. The nun had elevated the marriage act, too, by using such euphemisms as *temple* and *worship,* and even *noble* and *worthy,* and because of her attitude, Alesandra hadn't believed it was degrading or foul.

His sweet bride was like a butterfly emerging from her isolated shelter. Her own sensuality and her passionate response probably scared the hell out of her.

"I'm fortunate the nuns didn't warp you by planting fears in your head," he remarked.

"Why would they?" she asked, clearly puzzled. "The wedding vows we took are sacred. It would have been a sin to mock the sacrament."

Colin was so pleased with her, he hugged her. He apologized again because she had fretted needlessly, and then explained in detail exactly why she was supposed to bleed. He didn't stop there. The mother superior had told Alesandra that a child was the noble and worthy result of the union. Colin explained exactly how conception occurred. He talked about the differences in their bodies while he rubbed her back in a lazy fashion. The spontaneous lecture lasted nearly twenty minutes. She'd been embarrassed when he began his explanation, but his matter-of-fact attitude soon helped her get over her shyness. She was extremely curious about his body and plied him with questions. He answered all of them.

She was vastly relieved when he'd finished. She leaned away from him, thinking to give him her thank you for explaining, but the warm glint in his eyes made her forget what she was about to say. She kissed him instead.

"Did you honestly believe we would never . . ."

She wouldn't let him finish. "I worried we couldn't."

"I want you now."

"I'm too tender," she whispered. "And you did just say it would take a few days to feel better."

"There are other ways to find fulfillment."

Her curiosity was pricked. "There are?" she asked in a breathless whisper.

He nodded. "Lots of ways."

The way he was staring at her made her restless with desire. A warm glow was forming in the pit of her stomach and she suddenly wanted to get a little closer to him. She put her arms around his neck, threaded her fingers through his hair, and smiled at him. "How many ways?"

"Hundreds," he exaggerated.

The way he was smiling at her told her he was teasing. She responded in kind. "Then I should probably take notes while you explain them to me. I wouldn't want to forget one or two."

He laughed. "Demonstration is more fun than taking notes."

"Begging your pardon, milord, but you have a visitor downstairs."

Alesandra almost jumped off Colin's lap when the sound of Flannaghan's voice reached her. Colin wouldn't let her go. He continued to look at his bride when he spoke to his servant. "Who is it?"

"Sir Richards."

"Damn."

"Don't you like him?" asked Alesandra.

Colin let out a sigh. He lifted Alesandra off his lap and stood up. "Sure I like him," he replied. "The damn was because I know he won't be put off. I'll have to see him. Flannaghan, send him up."

The butler immediately left to fetch the director. Alesandra turned to leave. Colin grabbed her hand and pulled her back. He put his arms around her, leaned down, and gave her a long kiss. His mouth was hot, wet, demanding, and when he pulled back, she was trembling with desire. Her uninhibited response pleased him. "Later," he whispered before he let her go.

The dark promise in his eyes left no doubt as to what he was talking about. Alesandra didn't trust her voice yet, so she simply nodded her agreement. She turned and walked out of the study. Her hands shook when she brushed her hair back over her shoulders and she bumped into the wall when she turned to go back down the hallway. She let out a little sigh over her own sorry condition. All the man had to do was look at her and her mind turned into lettuce. One kiss and she wilted in his arms.

It was a fanciful thought, she admitted, yet all too true. Perhaps, once the newness of having a husband had worn off, she would become accustomed to Colin. She certainly hoped so, for she didn't want to spend the rest of her life bumping into walls and walking around in a daze.

She didn't want to ever take him for granted either. That thought made her smile. Colin would never let her become lax. He was a demanding, lustful man, and if last night was any indication, she also had those same qualities.

Alesandra went back into Colin's bedroom and stood by one of the windows looking out. It was a glorious day and all because Colin wanted her. She must have been perfect last night, she thought to herself. It hadn't been idle praise on his part, or he wouldn't have wanted her so soon again today, would he?

Wanting and loving weren't the same. Alesandra understood that truth well enough. She thought of herself as a realist. Yes, Colin had married her because of duty. She couldn't change that fact. She couldn't make him love her either, of course, but she believed that in time his heart would belong to her. She had already become his friend, hadn't she?

It was going to be a good, strong marriage. Both of them had taken a vow in front of God and witnesses to live as husband and wife until death did they part. Colin was too honorable to break his commitment to her, and surely in the years to come he would learn to love her.

She was already falling in love with him. Alesandra immediately shook her head in denial. She wasn't ready to think about her own feelings.

Alesandra's own vulnerability frightened her. Marriage, she decided, was far more complex than she'd ever imagined.

"Princess Alesandra, will I disturb you if I put fresh sheets on the bed?"

She turned and smiled at Flannaghan. "I would be happy to help you."

He reacted as though she'd just called him a foul word. He looked appalled. She laughed. "I do know how to change sheets, Flannaghan."

"You've actually . . ."

He was too flabbergasted to continue. She found his behavior puzzling. "Where I lived before I came to England I was fully responsible for my clothes and my bedroom. If I wanted the luxury of clean sheets, I changed them."

"Who would demand such a thing from a princess?"

"The mother superior," she answered. "I lived in a convent," she explained. "And I wasn't given special treatment. I was happy not to be thought of as different."

Flannaghan nodded. "Now I understand why you're so unspoiled," he blurted out. "I—I meant that as a compliment," he added in a stammer.

"Thank you," she answered.

The butler hurried over to the bed and began to unfold the linens. "I've already put fresh sheets on your bed, Princess. I'll turn the covers down for you directly after dinner."

His explanation confused her. "Why would you go to the trouble? I thought I would sleep with my husband in his bed."

Flannaghan didn't notice the worry in her voice. He was busy with his task of tucking the bottom sheet into a perfect corner fold. "Milord told me you would be sleeping in your own room," he told her.

The half-given explanation confused her even more. She turned around and pretended to look out the window so Flannaghan wouldn't see her expression. She doubted she could keep the hurt from showing in her eyes.

"I see," she replied for lack of anything better to say. "Did Colin explain why?"

"No," Flannaghan answered. He straightened up and walked around to the other side of the bed. "In England, most of the husbands and wives sleep in separate quarters. It's just the way it's done here."

Alesandra started to feel a little better. Then Flannaghan continued with his explanation. "Of course, Colin's brother, Caine, doesn't follow that dictate. Sterns is the marquess's man. He's my uncle, too," he added with a note of pride in his voice. "He let it slip once that his employer and his wife never sleep apart."

She was instantly miserable again. Of course Caine and Jade slept in the same bed. They happened to love each other. She wagered the duke and duchess only shared one bedroom, too, for they, too, held great affection for each other.

Alesandra straightened her shoulders. She wasn't going to ask Colin why he didn't want her in his bed. She did have her pride, after all. The man was making it perfectly clear how he felt about their marriage. First he cut his hair and now he was going to make her sleep alone. So be it, she decided. She certainly wasn't going to have hurt feelings. No, of course not. It would be a bother having to share a bed. She didn't need his warmth during the night and she certainly wouldn't miss being held in his arms.

The lies weren't working. Alesandra finally quit trying to make herself feel better. She decided she needed to get busy so her mind would be better occupied.

Flannaghan finished making the bed. She followed him down the hall. The door to the study was closed. Alesandra waited until she was well past the entrance to ask the butler how long she thought Colin would be in conference.

"The director had a stack of papers with him," Flannaghan said. "I'd wager it will take a good hour before they're finished."

Flannaghan had miscalculated by several hours. It was well after two that afternoon when he carried the tray of food Cook had prepared up the stairs. He came back down and told Alesandra that the men were still pouring over the documents.

Dreyson was scheduled to call at three, and Alesandra was trying to hurry through the correspondence she and her husband had received that morning. There were over fifty letters of congratulations and almost as many invitations to sort through. Alesandra had divided the papers into stacks, then made lists for each. She gave Flannaghan the stack of invitations to decline while she penned another note to Neil Perry, pleading for him to give her just one hour of his time to discuss his sister.

"I must speak to milord about hiring you both a lady's maid and a full-time secretary," Flannaghan remarked.

"No," Alesandra countered. "I don't have need for either, unless you dislike helping me out now and again, Flannaghan, and your employer is busy building his company. He doesn't need the added expense."

The vehemence in her tone told the butler she would be pricked if he went behind her back. He nodded acceptance. "It is good of you to be so understanding about your husband's financial affairs. We won't be poor for long," he added with a smile.

They weren't poor now, Alesandra thought to herself. If Colin would take advantage of her own funds, of course, she qualified to herself. "Your employer is very stubborn," she whispered.

Flannaghan didn't know what had caused that remark. The knocker sounded at the door and he excused himself from the table immediately.

Morgan Atkins walked into the foyer. He spotted

Alesandra in the dining room and turned to smile at her. "Congratulations, Princess. I just heard the news of your wedding. I hope you'll be very happy."

Alesandra started to stand up but Morgan motioned her to stay seated. He explained he was already late for a meeting with Colin and the director.

He really was a charming gentleman. He bowed low before turning to follow Flannaghan up the steps. She watched him until he disappeared from view, then shook her head. Colin had been wrong. Morgan Atkins wasn't the least bit bowlegged.

Another twenty minutes passed before Sir Richards and Morgan came downstairs together. They exchanged pleasantries with Alesandra and took their leave. Dreyson was given entrance just as the director and his new recruit left.

"I'm most alarmed, Princess," Dreyson announced as soon as he'd finished his greeting. "Is there someplace where we might have a bit of privacy?"

Raymond and Stefan were both standing in the foyer with Flannaghan. The guards always came running whenever a visitor wished entrance. Alesandra didn't believe their protection was necessary any longer, as she was married now and surely out of the general's reach, but she knew both guards would continue to do their duty until they were dismissed. She wasn't going to let them go, however, until she'd found suitable positions for them in London. Raymond and Stefan had let it be known they wanted to stay on in England, and she was determined to find a way to accommodate them. It was the very least she could do for such loyal men.

"Shall we go into the salon?" Alesandra suggested to the agent.

Dreyson nodded. He waited until the princess had walked past him, then turned to Flannaghan. "Is Sir Hallbrook at home today?" he asked.

Flannaghan nodded. Dreyson looked relieved. "Would you mind getting him for me? I believe he'll want to hear this distressing news."

The butler turned and hurried up the steps to see the task completed. Dreyson went inside the salon and sat down across from Alesandra.

"Your frown is very fierce," she said. She folded her hands in her lap and smiled at the agent. "Could the news be that terrible, sir?"

"I've come with two bits of bad news," Dreyson admitted. His voice sounded weary. "I'm sorry to have to bother you at all on your second day of marriage." He let out a sigh before continuing. "My contact has just informed me a substantial amount of your funds—in fact, all of the funds in the account back home—won't be released, Princess. It seems a general named Ivan has cleverly found a way to confiscate the near fortune."

Alesandra showed very little reaction to the news. She was mildly confused by his explanation. "I understood the money had already been transferred to the bank in Austria," she said. "Is that not correct?"

"Yes, it was transferred," Dreyson replied.

"General Ivan has no jurisdiction there."

"His tentacles are far-reaching, Princess."

"Has he actually taken the money out of the bank or frozen the account?"

"What difference does it make?"

"Please answer me and then I'll explain the reason behind my question."

"It was frozen. The bank won't let Ivan touch the money, but the officers have been intimidated by the unethical man and won't release the funds to England's bank."

"That is a dilemma," Alesandra agreed.

"Dilemma? Princess, I would call it a disaster. Have you no idea how much money sits idle in that bank? Why, it's most of your fortune."

Dreyson looked in jeopardy of weeping. She tried to soothe him. "I still have quite enough to live a comfortable life," she reminded him. "Thanks to your sound investments, I'll never become a burden to anyone, least of all my husband. I am confused by this news, however. If the general believed I would marry him, why would he . . ."

"He knew you'd left the convent," Dreyson explained. "And I imagine he knew you were running away from him. He's out to punish you, Princess, for defying him."

"Revenge is always a nice motive."

Colin made that announcement from the entrance. Both Alesandra and Dreyson turned to look at him. The agent stood up. Colin turned, closed the doors behind him, and then walked over to take his place on the settee next to Alesandra. He motioned to Dreyson to sit down again.

"There isn't anything nice about revenge, Colin," Alesandra announced.

She turned her gaze back to the agent. "I believe I know how we might get the funds released. I shall write to Mother Superior and give her a note for the full amount. The bankers might very well be intimidated by the general, but they'll be quite terrified of the superior when she calls on them to collect. Oh, yes, I do believe that's just the ticket, Dreyson. Holy Cross needs the money. I don't."

Colin shook his head. "Your father worked hard to build up his estate. I don't want you to give it away."

"Why do I need it?" she countered.

Dreyson interjected the sum of money under discussion. Colin visibly blanched. Alesandra shrugged. "It will go to a worthy cause. My father would approve. Mother Superior and the other nuns took care of my mother while she was ill. They were very loving to her. Yes, father would approve. I'll write the letter and sign the note before you leave, Matthew."

Alesandra turned back to her husband. He still didn't look pleased by her decision, and she was thankful he wasn't going to argue about it.

"About the ship, Princess," Dreyson interjected. "They have agreed to your terms and arrival date."

"What ship?" Colin asked.

Alesandra hastened to turn the topic. "You said there was another bit of bad news, Matthew. What was it?"

"First he's going to explain about the ship," Colin insisted.

"It was supposed to be a surprise," she whispered.

"Alesandra?" Colin wouldn't be put off.

"When I was in your father's library, I happened to read about a wonderful new invention. It's called a steam vessel, Colin, and it can cross the Atlantic in just twenty-six days. Isn't that amazing," she added in a rush. "Why, my letter to the mother superior will take at least three months to reach her, perhaps longer."

Colin nodded. He was well aware of the new invention, of course. He and his partner had already discussed the possibility of purchasing one to add to their fleet. The cost was prohibitive, however, and the idea was put on hold.

"And you purchased one, is that it?" Colin's voice shook with anger. He didn't give his wife time to answer his question but turned his attention, and his scowl, to her agent. "Cancel the order," he commanded.

"You cannot mean it," Alesandra cried out, her distress apparent. She was suddenly so angry with Colin she wanted to kick him. The steam vessel would increase revenues considerably and he was just being stubborn because the money came from her inheritance.

"I do mean it," he snapped. He was furious with her now because he had been quite explicit when he'd told her he wouldn't touch her money and she had blatantly disregarded his decision.

The set of his jaw told her he wasn't going to listen to reason. She was about to tell Dreyson to cancel the order when the agent intervened.

"I'm having trouble understanding," he remarked. "Sir Hallbrook, are you telling me you're going to refuse her uncle Albert's wedding gift? I believe it is customary to receive gifts."

"Who is Uncle Albert?"

Colin asked Alesandra that question. She didn't know what to do. If she told him the truth, that Albert didn't exist, Dreyson would be insulted. He would probably refuse to do further business with her, too, and she certainly didn't want to jeopardize that relationship.

She didn't want to lie to her husband either.

Truth won out. "He isn't my uncle," she began.

Dreyson enthusiastically cut her off. "But he likes to believe he is," he interjected. "He's a friend of the family. Why, I've known him for years," he added as a boast. "And made a pretty profit from his investments, I might add. Albert handles some of your wife's funds, you see, and I believe he would be very offended if you didn't accept his gift."

Colin's gaze stayed on Alesandra. Her expression didn't tell him anything. She looked very serene. Her hands told a different story, however. They were clenched tight in her lap. Something wasn't quite right, but Colin couldn't put his finger on what that might be.

"Why haven't you mentioned this uncle Albert to me? And why wasn't he invited to the wedding?"

She was going to have to lie after all. The truth wasn't going to do anyone any good.

Alesandra could also see the mother superior shaking her head with displeasure. She forced herself to block the image. She would have plenty of time to feel guilty later.

"I thought I had mentioned Albert to you," she said. She looked at his chin while she gave that lie. "Albert wouldn't have come to the wedding. He never goes anywhere. He won't receive visitors either," she added with a nod.

"He's a recluse, you see," Dreyson interjected. "Alesandra's his only connection to the outside world. He doesn't have any family. Isn't that right, Princess? If your hesitation stems from the cost of his gift, rest assured. He can well afford it, Sir Hallbrook."

"You've known this man for years?" Colin asked Dreyson.

"Yes, of course."

Colin leaned back against the cushions. He knew he probably owed Alesandra an apology for jumping to the wrong conclusion. He decided he would get to that later, when they were alone.

"Convey my appreciation in your next letter," Colin told Alesandra.

"Then you accept . . ."

She stopped her question when Colin shook his head. "It

was thoughtful of him, but much too extravagant. I—or, rather, we—cannot accept it. Suggest something else to him."

"Such as?"

Colin shrugged. "You'll think of something," he told her. "What was the other matter you wished to discuss?"

Dreyson became agitated. He started to explain, then suddenly stopped. While he threaded his fingers through his thinning gray hair, he cleared his throat. Then he started again. "A delicate situation has developed," he announced. "A nasty piece of business, I warn you."

"Yes?" Colin urged when the broker didn't immediately continue.

"Is either of you familiar with the Life Assurance Act of 1774?"

He didn't give Colin or Alesandra time to answer. "No one pays much attention to the ruling these days. It was passed such a long time ago."

"For what purpose?" Alesandra asked, wondering where in heaven's name this discussion was leading.

"A shameful practice was found out," Dreyson explained. "There were immoral men who would insure a life and then hire out the murder so they could collect the profit. Yes, it's shameful, but true, Princess."

"But what does this have—"

Colin interrupted her. "Give him time to explain, Alesandra."

She nodded. "Yes, of course," she whispered.

Dreyson turned his attention to Colin. "Not too many of the firms pay any attention to the Act anymore. It served its purpose, you see . . . for a time. However, it has just come to my attention that an insurance policy was taken out on your wife. The date was set at noon yesterday, and the sum is quite high."

Colin let out a low expletive. Alesandra leaned into his side. "Who would do such a thing? And why?"

"There are stipulations," Dreyson added with a nod. "And a time allowance as well."

"I heard that Napoleon's life was insured, but only for one month's time," Alesandra whispered. "And the Duke of Westminster insured his horse. Is that what you mean when you speak of a time allowance, Matthew?"

The broker nodded. "Yes, Princess. That is what I mean."

"Who underwrote this policy?" Colin demanded. The anger in his voice was barely controlled.

"Was it Lloyd's of London?" Alesandra asked.

"No," Matthew answered. "They're too reputable to become involved in a common wager. Morton and Sons underwrote the policy. They're the culprits, all right. They'll take any contract if the sum is high enough. I certainly don't deal with them," he added with a nod. "But a friend of mine does and he's the one who gave me the news. Thank the Lord I happened to run into him."

"Give me the particulars," Colin commanded. "What is the time limit?"

"One month."

"Who benefits if she dies?"

"The man who purchased the contract wishes anonymity" he answered.

"Can he do that?" Alesandra asked.

"Yes," Dreyson answered. "Your uncle Albert does the very same by using his initials and he wouldn't have to put those down if he didn't want to, Princess. The underwriters are sworn to secrecy."

The agent turned his attention back to Colin. "Thus far my friend and I haven't been able to find out who is behind this foul scheme. I'd wager, however, that it is the same scoundrel who blocked your wife's funds."

"General Ivan? It can't be," Alesandra argued. "Colin and I have been married only one day. He can't know yet."

"Precautions," Dreyson speculated.

Colin understood what the broker was trying to tell Alesandra. He put his arm around his wife, gave her an affectionate squeeze, and then said, "He probably gave orders to one of the men he sent after you. He's just having his fun, wife. He's a damned poor loser. He obviously knew you didn't want to marry him. You did run away in the dead of night."

"He's cruel-hearted, isn't he?"

Colin could think of at least a hundred better descriptions. "Yes, he is cruel," he agreed, just to please her.

"Matthew, did you mean it when you said Morton and Sons will issue any sort of policy?"

"Not policy, Princess, but contract," Dreyson corrected.

"What is the difference?"

"Your husband would insure his ship," he answered. "He would take out a policy to protect against disaster. A contract is another matter altogether. At least the type of voucher Morton and Sons issues is different," he added in a mutter. "It's nothing but a wager, but cloaked as insurance protection so it doesn't violate the Act of 1774. Now then, in answer to your question, yes, they will issue any sort of wager. I remember one in particular. Everyone in London was talking about it. The Marquess of Covingham's wife delivered him a son, and a contract was immediately taken out on the infant's life for one year. The amount was high and payable only if the infant died."

"Do you mean to say the contract could have been issued for the opposite? To pay if the infant lived?"

"Yes, Princess," Dreyson agreed. "Everyone was appalled, of course. The Marquess was in a rage. Speculation grew during the course of the year, for you see, although the buyer of the contract can remain unknown at the time of purchase, his identity will be found out when he collects the sum due him. He must present himself at Morton and Sons and personally sign the voucher. He cannot send a representative."

"So we will know, in one month's time, if General Ivan was behind the purchase," Alesandra said.

Colin shook his head. "It will only pay if you die, remember? And since you're going to stay fit, the general won't have anything to collect. He'll have no reason to come to England."

She nodded. "Yes, of course. Matthew? Did the son live or

die?" she asked, her mind still centered on the story about the Marquess of Covingham.

"He lived."

"Who took the contract out?"

"To this day no one knows," he answered. "Princess, I'm pleased to see you're taking this news calmly," he added.

Colin almost smiled. Alesandra really was very good at hiding her reactions. He could feel her trembling in his arms, but the expression on her face never faltered. She looked quite serene.

He knew better. "She has no reason to worry," he said. "She knows I'll protect her. Matthew, I want you to continue to try to find out who is behind this," he ordered then. "We can assume it's the general, but I want actual proof."

"Yes, of course. I won't give up."

"I wonder if everyone in London knows about this contract yet," Alesandra said. "If so, someone might have heard of a boast . . ."

"If a boast's been made, I'll hear about it," Dreyson assured her. "I wouldn't hold out hope that it's getting much notice, however, what with the fresh scandal making the rounds."

"What scandal?" Alesandra asked, her curiosity pricked.

"Why the Viscount of Talbolt's trouble, of course. His wife has caused the scandal. She left her husband. Astonishing, isn't it?"

Colin had never heard of anything so preposterous. Husbands and wives stayed together no matter how difficult the marriage became. "There has to be another explanation," he said.

"Do you know the viscount?" Alesandra asked her husband.

"Yes. He went to Oxford with my brother. He's a good man. Lady Roberta probably just went back to their country estate for a few days. The *ton* is always looking for reasons to gossip."

Dreyson nodded his agreement. "I heard the rumor from

Lord Thorton and I'll be the first to admit he's one to gossip. Still, the facts tell. Lady Roberta seems to have vanished into thin air. The viscount is beside himself with worry."

A shiver rushed down Alesandra's arms. "Vanished?" she whispered.

"She'll turn up," Dreyson rushed out as soon as he saw how worried the princess was becoming. "I'll wager they had a little marital spat and she's punishing him. She'll come out of hiding in a day or two."

The broker stood up. Colin walked by his side to the foyer. Alesandra stopped the two of them when she called out, "Matthew, no matter how outrageous the contract, if the sum is high enough Morton and Sons will agree?"

"Yes, Princess."

Alesandra smiled at Colin. "Husband, I would like for you to prove to me you mean to protect me."

His wife dared to keep right on smiling at him after she'd given him that insult. He knew she was up to something but he didn't have the faintest notion what it was.

"What do you have in mind?" he asked.

She walked over to Colin's side. "Take a contract out on me, naming yourself as beneficiary, for the exact sum and the exact time limit."

Colin was already shaking his head before she'd finished her request.

"It's a clever plan," she argued. "Do quit shaking your head at me."

"And will the policy pay if you live or die, Alesandra?"

She gave him a disgruntled look. "If I live, of course."

She turned her attention to Dreyson. "I know you dislike doing business with Morton and Sons, but couldn't you see to this little transaction?"

"I haven't agreed to this—"

"Please, Matthew," she interrupted, ignoring her husband's protest.

"Then you want his name on the voucher for everyone to read?" Dreyson asked.

"Yes, of course," she answered.

"You'll have to pay a high premium, and I'm not at all certain there's an underwriter willing to sign his initials alongside yours," he told Colin.

"You told me once that Lloyd's of London would insure a sinking ship if the price was high enough," Alesandra reminded the broker. "I'm certain Morton and Sons, with its tainted reputation for common wagering, would leap at the chance to make a profit."

"Perhaps . . . if you were married to anyone but Sir Hallbrook, that would be true. However, your husband's reputation will defeat your plan, Princess. No one's going to wager against him."

"Why is that?" she asked.

Dreyson smiled. "Your husband has become a legend of sorts. He's feared in most circles. His work, you see, for the War Department—"

"That's enough, Dreyson," Colin interrupted. "You're worrying my wife."

The agent immediately apologized. "Do I try to find someone to underwrite the voucher, Sir Hallbrook?"

"Call it what it is," Colin said. "A wager."

"If you have any doubts about your ability to keep me safe, then I would of course understand your reluctance to put your hard-earned money—"

"You know damned good and well I'm going to protect you," he snapped. "Honest to God, Alesandra, most women would be weeping with fear after finding out someone has taken a contract out on them, but you . . ."

"Yes?"

He shook his head. He finally accepted defeat, though not at all gracefully. "Do it then," he grumbled. "If my wife wants everyone in London to know there are two vouchers in effect, we'll let her have her way."

Alesandra smiled. "Do you know, Colin, you're actually wagering on your own ability. It's quite sporting, really," she added. "And in my opinion, a certain profit for you. You really shouldn't act so surly about this. I have ultimate faith in you. I therefore see no reason to fret."

Alesandra didn't wait to hear what Colin had to say about her opinions. She bid the agent good-bye and then went upstairs.

Flannaghan appeared out of the shadows. He let Dreyson out the front door and then hurried over to his employer.

"She isn't at all worried, is she, milord?"

"How much did you overhear?"

"All of it."

Colin shook his head. "Your uncle would be pleased. You're picking up all of his unsavory habits."

"Thank you, milord. Your princess's loyalty must please you."

Colin smiled. He didn't answer his servant but went up the stairs to his study. Flannaghan's words echoed in his mind.

My princess, he thought to himself. Yes, she was his princess now, and, oh, how she pleased him.

# Chapter

# 10

He infuriated her. They had their first argument late that night. Alesandra had already gone to bed, but she couldn't sleep, so she worked on the list of duties she wanted to accomplish the following day. She was in her own bedroom, of course, because that was where Flannaghan had told her Colin wanted her to sleep, and she was desperately trying not to become upset with her husband because he happened to be such an unfeeling clout. He couldn't help the way he was, could he? Their marriage wasn't a love match either, and if Colin wanted to sleep apart from her, she shouldn't take exception. She did, though. She felt vulnerable—frightened, too—and she couldn't understand why she would be plagued by either emotion.

She tried to understand what was happening to her. She decided she was feeling so insecure because Colin had put her in a much weaker bargaining position. Then she shook her head over that fanciful thought. What did she have to bargain? Her husband had rejected everything she had to give.

Heaven help her, she was beginning to feel sorry for herself. Mother Superior, in one of her daily lectures, had told her that men and women often wanted things they could never have. Envy, she explained, soon turned into jealousy, and once the tentacles of that sinful emotion had taken hold, misery soon followed. Jealousy burned, consumed, until there wasn't room for joy or love or happiness of any sort.

"But I'm not jealous," she whispered to herself. She was envious, though, and let out a little worried sigh over that admission. She was already envious of Colin's brother's happy marriage, and, Lord, did that mean she would soon turn into a jealous shrew and be miserable for the rest of her days?

Marriage, she decided, was a complicated business.

Colin didn't have time for it. He had disappeared into his study directly after dinner to work on his accounts. Having a wife wasn't going to change his habits. He was building an empire, and no one, especially an unwanted bride, was going to interfere with his plans. Colin hadn't had to sit her down and explain his views to her. His actions spoke for him.

Alesandra wasn't upset by his attitude. In truth, she approved of his dedication. She didn't have any doubts, either. Colin would achieve any goal he set. He was strong, terribly clever, and wonderfully disciplined.

She didn't have any intention of getting in his way. She wouldn't distract him, either. The last thing Colin needed was a clinging wife. Still . . . at night, when the work was done, she wished he wanted to be with her then. It would be nice to fall asleep in his arms, to feel him pressed against her during the dark hours of the night. She liked the way he touched her, kissed her . . .

She let out a groan. She was never going to be able to concentrate on her lists if she didn't quit daydreaming about her husband. She shook herself out of her daze and forced herself back to work.

It was almost midnight when Colin walked into her room through the connecting doorway to his own chamber. He wore only a pair of black pants, but he had those stripped off before he reached the side of the bed.

He was very casual about his nudity. She tried to be casual

about it, too. "Have you finished working on your accounts?"

She asked the bed that question. Color flooded her face and her voice sounded as though she were being strangled.

Colin grinned. "Yes," he answered. "I'm completely caught up now."

"Caught up on what?"

He tried not to laugh. "Alesandra, there isn't anything to be embarrassed about."

"I'm not embarrassed."

She was actually able to look directly into his eyes when she told that blatant lie. Colin thought it was an improvement. He pulled the covers back and got into bed. She hurried to move her papers out of his way.

He propped his back against the headboard and let out a loud sigh. He was deliberately giving her time to calm down. If she turned any redder, he thought she might ignite. Her hands shook when she reached for her papers. He didn't understand why she was acting so nervous with him, but he decided he'd have to wait to ask her. Questions now would only make her condition worse.

"Are you cold?"

"No."

"Your hands are shaking."

"Perhaps I am a little cold. My hair was still damp after my bath and I didn't take time to dry it."

He reached over and cupped the back of her neck with his hand. He could feel the tension and began to massage the knots away. She closed her eyes and let out a sigh of pleasure.

"What are you working on?" he asked.

"My list of duties for everyone. I made a list for Flannaghan, another one for Cook, one each for Raymond and Stefan, and several lists for myself. Oh, and the master list, of course. I just finished that one."

She made the mistake of turning to look at him. Her train of thought went flying out the window then. She couldn't even remember if she'd finished her explanation or not.

It was all his doing. If he hadn't had such beautiful eyes, and if he hadn't had such a wonderful smile, and if his teeth hadn't been as white as God's surely were, she wouldn't have taken the time to notice and forget every other thought. Closing her eyes wouldn't help. She would still be able to feel the heat from his body, still inhale his clean male scent, still . . .

"What is a master list?"

"I beg your pardon?"

He grinned. "A master list," he repeated.

He knew she was rattled. He was enjoying her discomfort, too, if his smile was any indication. That realization helped her regain a little of her composure.

"It's a list of my lists," she explained.

"You made a list of your lists?"

"Yes, of course."

He burst into laughter. The bed shook with the force of his amusement. She took immediate exception to his attitude. "Colin, lists are the keys to true organization."

Her voice reeked with authority. Because she was acting so sincere, he tried to control his laughter. "I see," he drawled out. "And where did you learn this important fact?"

"Mother Superior taught me everything I needed to know about organization."

"Was she as thorough as she was when she explained the intimate . . ."

She didn't let him finish. "She was much more thorough. It was very difficult for her to talk about . . . the other. She's a nun, after all, and had taken the vow of chastity years ago. You can understand her reticence, can't you? She didn't have much experience."

"No, I don't imagine she did have much experience," he agreed.

Colin was swallowing up the bed. She kept edging closer to the side to give his legs more room and he kept . . . expanding until he was comfortable. He stretched and yawned and soon took up all the space.

He took her papers, too. He put them on the table next to

his side of the bed, then blew out the two candles and turned back to her.

She folded her hands in her lap and ordered herself to quit being so nervous.

"Without organization we would have anarchy."

It was a stupid thing to say, but she couldn't think of anything better. She was dying to ask him why he was in her bed. Was he going to sleep with her in her chamber every night? No, she thought to herself. That didn't make any sense. His bed was much larger—much more comfortable, too.

Alesandra decided to ease into the topic of their sleeping arrangement. She was calm now, and in total control. He was her husband, after all, and she should be able to ask him any questions, no matter how personal the topic.

A clap of thunder sounded in the distance. She almost fell out of bed. He grabbed her before she went over the side and hauled her up close to him.

"Does thunder make you nervous?"

"No," she answered. "Colin, I was wondering . . ."

"Take your nightgown off, sweetheart," he ordered at the very same time.

His command gained her full attention. "Why?"

"I want to touch you."

"Oh."

She didn't move. "Alesandra? What's wrong?"

"You confuse me," she whispered. "I thought you did like to . . . and then when Flannaghan told me to . . . well, I didn't."

She knew she wasn't making any sense. She quit trying to explain and considered his order instead. She wished he wasn't watching her. She wished it was darker inside the chamber, too. The fire burning in the hearth was still bright enough to cast a golden glow on the bed. She knew she shouldn't be embarrassed. Colin was her husband, and he'd already seen every inch of her body. She hated being shy and wished she could be as uninhibited as he was.

Still, they'd only been married less than two full days. Alesandra decided to tell him how awkward she was feeling and perhaps gain a few pointers on how to get past her shyness.

He turned her attention, then, when he tugged her nightgown up over her hips. She had to force herself not to slap his hands away.

"What are you doing?" She sounded breathless, felt like a complete fool. She knew exactly what he was doing.

"I'm helping you."

"Do you notice how nervous I seem to be tonight?"

"Yes, I noticed," he replied. The laughter was in his voice, but there was heat there, too. The craving to touch her had been plaguing him all day, breaking through his concentration at the oddest moments, and now, finally, he was going to satisfy the intense desire building inside him.

"You're still a little shy with me, aren't you, Alesandra?"

She rolled her eyes heavenward. A little shy? She felt as though she was about to explode with her embarrassment.

Colin pulled the gown up over her head and tossed it over the side of the bed. She immediately tried to cover herself with the blankets. He wouldn't let her shield herself from his gaze, however, and gently tugged the covers down to her waist.

She was perfectly formed. Her breasts were full, lush, beautiful. The pink nipples were already hard, ready, and he arrogantly believed it was his nearness that caused that reaction. He didn't think the goose bumps on her arms were due to the chill in the room, either. Her body was already responding to him, and he hadn't even touched her yet.

He took his time looking at her. She stared at the covers. "I'm not used to sleeping without a gown."

"We aren't going to sleep, sweetheart."

She found her first smile. "I know," she whispered. She decided she had had quite enough of her own awkwardness, and although it took every bit of determination inside her, she turned to him. The look in his eyes—so warm, so caring—made her boldness easier. She wrapped her arms around his neck and pressed herself against him.

It felt wonderful to hold him so close, so intimately. The

hair on his chest tickled her breasts. She let out a little sigh of pleasure and deliberately rubbed against him again. He grunted in reaction. His hands cupped her backside and he pulled her tight against his hard arousal. Her face was tucked under his chin. He nudged her chin up, then lowered his head to hers.

He kissed her forehead first, the bridge of her nose next, and then teased her mouth open by pulling on her lower lip with his teeth. His mouth settled over her parted lips. Her mouth felt so wondrously soft against his own, and the sweet taste of her made him ravenous for more. The slow penetration of his tongue made her shiver. She let out a tiny whimper when he withdrew and then his tongue penetrated deeper inside again. The lazy love play went on and on, for the kiss seemed endless as his mouth slanted over hers again and again. The broken sighs of her pleasure intensified his own. He'd never had a woman respond with such abandon. Her sensuality intoxicated him, and, dear God, he hadn't understood until last night, when he'd first taken her, that such passion was possible between a man and a woman. She held nothing back, and that honest response forced him to let go of his own shields, his own barriers.

He rolled her onto her back, kissed her again, then turned his attention to the side of her neck. His breathing was ragged against her ear. "You make me burn," he whispered, his voice rough with need. "You get so hot so fast it makes me a little crazy."

He sounded almost angry when he told her how she made him feel, but she still took his confession as a compliment. "It's the way you touch me, Colin," she whispered back. "I can't help how I . . . ."

The last of her words ended in a low whimper, for Colin had just taken one straining nipple into his mouth and began to suck it. His hand slid between her thighs and he began to stroke the fire inside her. His fingers slowly penetrated her tight sheath. She cried out, in pain and pleasure, and reached down to take hold of his hand. She wanted to push him away, for she was still terribly tender, but she couldn't seem to make herself do that. She couldn't quit twisting in his arms either. The pad of his thumb made circles around and around the soft curls at the junction of her thighs. He delved deeper and brushed against the hot nub of flesh hidden between the sleek folds of skin. She moaned his name.

"Colin, we shouldn't . . . I can't . . . Don't do that," she cried out when his fingers penetrated her again. "It hurts. Oh, God, don't stop."

She clung to her husband while she gave him her contradictory orders. She knew she wasn't making any sense, but she couldn't seem to find the right words to explain how he made her feel. Colin stopped her protest by covering her mouth with his. The kiss was ravenous, unending, consuming. When he next pulled back, she was so overwhelmed by her own desire, she couldn't think about the pain.

She could barely think at all.

Colin stared down at the beautiful woman in his arms and was almost undone by the passion in her eyes. Her lips, swollen and rosy from his kisses, beckoned him again. He gave into the need and kissed her once again.

"Do you remember I told you there was more than one way to make love?" he asked her, his voice thick with emotion.

She tried to concentrate on what he was asking her, but it was terribly difficult. Everything about Colin overwhelmed her. His skin was so hot against hers and she moved restlessly against him, trying to get closer and closer. His scent, an erotic mixture of male and sex, aroused her as much as his magical touch. Her toes curled into the hair on his muscular legs and her breasts rubbed against the crisp hair on his chest. Her hands stroked the bulge of muscle along his upper arms. He felt like hot steel and the sheer power she felt beneath her fingertips was an intoxication all its own. He was such a strong man, yet he was being terribly gentle with her.

Colin didn't wait for an answer to his question. The need to know all of her overwhelmed his every other thought. He kissed the flat of her stomach, traced her navel with his wet tongue, and then, before she could understand his intent, he pushed her thighs apart with his hands and moved lower to taste the liquid heat of her.

"No, you mustn't." She whimpered the denial, for what he was doing to her was surely forbidden. It was appalling . . . and wonderful. Her control slipped further and further away with each erotic stroke of his tongue against the most private part of her. White-hot pleasure spiraled through her. She knew she was going to die from the sweet agony. The intimate sparing of his rough tongue against the sensitive nub of her desire drove her wild. She tried to tell him to stop even as she held him there and arched up against him for more of his erotic touch.

Her response drove him crazy. He wanted to give her fulfillment first, then teach her how to pleasure him, but the uninhibited way she moved beneath him made his own control snap. Her sexy moans made him wild to be inside her. He barely knew what he was doing now. The need overwhelmed him, ruled his every thought. His movements became rough, forceful, as he knelt between her silken thighs, dragged her arms around his neck, and plunged deep inside her. Perspiration beaded his brow, his breathing became choppy, and he clenched his jaw tight against the incredible feeling of her tight sheath squeezing every inch of his arousal. She fit him completely and the wet heat surrounding him made him shudder with raw pleasure. He heard her cry out. He stilled his movements, grimacing over that sweet torture.

"Am I hurting you, baby?"

She couldn't have answered him if she'd wanted to, for his mouth covered hers again, cutting off words and thoughts. The worry in his voice cut through the sensual haze of passion and she wanted to tell him yes, he was hurting her, but it didn't matter. The pleasure he gave her was far more intense—more demanding, too. She throbbed for release now. He wasn't moving quickly enough to suit her. She wrapped her legs around his thighs and arched up against him, telling him without words that she wanted more, and more, and more.

Colin understood. He buried his face in the crook of her

neck and began to move within her. His thrusts weren't measured but hard, fast, because it was impossible for him to control anything now. The fire inside her beckoned him, burned him, and he wanted and needed to get closer.

He never wanted the agony and the ecstasy to end. He sank into her again and again. And yet, when he felt her tighten around him even more, heard her cry out his name, and knew then she was finding her own release, he thrust deep one last time and let out a low grunt of acceptance as he poured his seed into her.

He thought he had died. And gone to paradise. He collapsed against her, took a long gulp of air, and groaned again. He was so damned satisfied, he felt like smiling. He couldn't, though. He didn't have the strength.

It took Alesandra long minutes to recover. She felt safe and warm held so tenderly in her husband's arms. The terror she'd felt seconds before subsided with each ragged breath Colin took.

"Damn, you're good," he said and rolled onto his back. The man wasn't much for flowery speech, Alesandra thought with a smile. It didn't matter. She was arrogantly proud of herself because she'd pleased him. Perhaps she should give him a little praise too. She rolled onto her side to face him, put her hand on his chest directly over his pounding heart, and whispered, "You're good, too. 'Tis the truth, you're the best I've ever had."

He opened his eyes to look at her. "I'm the *only* one you've ever had, remember?" His voice was gruff with affection.

"I remember," she said.

"No other man is ever going to touch you, Alesandra. You're mine."

She wasn't bothered by his possessiveness. In truth, she found comfort in his attitude, for it made her think he must care for her. She belonged to him now, and the thought of doing what she had just done with any other man repelled her. There was only one Colin, and he belonged to her.

She rested the side of her face on his shoulder. "I wouldn't want anyone but you."

He liked hearing her fervent admission and leaned up to kiss the top of her forehead to let her know how pleased he was.

Long minutes passed in silence. Alesandra thought about what had just happened to her and tried to make logical sense out of her behavior. It proved to be an impossible task, however, for her response to her husband was most illogical.

"Colin?"

"Yes?"

"When you touch me, my control seems to vanish. It felt as though my mind had become separated from my body. That doesn't make sense, does it?"

She didn't wait for his answer. "It was frightening—overwhelming, too—but it was also . . . splendid."

Colin smiled in the darkness. His wife sounded thoroughly confused—worried, too. "It's supposed to feel good, sweetheart," he whispered.

"Mother Superior didn't mention that fact."

"No, I don't imagine she would," he countered.

"I would like to make sense out of this bizarre mating ritual," she announced.

"Why?"

"So that I can understand," she replied. She leaned up to look at him. His eyes were closed and he looked very peaceful. She thought he was about to fall asleep. Alesandra decided to let the matter drop. She cuddled up against her husband and closed her eyes. Her mind wouldn't cooperate, however, and one question after another raced through her thoughts.

"Colin?"

He grunted his reply.

"Have you taken other women to your bed?"

He didn't immediately answer her. She nudged him in his side. He let out a sigh. "Yes."

"Very many?"

He almost shrugged her off his shoulder. "Depends on who's doing the counting."

She disliked that answer intensely. Was it two others, or twenty? The thought of Colin being intimate with even one other woman made her stomach tighten. Her reaction wasn't at all reasonable. His past shouldn't concern her. It did, though. "Was it lust or love that made you want them?"

"Alesandra, why are you asking me all these questions?"

He sounded irritated now. Realizing that made her annoyed as well. She was feeling vulnerable, but her insensitive husband was too obtuse to understand.

Her burst of anger vanished almost as soon as it appeared. How could Colin understand when she didn't understand herself? She wasn't being at all fair with him—or logical.

"I was just curious," she whispered. "Did you love any of those women?"

"No."

"Then it was lust?"

He sighed again. "Yes."

"Was it lust with me?"

Or love, she'd wanted to ask. She'd been too afraid to add that word to her question, fearing the answer wouldn't be what she wanted to hear. Oh, God, she wasn't making any sense at all. She knew Colin didn't love her. Why then did she have this consuming need to hear him tell her so?

What in heaven's name was the matter with her?

Colin wanted to put an end to her inquisition. She was prodding him to answer questions he wasn't ready to think about. Hell, yes, it had been lust when he bedded her, he decided. From the moment he'd first seen her, he'd wanted her in his bed.

Yet putting Alesandra into the same category with the other women he'd bedded seemed an atrocity to him. Making love to her had been completely different, and much, much more fulfilling. No other woman had made him burn the way she did; no other woman had made him lose himself so completely.

There was more than lust involved. Colin admitted that much to himself. He cared about Alesandra. She belonged to him now and it was a natural inclination for a husband to want to protect his wife.

But love? Colin honestly didn't know if he loved her or not. He didn't have enough experience to draw upon to know what the hell love was anyway. His gut reaction to the nagging question was that he wasn't capable of letting himself love anyone with real intensity. He remembered the agony his friend and partner, Nathan, had gone through when he'd fallen in love with his wife. Colin blanched over the mere possibility that he wasn't any stronger emotionally than Nathan was. He hadn't believed it was possible for such a tough-skinned giant to fall so hard. Nathan had, however. He'd become damned vulnerable, too.

Colin forced the dour thoughts aside and reached for his wife. She was trying to scoot over to the far side of the bed, away from him. He wasn't about to let her go. He pulled her into his arms, gently pushed her onto her back, and then covered her from head to toes with his body. He propped his weight with his arms and stared down at her. He frowned with concern when he saw the tears in her eyes. "Did I hurt you again, sweetheart? When I'm inside you I go a little crazy. I . . ."

His voice was gruff with emotion. She reached up to stroke the side of his face. "I went a little crazy too," she confessed. "You made me forget all about my tenderness."

"Then why are you upset?"

"I'm not. I was just trying to sort things out in my mind."

"Sort out things like love and lust?"

She nodded. He smiled. "Sweetheart, I've lusted after you for a long, long time. And you've lusted after me," he added with a nod.

He thought his admission would please her. She surprised him with a frown. "Lust is a sin," she whispered. "I will admit I found you very attractive, but I certainly didn't want you in my bed."

"And why the hell not?"

She couldn't believe he was getting pricked over her admission. The man's ego was involved, she supposed, and she'd just inadvertently stomped on it.

"Because I didn't know what would happen there. No one told me how wonderful making love would be. Now do you understand?"

He grinned, looked sheepish.

"Do you know, Colin, I've just worked it all out in my mind," she announced. "I couldn't understand why I was feeling vulnerable but now I know the reason and I'm feeling much better."

"Explain it to me," he ordered.

"It's because this intimacy is new to me, of course. I didn't have a clue it would be so magnificent, and I didn't realize I would become so emotionally involved." She paused to smile up at him. "If I'd had your experience, I probably wouldn't have felt vulnerable at all."

"It isn't a sin for a wife to feel vulnerable," he announced. "It doesn't make any sense in your situation, however."

"Why doesn't it make sense?"

"Because you certainly realize I'm going to take care of you and you therefore have no reason to feel vulnerable at all."

"That's an extremely arrogant thing to say, husband."

He shrugged. "I'm an arrogant man."

"Do husbands ever feel vulnerable?"

"No."

"But, Colin, if . . ."

He didn't let her finish her argument. His mouth covered hers, cutting off all conversation. He thought only to take her mind off the bizarre topic, but she opened her mouth for his tongue and put her arms around his neck and he was suddenly caught up in a burst of passion he didn't feel like squelching.

He made love to her again, tried to be gentle and take it slow and easy, but she waylaid his noble intentions by responding with abandon. Although it didn't seem possible to him, each time was better, even more fulfilling. His own climax almost killed him, and when he felt her tears on his shoulder, he believed he'd really hurt her.

Colin lit the candles and turned back to her. He took her into his arms and soothed her with honeyed words. She promised him he hadn't injured her, but she couldn't explain why she'd started crying.

He didn't prod her into another conversation. Her lusty yawns told him she was exhausted. Odd, but he was wide awake now. The scare that he might have harmed her jarred him and he knew it would take more than just a few minutes to relax again. Her lists drew his attention when he turned to blow out the candles. On the top sheet were two names. Lady Victoria was first, followed by Lady Roberta. Alesandra had placed question marks after each name.

Needless to say, his curiosity was caught. She was just drifting off to sleep when he nudged her.

"What is this all about?"

She didn't open her eyes. Colin read the names to her and asked her to explain.

"Can't we discuss this in the morning?"

He was about to give in to her request when she muttered, "There might be a connection between the two women. Both have disappeared, after all. After I've talked to Lady Roberta's husband, I'll explain everything to you. Good night, Colin."

"You are not going to talk to the viscount."

The tone of his voice cut through her sleepy haze. "I'm not?"

"No, you're not. The man has enough to deal with now. He doesn't need you grilling him with questions."

"Colin, I . . ."

He didn't let her finish. "I forbid it, Alesandra. Give me your word you won't bother him."

She was astonished by his high-handed attitude—angry, too. She wasn't a child who had to gain her parent's permission to pursue an interest or a worry, and Colin had best understand she had a mind of her own and could use it upon occasion.

"Promise me, Alesandra," he demanded again.

"No."

He couldn't believe what he'd just heard. "No?"

Because her face was still tucked under his chin and he couldn't possibly see her expression, she felt it safe to grimace. Lord, he sounded surly. His arm tightened around her. A good wife probably would try to placate her husband, she supposed.

She guessed she didn't have it in her to be a good wife,

however, for no man—not even Colin—was going to direct her actions.

Ask his permission indeed! She pushed herself away from him and sat up. Her hair covered half her face. She brushed it back over her shoulder and matched him glare for glare.

"Marriage is new to you, Colin, and so you will have to take my word when I tell you . . ."

"Correct me if I'm wrong, but haven't we been married the exact length of time?"

"Yes . . ."

"Then marriage is just as new to you too, isn't it?"

She nodded.

"New or old, Alesandra, the vows haven't changed. Wives obey their husbands."

"Ours is not a usual marriage," she countered. "You and I settled upon an agreement of sorts before we spoke our vows. You've obviously forgotten and for that reason I will not take exception to your outrageous command. I will remind you, however, that we both agreed not to hover."

"No we didn't."

"It was an unspoken promise we gave to each other. I told you I didn't want a husband who hovered and you admitted you didn't want a wife who hovered, either."

"What the hell does that have to do with . . ."

"By hover I meant someone who interferes," she told him. "You've made it perfectly clear on several occasions that you don't wish my help or interference in your business affairs and I would now like to take this opportunity to insist you not interfere in my affairs."

She couldn't quite look into his eyes. His incredulous expression made her nervous. She turned her gaze to his chin. "My father would never have forbidden my mother anything. Their marriage was based upon a foundation of mutual trust and respect. In time I hope we can achieve the same kind of arrangement."

"Are you finished?"

She was pleased that he didn't sound angry with her. Colin was going to be reasonable about this after all. He had listened to what she had to say and hadn't allowed his arrogant nature to get in the way.

"Yes, thank you."

"Look at me."

She immediately lifted her gaze to his eyes. He didn't say another word for a long minute. His stare made her worry, though. His expression didn't give her a hint of what he was thinking and his amazing ability to mask his thoughts and his feelings did impress her. She was a little envious, too. She wished she had that much control.

"Did you want to say something to me?" she asked when she couldn't stand the silence a second longer.

He nodded. She smiled.

"You will not talk to the viscount about his wife."

They were right back where they'd started. Colin obviously hadn't heard a word she'd said. She felt like kicking the stubborn man. She didn't, of course, because she was a lady, and her impossible husband was never going to know how furious she was.

God's truth, he could make Mother Superior curse in vexation.

Colin forced himself not to smile. The issue was too important to turn into a laughing matter, but, dear God, her expression was priceless. She looked like she wanted to kill him.

"Give me your promise, wife."

"Oh, all right," she cried out. "You win. I won't bother the viscount."

"This isn't about winning or losing," he countered. "The viscount has enough on his mind. I don't want you adding to his misery."

"You don't trust my judgment at all, do you, Colin?"

"No."

That answer hurt her far more than his high-handed command. She tried to turn away from him, but he reached out and grabbed hold of her chin. "Do you trust my judgment yet?"

He fully expected to hear the same denial. She didn't

know him well enough to give him her complete trust. In time, of course, when they had both learned the other's ways, she would begin to give him her trust.

"Yes, of course I trust your judgment."

He couldn't contain his surprise or his pleasure. He grabbed her by the back of her neck, pulled her toward him, and leaned up at the same time to kiss her hard.

"I'm pleased to know you have instinctively put your faith in me already," he told her.

She leaned back and frowned at him. "It wasn't instinctive," she said. "You had already proven to me that you can upon occasion use sound judgment."

"When was that?"

"When you married me. You used sound judgment then. I understand now, of course, that you knew something I didn't."

"And what did I know?"

"That no one else would have you."

She'd deliberately tried to prick his temper with that remark, for she was still irritated with him, but Colin wasn't at all offended. The slap at his arrogance went unnoticed. He either didn't know she'd just insulted him or he didn't care, she decided when he burst into laughter.

"You please me, Alesandra."

"Of course I please you. I just gave in."

She fluffed her pillow, then got back under the covers to rest on her side. "Marriage is more complicated than I anticipated," she whispered. "Will I always have to be the one to concede?"

God, she sounded forlorn. "No, you won't always have to concede."

Her unladylike snort told him she didn't believe him. "Marriage is a give-and-take arrangement," he speculated.

"With the wife doing all the giving and the husband doing all the taking?"

He didn't answer that question. He turned on his side and pulled her up against him. Her shoulders rested against his chest and her bottom was pressed against his groin. The backs of her thighs, so smooth and silky, covered the tops of his thighs, and, God, how he loved the feel of her against him. He draped one arm over her hip, dropped his chin to rest on top of her head, and closed his eyes.

Long minutes passed in silence. He thought Alesandra had already fallen asleep and was just easing away from her when she whispered, "I dislike the word *obey,* Colin."

"I gathered as much," he told her dryly.

"A princess really shouldn't have to obey anyone."

It was a paltry argument. "But you're my princess," he reminded her. "And you will therefore do what I think is best. We're both going to have to bow to tradition for a while," he added. "Neither one of us has any experience being married. I'm not an ogre, but the fact is you did promise to obey. I specifically remember hearing your pledge when you were reciting your vows."

"I wish you would be more reasonable."

"I'm always reasonable."

"Colin?"

"Yes?"

"Do go to sleep."

He let her have the last word. He waited a long while until he was certain she had fallen asleep before he left her bed and went back to his own chamber.

She felt him leave. She almost called out to him to ask him why he didn't want to sleep with her the rest of the night, but pride stopped her. Tears filled her eyes and she felt as though she had just been rejected by her husband. Her reaction didn't make much sense, especially after the passionate way he'd made love to her, but she was too tired to sort it all out in her mind.

Alesandra's sleep was fitful. She was awakened just an hour later by a scraping sound coming from Colin's bedroom. She immediately got out of bed to investigate. She didn't have any intention of intruding and therefore didn't bother with her robe or her slippers.

She heard a low expletive just as she pulled the door open and peeked inside. Colin stood in front of the fireplace. He'd dragged the footrest over and, while she watched, he put one foot on the cushion and bent over to massage his injured leg with both hands.

He didn't know she was there, watching him. She was certain of that fact because of his expression. It wasn't guarded now, and though she could only see one side of his face, it was enough for her to know he was in agony.

It took all the strength she had not to rush into his room and offer whatever paltry help she could give. His pride was involved, however, and she knew he would be furious with her if he realized she'd been watching him.

Rubbing the injured muscles wasn't easing the pain. Colin straightened up and began to pace back and forth in front of the hearth. He was trying to work out the knot of twisted muscle in what was left of the calf of his left leg. Forcing his full weight on the injured limb caused a spasm of pain to shoot all the way up to his chest. It felt like lightning had just struck every nerve in his body, and it damn near doubled him over. Colin refused to give in to the torment. He clenched his jaw tight, drew a deep breath, and continued walking. He knew from past experience that eventually he would be able to walk the cramp out. Some nights it only took an hour. Other nights it took much, much longer.

Colin walked over to the connecting door to Alesandra's room. He reached for the doorknob, then stopped. He wanted to look in on her, but he didn't want to wake her up and he knew she was a light sleeper. He'd learned that fact when he'd become ill and she slept with him.

Alesandra needed her rest. He turned around and resumed his pacing. His mind was suddenly filled with fragments of their conversation regarding his order and her compliance. He remembered how she had sounded when she'd told him she disliked the word *obey*. Hell, he didn't blame her. He thought it was a bit barbaric for a woman to have to promise to obey her husband for the rest of her life. Such radical opinions would land him in Newgate Prison if the conservatives got wind of his subversive thoughts, and Colin was honest enough to admit that there was a part of him—a very small part—that found the idea of a woman obeying his every command appealing. The appeal wouldn't last long, however. There were paid servants to do his bidding. And perhaps there were wives who would be just as accommodating. Alesandra didn't fit into that group. Thank God for that, he decided. She was feisty and opinionated, and he wouldn't have her any other way. She was so damned passionate about everything.

His princess, he decided, was flawed to perfection.

Alesandra hadn't made a sound when she hurried back to her bed and got under the covers. She couldn't get the picture of Colin's anguished expression out of her mind. Her heart ached for her husband. She hadn't realized until tonight how terrible his pain was, but now that she was aware, she vowed to find a way to help him.

She suddenly had a mission. She lit the candles and made a list of what she needed to do. First she would read whatever literature was available. Second on her list was a visit to the physician, Sir Winters. She would ply him with questions and ask him for suggestions. Alesandra couldn't think of anything else to add to her list now, but she was tired, and surely after some much needed sleep, she would think of other plans of action.

She put the list back on the side table and blew out the candles. Her cheeks were wet from her tears. She used the bed cover to wipe them dry, then closed her eyes and tried to go back to sleep.

A sudden realization rushed into her mind just as she was drifting off. Colin didn't want her to sleep in his bed because of his leg. He didn't want her to know about his agony. Yes, that made sense. His pride was the issue, of course, but he was also probably being thoughtful, too. If he needed to walk every night, he would wake her. That made sense, too. Alesandra let out a loud sigh of relief.

Colin hadn't rejected her after all.

# Chapter
# 11

Colin shook Alesandra awake early the next morning. "Sweetheart, open your eyes. I want to talk to you before I leave."

She struggled to sit up. "Where are you going?"

"To work," he answered.

She started to sink back down under the covers. Colin leaned over the side of the bed and grabbed hold of her shoulders. He couldn't tell if her eyes were open or not, for her curly hair hung over her face, blocking his view. He held on to her with one hand and brushed her hair back over her shoulders with his other. He was both exasperated and amused. "Are you awake yet?"

"I believe I am."

"I want you to stay inside until I return home. I've already given Stefan and Raymond their orders."

"Why do I have to stay inside?"

"Have you already forgotten about the policy in effect for thirty days?"

She let out a loud yawn. She guessed she had forgotten. "Do you mean to tell me I have to stay under lock and key for a full month?"

"We'll take it one day at a time, wife."

"Colin, what time is it?"

"A few minutes past dawn."

"Good God."

"Have you heard my instructions?" he demanded.

She didn't answer him. She got out of bed, put her robe on, and walked into his bedroom. Her husband followed her.

"What are you doing?"

"Getting in your bed."

"Why?"

"I belong here."

She buried herself under his covers and was sound asleep a minute later. He pulled the covers back, leaned down, and kissed her brow.

Flannaghan waited in the hall. Colin went over his instructions with the butler. The town house was going to become a fortress for the next thirty days, and no one other than immediate family was going to be allowed entrance.

"Keeping company out will be easy, milord, but keeping your princess inside is going to be most difficult."

Flannaghan's prediction proved accurate. The battle began late that morning. The butler found his new mistress sitting on the floor in Colin's bedroom. She was surrounded by a stack of her husband's shoes.

"What are you doing, Princess?"

"Colin needs new boots," she replied.

"But he has at least five pairs now he never wears. He's partial to the old Hessians even though the Wellingtons have become more fashionable."

Alesandra was looking at the soles of the boots. "Flannaghan, do you notice the heel on the left boot is barely worn?"

The butler knelt down beside his mistress and looked at the boot she held up for him. "It looks brand-new," he remarked. "But I know he's worn . . ."

"Yes, he has worn these boots," she interrupted. She held up the right-footed boot. "This one's well worn, isn't it?"

"What do you make of it, Princess?"

"We're speaking in confidence now, Flannaghan. I don't want a word of this discussion to reach Colin. He's sensitive about his leg."

"I won't say a word."

She nodded. "It appears Colin's injured leg is just a bit shorter than the other one. I would like a bootmaker to look at these shoes and make a few adjustments."

"Do you mean to make one heel thicker? Colin will notice, Princess."

She shook her head. "I was thinking along the lines of an insert of some kind—perhaps a soft leather pad running the length. Who makes Colin's boots now?"

"Hoby made that pair," Flannaghan answered. "Every fashionable gentleman gives him his business."

"Then he won't do," she countered. "I don't want anyone to know about this experiment. We must find someone else."

"There's Curtis," Flannaghan remarked after a moment's consideration. "He used to make Colin's father's shoes. The man's retired now, but he lives in London and he might be persuaded to help you."

"I shall go and see him at once. I'll take only one pair of Colin's shoes with me. If luck is on our side, my husband won't even notice they're gone."

Flannaghan was vehemently shaking his head at her. "You cannot leave the town house. I would be happy to go on this errand," he added in a rush when she looked like she was about to argue with him. "If you'll write down what you wish Curtis to do . . ."

"Yes," she agreed. "I'll make a list of suggestions. What a fine idea. Could you go this afternoon?"

The butler immediately agreed. Alesandra handed him the pair of boots and then stood up. "If this plan works, I'll have Curtis make a pair of half Wellingtons for Colin. Then he'll have a pair to wear under his trousers. Now then, Flannaghan, I have one more request to ask of you."

"Yes, Princess?"

"Would you please take a note to Sir Winters? I would like him to call late this afternoon."

"Yes, of course," the butler agreed. "May I be bold and ask you why you wish to see the physician?"

"I'm going to be ill this afternoon."

Flannaghan did a double take. "You are? How can you know . . ."

She let out a sigh. "If I give you the full explanation and beg your confidence, you'll have to lie to your employer. We can't have that, now can we?"

"No, of course not."

"So you see, Flannaghan, it's best you not know."

"This has something to do with Colin, doesn't it?"

She smiled. "Perhaps," she replied.

She left Flannaghan to the task of putting the other shoes back in the wardrobe and went back to her room to make her list for the bootmaker. The boots she was sending were made of soft black calfskin and she added in her note the hope that Curtis would be able to stretch the bridge across the top of the boot enough to accommodate the insert she was certain he could make.

Alesandra then sent a note to Sir Winters requesting an audience. She set the time at four o'clock.

The physician was punctual. Stefan escorted him into the salon. He dared to frown at his mistress for insisting he let the man inside. She smiled at the guard.

"Your husband gave us specific orders that no one outside of immediate family be given admittance," he whispered.

"Sir Winters is like family," she countered. "And I'm not feeling at all well, Stefan. I have need of his services."

The guard was immediately contrite. Alesandra felt a bit guilty for telling the blatant lie. She got past the feeling quickly, however, when she reminded herself she only had Colin's best interests at heart.

She closed the guard out by pulling the French doors to the salon closed. Sir Winters stood by her side. He held a brown leather bag under one arm. She ushered him over to the settee.

"If you're indisposed, shouldn't you be in bed, Princess?"

She smiled at the physician. "I'm not that ill," she announced. "I have a little tickle in my throat. That's all."

"Hot tea is just the ticket, then," Sir Winters returned. "A spot of brandy would also do the trick."

Because the white-haired man was being so sincere and looking so concerned, she couldn't continue with the lie any longer. "I had another purpose for asking you to come here," she admitted. "I would like to talk to you about Colin."

Alesandra sat down in the chair across from the physician and folded her hands in her lap. "I used trickery to get you to come here," she admitted. She acted as though she had just confessed a dark sin. "My throat really isn't paining me. 'Tis the truth, the only time it hurts is when I want to shout at my stubborn husband and I know I can't."

Sir Winters smiled. "Colin can be stubborn, can't he?"

"Yes," she whispered.

"He's ill, then?" the physician asked, trying to understand the real motive behind his summons.

She shook her head. "It's his leg," she explained in a whisper. "He won't talk about his injury. He's sensitive about it, you see, but I know he's in terrible pain. I was wondering if something could be done to ease his discomfort."

The physician leaned back against the cushions. The worry on the princess's face told him her concern was genuine. "He hasn't told you how he came by the affliction, has he?"

"No."

"A shark took a bite out of his leg, Princess. I tended him, and there was a time when I considered taking the leg off. Colin's partner, Nathan, wouldn't let me. Your husband, you see, wasn't in any condition to give me his opinion. He blessedly slept through the worst of it."

A knock on the door interrupted their conversation. Flannaghan came inside carrying a silver tray. Neither Alesandra nor Sir Winters said another word until the butler had served both of them cups of hot tea and left the salon again.

Sir Winters pushed his bag out of his way and leaned forward to help himself to the assortment of sweet biscuits from the tray. He popped one into his mouth and then took a long swallow of the tea.

"Colin would be extremely upset if he knew we were discussing his condition," she admitted. "And I do feel guilty because I know he'll be displeased with me."

"Nonsense," Sir Winters countered. "You have his best interests at heart. I won't be telling him about our talk. Now, then, as to your question. How do you help him? I would suggest laudanum or brandy when the pain becomes insistent, but I know Colin won't take either."

"Is pride the reason?" she asked, trying to understand.

Winters shook his head. "Dependency," he countered. "Laudanum is addictive, Princess, and some say spirits can be addictive as well. Regardless, Colin won't take the chance."

"I see," she replied when the physician didn't immediately continue.

"I also suggested a brace of steel be made to fit from the knee to the ankle. Your husband was appalled by that suggestion."

"He's a proud man."

Winters nodded. "He's a sight more clever than I am too," he remarked. "I didn't believe he'd ever walk again without assistance. He's proven me wrong. What muscle is left has strengthened enough to support him. He barely limps now."

"At night, when he's weary, then he limps."

"Hot towels should be applied then. It won't make the leg stronger, of course, but it will ease his discomfort. A soothing massage would also help."

She wondered how in heaven's name Colin would ever allow her to follow those suggestions. That was her problem, however, not Sir Winters', and she would worry about it after he'd left.

"Anything else?" she asked.

"He should get off his feet when the pain intensifies," Sir Winters announced. "He shouldn't wait until it's agonizing."

Alesandra nodded agreement. She was thoroughly discouraged, but she kept her expression serene so the physician wouldn't know how disappointed she was feeling. His suggestions were superficial at best.

"You give me recommendations meant to deal with the symptoms, Sir Winters, but I was hoping you might have an idea or two regarding the cause."

"You're hoping for a miracle," Sir Winters replied. "Nothing can be done to make the leg fit again, Princess." His voice was filled with kindness.

"Yes," she whispered. "I was hoping for a miracle, I suppose. Still, your suggestions will prove helpful. If you think of anything more to add, will you pen me a note? I could use all the advice you can give."

Sir Winters took the last biscuit from the tray. His mind was fully occupied with Colin's condition and he didn't realize he'd eaten all of the treats. Alesandra filled his cup with more tea.

"Are all husbands stubborn?" she asked the physician.

Sir Winters smiled. "It seems to be a trait most husbands share."

He told her several amusing stories concerning titled men who refused to acknowledge they were in need of a physician. His favorite was the tale about the Marquess of Ackerman. The gentleman had been involved in a duel. He'd been shot in the shoulder and wouldn't allow anyone to see to the injury. Winters had been called by his brother to tend to the man.

"We found him at White's at one of the gaming tables," he told her. "It took three of his friends to drag him away. When we got his jacket off, why, there was blood everywhere."

"Did the marquess recover?"

Winters nodded. "He was too stubborn to die," he remarked. "Kept referring to the injury as a paltry nick until he passed out. I advised his wife to tie him to the bed until he recovered."

Alesandra smiled over that picture. "Colin's every bit as stubborn," she announced. She let out a sigh. "I would appreciate it if you would keep this conference secret, please. As I said before, Colin is quite sensitive about his leg."

Sir Winters placed his teacup and saucer back on the tray, picked up his satchel, and stood up to take his leave. "You needn't worry, Princess. I won't say a word about this visitation. You'd be surprised if you knew how many wives seek my advice concerning their husbands' welfare."

The door to the salon opened just as the physician was reaching for the handle. Colin moved out of the way to allow Winters room. He gave the physician a quick nod in greeting and turned to his wife.

"Flannaghan said you were ill."

He didn't give her time to answer but turned to Winters. "What's wrong with her?"

Alesandra didn't want the physician to lie for her. "I had a tickle in my throat, but it's better now. Sir Winters suggested hot tea," she added with a nod.

"Yes, I did," Winters agreed.

Something wasn't quite right, but Colin couldn't put his finger on what was wrong. Alesandra couldn't look him in the eye. He knew her well enough to know she wasn't telling him the truth. She didn't look ill. Her cheeks were high with color, indicating she was embarrassed about something. He decided then he would have to wait until they were alone to find out what was really wrong.

Alesandra stood by Colin's side while he visited with the physician. She happened to glance over her shoulder and found Flannaghan standing just a few feet away. The butler was giving her a sympathetic expression.

She already felt guilty because she'd lied to her husband and Flannaghan's expression made her feel worse.

Her motives were pure, she immediately told herself. She let out a little sigh then. She'd used that very excuse when she'd made the second set of books for the mother superior.

A sin is still a sin, or so the nun had proclaimed when she'd found out about the little deception. Large or little, it didn't matter. God, the mother superior assured her with great authority in her voice, kept an accurate list of each and every sin committed by every man and woman on this earth. Alesandra's list, the nun speculated, was probably long enough to reach the bottom of the ocean.

Alesandra didn't believe she'd sinned that much or that often. She imagined her list was about the length of her shadow by now. She wondered if her Maker had two columns on his sheet of paper for her—one for small infractions and the other for more substantial offenses.

She was pulled back to the present rather abruptly when Sir Winters said, "I was sorry to hear about the loss of the *Diamond*, Colin. Bad piece of luck, that."

"You've lost a diamond?" Alesandra asked, trying to understand.

Colin shook his head. "It's a ship, Alesandra. She went down with a full cargo. Winters, how did you hear about it so soon? I only just found out yesterday."

"A friend of mine had some business dealings at Lloyd's today. One of their agents mentioned it. They insured the loss, didn't they?"

"Yes."

"Is it true it was the second vessel this year you and Nathan have lost?"

Colin nodded.

"Why didn't you tell me?" Alesandra asked.

She tried to keep the hurt out of her voice. It was a difficult task.

"I didn't want you to worry," Colin explained.

She didn't believe he'd given her the full reason. Yes, it was probably true that he didn't want to worry her, but more important, he didn't want to share his burdens with her. She tried not to be offended. Colin had kept his own counsel for a long while and it surely wasn't easy for him to take anyone into his confidence, not even his wife.

She was going to have to be patient, she decided. Colin would have to get used to having her around before he felt comfortable enough to confide in her.

Her husband was still talking to the physician when she excused herself and went upstairs. She went to her room and started her list of suggestions Winters had given her to help ease the pain in Colin's leg, but her mind wasn't on the task.

He should have told her about the ship, damn it. If he was worried, she had every right to be worried too. Husbands and wives were supposed to share their problems, weren't they?

Flannaghan came to fetch her for dinner. On the way downstairs, she asked him for another favor.

"Have you heard about the Viscount of Talbolt's troubles?"

"Oh, yes," Flannaghan replied. "Everyone's talking about it. Lady Roberta left her husband."

"Colin has forbidden me to talk to the viscount and I must go along with his wishes. My husband believes I'll upset the man."

"Why do you want to talk to him?"

"I believe there might be a connection between his wife's sudden disappearance and that of my friend, Lady Victoria. She disappeared, too, Flannaghan. I was wondering if you would mind talking to his servants for me. I want to find out if Lady Roberta received any little presents from an unknown admirer, you see."

"What kinds of gifts, Princess?"

She shrugged. "Flowers—perhaps chocolates," she said. "Wouldn't the maids notice such gifts?"

Flannaghan nodded. "Yes, of course they'd notice. They would talk amongst themselves, too. They won't talk to me, though. Now Cook could learn a thing or two when she goes to market tomorrow. Shall I put the request to her?"

"Yes, please," Alesandra replied.

"What are you two whispering about?"

Colin asked that question from the entrance to the dining room. He smiled over the startle he gave his wife. She jumped a good foot. "You seem a bit nervous tonight," he remarked.

She didn't have a quick answer for that remark. She followed Flannaghan into the dining room. Colin held her chair out for her and then took his place at the head of the table, adjacent to her.

"Am I going to have to stay locked inside for a full month?" she asked.

"Yes."

He was occupied sorting through a stack of correspondence and didn't bother to glance her way when he answered her.

The man couldn't even take time away from his work to eat a proper meal. She wondered if he had digestive problems and almost asked him that personal question. She changed her mind and turned the topic to a more pressing matter.

"What about Catherine's first ball? It's only a week away, Colin. I don't want to miss it."

"I'll tell you all about it."

"You'd go without me?"

She sounded wounded. He smiled. "Yes," he answered. "I have to attend," he added. "And you have to be reasonable about this."

The set of his jaw told her he wasn't going to give in. She drummed her fingertips on the tabletop in agitation.

"It's rude to read your correspondence while at the table."

Colin was so occupied reading the letter from his partner, he didn't hear his wife's rebuke. He finished the long missive, then put the papers on the table.

"Nathan's wife has given him a baby girl. They've named her Joanna. The letter's almost three months old and he mentioned that as soon as Sara is feeling well enough, he's going to bring her and the baby back to London for a brief visit. Jimbo will watch the offices while he's gone."

"Who is Jimbo?" Alesandra asked, smiling over the odd name.

"A very good friend," Colin answered. "He's captain of one of our ships, the *Emerald,* but the vessel is undergoing some much needed repairs so Jimbo has time on his hands."

"This is all good news, Colin," she remarked.

"Yes, of course."

"Then why are you frowning?"

He hadn't realized he was frowning until she asked him why. He leaned back in his chair and gave her his full attention. "Nathan wants to offer ten or twenty shares of stock for sale. I hate the idea and I know that deep down Nathan feels the same way. I understand, however. He has a family now and wants to provide for them. He and Sara have been living in rented rooms, and now that the baby's here he wants more permanent quarters."

"Why are you two so opposed to stockholders?"

"We want to maintain control."

She was exasperated with him. "If only ten or twenty shares are sold, you and Nathan will still be the major stockholders and therefore in complete control."

He didn't seem impressed with her logic, for he continued to frown. She tried another approach. "What if you sold the stock to family members?"

"No."

"Why, in heaven's name, not?"

He let out a sigh. "It would be the same as a loan."

"It would not," she argued. "Caine and your father would make a handsome profit eventually. It would be a sound investment."

"Why did you send for Winters?"

He was deliberately changing the topic on her. She wasn't ready to let him. "Has Nathan given permission for this sale?"

"Yes."

"And when will you decide?"

"I've already decided. I'll have Dreyson handle the transaction. Now, enough about this. Answer my question. Why did you send for Winters?"

"I already explained," she began. "My throat . . ."

"I know," Colin said. "You had a scratch in your throat."

Alesandra was folding and refolding her napkin. "Actually it was a little tickle."

"Yes," he agreed. "Now I want you to tell me the truth. And look at me while you explain."

She dropped the napkin in her lap and finally looked up at him. "It's rude of you to suggest I would lie."

"Did you?"

"Yes."

"Why?"

"Because if I told you the truth, you'd become irritated with me."

"You will not lie to me in future, wife. Give me your word."

"You lied to me."

"When?"

"When you told me you didn't work for Sir Richards any longer. I saw the cash entries in the ledgers, Colin, and I heard him talk to you about a new assignment. Yes, you lied to me. If you give me your promise not to lie in future, I'll be happy to give you my word."

"Alesandra, it isn't at all the same."

"No, it isn't."

She was suddenly furious with her husband. She tossed the napkin down on the table just as Flannaghan came through the swinging door with a tray laden with food in his hands. "I don't take risks, Colin. You do. You don't give a twit about me, do you?"

She didn't give him time to answer her question but rushed on. "You've deliberately involved yourself in danger. I would never do such a thing. Now that we are married, I not only think about my well-being, I think about yours. If something happened to you, I would be devastated. Yet if something happened to me, I believe you would only be mildly inconvenienced. My funeral would force you to put your work aside for a few hours. Do excuse me, sir, before I say something more I know I'll regret."

She didn't wait for his permission to leave the table. She ignored his command to sit back down, too, and ran all the way up to her bedroom. She wanted to vent her frustration by slamming the door shut. She didn't give in to that urge, however, for it wouldn't be dignified.

Thankfully, Colin didn't follow her. Alesandra needed to be alone now so she could get a grip on her own rioting emotions. She was a bit stunned she'd become so angry with Colin so quickly. She wasn't Colin's keeper, she told herself. If he wanted to work for Richards, she couldn't and wouldn't try to talk him into quitting.

But he shouldn't want to take such risks, she decided. If he cared at all about her, he wouldn't deliberately hurt her this way.

Alesandra tried to walk the anger away. She paced back and forth in front of the hearth for a good ten minutes, muttering all the while.

"Mother Superior would never place herself in danger. She knew how I depended upon her and she never would have taken risks. She loved me, damn it."

Even though she wasn't Catholic, Alesandra still made the sign of the cross after muttering that blasphemy.

"I doubt Richards would ask the nun to work for him, Alesandra."

Colin made that comment from the doorway. She had been so intent on her ranting and raving she hadn't heard the door open. She turned around and found her husband lounging against the frame. His arms were casually folded across his chest. He was smiling, but it was the tenderness she saw in his eyes that almost did her in.

"Your amusement displeases me."

"Your behavior displeases me," he countered. "Why didn't you tell me you were upset about all this business with Richards?"

"I didn't know I was."

He raised an eyebrow over that odd admission. "Do you want me to quit?"

She started to nod, then changed her mind and shook her head instead. "I want you to want to quit. There's a difference, Colin. God willing, someday you might understand."

"Help me understand now."

She turned around to face the hearth before she spoke again. "I never would have taken deliberate risks while I lived at the convent—at least, not after the lesson I learned. There was a fire, you see, and I was trapped inside. I got out just as the roof collapsed. Mother Superior was beside herself with worry. She actually wept. She was so thankful I was all right and so furious with me because I'd taken one of the candles out of the holder so I could read Victoria's letter instead of praying like I was supposed to be doing . . . and I felt terrible because I'd caused her so much distress. The fire was an accident, but I made a promise to myself not to act foolish again."

"How did you act foolish if it was an accident?"

"I kept going back inside to save the pictures and the smaller statues the nuns put such store in."

"That was foolish."

"Yes."

"The mother superior loved you like a daughter, didn't she?"

Alesandra nodded.

"And you loved her."

"Yes."

A long minute passed in silence. "With love comes responsibility," she whispered. "I didn't realize that truth until I saw how upset Mother was with me."

"Do you love me, Alesandra?"

He'd cut right to the heart of the matter. She turned around to face him just as he pulled away from the doorway and started walking toward her. She immediately started backing away.

"I do not wish to love you."

The panic in her voice didn't stop him. "Do you love me?" he asked again.

It was a blessing there wasn't a fire burning in the hearth tonight. Her gown would have gone up in flames by now because she'd backed herself up against the stones.

Was she trying to get away from him or from his probing question? Colin wasn't certain. He was relentless, however, in his attempt to make her answer him. He wanted . . . no, he needed to hear her admit the truth.

"Answer me, Alesandra."

She suddenly quit trying to get away from him. She folded her arms in front of her and walked over to stand directly in front of him. Her head was tilted all the way back so she could look into his eyes.

"Yes."

"Yes, what?"

"Yes, I love you."

His satisfied grin said it all. He didn't seem at all surprised, and that thoroughly confused her.

"You already knew I loved you, didn't you?"

He slowly nodded. She shook her head. "How could you know when I didn't?"

He tried to take her into his arms. She quickly backed up a step. "Oh, no you don't. You want to kiss me, don't you? Then I'll forget my every thought. You will answer me first, Colin."

He wouldn't be denied. He pulled her into his arms, nudged her chin up, and kissed her long and hard. His tongue swept inside to rub against her own. She let out a loud sigh when he finally lifted his head. She collapsed against his chest and closed her eyes. His arms were wrapped around her waist. He hugged her tight and let his chin drop to rest on the top of her head.

It felt so damn good to hold her. The end of his workday was now something he looked forward to, because he knew she would be home waiting for him.

It suddenly dawned on Colin that he liked having a wife. Not just any wife, he qualified to himself. Alesandra. He used to dread the evenings, and all because the pain in his leg was usually excruciating by then. His gentle little bride had taken his mind off his aches, however. She exasperated him and she enchanted him, and he was usually so busy reacting to her, there wasn't room in his mind for anything else.

And she loved him.

"Now I'll answer your question," he said in a husky whisper she found wonderfully appealing.

"What question?"

He laughed. "You really do forget your every thought when I touch you, don't you?"

"You needn't sound so happy over that shameful fact. You're above such behavior though, aren't you? Why, I imagine you're full of thoughts while you're kissing me."

"Yes, I am."

"Oh." She sounded crestfallen.

"And every one of them is centered on what I want to do to you with my mouth, my hands, my . . ."

She reached up and clamped her hand over his mouth as a precaution against hearing something indelicate. Her reaction made Colin laugh again.

He pulled her hand away and said, "You wondered when I realized you loved me."

"Yes, I did wonder."

"It was on our wedding night," he explained. "The way you responded to me made it obvious you were in love with me."

She shook her head. "It wasn't obvious to me."

"Sure it was, sweetheart," he replied. "You couldn't hold anything back. Your every reaction was so damn honest. You couldn't have let yourself go that completely unless you loved me."

"Colin?"

"Yes?"

"You really should do something about your arrogance. It's getting out of hand."

"You like my arrogance."

She didn't reply to that outrageous remark. "I won't interfere in your schedule, Colin. I promise you."

"I never thought you would," he replied, smiling because she'd sounded so fervent.

"You haven't changed your plan, have you? You still need five full years before you . . ." She didn't go on.

"Before I what?"

Before you turn your attention to falling in love with your wife, you dolt, she thought to herself. And children, she added. In five years he would probably decide to have one or two. She wondered if she would be too old to have babies by then.

She definitely couldn't have one now. A baby would put too much pressure on Colin. Why, look how his partner, Nathan, had changed. He was now willing to do something he'd found unacceptable before. Selling stock was certainly a last resort, and it was the birth of his daughter that had changed his mind.

"Alesandra, before I what?" Colin asked again. The wistfulness in her voice puzzled him.

"Before you reach your goals," she blurted out.

"Yes," Colin said. "It's still five years."

He made that comment on his way over to the bed. He sat down on the side and bent to take his shoes off. "I didn't realize you were worried about my working for Richards," he said, turning the topic back to that issue. "You should have said something."

He tossed his shoes and socks aside, then turned his attention to his shirt. "And you were right when you said we're both responsible for each other. I haven't taken the time to consider your feelings. I'm sorry about that."

She watched him pull his shirt out of his waistband and work it up over his head. She couldn't take her gaze off him. She hung on his every word, hoping he would tell her how he felt about her. She didn't have enough gumption to ask him if he loved her. Colin hadn't had any problem asking *her,* she thought to herself. But then, he already knew her answer.

She didn't know his.

She had to shake her head over her own fanciful thoughts. Men didn't think about such things as love, or at least she didn't think they did. If Colin hadn't taken the time to consider her feelings regarding his dangerous work for Richards, why in heaven's name would he take the time to think about loving her? His mind was already completely full with his plans to build his company into an empire, and there simply wasn't room for anything else.

Alesandra straightened her shoulders and her resolve. She reminded herself that she found her husband's dedication admirable. She could be patient. Colin would get around to her in five years or so.

He drew her attention away from her thoughts when he said, "I've given my word to Richards I'd pass on a few papers for him." He paused to toss his shirt on the chair and stood up. "As for the other assignment I was offered, I'll let Morgan have it. In truth, I'd already decided against taking on the mission because it would have meant I'd have to be away from London for at least two weeks, possibly even three. Borders could have handled the office, of course, but I didn't want to leave you alone."

She thought that was the sweetest thing Colin had ever said to her. He would have missed her. She decided she wanted to hear him say the words.

"Why didn't you want to leave me alone?"

"Because of the policy, of course."

Her shoulders slumped. "Stefan and Raymond could watch out for me."

"You're my responsibility, Alesandra."

"But I don't wish to be your responsibility," she muttered. "You have enough on your mind. You don't need to add me to your list."

He didn't remark on that little speech. He unbuttoned his pants and stripped out of the rest of his clothes.

Her thoughts became fragments. She couldn't stop staring at her husband. Lord, he was magnificent. He was what she envisioned a warlord from bygone days must have looked like. Colin was all muscle, all power, and he had such sleek, smooth lines.

She followed him with her gaze as he crossed the room and bolted the bedroom door. He walked past her again on his way back to the bed. He pulled the covers back, straightened back up, and crooked his finger at her.

She didn't hesitate. She walked over to stand directly in front of him. Her hands were demurely folded in front of her. She looked serene, composed, but Colin knew better. The pulse in the base of her neck was beating frantically. He noticed when he lifted her hair away from her neck and bent down to kiss her.

She started to undress. Colin gently pushed her hands away from the bodice of her gown. "Let me," he whispered.

Her hands dropped back down to her sides. Colin was much quicker getting her clothes off than she was. He wasn't nearly as careful though. He didn't take the time to fold her garments but tossed them in a heap on top of his shirt. He was anxious to get to her bare skin. He noticed his hands shook when he untied the lace ribbon holding the neckline of her chemise in place and smiled over his lack of discipline.

He was surprised by his own quick response to her. His breathing was already ragged, his heartbeat was slamming inside his chest, and he hadn't even touched her yet—at least, not the way he wanted to touch her. Anticipation made him hard, aching.

Alesandra's thoughts were a little more centered. She was determined to get him to tell her he would have missed her if he'd taken the assignment.

When the last of her clothes had been discarded, she turned her gaze to her husband's chin and whispered his name.

"Colin?"

"Yes?"

"If you'd left London, would you have missed me?"

He lifted her chin up so she would look at him. His smile was filled with tenderness. "Yes."

She was so pleased with his answer, she let out a little sigh. Colin leaned down and brushed his mouth over hers.

"Do you wonder if I would have missed you?"

"No."

"Why not?"

He distracted her by taking her hands and placing them around his neck. Then he began to nibble on her earlobe. "Because I already know you'd miss me. You love me, remember?"

She couldn't fault that reasoning. Her husband certainly didn't have a problem with self-esteem. She thought to tell him so, and just as soon as he quit turning her thoughts into mush with his kisses, she would.

Colin placed wet kisses along the column of her throat. Her pulse was beating frantically now and she was already trembling in his arms. He thought that was a nice start.

He was slowly driving her crazy with his touch, and he knew it. That realization settled in her mind all at once.

Alesandra pushed herself away from him. He let her go, but the look on his face showed his confusion.

"What is it, sweetheart? Why did you push me away? I know you want me, and you sure as hell have to know how much I want you."

Alesandra was determined to turn the tables on her husband. She got into bed, moved to the center, and then knelt on her knees, facing him. She could feel herself blushing, but she absolutely refused to give in to her embarrassment. Colin was her husband and her lover, and she should be able to do anything she wanted with him.

She crooked her finger at him. He was so surprised by her boldness, he laughed. He got into bed and reached for her. She shook her head at him and pushed against his shoulders, telling him without words she wanted him on his back.

"Does my boldness please you?"

"Yes," he answered. "It pleases me."

It wasn't what he'd said as much as how he'd said it that gave Alesandra the courage to continue her game. She trailed her fingers down his chest.

"When you touch me, I go a little crazy," she whispered. "But tonight . . ."

She didn't go on. Her fingertips slowly circled his navel. She smiled over his quick indrawn breath when her hand moved lower.

"Yes?" he asked, his voice rough with need.

"You're going to lose your control before I lose mine. Do you accept my challenge, husband?"

In answer Colin stacked his hands behind his head and closed his eyes. "I'll win, Alesandra. I have far more experience."

She laughed over that boast. Odd, but admitting she loved him had somehow freed her from all restraint. She felt wild, wanton, and she didn't care at all that she wasn't being dignified. She really didn't think it was possible to maintain decorum when she was stark naked.

"Thank you for telling me I love you, Colin."

"You're welcome, sweetheart."

He was tense with anticipation. His voice was gritty when he said, "Are you about finished working up your courage?"

"I'm planning my attack," she countered.

That remark made him smile. She was highly curious about his body. She wanted to learn the taste of him just as he had learned the taste of her. The thought of what she wanted to do to him made her blush intensify, but Colin's eyes were closed so she didn't worry about hiding her embarrassment.

"Colin, is . . . everything permitted or is there something I shouldn't do?"

"Nothing's forbidden," he replied. "Our bodies belong to each other."

"Oh, that's nice."

She leaned back on her heels while she considered where she would like to start. His neck appealed to her, but then so did the rest of his body.

"Sweetheart, I'm going to fall asleep if you don't get started," he announced.

Alesandra decided not to waste time getting to the area that most intrigued her.

He should have kept his eyes open. When he felt her mouth on the tip of his erection, he damn near came off the bed. His groan of pleasure came out as a raw shout.

He came undone. It took every ounce of discipline he possessed not to spill his seed then and there. Perspiration broke out on his brow. Her sweet tongue flicked over his sensitive skin until he was in acute agony to let himself climax.

He couldn't take the torment long. He suddenly let out a low growl as he grabbed hold of her shoulders and lifted her upward. He forced her thighs apart with his knee so that she would straddle his hips, cupped the back of her neck with his hand to bring her mouth down to his, and then sealed her soft lips with his as he thrust inside her with one hard surge. The liquid heat he felt told him she was ready for him. His hands dropped to the sides of her hips and he forced her upward so that he could thrust back inside again. He was beyond reason now, and as soon as he felt her instinctively tighten around him, he was powerless to control his body's reaction. His climax caught him by surprise. He let out another loud groan as he poured his seed into her.

Touching her husband so intimately and watching his own uninhibited response had heightened Alesandra's pleasure. He found his own release before she did, but he didn't stop moving inside her. The ecstasy was almost too much to endure. She whimpered his name when the heat began to uncoil and spread like wildfire through her body. Her head fell back in surrender to the bliss. Colin felt the first tremors of her release and reached down between their joined bodies to stroke her. His touch helped her gain her own fulfillment. She arched against him, rigid with the consuming pleasure cascading down her limbs.

The tremors seemed to go on and on, overwhelming in their intensity, yet she wasn't at all afraid because Colin wrapped his arms around her and pulled her down against his chest. He held her close, keeping her safe until the storm of passion eased.

The beauty of their lovemaking was too much for her. She was so shaken by what had just happened she began to cry great gulping sobs against his neck.

Colin was just as shaken. He stroked her back and whispered honeyed words in a voice as ragged as a winter's wind until she regained a bit of her composure.

"Each time it gets better," she whispered.

"Is that so terrible?" he asked.

"I'll be dead in a week," she countered. "Can't you feel how my heart is hammering away? I'm certain this can't be at all good for me."

"If you die, sweetheart, you'll die happy," he boasted. "You liked being on top, didn't you?"

She slowly nodded. "I won the challenge, didn't I?"

His laughter filled the room. "Yes," he conceded.

She was content. She closed her eyes and snuggled against her husband.

"We forgot to eat our supper," she whispered.

"We'll eat later," he replied. "After I have my turn."

She didn't understand what he meant. "After you have a turn at what?"

Colin rolled her onto her back and covered her with his body. He braced his weight on his elbows and smiled down at her.

When his mouth was just an inch away from hers, he answered her.

"Winning."

# Chapter

# 12

❧

Loving and liking Colin were two different kettles of fish altogether. The man was impossible to reason with but extremely easy to kiss. She knew better than to offer him what was left of her inheritance to put into his company, and she finally had to resort to plain old-fashioned trickery in order to help him. She followed her father's example, and she told herself more than once that God would understand even if Colin didn't. Her husband would eventually get over his stubbornness, but she wasn't willing to let outsiders buy into his company while she waited for him to come to his senses.

The stock went public at ten o'clock on a Wednesday morning. Two minutes later, the transactions were complete and all twenty shares were sold. The price was extremely high.

Colin was stunned by the amount. He was suspicious, too. He demanded to know the names of the new stockholders. Dreyson would only tell him there was a single buyer of all twenty shares, but that he wasn't at liberty to divulge the buyer's name.

"You will answer one question for me," Colin demanded. "I want to know if my wife's name is on the shares as owner."

Dreyson immediately shook his head. "No, Sir Hall-brook," he was able to admit quite honestly. "Princess Alesandra isn't the owner."

Colin was satisfied the broker was telling the truth. A sudden possibility then occurred to him. "And her adviser, the man she calls Uncle Albert? Is he the owner."

"No," Dreyson immediately answered. "I'm certain he would have snapped at the chance but the shares were all sold within a blink of the eye. There wasn't time to notify him."

Colin finally let the matter drop. Alesandra said a prayer of thanksgiving because her husband wasn't going to probe deeper.

She felt extremely guilty because she'd used trickery. She knew it was wrong to manipulate her husband, but she blamed her sin on his stubbornness. She thought she could put the deceit behind her, too, yet found that the longer she went without confessing the truth to her husband, the more miserable she became. She did a lot of muttering to herself. Thankfully, Colin wasn't there to hear her. He was working twelve-hour days at the shipping company. Flannaghan heard her carrying on, of course, but he believed she was just in an irritable mood because of her long confinement.

The month actually did hurry by. Catherine's ball was reported to have been a smashing success, and the event was recounted in vivid detail by both the duchess and her daughter-in-law, Lady Jade. They were sorry Alesandra couldn't attend, of course, but they understood the reason behind Colin's decision to make her stay under lock and key.

Catherine stopped by the following afternoon to add her own descriptions. She announced she was already in love with a marquess and two earls. She was anxiously waiting to receive notes through her father for permission for the gentlemen to call on her.

Because Colin was working such long hours, Alesandra treasured their time together and didn't like bringing up business matters. Still, there were times when it was necessary. The rental agent notified Flannaghan that the owners had decided to stay abroad and wished to sell their town house. Alesandra had become attached to her home and wanted to purchase it. She eased into the topic at the dinner table.

Colin's attitude toward her inheritance hadn't changed. He told her he didn't care what she did with her money.

Then she became more specific. "I would like to purchase this town house," she announced.

She didn't give him time to deny her request right away, but hurried on with her explanation. "Because of your ignorant English law, it's almost impossible for a married woman to make a contract on her own. I wouldn't bother you with this matter, but I need your signature on the papers."

"The reason for that law is simple to understand," he countered. "Husbands are legally responsible for any and all ventures their wives enter into."

"Yes, but the issue under discussion . . ."

"The issue is rather or not I can provide for you," he interrupted. His voice had gone hard. "Do you doubt I'll be able to provide for you?"

"No, of course not," she replied.

He nodded, satisfied. She let out a sigh. He wasn't going to be at all reasonable about this. She briefly considered using her initials and claiming Uncle Albert had purchased the town house for them, then discarded the idea. Colin was bound to pitch a fit. Besides, such trickery would be an out-and-out lie, and she doubted God would forgive her this transgression where her motives were only selfish ones. Using a little bit of deceit to secure the stocks and keep them in the family in order to help Colin and his partner was one thing, but manipulating the purchase of a home just because she'd taken a fancy to it was quite another. Her list of sins had grown by leaps and bounds since she'd married Colin, she supposed, but most of her offenses were surely under God's column of minor transgressions. A blatant lie told to get her own way would definitely come under the heading of more serious sins.

She couldn't deceive him. "As you wish, Colin. I would

like you to note that I believe you're being extremely unreasonable about this."

"So noted," he replied dryly.

He didn't even let her have the last word this time. Yet although he was frequently insensitive to her needs, he was quite the opposite with other people. He could actually be very thoughtful upon occasion. After the month was over and Raymond and Stefan were no longer needed to guard her, Colin offered them employment with his company. The men were eager to work on a ship and travel the world, as they were both young and unattached, and Colin put them under the supervision of his friend, Jimbo, so they would be properly trained.

Colin continued to be a very passionate lover. He spent every night in her bed, and after he made love to her, he held her close until he thought she had fallen asleep. Then he went back to his own room. Alesandra was afraid to make an issue out of the ritual because her husband had made it quite clear he didn't want to talk about his leg. He all but pretended he didn't even have a problem. She didn't understand how his mind worked. Did it make him feel inferior if he acknowledged a human frailty? And if he loved her, wasn't it his duty to share his joys and his sorrows with her?

But Colin didn't love her—at least, not yet, Alesandra reminded herself. She wasn't disheartened, however, because she had complete faith in her husband. He was an intelligent man, after all, and in time she felt certain his attitude would soften and he'd realize what a fine wife she was. If he didn't get around to the realization for five years, that was all right. She could wait. She would keep her promise to him, too. She wouldn't interfere.

The inserts she'd had made for her husband's shoes didn't qualify as interference in her mind, however. She took great delight in the fact that he was now wearing the special pair of Wellingtons almost every day. The bootmaker had made two leather inserts. The first was too thick, or at least she thought it must have been too thick because Colin only wore the boots for a few minutes before taking them off and putting on another pair. The second insert she'd slipped under the lining worked much better. Colin believed he'd broken in the boots and they were now comfortable. She knew better, of course, but she didn't say a word. Neither did Flannaghan. The butler whispered to Alesandra that he'd noticed his employer's limp wasn't quite as pronounced at the end of the day. Alesandra agreed. She was so pleased with the success of her plan she immediately ordered two extra inserts made so that her husband would have comfortable walking shoes and evening dress shoes as well.

To the outside world, Colin appeared to be a man without a care in the world. He always wore a devil-may-care smile, and he was one of the most popular men in London. When he entered a room, he was immediately surrounded by friends. The women wouldn't be left out either. It didn't matter to most of the ladies that he was now married. They continued to flock to his side. Colin was a charmer, yes, but he wasn't a flirt. He usually had hold of Alesandra's hand while he went about the task of mixing business with pleasure. Colin wasn't just intelligent—he was clever, too. Most of the shipping deals were negotiated in the ballrooms. When she realized that fact, she didn't mind the late hours they kept every night.

She did do quite a bit of napping, though. She and Colin attended parties almost every night for two full months, and she was so exhausted she was seized with attacks of nausea.

She was looking forward to tonight's affair, however, because Colin's family was also going to be attending the Earl of Allenborough's bash. The duke and duchess were escorting their daughter Catherine, and Colin's brother, Caine, and his wife were also going to be there.

The earl had rented Harrison House for the ball. The magnificent marble and stone estate was almost as large as the prince regent's palace.

Alesandra wore her ivory-colored gown. The neckline wasn't overly revealing, but Colin still felt compelled to grumble about it. Her only adornment was a beautiful gold and sapphire necklace that fit like a choker around her neck. There was only one sapphire in the center of the looped chain. The precious jewel was at least two carats in size and appeared to be flawless. Colin knew the thing was worth a bloody fortune, and he didn't like the idea of Alesandra wearing it.

"I have a special fondness for this necklace," she remarked once they were settled inside the carriage and on their way to the ball. "But I can tell from your frown you don't care for it. Why is that, Colin?"

"Why do you like it?"

Her fingertips brushed the necklace. "Because it belonged to my mother. Whenever I wear it, I'm reminded of her. The necklace was a gift to her from my father."

Colin's attitude immediately softened. "Then you should wear it."

"But why did it displease you? I saw the way you frowned when you first noticed it."

He shrugged. "I was displeased because I didn't buy it for you."

She didn't know what to make of that remark. She reached behind her neck and started to undo the clasp so she could take the necklace off. Colin stopped her. "I was being foolish. Leave it. The color matches your eyes."

From the look on her husband's face, she concluded he'd just given her a compliment and not a criticism. She folded her hands in her lap, smiled at her husband, and changed the subject. "Shouldn't your partner be home any day now?"

"Yes."

"Will I like him?"

"Eventually."

"Will I like his wife?"

"Yes."

She wasn't upset by his short answers. She could tell from his expression he was in pain. His leg was obviously acting up tonight, she speculated, and when Colin propped his foot up on the cushion next to her, she knew her guess was right.

It took all the self-control she could muster not to reach over and touch his leg. "We don't have to attend the affair tonight," she said. "You look weary to me."

"I'm fine." he said in a clipped, no-nonsense tone of voice. She decided not to argue with him.

She changed the topic again. "It's appropriate for us to give a gift to Nathan and Sara for their baby."

Colin had leaned back against the seat and closed his eyes. She wasn't certain if he was paying attention to what she was saying or not. She lowered her gaze to her lap and began to adjust the folds of her gown. "I didn't think you wanted to be bothered with the chore so I took care of it. Since you and Nathan own a shipping company, I thought it would be nice to have a replica of one of the ships made. What do you think of that idea? When they purchase a home, Sara could put our gift on her mantel."

"I'm sure she'll like it," Colin replied. "Whatever you decide is fine with me."

"There were several drawings of your ships in your library," she said then. "I hope you don't mind that I borrowed one of the *Emerald* to give to the craftsman."

The carriage came to a quick stop in front of Harrison House. Colin had looked half asleep until the door was opened by the coachman. Then his manner changed. He helped Alesandra out, took hold of her arm, and started up the steps. He spotted his brother and his wife walking toward them and immediately smiled.

Colin hadn't made a miraculous recovery. His smile was forced, but Alesandra knew she was the only one who realized how much pain he was in. The physician had told her that Colin should get off his leg when it pained him. Her husband wouldn't listen to such advice, however. He would probably dance the night away just to prove he was all right.

The night air was damp and chilly. Alesandra suddenly felt a bit lightheaded. Her stomach turned queasy, too, and she was thankful she hadn't eaten much of the light supper Cook had prepared. Exhaustion was surely the reason she wasn't feeling well, she told herself.

Jade noticed how pale Alesandra's complexion was and made that mention in front of their husbands. Both Caine and Colin turned to look at her.

"Why didn't you tell me you didn't feel well?" Colin asked.

"I'm just a little weary," she hastily replied. "Do quit frowning at me, Colin. I'm not accustomed to going out every night and that's why I'm a bit fatigued. 'Tis the truth, I would rather stay home every now and then."

"You don't like the parties?"

Her husband looked surprised. She lifted her shoulders in a shrug. "We do what we must," she replied.

"Explain what you mean, sweetheart."

He wasn't going to let the matter drop. "All right then," she said. "No, I don't particularly like the parties . . ."

"Why didn't you say something?"

He was exasperated with her. She shook her head at him. "Because each affair is a business opportunity for you and Nathan," she explained. "You don't like going out either," she added. "And that is why I said that we do what we must. I would have said something eventually."

His wife was an extremely astute woman. She'd understood his motives and known exactly how he'd really felt about all the parties he dragged her to. "Eventually?" he repeated with a grin. "When, exactly, would you have offered a complaint?"

"I would never complain and you should apologize for even suggesting I would," she countered. "Eventually would be exactly five years from now. Then I would mention my preference to stay home."

Caine smiled at Alesandra and said, "Be sure to thank your friend, Albert, for his advice regarding that investment. The stock has already increased threefold."

She nodded.

"What investment?" Colin asked.

Caine answered. "I mentioned I was interested in investment opportunities the last time I was over at your house, and Alesandra told me Albert had recommended shares in Campton Glass. It just went public."

"I thought you were investing in Kent's garment factory," Jade interjected.

# Julie Garwood

"I'm still considering it," Caine replied.

Alesandra shook her head before she could stop herself. "I don't believe that would be a wise investment, Caine. I do hope you'll give the matter careful consideration first."

She could feel Colin's gaze on her but didn't turn to look at him. "Albert was also interested in the garment factory. He had his broker, Dreyson, go and look at the place. Dreyson reported it was a fire trap and ill run. There are hundreds of women and children employed there and conditions are deplorable. Albert wasn't about to make the owner rich or get rich himself on such a venture. Why, he would be profiting from other people's misery—at least, that's what he told me in his last letter."

Caine immediately agreed. The topic was dropped when they entered the foyer of Harrison House. The duke and duchess were waiting in a nearby alcove with Catherine and immediately motioned for Caine and Colin and their wives to join them. Business matters were put aside. Catherine hugged Jade, then turned to hug Alesandra. She noticed the sapphire necklace right away and declared she was about to swoon with envy. Catherine wore a single strand of pearls around her neck. She absentmindedly fingered her necklace as she mentioned that her violet gown would look far more smashing if her father had given her a sapphire to wear.

Alesandra laughed over the not-too-subtle hint. Since no one was observing them, she quickly took off her necklace and handed it to Catherine.

"This belonged to my mother, so you must be very careful with it," Alesandra whispered so Colin wouldn't overhear her. "The clasp is quite secure and as long as you leave it on, you won't lose it."

Catherine gave a halfhearted protest as she unclasped her own necklace and handed it to Alesandra. Jade held on to Catherine's dance card while her sister-in-law put on the necklace, then made her turn around so that she could make certain the clasp was secure.

"You be careful with this," she ordered her.

Colin didn't notice the switch in jewelry for a good hour. Sir Richards came hurrying over to greet the family, and when Caine was occupied answering a question from his father, the director gave Colin the signal that he wanted to speak in private to him. The look on Richards's face indicated the matter was serious.

The opportunity for a quick conference arose when Colin's father requested a dance with Alesandra. As soon as they walked toward the center of the ballroom, Colin went over to the director. Richards stood at the entrance of a triangular alcove, watching the crowd.

The two men stood side by side without speaking for several minutes. Colin noticed Neil Perry across the floor and immediately frowned with displeasure. He hoped Alesandra wouldn't notice the man. She was bound to try to corner him as soon as she spotted him and demand answers about his sister. Neil would turn insulting, of course, and Colin would probably have to smash his face in.

That possibility made Colin smile.

His sister drew his attention then. She was partnered with Morgan. Colin clasped his hands behind his back and watched the pair. Morgan spotted Colin and nodded to him. Colin nodded back.

Sir Richards also nodded to the new recruit. He smiled, too. For that reason Colin was surprised by his angry tone of voice when he spoke. "I shouldn't have given the assignment to Morgan," he whispered. "He made a muck of it. Do you remember Devins?"

Colin nodded. The man Richards referred to was an agent who was occasionally used to transfer information for the government.

"He's dead now. From what I can sort out, he got caught in the middle of what turned into a bloody fight. Morgan said Devins panicked. They were waiting for their contact when Devins's daughter came along. It was a bad piece of luck. The girl was killed in the cross fire. Damn it all, Colin, it should have gone as smooth as ice, but Morgan's eagerness and inexperience turned a simple, uncomplicated mission into a fiasco. Bad luck or not, the man doesn't have the instincts for this line of work," he added with a nod.

"Don't use him again." Colin's voice shook with anger.

"Devins wasn't the type to panic. He had a temper, yes, but he could always be relied on to use sound judgment."

"Yes, under usual circumstances I would agree with your evaluation. However, he was also a protective father, Colin. I can imagine he did panic if he thought she was in danger."

"I would think a father would react in just the opposite manner. He had more reasons not to panic."

Richards nodded. "I've told Morgan he's out. He felt bad about my decision, of course. He was sorry it went sour and admitted he'd overreacted. He blamed you too, son, because you didn't go along and show him the ropes, so to speak."

Colin shook his head. He wasn't buying that excuse. From the look on the director's face, he wasn't buying it either.

"You're right, Richards. He doesn't have the instincts."

"It's a pity," the director remarked. "He's eager to please and he needs the money. I imagine he'll marry well. He's quite a charmer with the ladies."

Colin looked back at the dance floor. He found Morgan right away. He was smiling down at Catherine as he whirled her around the floor. His sister was laughing and obviously having the time of her life.

Colin noticed the necklace Catherine was wearing then. He immediately turned to find Alesandra in the crowd. He spotted his father first, then saw Alesandra. She was now wearing Catherine's pearls. Colin frowned with concern. The switch in jewelry wasn't the cause, however. His wife's complexion had turned as white as her gown. She looked ready to faint.

Colin excused himself from the director and went to his wife. He tapped his father on his shoulder and took Alesandra into his arms. She forced a smile and leaned into her husband's side.

The waltz ended just as Colin turned to take his wife out on the front terrace.

"You're really ill, aren't you, sweetheart?"

Caine was standing with his wife next to the doors leading outside. He took one look at Alesandra's complexion and immediately backed up a step. His sister-in-law's face was turning green. He hoped to God whatever was ailing her wasn't the catching kind.

Alesandra couldn't make up her mind whether she wanted to swoon or throw up. She prayed she wouldn't do either until she was home. The fresh air seemed to help, however, and after a minute or two, her head quit spinning.

"It was all that twirling around and around," she told her husband.

Caine let out a loud sigh of relief and stepped forward to offer his assistance. Colin left Alesandra leaning against his brother while he said their good-byes, then came back to collect her. She hadn't worn a cloak, so he took off his jacket and put it around her shoulders on the way down the steps to their waiting carriage.

Feeling better was short-lived. The rocking motion of the carriage made her stomach start acting up again. She gripped her hands together in her lap and took several deep breaths to calm herself.

Colin reached over and hauled her onto his lap. He tucked her head under his chin and held her tight.

He carried her inside the town house and up to her bedroom. He left her sitting on the side of the bed while he went to fetch a drink of cool water she'd requested.

Alesandra stretched out on top of the covers and closed her eyes. She was sound asleep a minute later.

Colin undressed her. Flannaghan was pacing with worry outside the door, but Colin wasn't about to let him help. He stripped his wife out of her garments and put her under the covers. She really was exhausted, for she slept like a baby now and didn't even open her eyes when he lifted her up so he could pull the blankets back.

He decided to spend the full night with her. If she became ill he wanted to be close by in case she needed his help. And, Lord, he was suddenly feeling exhausted, too. He stripped out of his own clothes and got into bed beside her. She instinctively rolled into his arms. Colin kissed her forehead, wrapped his arms around her, and closed his eyes. He, too, was asleep less than a minute later.

He awakened a little before dawn when his wife rubbed

her backside against him. She was still asleep. Colin was barely awake enough to think about what he was doing. He made love to her, and when they'd both found fulfillment, he fell asleep again still joined to her.

Alesandra was feeling as fit as ever the next day. Catherine arrived on her doorstep at two that afternoon to personally return the necklace. She was full of news, too.

She was having a grand time with her season and wanted to tell Alesandra all about the offers for her hand in marriage her father had already received.

Catherine linked her arm through Alesandra's and pulled her along into the salon.

"Where is my brother on this fine Sunday afternoon?"

"He's working," Alesandra answered. "He should be home by dinner."

Catherine sat down in the chair adjacent to the settee. Flannaghan stood near the entrance, waiting to find out if he was needed.

"I can barely keep all the gentlemen straight in my mind," Catherine exaggerated.

"You must make a list of the gentlemen you're interested in," Alesandra advised. "Then you wouldn't be confused."

Catherine thought that was a sound plan of action. Alesandra immediately asked Flannaghan to fetch her paper and pen.

"I've already asked father to decline several gentlemen and he's been very accommodating. He isn't in any hurry to get me settled."

"You should probably start a list of your rejections, too," Alesandra suggested. "With your reasons by each name, of course, in the event you change your mind or forget why you discarded them."

"Yes, that's a wonderful idea," Catherine claimed. "It's so thoughtful of you to help."

Alesandra was thrilled to be of assistance. "Organization is the key, Catherine," she announced.

"The key to what?"

Alesandra opened her mouth to answer, then realized she

wasn't exactly sure. "To a well-structured, happy life," she decided aloud.

Flannaghan returned with the items she'd requested. Alesandra thanked him and then turned back to Catherine.

"Shall we begin with the rejections?"

"Yes," Catherine agreed. "Put Neil Perry at the top of the list. He offered for me yesterday. I don't like him at all."

Alesandra titled the list, then put Perry's name down. "I don't particularly like him either," she announced. "You've shown sound judgment in rejecting him."

"Thank you," Catherine replied.

"What specific reason should I put next to his name?"

"Disgusting."

Alesandra laughed. "He is that," she remarked. "He's the complete opposite of his sister. Victoria's a dear lady."

Catherine didn't know Victoria and therefore couldn't agree or disagree. She continued with the names of men she found unacceptable. She hurried through the task since she was anxious to concentrate on the appealing candidates. She also had additional news she was dying to share with Alesandra.

"All right, then, let's begin with the second list."

Catherine gave her four names. The last was Morgan. "He hasn't offered for me, of course, and I only just met him last night, but, Alesandra, he's so handsome and charming. When he smiles, I declare, my heart feels like it's going to stop beating. I doubt I'll stand a chance with him, though. He's extremely popular with the ladies. Still, he did mention he was going to ask father if he could call."

"I've met Morgan," Alesandra replied. "And I do agree he's charming. I believe Colin likes him, too."

"He would be a fine catch," Catherine decided. "Still . . . there is one other I would like to consider as well."

"What is his name and I'll add him to your list."

Catherine started blushing. "It's the most romantic thing," she whispered. "But Father wouldn't think so. You must promise not to tell anyone."

"Tell what?"

"Just promise me first, then I'll explain. Put your hand over your heart. That makes your promise more binding."

Alesandra didn't dare laugh. Catherine sounded so sincere. She didn't want to hurt her feelings. She did as she was instructed and placed her hand over her heart while she gave her pledge.

"Now will you explain?"

"I don't know the gentleman's name yet," Catherine said. "He was at the ball last night. I'm certain of it. I'm certain he's wonderful, too."

"How can you know he's wonderful if you've never met him? Or did you meet him? That's it, isn't it? You just don't know his name. Tell me what he looks like. Perhaps I've met the man."

"Oh, I haven't seen him yet."

"You're confusing me."

Catherine laughed. "He has a name we can put on the list for now."

Alesandra dipped her pen into the inkwell. Catherine waited until she'd completed that task, then whispered, "My Secret Admirer."

She let out a long happy sigh after whispering the name. Alesandra gasped at the very same time. She dropped her pen into her lap. Ink blotted her pink dress.

"Good heavens, look what you've done," Catherine cried out. "Your dress . . ."

Alesandra shook her head. "Forget the dress," she countered. Her voice shook with worry. "I want to hear about this secret admirer."

Catherine frowned. "I haven't done anything wrong, Alesandra. Why are you so upset with me?"

"I'm not upset . . . at least not with you," Alesandra said.

"You shouted at me."

"I didn't mean to shout."

She saw the tears in Catherine's eyes then. Her sister-in-law was high-strung, and her feelings were easily hurt. She was still more child than woman, Alesandra realized, and she made up her mind then and there not to tell her about her worries. She would talk to Colin first. He would know what to do about the secret admirer.

"I'm sorry I upset you. Please forgive me." She forced a mild tone of voice when she added, "I'm very interested in hearing all about this secret admirer. Will you explain?"

Catherine blinked away her tears. "There isn't much to explain," she said. "I received a lovely posey this morning with a notecard attached. There wasn't a message—just the signature."

"Which was?"

"Your Secret Admirer. I thought it was very romantic. I don't understand why you're acting so strange."

"Dear God." Alesandra whispered those words and collapsed against the back of the settee. Her mind raced with her fears. Colin would have to listen to her, she decided, even if she had to tie the man up while he slept to get her way.

"You're shivering, Alesandra," Catherine said.

"I'm just a little chilled."

"Mother told Jade she thinks you're carrying."

"I'm what?"

She hadn't meant to shout, of course, but Catherine's blurted-out remark did surprise a near scream out of her.

"They think you might be carrying Colin's baby," Catherine explained. "Are you?"

"No, of course not. It isn't possible. It's too soon."

"You've been married over three months now," Catherine reminded her. "Mother told Jade your nausea could be a symptom. She's going to be disappointed if you're not carrying. Are you sure, Alesandra?"

"Yes, I'm sure."

She wasn't telling Catherine the truth. She really wasn't sure at all. Good Lord, she could be pregnant. It had been quite a long time since her last monthly—over three months ago. She counted back just to be certain. Yes, that was right. She had had cramps two weeks before she got married . . . and none since. Was it possible the stomach upset wasn't due to exhaustion? She'd never napped before, she thought to herself, but now she could barely get through a day without an afternoon rest. Of course, she and Colin had had to go out every night, and she really believed the late hours they were keeping made the afternoon naps necessary.

Her hand dropped to her stomach in a protective gesture. "I would like to have Colin's children," she said. "But he has an important schedule and I promised not to interfere."

"What does a schedule have to do with babies?"

Alesandra tried to pull herself together. She felt as though she were in a daze. She couldn't seem to organize her thoughts. Why hadn't she realized . . . the possibility . . . the only logical answer . . . Oh, yes, she was pregnant.

"Alesandra, do explain," Catherine demanded.

"It's a five-year schedule," Alesandra blurted out. "I'll have children then."

Catherine thought she was jesting with her. She burst into laughter. Alesandra was able to maintain her composure until her sister-in-law took her leave a few minutes later. Then she hurried up to her bedroom, shut the door behind her, and promptly burst into tears.

She was filled with the most conflicting emotions. She was thrilled she was carrying Colin's son or daughter. A precious life growing inside her seemed a true miracle to her and she was fairly overwhelmed with her joy—and her guilt.

Colin might not be happy about the baby at all. Alesandra didn't have any concerns about his ability to be a good father, but wouldn't a child now be an added burden? Oh, God, she wished he loved her. She wished he wasn't so stubborn about her inheritance, too.

She didn't want to feel guilty, and how in heaven's name could she feel so euphoric and frightened at the same time?

Flannaghan came upstairs with a cup of hot tea for his mistress. He was about to knock on her door when he heard her crying. He stood there, uncertain what to do. He wanted to find out what was wrong, of course, so that he could try to help, but she had closed the door, indicating she wanted privacy.

He heard the front door open and immediately turned

back to the steps. He'd reached the landing when Colin walked inside. He wasn't alone. His partner, Nathan, followed behind him. The man was so tall, he had to duck his head under the arch of the doorway.

Flannaghan knew better than to blurt out his worry about his mistress in front of company. He hurried down the steps, bowed to his employer, and then turned to greet his partner.

"We'll go into the salon," Colin said. "Caine and his wife are going to be joining us shortly. Where's Alesandra?"

"Your princess is above the stairs resting," Flannaghan answered. He was trying to act like a dignified man of the house. He had met Nathan before, of course, yet was still a bit intimidated by the man.

"Let her rest until my brother gets here." He turned to his partner and said, "We've had to go out every damn night. Alesandra is exhausted."

"Does she like going out every night?" Nathan asked.

Colin smiled. "No."

A knock sounded at the door just as Colin and his partner walked into the salon. Flannaghan assumed the callers were Colin's family. He hurried to open the door and was in the process of bowing low when he realized it was just a messenger boy standing on the stoop. The messenger held a white gift box tied with a red ribbon. He thrust the package at Flannaghan.

"I've been given a coin to see Princess Alesandra gets this," he announced.

Flannaghan took the box, nodded, and then shut the door. He turned to go up the stairs, smiling now, for he had a good reason to interrupt his princess and hopefully, once he was inside her room, he could nag out of her the reason why she was so upset.

The door knocker sounded again. Flannaghan put the box down on the side table and went back to the front door. Less than a minute had passed and he thought the messenger had returned.

Colin's brother and his wife waited entrance. Lady Jade gave Flannaghan a nice smile. Caine was barely paying attention to the butler, however. He was diligently frowning down at his wife.

"Good afternoon," Flannaghan announced as he pulled the door wide.

Jade hurried inside. She greeted the butler. Caine gave him a nod. He seemed preoccupied.

"We are not finished with this discussion," he told his wife in a hard, no-nonsense tone of voice.

"Yes, we are finished," she countered. "You're being extremely unreasonable, husband. Flannaghan, where are Colin and Nathan?"

"They're waiting for you in the salon, milady."

"I'm going to get to the bottom of this, Jade," Caine muttered. "I don't care how long it takes."

"You're being unreasonably jealous, Caine."

"Damn right I am."

He made that emphatic statement of fact in a loud voice as he followed his wife into the salon.

Both Nathan and Colin immediately stood up when Jade entered the salon. Nathan took his sister into his arms and hugged her tight. He glared at Caine because he had raised his voice to his sister, then added a rebuke.

"A husband shouldn't raise his voice to his wife."

Caine laughed. Colin joined in. "You've done a complete turnaround," Caine remarked. "I seem to remember you were always shouting."

"I'm a changed man," Nathan replied in a calm, matter-of-fact voice. "I'm content."

"I'll wager your Sara's probably doing all the yelling now," Colin said.

Nathan grinned. "The little woman does have a temper," he remarked.

Jade sat down in the chair next to Nathan's. Her brother resumed his seat and turned his attention back to Caine. "Are you two having a difference of opinion?"

"No," Jade replied.

"Yes," Caine answered at the very same moment.

"I don't wish to speak about this now," Jade announced.

She deliberately turned the topic. "I'm dying to see the baby, Nathan. Does she look like you or Sara?"

"She's got my eyes and Sara's feet, thank God," Nathan replied.

"Where are they now?" Colin asked.

"I dropped Sara at her mother's so she could show off the baby."

"Are you staying with her family while you're in London?" Caine asked.

"Hell, no," Nathan answered. There was a true shudder in his voice. "They would drive me daft and I'd probably kill one of them. We're staying with you."

Caine nodded. He smiled, too. How like Nathan to instruct instead of ask. Jade clasped her hands together with joy. She was obviously thrilled with the news.

"Where is your wife?" Nathan asked Colin.

"Flannaghan went upstairs to get her. She'll be down in a minute."

One minute turned into ten. Alesandra had already taken off her ink-stained gown and put on a pretty violet-colored dress. She was sitting at her writing table, absorbed in her fanciful task of making a list of duties for Colin. She would never show the list to her husband, of course, because none of the orders were appropriate. Wives, she was learning, did better to suggest to their husbands. Most, including Colin, didn't like being ordered to do anything.

Still, it was quite all right to pretend, and it did make her feel better to write down her expectations. She put Colin's name at the top of the paper. The list of orders followed.

First, he should listen to his wife explain her concerns about the alarming coincidences involving Victoria and a man who called himself a secret admirer. In brackets she wrote Catherine's name.

Second, Colin should do something about his attitude toward her inheritance. In brackets she added the words *too stubborn*.

Third, Colin shouldn't wait five years to realize he loved her. He should realize it now, and tell her so.

Fourth, he should try to be happy he was going to become a father. He shouldn't blame her for interfering with his schedule.

Alesandra read over her list and let out a loud sigh. She was so thrilled she was going to have Colin's baby and so afraid he would be unhappy, she wanted to weep and shout at the same time.

She let out a long sigh. It wasn't like her to be so disorganized or so emotional.

She added a question to her list: "Can pregnant wives become nuns?"

She wasn't quite finished and added one more sentence: "Mother Superior loves me."

There—that important reminder made her feel a little better. She nodded, calmer now, and lifted the sheet of paper in her hands with the intent of tearing it up.

Flannaghan interrupted her. He knocked on her door and when she bid him enter he rushed inside.

He was relieved to see his princess had quit weeping. Her eyes still looked a bit swollen, but he didn't mention her condition and neither did she.

"Princess, we have . . ."

She didn't let him finish. "Pray forgive me for interrupting, but I don't want to forget my question to you. Has Cook been able to talk to anyone in the viscount's household yet? I know I've been pestering you with this matter and I do apologize, but I have sound reasons for wanting to know my answers, Flannaghan. Please be patient with me."

"She still hasn't run into any of the staff at market," Flannaghan replied. "May I offer a suggestion?"

"Yes, of course."

"Why not send her over to the viscount's town house? If she goes to the back door, the viscount won't know she called. I don't believe the staff would mention it to him."

She immediately nodded agreement. "That's a fine idea," she said in praise. "This is too important to put off any longer. Please ask Cook to go now. She can use our carriage."

"Oh, no, Princess, she wouldn't wish to ride in the

carriage. It wouldn't be proper. The viscount's residence is just a stone's throw away," he exaggerated. "She'll enjoy the brisk walk."

"If you're certain," Alesandra replied. "Now what was it you wanted to speak to be about before I interrupted you?"

"We have company," Flannaghan explained. "Your husband's partner is here. Milord's brother and his wife are with him."

She started to stand up, then changed her mind. "Wait just a minute and I'll follow you down. I've made a fresh list for you."

Flannaghan smiled in anticipation. He'd learned to love her lists, because in his heart he knew she cared about him enough to help him become organized. She always included little bits of praise along with her suggestions for tasks she believed he would wish to complete for the day. His princess was always most appreciative, too, and gracious with her compliments.

He watched as she sorted through her pile. Alesandra finally found the sheet of paper with Flannaghan's name on it and handed it to him.

He tucked the list in his pocket and escorted her down the stairs. He spotted the package on the table in the foyer and only then remembered he was supposed to give it to her.

"That box arrived a few minutes ago," he told her. "Would you like to open it now or wait until later?"

"Later, please," she answered. "I'm most curious to meet Colin's partner first."

Colin was about to get up and go after his wife when she walked into the salon. The men immediately stood up. Alesandra went over to Jade, took hold of her hand, and told her how pleased she was to see her again.

"Damn, but you did all right, Colin."

Nathan whispered that praise. Alesandra didn't hear his remark. She finally gained enough courage to walk over to the huge man and smile up at him.

"Do I bow my head to a princess?" Nathan asked.

"If you do, I'll be able to kiss your cheek in appreciation. I'll need a ladder otherwise."

Nathan laughed. He leaned down, received a kiss on his cheek, and then straightened up again. "Now explain what you meant by appreciation," he ordered.

Lord, he was a handsome devil. Terribly soft-spoken too. "In appreciation for putting up with Colin, of course. I understand how your partnership works so well now. Colin's the stubborn one, and you're surely the peacemaker in the company."

Colin threw back his head and laughed heartily. Nathan looked a little sheepish.

"You've got it backwards, Alesandra," Caine explained. "Nathan's the stubborn one and Colin's the peacemaker."

"She calls me a dragon," Colin announced.

Alesandra frowned at her husband for giving away that secret, then walked over to sit on the settee next to him.

"Caine, quit glaring at your wife," Colin ordered.

"He's extremely upset with me," Jade explained. "And that's ridiculous, of course. I didn't encourage the attraction."

"I never said you did," Caine argued.

Jade turned to Colin. "He threw out the flowers. Can you imagine?"

Colin shrugged. He put his arm around Alesandra's shoulders and stretched out his legs in front of him. "I haven't the faintest idea what you're talking about."

"You had better get this argument settled before I bring Sara and Joanna into your home. Daughters need a peaceful environment."

Nathan made that announcement. Caine and Colin turned to stare at him. They both looked incredulous. Nathan ignored them.

"Were you pleased when you found out you were going to become a father?" Alesandra tried to sound very nonchalant when she asked Nathan that question. She gripped her hands together in her lap.

If Nathan thought her question odd, he didn't remark on it. "Yes, I was very pleased."

"But what about your five-year schedule?" Alesandra asked.

"What about it?" Nathan countered, his confusion obvious.

"Didn't the baby interfere with your company plans?"

"No."

She didn't believe him. Nathan never would have sold company stock if it weren't for the baby. Colin had told her he wanted to purchase a home for his family.

She wasn't about to bring up that tender topic, however. "I see," she said. "You made allowances for such an eventuality in your schedule."

"Colin, what is your wife talking about?"

"When I first met Alesandra, I explained I wasn't going to get married for five years."

"Or have a family," she interjected with a nod.

"Or have a family," he repeated just to please her.

Caine and Jade shared a look. "How organized of you," Caine told his brother.

Alesandra believed Colin's brother had just given a compliment. "Yes, he is very organized," she enthusiastically agreed.

"Plans have a way of changing," Jade said. She was looking at Alesandra when she made that remark. Her expression was filled with sympathy. Alesandra was suddenly looking quite miserable. Jade believed she knew why.

"A baby is a blessing," she blurted out.

"Yes," Nathan agreed. "Jade's correct, too, when she says plans have a way of changing," he added with a nod. "Colin and I were counting on my wife's inheritance from the king to strengthen the company funds, but the prince regent decided to keep the money and we had to turn our minds to finding other solutions."

"Hence the five-year schedule," Colin explained.

Alesandra looked like she was about to burst into tears. Caine felt like throttling his brother. If Colin would only look at her face, he would know something was terribly wrong. His brother obviously didn't have a clue, however, and Caine didn't believe he should interfere . . . yet.

Alesandra was caught up in her own thoughts. She could feel herself getting angry over Nathan's casually given remark. He had made it quite clear that neither he nor Colin had any qualms about using Sara's inheritance. Why, then, was Colin so stubbornly resistant to using some of hers?

Colin drew her attention when he spoke again. "Caine, will you quit scowling at your wife."

"He blames me," Jade announced.

"I do not blame you," Caine argued.

"Blames you for what?" Colin asked.

"I received a bundle of flowers this morning. There wasn't a note, just a signature."

Nathan and Colin frowned in unison.

"You received flowers from another man?" Nathan asked, his astonishment clear.

"Yes."

Nathan turned to glare at his brother-in-law. "You damn well better do something about this, Caine. She's your wife. You can't allow another man to send her flowers. Why the hell haven't you killed the bastard?"

Caine was thankful Nathan had taken his side. "I'm damn well going to kill him just as soon as I find out who he is."

Colin shook his head. "You can't kill anyone," he announced in exasperation. "You're going to have to be reasonable about this, Caine. Sending flowers isn't a crime. He's probably just some young pup caught up in an infatuation."

"It's fine for you to be reasonable, Colin. Jade isn't your wife."

"I would still be reasonable if the flowers had been sent to Alesandra," Colin argued.

Caine shook his head.

"Tell us his name, Jade," Nathan demanded.

No one was paying any attention to Alesandra. She was thankful for their inattention. Her mind raced with speculations. She'd shaken her head when Colin had guessed it was just a young man caught up in an infatuation.

"Yes," Colin asked Jade then. "Who sent them?"

"He signs all his cards Your Secret Admirer," said Alesandra.

Everyone turned in unison to stare at her. Jade's mouth dropped open.

"Isn't that right, Jade?"

Her sister-in-law nodded. "How did you know?"

Nathan leaned back in his chair. "There's more to this than admiration, isn't there?"

No one said a word for a long minute. Alesandra suddenly remembered the package Flannaghan had told her had been delivered. She tried to go and get it. Colin wouldn't let her move. He tightened his hold on her shoulder.

"I believe the man might have sent something to me," she explained. "There's a package in the foyer."

"The hell he did. Flannaghan!"

Colin roared the summons. Alesandra's ears started ringing. Flannaghan came running. He had the package in his hands, indicating he'd been listening to the conversation. He all but tossed the thing to Colin.

Alesandra reached for the package. Colin's glare changed her mind. She leaned back against the settee and folded her hands. Colin leaned forward to attack the box. He ripped the bow off, muttering under his breath, then tore the lid free and looked inside. Alesandra peeked around her husband's shoulder to see what was there. She got a glimpse of the ornately painted fan before Colin slammed the lid back down on the box.

"Son of a bitch!" Colin roared. He repeated the shameful blasphemy a second time. Nathan, Alesandra noticed, nodded each time the foul words were said. Apparently those were his sentiments as well.

Colin held the notecard in his hand and glared at it.

"Aren't you going to be reasonable about this?" Caine challenged.

"Hell, no."

"Exactly," Caine muttered.

"One more and you'll have enough for a lynch mob," Jade announced. "Will you look at our husbands, Alesandra? They're blowing this all out of proportion. Such jealousy is unfounded," she added.

She expected Alesandra's agreement and was therefore surprised when her sister-in-law shook her head.

"Colin and Caine shouldn't be jealous," Alesandra whispered. "But they should be worried."

"How did you know what was signed on the card?" Nathan asked. "Have you received other gifts?"

Colin turned to look at her. His expression was chilling. So was his tone of voice when he said, "You would have told me if you'd received any other gifts. Isn't that right, Alesandra?"

She was thankful she could agree with him. Colin's fury was actually a little frightening. "Yes, I would have told you, and no, I haven't received any other gifts."

Colin nodded. He leaned back, put his arm around her shoulders again, and hauled her up tight against his side. She found his possessiveness a comfort now and didn't mind at all that he was inadvertently squeezing the breath right out of her.

"You know more than you're telling," Nathan announced.

Alesandra nodded. "Yes," she answered. "And I've been trying to get someone to listen to me for a good long while. I even asked Sir Richards for help."

She turned to frown at her husband. "Are you ready to hear what I have to say?"

Colin was a bit surprised by his wife's comments, of course, but he was astonished by her angry tone of voice.

"What have you been trying to tell me?"

"Victoria received letters and gifts from a secret admirer."

Colin was taken aback by that reminder. Alesandra had tried to explain why she was worried about her friend and he hadn't let her. He should have listened, he realized now.

"Who is Victoria?" asked Caine.

Alesandra answered him. She explained how she'd met Victoria. "After she returned to England, she wrote to me at least once a month. I would immediately write back, of course, and I did love hearing from her. She had such an exciting life. In the last few letters, however, she mentioned an admirer who was sending her gifts. She thought it all very romantic. I received her last letter in early September."

"And what did she say in that letter?" Caine asked.

"She had decided to meet the man," Alesandra answered. "I was appalled, of course, and wrote back to her right away. I advised caution and suggested she take her brother with her if she was determined to find out who her admirer was."

Alesandra started to shiver. Colin instinctively hugged her. "I don't know if Victoria received my letter or not. She might have already been gone by then."

"Gone? Gone where?" Jade asked.

"It was reported Victoria ran off to Gretna Green," Colin explained. "Alesandra doesn't believe that."

"There isn't any record of a marriage," Alesandra countered.

"What do you think happened to her?"

Nathan asked her that question, and until that moment she hadn't allowed herself to voice her true fear. She took a calming breath and turned her gaze to her husband's partner.

"I think she was murdered."

*He paced the library in a rage. None of it was his fault. None of it. He had stopped. He'd ignored the craving, hadn't given in to the urge. It wasn't his fault. No, it was the bastard who was responsible. He never would have killed again . . . he never would have given in to the urge.*

*Revenge. He would show him. He would get even. He would destroy him. He would begin by taking away everything he valued. He would make him suffer.*

*He smiled in anticipation. He would start with the women.*

# Chapter
# 13

That statement got an immediate reaction. "Good God," Caine whispered.

"Could it be possible?" Nathan asked.

"I hadn't realized . . ." Jade whispered that remark and placed her hand over her heart.

Colin was the last to react and the most logical in his response. "Explain why you believe this," he commanded.

"Flannaghan, will you please go upstairs and fetch my list for me?"

"You have a list of reasons why you suspect your friend was murdered?" Caine asked.

"She has a list for everything."

Colin made that remark but she was pleased that he didn't sound at all condescending.

"Yes, I do have a list," Alesandra said. "I wanted to organize my thoughts about Victoria's disappearance and try to come up with some sort of plan. I knew something was wrong as soon as I heard she'd eloped. Victoria never would have done such a thing. Appearances were more important to her than love. Besides, I don't think she would have allowed herself to fall in love with someone she believed inferior to her station in life. She was sometimes a little shallow-headed and a bit of a snob as well, but those were her only faults. She was also very kindhearted."

"He has to be someone in society," Nathan decided aloud.

"Yes, I think so, too," Alesandra agreed. "I also think this man begged her to meet him somewhere and that her curiosity led her to forget caution. She was certainly flattered by his attention."

"She must have been terribly naive," Jade remarked.

"So is Catherine."

"Catherine? What does my sister have to do with this?"

"She made me promise not to tell, but her safety is at issue and I must break her confidence. She also received flowers this morning."

"Hell, I need a brandy," Caine muttered.

Flannaghan returned to the salon just then. He handed a pile of papers to Colin to pass along to Alesandra. He'd heard Caine's request and immediately announced he would fetch the brandy.

"Bring the bottle," Caine ordered.

"I hope to God we're all jumping to the wrong conclusion," Nathan said.

"Better that we are," Caine countered. "Three women in our family are being courted by the bastard. Think the worst and plan accordingly," he added with a hard nod.

Colin was sorting through the stack of papers, looking for the list pertinent to their discussion. He was given pause when he saw his name at the top of one sheet.

Alesandra wasn't paying any attention to her husband now. Her gaze was centered on his brother.

"Caine, you don't have sufficient information to assume there are only three," she explained. "This man could have sent dozens of gifts to women all over London."

"She's right about that," Nathan agreed.

Caine shook his head. "My gut feeling is that he's coming after one of ours."

Colin had just finished reading Alesandra's list. It took everything he possessed not to show any reaction. His hand shook when he placed the paper on the bottom of the pile.

He was going to become a father. He was so damn pleased he wanted to take Alesandra into his arms and kiss her.

And what a time to find out, he thought to himself. Colin wouldn't let her know he'd read the list, of course. He would wait until she told him. He'd give her until tonight, when they were in bed together . . .

"Why are you smiling, Colin? It's a damn bizarre reaction to this topic," Caine told him.

"I was thinking about something else."

"Do pay attention," Alesandra requested.

Colin turned to look at her. She saw the warm glint in his eyes and wondered what in heaven's name he'd been thinking about to cause that reaction. Before she could ask him, he leaned down and kissed her.

It was a quick, hard kiss that was over and done with before she could react.

"For God's sake, Colin," Caine muttered.

"We're newly married," Alesandra blurted out, trying to find some excuse for her husband's display of affection.

Flannaghan came in with a tray loaded with goblets and a large decanter of brandy. He placed the tray on the table near Alesandra and leaned over to whisper close to her ear.

"Cook's back."

"Does she have news?"

Flannaghan eagerly nodded. Caine poured himself a drink and downed it in one long swallow. Both Nathan and Colin declined the brandy.

"May I have a drink, please?" Alesandra asked. She didn't particularly like the taste of brandy but she thought the warm liquid might take some of the chill out of her. She was feeling queasy, too, and she was certain the distressing talk about murder was the cause.

"Flannaghan, get Alesandra some water," Colin ordered.

"I would rather have brandy," she countered.

"No."

She was clearly astonished by his emphatic denial. "Why not?"

Colin didn't have a quick answer for her question. He

wanted to tell her brandy probably wasn't good for her delicate condition. He couldn't, of course, because she hadn't told him about the baby yet.

"Why are you smiling? I do declare, Colin, you're the most confusing man."

He forced himself back to the matter at hand. "I don't like you drinking," he announced.

"I never drink."

"That's right," Colin agreed. "And you aren't going to start now."

Flannaghan tapped Alesandra on her shoulder, reminding her of his message.

"Will you excuse me for a moment?" she asked. She noticed her lists were in his hands then. "What are you doing with those?"

"I'm holding them for you," he replied. "Would you like me to look through them for the list you made concerning Victoria?"

"No, thank you," she replied. She took the papers, found Victoria's list second from the top, and then started to stand up. Colin shook his head at her and hauled her back.

"You aren't going anywhere."

"I must speak to Cook."

"Flannaghan can answer her questions."

"You don't understand," Alesandra said in a low whisper. "She went on a little errand for me and I wanted to find out the results."

"What errand?" Colin asked.

She debated answering him for a minute or two. "You'll get angry," she whispered.

"No, I won't."

Her expression told him she didn't believe him.

"Alesandra?"

He said her name in that warning tone of voice he was certain would make her wish to answer him with all possible haste, but when she smiled at him he knew she wasn't at all impressed.

"Please tell me," he asked.

He had asked, not ordered, and that made all the difference in her mind. She immediately answered him. "I sent her to the Viscount of Talbolt's town house. Before you get upset over this, Colin, do remember you ordered me not to talk to the viscount. I adhered to your wishes."

He was thoroughly confused. "I still don't understand," he admitted.

"I sent Cook to talk to Lady Roberta's staff. I wanted to find out if she'd received any gifts before she disappeared. Husband, we both know she didn't run away from her husband. Such an excuse is unthinkable."

"She did receive gifts," Flannaghan blurted out. "The viscount pitched a tantrum, too. Staff believes Lady Roberta ran off with the suitor. The viscount isn't talking but his employees believe he thinks his wife ran off, too. The upstairs maid told Cook the viscount has turned to drink to ease his torment and stays locked up in his library day and night."

"What the hell is going on here?" Caine asked. "Could there be a connection between the two women?"

"They both disappeared," Jade reminded her husband. "Isn't that connection enough?"

"That isn't what I meant, sweetheart."

"Maybe he's being random in his selection," Nathan suggested.

"There's always a motive," Colin argued.

"Perhaps with the first one," Nathan agreed.

Alesandra was confused by that comment. "Why a motive with the first and not the second?"

Nathan looked at Colin before answering. Colin nodded. "There was probably a motive behind the first murder," Nathan explained. "But then he got a taste for killing."

"Some do," Caine admitted.

"Dear God," Jade whispered. She visibly shivered. Caine immediately got up and went over to his wife. He pulled her out of the chair, sat down, and then settled her on his lap. She leaned against him.

"Do you mean to tell me he likes killing?" Alesandra asked.

"Could be," Nathan answered.

Alesandra's stomach turned queasy again. She leaned closer into her husband's side in an attempt to gain more of his warmth. She felt safe when she was near him— comforted, too. That was what love was all about, she thought to herself.

"We're going to have to get a lot more information," Caine announced.

"I tried to talk to Victoria's brother, but he wasn't at all helpful," Alesandra said.

"He'll be helpful when I talk to him," Colin snapped.

"I can't imagine why he would cooperate," Alesandra replied. "You threw him out on the pavement the last time you spoke to him."

"What about asking Richards for some help?" Nathan suggested.

Alesandra closed her eyes and listened to the discussion. Colin was rubbing her arm in an absentminded fashion. His touch was wonderfully soothing. The men's voices were low and while they formulated their plans of action, she thought about how nice it was to finally have her husband's coopera- tion. She knew he would find out what happened to Victoria . . . and why. She didn't have any doubts about Colin's ability to find the culprit, because she was certain she was married to the most intelligent man in all of England. He was probably the most stubborn, too, but that flaw would come in handy now. He wouldn't quit until he had his answers.

"What the hell else do we do?" Caine asked.

Alesandra looked down at her list before she answered him. "You find out who profited from Victoria's death. Colin, you could find out if any policies were taken out. Dreyson would be happy to help you."

All three men smiled in unison. "I thought you were asleep," Colin remarked.

She ignored that comment. "You should also consider all the other motives . . . in the general sense," she explained. "Jealousy and rejection are two motives. Neil mentioned his sister had turned down several proposals. Perhaps one of those men didn't like being told no."

It occurred to Jade that Alesandra was actually very astute. Colin was grinning, suggesting to Jade that he was also aware of his wife's cleverness, but Nathan and Caine hadn't realized it yet.

"Yes, of course, we'll look into every possible motive," Caine said. "I just wish we had a clue or two."

"Oh, but you do," Alesandra replied. "The fact that three women in your family have received gifts is clue enough, Caine. It occurs to me that one of you men or one of us women has offended the man."

Colin nodded. "That thought had already occurred to me," he said. "He's getting careless."

"Or more bold," Nathan interjected.

"Isn't everyone forgetting one important fact?" Jade asked.

"What's that?" Caine asked his wife.

"There aren't any bodies. We really could be jumping in the wrong direction."

"Do you think we are?" Alesandra asked.

Jade thought about it a long minute, then whispered, "No."

Colin took charge then. He gave everyone but Alesandra an assignment. He told Jade to talk to as many of the ladies of the *ton* as possible to find out if anyone else had received a gift. He warned her not to tell the women about the gifts she, Catherine, and Alesandra had received because some of the more foolish women might think this was all some sort of competitive game.

Nathan was given the duty of taking over the offices while Colin concentrated on finding answers.

"Caine, Alesandra's right. Neil won't talk to me. You'll have to deal with him."

"I will," Caine agreed. "I should also talk to Talbolt," he added. "We went to Oxford together and he might be more receptive to hearing me out."

"I'll talk to Father," Colin said then. "He's going to have to keep a watchful eye on Catherine until the bastard is caught."

Alesandra waited to hear what Colin wanted her to do. A few minutes passed before her impatience got the better of her. She nudged her husband to get his attention.

"Haven't you forgotten me?"

"No."

"What is my assignment, Colin? What do you want me to do?"

"Rest, sweetheart."

"Rest?"

She'd sounded incensed. Colin wouldn't let her argue with him. Caine was ready to leave. He lifted his wife off his lap and stood up. Nathan also stood and started for the door.

"Come along, Alesandra. You need a nap," Colin said.

She certainly did not need a nap, she thought to herself, and if she hadn't been so tired she would have told him so. Arguing with her husband required stamina, however, and Alesandra didn't seem to have any left. The dark discussion had taken all of her energy.

Caine was smiling at her. Alesandra didn't want him to think she was a weakling, and she knew he'd heard Colin insist she rest. She shoved the list into his hands. "There are other motives I've written down you might wish to consider," she said.

Before Caine could thank her, she blurted out, "I am a little tired, but only because Colin and I have been keeping such late hours every night. He's weary, too," she added with a nod.

Caine winked at her. She didn't know what to make of that. Colin turned her attention then when he nudged her up the steps. Flannaghan saw their guests out.

"Why are you treating me like an invalid?"

She asked him that question in her bedroom. Colin was unbuttoning her dress for her. "You look worn out," he said. "And I like undressing you."

He was being terribly gentle with her. After she'd been

295

stripped down to her white silk chemise, he leaned down, lifted the hair away from the back of her neck, and kissed her there.

He pulled the covers back and tucked her in bed. "I'm only going to rest for a few minutes," she said. "I don't dare fall asleep."

He bent over the bed and kissed her brow. "Why not?"

"If I sleep now, I won't be able to sleep tonight."

Colin started for the door. "All right, sweetheart. Just rest."

"Wouldn't you like to rest too?"

He laughed. "No. I have work to do."

"I'm sorry, husband."

He'd just pulled the door open. "What are you sorry about?"

"I always seem to interfere in your work. I'm sorry about that."

He nodded, started out the doorway, then changed his mind. He turned around and walked back to the side of the bed. It was ridiculous for her to apologize for interfering and he wanted to tell her so. She was his wife, after all, not some distant relative making a nuisance of herself.

He didn't say a word. He would have to wait until later to instruct his wife when she would listen to him. She was sound asleep now. He was a little amazed at how quickly she'd fallen asleep and immediately felt a little guilty because he'd kept her out every night. Damn, she looked so delicate and vulnerable to him.

Colin didn't know how long he stood there staring down at Alesandra. His mind was consumed with the need to protect her. He'd never felt this possessive . . . or this blessed, he suddenly realized.

She loved him.

And, Lord, how he loved her. The truth didn't sneak up on him and clobber him over the head, though the picture was fanciful enough to make him smile. He had known for a long time that he loved her, even though he had stubbornly refused to openly acknowledge it. God only knew he had all the symptoms of a man in love. From the moment he'd met her, he'd been acting terribly possessive and protective. He hadn't been able to keep his hands off her and for a long while he believed he was just consumed with a simple case of lust. After a time, he knew better. It wasn't lust at all.

Oh, yes, he'd loved her for a long time. He couldn't imagine why she loved him. Had she been awake, he might have asked her that question then and there. She certainly could have done better with someone else. Someone with a title . . . someone with land and inheritance . . . someone with a sound, healthy body.

Colin didn't think of himself as a romantic. He was a logical, practical man who had learned that he could achieve success if he worked hard enough. In a dark corner of his mind he had harbored the thought that God had turned his back on him. It was an unreasonable belief, and it had taken root right after his leg had been nearly destroyed. He remembered hearing the physician whisper the need to amputate the limb—remembered, too, his friend's vehement refusal. Nathan wouldn't let Sir Winters touch the leg, but Colin had still been so damned afraid to sleep for fear that when he awakened he wouldn't be whole again.

The leg had survived, but the constant pain he now lived with made the victory hollow indeed.

Miracles were for other people, Colin had always believed —until Alesandra came into his life. His princess actually loved him. In his heart he knew there weren't any restrictions or conditions surrounding her love. Had she met a man with only one leg, she would have loved him just as much. He would have gained her sympathy, perhaps, but certainly not her pity. Her every action showed her strength and her determination to take care of him.

She would always be there for him, nagging him and arguing with him—and loving him no matter what.

And that, Colin decided, was definitely a miracle.

God hadn't forgotten him after all.

She wanted to leave him. Alesandra knew she wasn't being reasonable, but she was so upset inside she could barely think what to do. Nathan's casual remark about how he and Colin had both counted on Sara's inheritance to help their shipping company played on her mind until she was ready to weep.

Colin, she decided, had rejected her on every level possible. He didn't want her to help him with his company books, he didn't want her inheritance, and he didn't particularly want—or need—her love. His heart seemed to be surrounded by shields, and Alesandra didn't believe she would ever be able to get him to love her.

She knew she was being pitiful. She didn't care. Mother Superior's letter had arrived that morning, and Alesandra had already read the thing at least a dozen times.

She wanted to go home. She was so horribly homesick for the nuns and the land, she burst into tears. It was quite all right, she decided. She was alone, after all, and Colin was working in his study with the door closed. He wouldn't hear her.

Dear God, she wished she wasn't so emotional these days. She couldn't seem to apply logic to anything. She stood at the window in her robe and gown, looking out, and her mind was so engrossed with her worries she didn't even hear the door open.

"What is it, sweetheart? Don't you feel well?"

Colin's voice was filled with concern. She took a deep, calming breath and turned to look at him.

"I would like to go home."

He hadn't been prepared for that request. He looked quite astonished. He was quick to recover. He shut the door behind him and walked toward her.

"You are home."

She wanted to argue with him. She didn't. "Yes, of course," she agreed. "But I would like your permission to go back to Holy Cross for a visit. The convent is just a walk away from Stone Haven, and I would like to see my parents' home again."

Colin walked over to her writing desk. "What is this really all about?" he asked her. He leaned against the edge of the table while he waited for her to answer him.

"I received a letter from Mother Superior today, and I'm suddenly very homesick."

Colin didn't show any outward reaction to her plea. "I can't take the time right now to . . ."

"Stefan and Raymond would go with me," she interrupted. "I don't expect you to go along. I know how busy you are."

He could feel himself getting angry. The very idea of his wife leaving on such a journey without him at her side appalled him. He stopped himself from immediately denying her request, however, because in truth he had never seen her this upset. It worried the hell out of him, given her delicate condition.

She was out of her mind if she thought he would ever let her go anywhere without him. He didn't tell her that opinion either.

He decided to use reason to make her understand. "Alesandra . . ."

"Colin, you don't need me."

He was taken aback by that absurd comment. "The hell I don't need you," he countered in a near shout.

She shook her head. He nodded. Then she turned her back on him.

"You have never needed me," she whispered.

"Alesandra, sit down."

"I don't wish to sit down."

"I want to talk to you about this . . ." He almost said he wanted to talk to her about her "ridiculous notion," but he caught himself in time.

She ignored him and continued to stare out the window.

He noticed the stack of papers on her desk and suddenly knew what he was going to do. He quickly sorted through her lists until he found the one with his name on the top.

She wasn't paying any attention to him. He folded the sheet in half and tucked it in his pocket. Then he ordered her to sit down again. His voice was harder, more insistent.

She took her time obeying. She mopped the tears away from her face with the backs of her hands and finally walked over to the side of the bed. She sat down, folded her hands in her lap, and bowed her head.

"Have you suddenly stopped loving me?"

He hadn't been able to keep the worry out of his voice. She was so surprised by his question, she looked up at him. "No, of course I haven't stopped loving you."

He nodded, both pleased and relieved to hear her fervent answer. Then he straightened away from the desk and walked over to stand in front of her.

"There isn't any Uncle Albert, is there?"

The switch in topic confused her. "What does Albert have to do with my request to go home?"

"Damn it, this is your home," he countered.

She lowered her head again. He immediately regretted the burst of anger and took a breath to calm himself. "Bear with me for just a moment, Alesandra, and answer my question."

She debated telling him the truth for a long minute. "No, there isn't any Uncle Albert."

"I didn't think so."

"Why didn't you think so?"

"There were never any letters delivered here from the man, yet I heard you tell Caine you'd received a missive. You made him up, and I think I know why."

"I really don't wish to talk about this. I find I'm weary tonight. It's quite late, almost ten."

He wasn't about to let her run away from this discussion. "You had a four-hour nap today," he reminded her.

"I was catching up on my sleep," she announced.

"Dreyson wouldn't take stock orders from a woman, would he? So you invented Albert, a convenient recluse who just happened to have your same initials."

She wasn't going to argue with him. "Yes."

He nodded again. He clasped his hands behind his back and frowned down at her. "You hide your intelligence, don't you, Alesandra? You obviously have a knack for the market, but instead of boasting about your cleverness with investments, you invented another man to take the credit."

She looked up at him so he could see her frown. "Men

listen to other men," she announced. "It isn't acceptable for a woman to have such interests. It isn't considered ladylike. And it isn't a knack, Colin. I read the journals and listen to Dreyson's suggestions. It doesn't take a brilliant mind to be guided by his advice."

"Will you agree you're at least fairly intelligent and can reason most things through logically?"

She wondered where in heaven's name this discussion was leading. Her husband was acting terribly uncomfortable. She couldn't imagine why.

"Yes," she answered. "I will agree I'm fairly intelligent."

"Then why in God's name haven't you been able to reason through all the obvious facts and figure out that I love you?"

Her eyes widened and she leaned back. She opened her mouth to say something to him, but she couldn't remember what it was.

"I love you, Alesandra."

It had been difficult telling her what was in his heart, yet once the words were spoken, he felt incredibly free. He smiled at his wife and said the words again.

She bounded off the bed and frowned up at him. "You do not love me," she announced.

"I sure as hell do," he argued. "If you would apply a little reason . . ."

"I did use reason," she interrupted. "And came to the opposite conclusion."

"Sweetheart . . ."

"Don't you dare 'sweetheart' me," she cried out.

Colin reached for her but she eluded him by sitting down again. "Oh, I reasoned it through and through and through. Shall I tell you my conclusions?"

She didn't give him time to answer her. "You have turned your back on everything I had to give you. It would be illogical for me to assume you love me."

"I've what?" he asked, stunned by the vehemence in her voice.

"You've rejected everything," she whispered.

301

"Exactly what have I rejected?"

"My title, my position, my castle, my inheritance—even my help with your company."

He finally understood. He pulled her to her feet and wrapped his arms around her. She tried to push herself away from him. They fell onto the bed. Colin protected her from his weight as he stretched out on top of her. He pinned the lower part of her body with his thighs and braced himself on his elbows so he could look down at her.

Her hair spilled out on the pillows and her eyes, cloudy with unshed tears, made her appear more vulnerable to him. Dear God, she was beautiful—even when she was glaring at him. "I love you, Alesandra," he whispered. "And I have taken everything you had to give me."

She started to protest. He wouldn't let her. He clamped his hand over her mouth so she couldn't interrupt him. "I rejected nothing of value. You offered me all a man could ever want. You gave me your love, your trust, your loyalty, your mind, your heart, and your body. None of those offerings is material, sweetheart, and if you lost all the financial trappings that came along with you, it wouldn't matter to me. You're all I have ever wanted. Now do you understand?"

She was overwhelmed by his beautiful words. His eyes were actually misty, and she knew then that it had been difficult for him to tell her how he felt. Colin did love her. She was so filled with joy, she burst into tears.

"Love, don't cry," he pleaded. "It's very upsetting for me to see you so miserable."

She tried to stop crying long enough to explain she wasn't miserable at all. Colin moved his hand away from her mouth and gently wiped her tears away.

"I didn't have anything to give you when I married you," he told her. "And yet . . . on our wedding night I knew you loved me. I had trouble accepting it at first. It seemed so damned unfair to you. I should have remembered a comment you made to me about the prince regent. That reminder would have saved both of us a good deal of worry."

"What comment did I make?"

"I told you I'd heard the prince regent was taken with you," he answered. "Do you remember what you said to me then?"

She did remember. "I told you he was taken with what I am, not who I am."

"Well?" he demanded in a rough whisper.

"Well, what?"

Her smile was radiant. She finally understood.

"I thought you were fairly intelligent," he drawled out.

"You love me."

"Yes."

He leaned down and kissed her. She sighed into his mouth. When he pulled away, she looked properly convinced.

"Have you also worked it out in your mind?" she asked.

He didn't understand what she meant by her question. He was busy unbuttoning the top of her gown. "Worked out what?"

"That I fell in love with who you are, not what you are," she answered. "It was your strength and courage that drew me to you, Colin. I needed both."

He was so pleased with his wife he had to kiss her again. "I needed you," he admitted.

He wanted to kiss her again. She wanted to talk. "Colin, you present yourself to the world as a man struggling to build a company."

"I *am* a man struggling to build a company."

He rolled to his side so he could get her robe and gown off her more quickly.

"You aren't a pauper," she announced. She sat up in bed and started tugging her robe off her shoulders. Colin helped her.

"I had a good look at your books, remember? You've made an amazing profit, but you poured every bit of it back into the operation and the result is very impressive. You've been trying to build an empire, but if you'll only step back and take a good look you'll realize you've already accomplished your goal. Why, you have close to twenty ships now with cargo orders stretching into next year and that must surely convince you that your company is no longer a struggling venture."

He was having trouble listening to what she was telling him. She'd shed her robe and was now inching her gown up over her head. His throat tightened up on him. She finally got rid of the barrier. He immediately reached for her. She shook her head at him. "First, I would like you to answer a question for me, please."

He might have nodded but he couldn't be certain. A fire burned inside him and all he wanted to do was bury himself in her. He was so damn anxious to touch her, he was literally destroying his shirt in his hurry to get the thing off.

"Colin, when is enough enough?"

Her question required concentration. He didn't have any to spare.

"I'll never be able to get enough of you."

"Nor I you," she whispered. "But that isn't what I was asking . . ."

Colin silenced her with his mouth. She couldn't resist him a moment longer. She wrapped her arms around his neck and gave in to the wonder of his passion . . . and his love.

He was demanding, yet incredibly gentle with her at the same time. His touch was magical, and while she was in the throes of her own blissful surrender, he told her again and again how much he loved her.

She would have told him she loved him, too, but Colin had worn her out and she couldn't find the strength to speak. She rolled onto her back, closed her eyes, and listened to her pounding heartbeat while the air cooled her feverish skin.

He rolled to his side, propped his head up on his hand, and grinned down at her. He looked thoroughly satisfied.

He stroked a path from her chin to her belly, and then his hand gently rubbed the flat of her stomach.

"Sweetheart, do you have something you want to tell me?"

She was feeling too content to think about anything other than what had just happened to her.

Colin was going to nag her until she told him about the

baby, but Flannaghan started banging on the bedroom door then, interrupting that intention.

"Milord, your brother's here. I put him in the study."

"I'll be right there," Colin shouted.

He muttered about his brother's bad timing. Alesandra laughed. She didn't bother to open her eyes when she said, "It would have been bad timing ten minutes ago. I would say he was being very considerate."

He agreed with that assessment. He started to leave the bed, then turned back to her. She opened her eyes just in time to watch him lean over her and place a kiss on her navel. She brushed her hand across his shoulder. The hair on the back of his neck curled around her fingers.

Colin was letting his hair grow long again. That sudden realization hit her all at once. She was so pleased she almost started crying again. She didn't, of course, because Colin had told her he found it upsetting to see her weep, and she doubted he would understand anyway. She understood, though, and that was all that mattered. Marriage hadn't turned out to be a prison for her husband.

He was puzzled by the look on her face. "Sweetheart?" he asked.

"You're still free, Colin."

His eyes widened over that remark. "You say the strangest things," he remarked.

"Your brother's waiting."

He nodded. "I want you to think about my question while I talk to Caine. All right, love?"

"What question?"

Colin got out of bed and pulled his pants on. "I asked you if you had anything else to tell me," he reminded her.

He slipped his bare feet into his shoes and started toward his bedroom in search of a fresh shirt. He'd shredded the one he'd been wearing.

"Think about it," he told her. He grabbed his jacket, winked at her, and then left the room.

Caine was sprawled out in the leather chair next to the hearth. Colin nodded and sat down behind his desk. He reached for his pen and paper.

Caine took one look at his brother and broke into a wide grin. "I see I interrupted you. Sorry," he added.

Colin ignored the laughter in his brother's voice. He knew he looked disheveled. He hadn't bothered with a cravat. He hadn't bothered to comb his hair, either.

"Marriage agrees with you, Colin."

Colin didn't pretend indifference. He looked up at his brother and let him see the truth in his expression. The shields were gone.

"I'm a man in love."

Caine laughed. "It took you long enough to realize it."

"No longer than it took you to realize you loved Jade."

Caine agreed with a nod. Colin went back to writing on his paper.

"What are you doing?"

Colin's grin was a bit sheepish when he admitted he was starting a list.

"I seem to have caught my wife's obsession for organization," he said. "Did you talk to the viscount?"

Caine's smile faded. He loosened his cravat while he answered. "Harold's a mess," he said, referring to the viscount. "He's barely coherent. The last time he saw his wife they had an argument and he has spent every minute since tormenting himself over the harsh words he said to her. His anguish is aching to see."

"The poor devil," Colin said. He shook his head, then asked, "Did he tell you what the argument was about?"

"He was certain she'd taken a lover," Caine answered. "She was receiving gifts and Harold jumped to the conclusion she was involved with another man."

"Hell."

"He still hasn't figured it out, Colin. I told him about the gifts our wives received but he was too sotted from drink to understand the ramifications. He kept saying his anger swayed Roberta into running away with her lover."

Colin leaned back in his chair. "Did he have anything helpful to add?"

"No."

The brothers lapsed into silence, each caught up in his

own thoughts. Colin pushed his chair back and bent over to take his shoes off. He tossed off his left shoe, then his right, and was about to straighten up again when he noticed the lining protruding from his left shoe.

"Damn," he muttered to himself. His most comfortable pair of shoes were already wearing out. He picked up the shoe to see if it could be repaired. The thick insert fell into his hands.

He'd never seen anything like it. He immediately picked up the other shoe and examined it. Flannaghan chose that moment to walk into the study with a fresh decanter of brandy so that Caine could have a drink if he was so inclined. He took one look at what Colin was holding in his hand and immediately turned around to leave.

"Come back here, Flannaghan," Colin ordered.

"Did you wish a drink, milord?" Flannaghan asked Caine.

"Yes," Caine answered. "But I want water, not brandy. After seeing Harold tonight, the thought of a hard drink turns my stomach."

"I shall fetch the water at once."

Flannaghan tried to leave again. Colin called him back.

"Did you wish some water?" the butler asked his employer.

Colin held up the insert. "I wish to find out if you know anything about this."

Flannaghan was torn between his loyalties. He was Colin's servant, of course, and was certainly loyal to him, but he had also promised his princess not to say a word about the bootmaker.

Flannaghan's silence was a bit damning. Caine started laughing. "From the look on his face, I would say he knows a great deal about something. What are you holding, Colin?"

He tossed the leather insert to Caine. "I just found this hidden under the lining of my shoe. It's been specifically made for the left foot."

He turned his gaze back to his butler. "Alesandra's behind this, isn't she?"

Flannaghan cleared his throat. "They have become your

favorite shoes, milord," he hastened to point out. "The insert made your shoe fit your heel much better. I pray you won't become too angry over this."

Colin wasn't at all angry, but his butler was too young and too caught up in his worry to realize that fact.

"Our princess realizes that you are a bit . . . sensitive about your leg," Flannaghan continued, "and for that reason she did resort to a little trickery. I do hope you won't berate her."

Colin smiled. Flannaghan's defense of Alesandra was pleasing to him. "Will you ask 'our princess' to come in here? Knock softly on her door, Flannaghan, and if she doesn't immediately answer, assume she's asleep."

Flannaghan hurried out of the study. He realized he was still holding the decanter in his hands and quickly turned back to the study. He put the brandy on the side table and once again left.

Caine tossed the insert back to his brother. "Does the contraption work?"

"Yes," Colin answered. "I didn't realize . . ."

Caine saw the vulnerability in his brother's eyes and was amazed. It wasn't like Colin to let anyone see beyond the smile. He suddenly felt closer to his brother, and all because Colin wasn't shutting him out. He leaned forward in his chair, his elbows braced on his knees.

"What didn't you realize?"

Colin stared at the thick heel of the insert when he answered. "That my left leg was shorter than my right. It makes sense. The loss of muscle . . ."

He forced a shrug. Caine didn't know what to say to him. This was the first time Colin had acknowledged his condition and Caine wasn't certain how to proceed. If he sounded too nonchalant, his brother might assume he didn't care. Yet if he sounded too earnest and prodded him with questions, Colin might slam the door on the subject for another five years.

It was damned awkward. And in the end he didn't say anything. He changed the topic. "Have you talked to Father about Catherine yet?"

"Yes," Colin answered. "He promises to be on his guard. He's alerted his staff, too. If anything else is delivered, Father will see it first."

"Is he going to warn Catherine?"

"He didn't want to worry her," Colin replied. "I insisted. She needs to understand this is a serious matter. Catherine's a bit . . . flighty, isn't she?"

Caine smiled. "She isn't completely grown up yet, Colin. Give her time."

"And protect her until she does grow up."

"Yes."

Alesandra appeared in the doorway with Flannaghan at her side. She wore a dark blue robe that covered her from chin to slippers. She walked inside the study, smiled at Caine, and then turned to her husband. Colin held up the insert for her to see. She immediately lost her smile and started backing out of the room.

She didn't look frightened, just wary. "Alesandra, do you know something about this?"

She couldn't tell from his expression if he was angry or merely irritated with her. She reminded herself that her husband had vowed his love for her just minutes before and took a step forward. "Yes."

"Yes, what?"

"Yes, I know something about the insert. Good evening, Caine. It's good to see you again," she added in a rush.

She was deliberately being obtuse. Colin shook his head at her. "I asked you a question, wife," he said.

"Now I understand your question," she blurted out. She took another step forward. "Just before you left my chamber you asked me if I had something to tell you and now I realize you'd found the insert. All right, then. I'll tell you. I interfered. Yes, I did. I had your best interests at heart, Colin. I'm sorry you're so prickly about your leg, and if you weren't, I could have discussed my idea with you before sending Flannaghan to the bootmaker. I had to force your man to take on the assignment. He's most loyal to you," she hastened to add lest he think Flannaghan had somehow betrayed him.

"No, Princess," Flannaghan argued. "I begged you to let me take on the assignment."

Colin rolled his eyes heavenward. "What made you think of the idea?" he asked.

She looked surprised by his question. "You have a limp . . . at night, when you're tired, you do tend to limp a little. Colin, you are aware you favor your right leg, aren't you?"

He almost laughed. "Yes, I'm aware."

"Do you agree you're a fairly intelligent man?"

She was turning his words back on him. He held his frown. "Yes."

"Then why didn't you try to reason why you were limping?"

He lifted his shoulders in a shrug. "A shark took a bite out of my leg. Call me daft, Alesandra, but I assumed that was the reason I limped."

She shook her head. "That was the reason for the injury," she explained. "I looked at the bottoms of your shoes. The left heel was barely worn on each pair. Then, of course, I knew what to do." She let out a sigh. "I do wish you weren't so sensitive about this issue."

She turned to look at Caine. "He is sensitive, though. Have you, by chance, noticed?"

Caine nodded.

She smiled because she'd gained his agreement. "He won't even talk about it."

"He's talking about it now," Caine told her.

She whirled around to look at her husband. "You are talking about it," she cried out.

She looked thrilled. Colin didn't know what to make of that. "Yes," he agreed.

"Then will you let me sleep in your bed every night?"

Caine laughed. Alesandra ignored him. "I know why you go back to your room. It's because your leg hurts and you need to walk. I'm right, aren't I, Colin?"

He didn't answer her.

"Will you please say something?"

"Thank you."

She was thoroughly confused. "Why are you thanking me?"

"For the insert."

"You aren't angry?"

"No."

She was astonished by his attitude.

He was humbled by her thoughtfulness.

They stared at each other a long minute.

"You aren't angry with Flannaghan, are you?" she asked.

"No."

"Why aren't you angry with me?"

"Because you had my best interests at heart."

"What a nice thing to say."

Colin laughed. She smiled. Flannaghan came running into the study and thrust a glass of water at Caine. His attention was centered on Alesandra. She saw his worried expression and whispered, "He isn't angry."

Caine drew her attention when he announced he was going home. Colin didn't take his gaze off his wife when he bid his brother good night.

"Alesandra, stay here. Flannaghan will see Caine out."

"As you wish, husband."

"God, I love it when you're humble."

"Why?"

"It's so damned rare."

She shrugged. He laughed again. "Is there something else you wanted to tell me?" he asked.

Her shoulders slumped. The man was too cunning by half. "Oh, all right," she muttered. "I talked to Sir Winters about your leg to gain suggestions. We spoke in confidence, of course."

Colin raised an eyebrow. "Suggestions for what?"

"For ways to make it feel better. I made a list of his ideas. Would you like me to fetch it for you?"

"Later," he answered. "Now, then, is there something else you wanted to tell me?"

The question covered a broad range of topics. Colin decided he'd have to remember to ask her that question every other week in future so that he could find out what she'd been up to.

She wasn't about to blurt out another confession until she knew what he was fishing for. "Could you be more specific please?"

Her question told him there were still more secrets. "No," he answered. "You know what I'm asking. Tell me."

She threaded her fingers through her hair and walked over to the side of his desk. "Dreyson told you, didn't he?"

He shook his head. "Then how did you find out?"

"I'll explain how I found out after you tell me," he promised.

"You already know," she countered. "You just want to make me feel guilty, don't you? Well, it won't wash. I didn't cancel the order for the steam vessel and it's too late for you to interfere. Besides, you told me I could do whatever I wanted with my inheritance. I ordered the ship for myself. Yes, I did. I've always wanted one. If, however, you and Nathan would like to use my ship every now and again, I would be happy to share it with you."

"I told Dreyson to cancel the order," he reminded her.

"I told him Albert had decided he wanted it."

"What the hell else have you kept from me?"

"You didn't know?"

"Alesandra . . ."

"You're pricking my temper, Colin. You still don't understand how much you hurt me," she announced. "Can you imagine how I felt when I heard Nathan say that he and you were all set to use Sara's inheritance to build the company? You made such an issue out of turning your back on my inheritance."

Colin pulled her onto his lap. She immediately put her arms around his neck and smiled at him.

He frowned at her. "The money was put aside by the king for both Nathan and Sara," he explained.

"My father put his money away for me and my husband."

She had him there, he thought to himself. She knew it, too. "Your father wonders why he's still in charge of my funds, Colin. It's embarrassing. You should take over the task. I would help."

His smile was filled with tenderness. "How about if I helped you manage it?"

"That would be nice." She leaned against him. "I love you, Colin."

"I love you, too. Sweetheart, isn't there something else you want to tell me?"

She didn't answer him. Colin reached into his pocket and pulled out her list. She snuggled closer to him.

He opened the paper. "I want you to be able to talk to me about anything," he explained. "From this moment on."

She started to pull away from him but he tightened his hold on her. "I made it impossible for you to talk about my leg, didn't I?"

"Yes."

"I'm sorry about that, sweetheart. Now stay still while I answer your questions for you, all right?"

"I don't have any questions?"

"Hush, love," he ordered. He held her close with one hand and lifted the sheet of paper with the other. He silently read her first order and then said, "I have listened to your concerns about Victoria, haven't I?"

"Yes, but why . . ."

Colin squeezed her. "Be patient," he commanded. He read the second order. "I will promise to soften in my attitude toward your inheritance." In brackets Alesandra had written the word *stubborn*. He let out a sigh. "And I won't be mule-headed about it."

The third order made him smile. She had instructed him not to wait five years to realize he loved her.

Since he'd already complied with that command, he moved on to the next order. He should try to be happy he was going to become a father and he shouldn't blame her because she was interfering with his schedule.

Could pregnant wives become nuns? Colin decided to answer the last first.

"Alesandra?"

"Yes?"

He kissed the top of her head. "No," he whispered.

The laughter in his voice confused her. So did his denial. "No, what, husband?"

"Pregnant wives can't become nuns."

She would have jumped off his lap if he'd let her. He held her tight against him until she finally calmed down.

She did a lot of ranting and raving, too. "You knew . . . all the time. . . . Oh, God, it was the list. You found it and that's why you told me you loved me."

Colin forced her chin up and kissed her hard. "I knew I loved you before I read your list," he told her. "You're going to have to trust me, Alesandra. Trust your heart, too."

"But . . ."

His mouth silenced her protest. When he pulled back, she had tears in her eyes. "I'm going to ask you one last time," he said. "Do you have something to tell me?"

She slowly nodded. He looked so arrogantly pleased. Dear God, how she loved him. From the way he was looking at her, she knew he loved her just as much.

Oh, yes, he was happy about the baby. She didn't have any worries about that. His hand had dropped to her stomach and he was gently patting her. She didn't think he was even aware of what he was doing. The action was telling, though. He was caressing his unborn son or daughter.

"Answer me," he commanded in a rough whisper.

He was looking so fiercely intent now. She smiled in reaction. Colin always tried to be so serious, so disciplined. She loved that trait in him, of course, but she found she delighted in making him forget himself every now and again.

She did love to tease him and all because he reacted with such surprise.

Colin couldn't hold on to his patience any longer. "Answer me, Alesandra."

"Yes, Colin. I do have something to tell you. I've decided to become a nun."

He looked like he wanted to throttle her. His glare made her laugh. She wrapped her arms around him again and tucked her head under his chin.

"We're going to have a baby," she whispered. "Have I mentioned that yet?"

# Chapter
# 14

An endless stream of visitors demanded Colin's attention during the following two weeks. Sir Richards was there so often he might as well have had his own bedroom. Caine stopped by every afternoon, and so did Nathan. Alesandra didn't see much of her husband during the daylight hours, but the evenings belonged to her. Colin would catch her up on all the latest developments in his investigation directly after dinner.

Dreyson proved to be very helpful. He found out a policy had been taken out on Victoria's life just four months before her disappearance. The beneficiary named on the contract was her brother, Neil. The policy was underwritten by Morton and Sons.

Through his sources, Colin found out Neil would inherit his sister's sizable dowry, set aside on the day she was born by a distant aunt, if she didn't return to London to claim it.

Sir Richards had joined them at the dinner table. He listened while Colin explained to Alesandra what he'd learned, then interjected a comment of his own.

"Until a body is found he can't collect the insurance money or the inheritance. If he's the culprit and his motive was money, why would he go to such lengths to hide her body?"

"It doesn't make much sense," Colin agreed. "He has a large bank account of his own."

Sir Richards agreed with a nod. "He might think he needed more," he said. "Alesandra did tell us Neil didn't particularly like his sister," he added. "There's another bit of damning evidence wagging its finger in Neil's direction, too, circumstantial though it is. You see, he offered for Roberta six years ago but she turned him down in favor of the viscount. Rumor has it Neil continued to pursue her even after she was married. Some believe she was having an affair with him. And there, you see, is the tie-in between the two women."

"I can't imagine any woman wanting to be with Neil Perry," Alesandra whispered. "He isn't at all . . . charming."

"Have you received any other gifts?" he asked.

She shook her head. "The gift I ordered made for Nathan and Sara arrived this morning. Colin almost destroyed the thing in a rage before he remembered I'd ordered the ship. Thankfully, he only shredded the box."

"You failed to mention you had the gift outlined with strips of gold," Colin said. "It would take five men to destroy it."

Caine interrupted the talk when he came rushing into the dining room.

"They found Victoria's body!"

Colin reached over and covered Alesandra's hand. "Where?" he asked.

"In a field about an hour's ride from here. A cropper happened upon the grave. Wolves had . . ." Caine stopped in midsentence. The look on Alesandra's face showed her anguish. Caine wasn't about to add to her heartache by going into more vivid detail.

"The authorities are certain it's Victoria?" she asked.

Her eyes filled with tears, but she forced herself to remain in control. She could weep for Victoria later—pray for her soul, too—and she would do both . . . after the man who'd hurt her had been caught.

"The jewelry she wore . . . it helped with the identification," Caine explained.

Sir Richards wanted to see where the body was found. He pushed his chair back and started to stand up.

"It's too dark to see anything," Caine told the director. He pulled out the chair next to Alesandra and sat down. "You're going to have to wait until tomorrow."

"Who owns the field where she was found?" Colin asked.

"Neil Perry."

"How convenient," Colin said.

"It's too damned convenient," Caine agreed.

"We take what we're given," Richards announced. "Then we pull it apart to find the truth."

"When will you have your men start digging?" Colin asked.

"Tomorrow at first light."

"Digging?" Alesandra asked. "Victoria's already been found. Why would you . . ."

"We want to see what else we'll find," Richards explained.

"You believe Roberta might also be buried there?"

"I do."

"So do I," Caine interjected.

"Neil wouldn't be so stupid as to bury his victims on his own land," she said.

"We believe he's probably the culprit," Caine said. "We don't believe he's clever."

She grabbed hold of Caine's hand so he would give her his full attention. "But that's just it," she argued. "He's been clever until now, hasn't he? Why would he bury either woman on his own land? It doesn't make sense. You're forgetting something else, too."

"What's that?" Caine asked.

"All of you are assuming there are only two women. There could be more."

"She's got a point, Caine," Colin agreed. "Sweetheart, let go of my brother."

She realized she was squeezing Caine's hand then and quickly let go. She turned her attention to the director. "What are your other plans?"

"Neil will certainly be charged," he announced. "It's just a start, Alesandra. Like you, I'm not completely convinced he's the one. I don't like conveniences."

She was satisfied with his answer. She excused herself from the table. Caine stood up and pulled her chair back for her. She turned to thank him. She was surprised when he put his hands on her shoulders and leaned down. Before she could ask him what he was doing, he kissed her on her forehead.

"Congratulations, Alesandra," he said. "Jade and I are both very happy over the news."

"What news?" Sir Richards asked.

She let Colin tell him. She smiled up at Caine. "We're both very happy, too," she whispered.

Richards was shaking Colin's hand when she started toward the entrance. A sudden thought made her stop. She turned around to look at Colin again. "Don't you still wonder why three women in your family were chosen? You did throw Neil out," she reminded him. "Would that make him angry enough to seek revenge?"

Colin didn't think so. She left him with Caine and Richards to mull over the possibilities and went upstairs. Flannaghan was waiting for her in the study. His younger sister, Megan, was waiting with him.

"Here she is," Flannaghan announced when Alesandra walked inside.

"Princess Alesandra, this is Megan," he announced. "She's eager to see to your needs."

Flannaghan nudged his sister in her side. She immediately stepped forward and made an awkward curtsy. "I would be happy to serve you, milady."

"Not milady," Flannaghan instructed. "Princess."

Megan nodded. She looked very like her brother. She had the same coloring, and her smile was almost identical to Flannaghan's. She looked up at her brother with true adoration, and such devotion warmed Alesandra's heart.

"We're going to get along just fine," she predicted.

"I'll teach her what she needs to know," Flannaghan announced.

Julie Garwood

Alesandra nodded. "Where is Kate? I thought we had agreed she would start helping me with the correspondence tomorrow?"

"She's still packing up her things," Flannaghan explained. "Have you mentioned my sisters to your husband yet?"

"No," Alesandra answered. "Don't worry so, Flannaghan. He'll be as pleased as I am."

"I've put Megan in the last bedroom along the hallway upstairs," Flannaghan said. "Kate can have the room next to hers if that is all right."

"Yes, of course."

"It's a fine room, milady," Megan blurted out. "And the first I've ever had all to myself."

"Princess, not milady," her brother corrected again.

Alesandra didn't dare laugh. She didn't want to undermine Flannaghan's position.

"We'll start your training tomorrow, Megan. I believe I'll go along to bed now. If you need anything, ask your brother. He'll take good care of you. He certainly takes good care of Colin and me. I don't know what we would do without him."

Flannaghan flushed over her praise. Megan looked properly impressed.

Colin laughed when she told him about the additions to their staff. He was quick to sober, however, upon hearing his ill-paid butler was the sole support of both Megan and Kate. He'd known Flannaghan's parents were both dead—Sterns had told him so when he'd implored Colin to hire his nephew, but he hadn't mentioned the two sisters. No, he hadn't known, and he was thankful Alesandra had taken the sisters in. He increased Flannaghan's salary the following morning.

Flowers arrived for Alesandra that afternoon. Dreyson had sent them with a note filled with sympathy over her tragic loss.

Alesandra was arranging the flowers in a white porcelain vase while Colin scowled over the note. "What's this about?" he asked.

"Albert died."

Colin burst into laughter. She smiled. "I thought you would be pleased."

"It's damned callous of you to laugh, Colin."

Caine stood in the entrance of the dining room, scowling at his brother. He turned to Alesandra to offer his sympathy and only then realized she was smiling.

"Isn't Albert a good friend of yours?"

"Not anymore," Colin drawled out.

Caine shook his head. Colin laughed again. "He never existed," he explained. "Alesandra made him up so Dreyson would take her stock orders."

"But he gave me sound advice. Damn it, I'm going to miss him. I . . ."

"Alesandra gave you *her* sound advice. Ask her in future," Colin suggested.

Caine looked astonished. Alesandra gave her husband an I-told-you-so look before turning back to his brother.

"Dreyson was far more willing to talk to me about investments because he believed I was sending the information on to Albert. Now he'll talk to Colin whenever he hears of good opportunities. He would be very upset if he found out Albert never existed and for that reason I beg you not to say anything."

"Why bother with a middleman?" Caine asked, still not certain if he believed her or not.

"Because men like to talk to men," she patiently explained.

"Why are you here?" Colin asked, switching the topic then. "Do you have more news?"

"Yes," Caine answered, drawn back now to his reason for calling. "They found Lady Roberta's body about fifty yards away from Victoria's grave."

"Dear God," Alesandra whispered.

Colin put his arm around his wife's shoulders. "Were there any others found?"

Caine shook his head. "They haven't found any so far but they're still looking. Neil's being charged with the second murder. He sent a request through his barrister to talk to Alesandra."

"It's out of the question."

"Colin, I think I should talk to him."

"No."

"Please be reasonable," she pleaded. "Don't you want to make certain he's the one?"

Colin let out a sigh. "Then I'll go and talk to him."

"Neil doesn't like you," she reminded her husband.

"I don't give a damn if he likes me or not," Colin replied. She turned to Caine. "Colin threw him out," she explained. "I can't imagine he would want to talk to him now."

"You'd be surprised how a man changes in Newgate Prison," Caine said. "I imagine he'll talk to anyone he thinks might be able to help him."

"You aren't going, Alesandra," Colin told her. "However," he hastened to add when she tried to argue with him again, "if you write down your questions I'll ask Neil whatever it is you want to know."

"I already have a list," she replied.

"Then go and get it for me."

"Colin, I'm going with you," Caine announced.

Alesandra knew it was useless to continue to argue with her husband. From the look in his eyes she knew he was going to be stubborn about this. She went upstairs to fetch her list, added a few more questions to the sheet of paper, and then hurried downstairs again.

"We'll take my carriage," Caine told his brother.

Colin nodded. He took the list from his wife, put it in his pocket, and kissed her good-bye. "Stay home," he ordered. "I shouldn't be gone long."

"She can't stay home," Caine interjected. "I've forgotten. Nathan's coming by to collect her in about an hour."

"Why?" Colin asked.

"Jade wants your wife to meet Sara," he explained. "Mother and Catherine are at the house, too."

"Nathan will be with Alesandra?" Colin asked.

"Yes."

Alesandra turned and started up the steps. She was in a hurry to change her dress. She wanted to look her best when she met Sara.

"Should I take our gift along?" she called down to her husband.

Colin was starting out the doorway. He told her that was a fine idea, but she could tell from the shrug in his answer he was barely paying attention to her.

Megan helped her change her clothes. Flannaghan's sister was nervous—awkward, too—but her enthusiasm to please her mistress was most apparent.

Nathan came to collect her a short while later. Alesandra carried the gift Flannaghan had rewrapped for her down the stairs. She handed the box to Nathan to carry for her but didn't explain what it was.

Colin's partner seemed preoccupied and barely said a word to her on the way over to Caine's town house.

She finally asked him if something was wrong.

"I've been going over the books," he explained, "and trying to figure out where all the entries came from. Colin's the one with a head for figures," he added. "I'm trying to keep the ledgers current but it's difficult."

"I entered the invoices while Colin was ill," she said. "Perhaps I made a mistake. Are you thinking the balances are wrong?"

Nathan shook his head. "Colin told me you caught him up," he said. He smiled then and stretched his long legs out. She moved her skirts out of his way so he would have more room.

"I couldn't find the invoices for some of the deposits made," he said.

She finally understood what was bothering him. The money Colin had transferred into the company account came from payment for services rendered for the War Department.

"There aren't any receipts for four entries," she remarked.

"Yes, four exactly," Nathan agreed with a nod. "Do you

know where Colin got the money? It doesn't make sense. The income from the ships is accounted for and I know he doesn't have a separate income."

"Have you asked him about it?"

Nathan shook his head. "I just discovered the puzzle this morning."

"Do you and Colin . . . share everything? I mean to ask, does either of you keep secrets?"

"We're partners, Alesandra. If we can't trust each other, who in thunder can we trust?"

He gave her a piercing look. "You know where the money came from, don't you?"

She slowly nodded. "Colin should probably tell you—not me," she reasoned aloud.

"Did the money come from you?"

"No."

"Then who?"

He wasn't going to let it drop. Because Nathan wasn't just Colin's partner but his best friend as well, Alesandra decided it wouldn't be disloyal to tell him.

"You must promise me not to say a word to Caine or anyone else in Colin's family," she began.

Nathan nodded. His curiosity was pricked, of course. "I promise."

"Colin was doing some work on the side to increase the accounts."

Nathan leaned forward. "Who did he work for?"

"Sir Richards."

His roar almost knocked her gift off the seat. Nathan had appeared to be only mildly interested and for that reason his furious reaction was a bit stunning. She visibly jumped. She flinched, too, when he muttered a dark expletive.

Nathan regained his control and apologized for using the foul word. The look in his eyes remained chilling.

"I believe it would be best if you let Colin explain," she stammered out. "He doesn't work for Richards any longer, Nathan."

"You're certain?"

She nodded. "I'm very certain."

Nathan let out a long sigh and leaned back. "Thank you for telling me."

"Colin would have told you, wouldn't he?"

The worry in his voice was very apparent. Nathan thought she was having second thoughts about telling him. He smiled. "Yes, he would have told me. In fact, I'll ask him about the missing invoices tonight."

He deliberately turned the topic so she would quit fretting. They arrived at Caine's town house a few minutes later.

Alesandra met Flannaghan's uncle Sterns when he opened the door for them. He was an extremely dour-faced elderly gentleman, stiff as starch in his manners, but there was a true sparkle in his eyes when he greeted her. Flannaghan, it seemed, had been singing her praises, and Sterns made mention that he'd just heard both Megan and Kate were also in her household now.

The doors to the salon were wide open. Caine's daughter spotted her first and came running into the entrance. The four-year-old grabbed hold of Sterns's hand so she wouldn't tumble when she executed a curtsy. Her ladylike behavior was short-lived. The second she'd finished with the bothersome formality, she let go of Sterns and threw herself at her uncle Nathan's legs. She let out a shriek of joy when he lifted her up and tossed her like a hat into the air.

"Thank God for tall ceilings," Sterns remarked.

Nathan heard the comment and laughed. He settled his niece in his arm and followed Alesandra into the salon.

Jade and Catherine were sitting side by side on the settee. The duchess was seated in the chair across from her daughters. All three women rushed to their feet and surrounded Alesandra.

"We just heard the wonderful news," the duchess announced.

Alesandra laughed.

"I heard it from Catherine," said the duchess.

"I heard it from Jade," Catherine interjected.

"I never . . ." Jade began to protest.

"I heard mother giving you her speculations," Catherine admitted then.

"Where is Sara?" Nathan demanded to know.

"She's feeding Joanna," Jade explained. "She'll be down in a minute or two."

Nathan immediately turned to go to his wife. He tried to put Olivia down, but she tightened her hold on his shoulders and announced she was going with him.

Alesandra put the gift box down on the side table and followed her relatives over to the chairs. She sat down next to her mother-in-law. The duchess was dabbing at her eyes with her linen square.

"I'm beside myself with joy," she announced. "Another grandchild. It's such a blessing."

Alesandra beamed with pleasure. The talk centered on children for several minutes. Catherine quickly became bored. Alesandra noticed and decided to change the topic.

"Are you angry with me for telling Colin about the flowers you received?"

"I was angry at first, but then Father explained everything. Then I became afraid. Now that Neil Perry's been locked away, I'm not at all afraid and Father is going to let me go to all the affairs again. Do you realize the season is almost over. I shall die of boredom when I have to go back to the country."

"You will do no such thing," her mother countered.

"I'm going riding in the park with Morgan Atkins today."

"Catherine, I thought we agreed you would decline the invitation and spend the afternoon with your family," her mother reminded her.

"It's only a short ride and everyone will notice if I don't go. Besides, I can see family anytime."

"Is Morgan coming here to collect you?" Jade asked.

Catherine nodded. "He's so divine. Father likes him, too."

Alesandra was uneasy about Catherine going anywhere. Oh, she knew Morgan was a friend of Colin's and would certainly watch out for Catherine, but she still wished her sister-in-law would stay home. Alesandra wasn't convinced Neil was the culprit. She didn't want to alarm her relatives, though. She wished Colin were here. He would know what to do.

He wouldn't let his sister leave. Alesandra came to that conclusion right away. But Colin was cautious to a fault, she thought to herself.

"Catherine, I believe you should stay here with us," Alesandra blurted out.

"Why?"

Why indeed? Alesandra's mind hunted for a reason. She turned to Jade, silently imploring her help.

Caine's wife was very astute. She caught the worry in Alesandra's eyes and immediately voiced her agreement.

"Yes, you should stay with us," she told Catherine. "Sterns will be happy to send a note to Morgan explaining a family matter has come up and you aren't able to keep your appointment."

"But I wish to keep my appointment," Catherine argued. "Mother, this isn't fair. Michelle Marie is going riding with the Earl of Hampton. Her sisters don't tell her what to do."

"We aren't telling you what to do," Alesandra countered. "We just don't want you to go."

"Why not?"

Catherine's frustration made her voice shrill. Thankfully, Alesandra was saved from having to come up with an answer, for Nathan and his wife walked into the room, drawing everyone's attention.

Alesandra literally bounded to her feet. She hurried across the room to meet Sara.

Nathan's wife was a beautiful woman. She had dark brown hair, a flawless complexion, and eyes the color of a clear blue sky. Her smile was enchanting, too. It was filled with warmth.

Nathan introduced her to his wife. Alesandra wasn't certain if she should formally curtsy or take hold of Sara's hand. Her dilemma didn't last long. The woman was openly affectionate. She immediately walked forward and embraced Alesandra.

It wasn't possible to feel awkward around Sara. She treated Alesandra as though she were a long-lost friend.

"Where is Joanna?" Alesandra asked.

"Olivia's bringing her down," Sara explained.

"With Sterns's assistance," Nathan interjected. He turned to his wife then. "Sweetheart, I'm going back upstairs to finish with the ledgers."

Jade called out to Sara and patted the cushion next to her. Alesandra didn't follow. She chased after Nathan. She caught him halfway up the stairs.

"May I please speak to you in private for just a moment?"

"Certainly," Nathan answered. "Will the study do?"

She nodded. She followed him up the rest of the stairs and into the study. Nathan motioned to a chair, but she declined the invitation to sit.

The room was a clutter of maps and ledgers. Nathan had obviously turned Caine's study into a secondary shipping office. She made that mention to him as he walked across the room.

"Caine's library is downstairs," Nathan explained. "He won't let me inside. He won't come inside this room, either," he added with a grin. "My brother-in-law is a fanatic about order. He can't stand the mess. Have a seat, Alesandra, and tell me what's on your mind."

She again declined the invitation to sit. "This will only take a minute," she explained. "Catherine wishes to go riding with Morgan Atkins. He's coming here to fetch her. I don't think it's a good idea to let her go, Nathan, but I can't come up with a suitable argument why. She's very determined."

"Why don't you want her to go?"

She could have gone into a lengthy and surely confusing explanation that wouldn't make any sense at all, but she decided not to waste Nathan's time.

"I'm just uneasy about it," she said. "And I know Colin wouldn't let her go. Neither one of us is convinced Neil Perry is the guilty man, and until we are convinced we don't want Catherine going anywhere. Colin isn't here to tell his sister no, and her mother won't be able to sway her. Will you please handle this? I don't believe Catherine would dare argue with you."

Nathan started for the door. "So Colin doesn't trust this Atkins?"

"Oh, no, I didn't mean to imply that," she said. "Morgan's a friend of Colin's." She lowered her voice when she added, "He's taken over Colin's position in the department under Sir Richards's supervision."

"But you believe Colin wouldn't wish her to go. All right. I'll take care of it."

"What excuse are you going to give her?" Alesandra asked as she hurried after the giant.

"None," Nathan answered. He smiled then, a rascal's smile to be sure. "I don't need a reason. I'll simply tell her she's staying here."

"And if she argues?"

Nathan laughed. "It isn't what I'm going to say to her, it's how I'll say it. Trust me, Alesandra. She won't argue. There are only two women in this world I can't intimidate. My sister and my wife. Don't worry, I'll take care of it."

"Actually, Nathan, there are three. You can't intimidate Jade, Sara, or me."

She smiled over the look of surprise in his eyes but didn't dare laugh.

The duchess was waiting in the foyer to say good-bye to both Alesandra and Nathan. She had an important dinner party to prepare for, she explained. She kissed Alesandra on her cheek, then made Nathan lean down so she could kiss him, too.

Alesandra assumed Catherine was still inside the salon. She turned to go inside before Nathan so she could pretend she hadn't interfered. Catherine was already a little irritated with her because she'd broken her word to her and Alesandra didn't want to add another sin to her list.

Sara was sitting on the settee. Little Olivia sat next to her and was holding the baby in her lap.

"I do hope Joanna turns out to be as pretty as you are," Sara told Olivia.

"Probably she won't," Olivia replied. "She doesn't have enough hair to be as pretty as me."

Jade rolled her eyes heavenward. Sara smiled. "She's still young," she said. "She might grow more."

"Where's Catherine?" Alesandra asked as she crossed the room. "Nathan wants to have a word with her."

"She left a few minutes ago," Jade answered.

Alesandra immediately jumped to the conclusion that Catherine had left with her mother. She sat down next to Olivia to look at the baby.

"Was she very angry we interfered with her plans? She's probably giving her mother a fit right about now. Oh, Sara, Joanna's beautiful. She's so tiny."

"She'll get bigger," Olivia announced. "Babies do. Mama says so."

"Alesandra, Catherine didn't go home with her mother. She left with Morgan. We did try to make her change her mind, but without a valid reason at hand her mother finally relented. Catherine can cry at the drop of a hat, and I believe her mother didn't want a scene."

The baby started fretting. Sara took her daughter into her arms and stood up. "It's time for her nap," she announced. "I'll be right back down. Sterns will snatch her out of my hands as soon as he can. The man's a wonder with infants, isn't he, Jade?"

"He's a wonder with four-year-old's too," Jade replied. She turned her attention to her daughter. "It's time for your nap, too, Olivia."

Her daughter didn't want to leave. Jade insisted. She took Olivia's hand and pulled her along.

"I'm not a baby, Mama."

"I know you're not, Olivia," Jade answered. "And that's why you only take one nap a day. Joanna takes two."

Alesandra sat down on the settee and watched Jade drag her daughter out of the room. Nathan stood in the doorway.

"Do you want me to go after Catherine?" he asked.

She shook her head. "I'm just a worrier, Nathan. I'm certain it will be all right."

The front door opened just then and both Caine and Colin walked inside. Caine stood in the foyer talking to

Nathan, but Colin immediately went into the salon to his wife. He sat down beside her, hauled her up against him, and kissed her.

"Well?" she demanded when he began to nuzzle on the side of her neck and didn't immediately tell her what happened.

"He's probably guilty," Colin announced.

Caine and Nathan walked inside to join them. Alesandra nudged Colin so he would quit nibbling on her earlobe. Her husband let out a sigh before straightening away from her. He smiled when he saw her blush.

"He had motive and opportunity," Colin remarked then.

Caine heard his brother's comment. "I think we're trying to make this more complicated than it really is. I'll admit it's . . . convenient."

Colin nodded. He pulled out his list. "All right, sweetheart. Here are your answers. First, Neil denies that he went with his sister to meet a man calling himself her admirer. Second, he swears he didn't know anything about an insurance policy. And third, he vehemently denies being involved with Lady Roberta."

"I expected those answers," Alesandra announced.

"He wasn't much of a brother to Victoria," Caine interjected. He sat down and let out a loud yawn.

"What about my other question to Neil?"

"Which one was that?" Colin asked.

"I wanted the names of the suitors Victoria turned down. He mentioned there were three when he visited me and I thought those rejections might be important. Honestly, Colin, did you forget to ask him?"

"No, I didn't forget. There was Burke—he's married now so he wouldn't count—and Mazelton."

"He's getting married soon," Caine interjected.

"And?" Alesandra asked when Colin didn't continue. "Who was the third man?"

"Morgan Atkins," said Caine. Colin nodded. Alesandra glanced over at Nathan. He was frowning. "Colin, isn't Morgan a friend of yours?" he asked.

"Hell, no," Colin answered. "He probably wants to throttle me about now. He blames me for a situation that developed and he messed up."

Nathan leaned forward. "Would he blame you enough to come after your wife?"

Colin's expression changed. He started to shake his head, then stopped himself. "It's a possibility," he admitted. "Remote, but . . . what are you thinking, Nathan?"

His partner turned to look at Alesandra.

They said her name in unison. "Catherine."

# Chapter

# 15

❧

"**W**e did not panic."

"Yes, we did," Alesandra replied. She smiled at her husband while she contradicted him, then turned her attention back to her task.

Both she and her husband were in bed. Colin was stretched out on his back and had pillows propped behind his head. Alesandra knelt at the foot of the bed. She wrung out another long strip of cotton and applied it to her husband's leg. The heat from the water made her fingers red, but the mild discomfort was certainly rewarded by Colin's loud sighs of pleasure.

Her husband had barely grumbled when she had handed him the list of suggestions Sir Winters had made. He refused both pain medication and liquor, but he took the time to explain why. He didn't wish to become dependent on either and so he went without, regardless of how painful the leg became.

The hot cloths helped take the cramp out of his calf, however, and as long as she kept him busy thinking about something else, he forgot to be sensitive or embarrassed about the scars.

He certainly wasn't embarrassed about the rest of his body. He was a bit of an exhibitionist, too. Alesandra wore a prim pink and white high-necked sleeping gown and matching robe. Colin wasn't wearing anything. His hands were stacked behind his head, and when he let out another long sigh, she decided her husband was thoroughly uninhibited with her . . . and just as content.

"I will admit Caine did run around a bit, but only because there was the slightest chance Morgan might somehow be involved."

"Ran around a bit? Surely you jest, Colin. The man picked up his wife and tossed her into his open carriage, then went racing toward the park after Catherine."

Colin grinned over the picture. "All right, he did panic. I didn't, however."

She let out an inelegant snort. "Then I didn't see you leap over the side of their carriage so you wouldn't be left behind?"

"Better safe than sorry, Alesandra."

"And all for nought," she said. "Catherine would have died of mortification if Caine and you had caught up with her. Thank heaven Morgan took her home before her brothers spotted her. This is all my fault, by the way."

"What's all your fault?"

"I got everyone all worked up," she admitted. "I shouldn't have made your relatives so worried."

"They're your relatives, too," he reminded her.

She nodded. "Why do you think Victoria turned Morgan down?"

The switch in topics didn't throw Colin. He was getting used to the way his wife's mind raced from one thought to another. She was an extremely logical woman—damned intelligent, too—and for those reasons he no longer shrugged off any concerns she might have. If she wasn't completely convinced Neil was the culprit, then he wasn't completely convinced either.

"Morgan's up to his neck in debt and could very well lose his estates."

"How do you know that?"

"Richards told me," he answered. "Maybe Victoria thought she could do better."

"Yes," Alesandra agreed. "That is possible, I suppose."

"Sweetheart, let's go to bed."

She scooted off the bed and put the bowl of water on the bench near the window. Then she removed the wet strips from his leg, folded them, and put them next to the bowl.

"Colin, are you feeling guilty because you wouldn't listen to me when I tried to talk to you about Victoria?"

"Hell, yes, I'm feeling guilty. Every time you brought up the topic, I told you to leave it alone."

"Good."

He opened one eye to look at her. "Good? You want me to feel guilty?"

She smiled. "Yes," she answered. She took off her robe, draped it over the edge of the bed, and began unbuttoning her gown. "It's good because I now have the upper hand in negotiating."

He grinned over her choice of words and her expression. She looked so serious. "What exactly do you want to negotiate?"

"Our sleeping arrangement. I'm going to sleep in your bed all night, Colin. It won't do you any good to argue."

Alesandra quit trying to get her sleeping gown off and hurried to get into bed. She thought it would be more difficult for Colin to deny her demand if she was already settled next to him. She pulled the covers over her, fluffed her pillow, and then said, "If guilt doesn't sway you, then I'll have to remind you of my delicate condition. You won't deny the mother of your child anything."

Colin laughed. He rolled to his side and put his arm around his wife. "You're quite the little negotiator," he drawled out. "Love, it isn't that I don't want you to sleep with me, but I get up off and on all night long and I don't want to wake you. You need your rest."

"You won't wake me," she replied. "A nice long letter arrived from Mother Superior today," she said then, turning the topic. "I left it on your desk so you could read it. The roses are in bloom all around Stone Haven now. Perhaps next year, when you take me to see our castle, all the flowers will be in their full glory. It's quite a sight, husband."

"Lord, I really do own a castle, don't I?"

She cuddled closer to his side. "Mother Superior was able to get the funds released from the bankers. I never doubted her ability, of course. She can be very persuasive when she wants to."

Colin was pleased with the news. He didn't want the general to get even a fraction of Alesandra's inheritance. "Dreyson will quit worrying," he remarked. "Once the money is safe in the bank here . . . ."

"Good Lord, Colin, you don't believe Mother Superior will send the funds on to us, do you?"

"I did think . . ."

Her laughter stopped him. "What is so amusing?"

"Getting the money away from the general wasn't difficult at all, but trying to get the Mother Superior to release the funds will be quite impossible."

"Why?" he asked, still confused.

"Because she's a nun," she answered. "And nuns solicit funds. They don't give them up. The general wasn't any match for the mother superior, and neither are you, husband. God wants them to have the money," she added. "Besides, it was a gift, remember? And they can certainly put the money to good use. Dreyson will pout for a little while and then he'll forget all about it."

Colin leaned down and kissed her. "I love you, Alesandra."

She'd been waiting to hear that declaration and immediately pounced on it. "Perhaps you do love me just a little, but certainly not as much as Nathan loves Sara."

Her announcement astonished him. He leaned up on one elbow so he could see her expression. She wasn't smiling, but there was a definite sparkle in her eyes. The little woman was up to something, all right.

"Why would you say such a thing?"

She wasn't the least affected by the growl in his voice or the scowl on his face. "I'm negotiating again," she explained.

"What is it you want now?" Colin was having difficulty controlling his frown. He wanted to laugh.

"You and Nathan were going to use Sara's gift from the king, and I ask—nay, I demand—you take the exact amount from my inheritance. It's only fair, Colin."

"Alesandra . . ."

"I don't like being slighted, husband."

"Slighted? Where in God's name did you come up with that notion?"

"I'm really very sleepy now. Think about the fairness in my request and let me know tomorrow. Good night, Colin."

*Request?* He scoffed over that word. She'd demanded, and that was that. He could tell her mind was set, and she was simply too stubborn for her own good. She wasn't going to let up on the issue, either. From the tone of her voice he knew her feelings had somehow been injured over what she considered a slight.

"I'll think about it," he finally promised.

She didn't hear him. She was already sound asleep. Colin blew out the candles, pulled his wife close, and fell asleep minutes later.

The household hadn't completely settled down for the night. Flannaghan was still downstairs putting the finishing touches on his sister's work. He had given Meg the task of dusting the salon and was now diligently cleaning the spots she'd missed. Flannaghan was a worrier, a perfectionist as well, and until both his sisters learned the routine of the household he would continue to scrutinize their work to make certain it was up to his standards.

It was after one in the morning when he finally finished with the salon and blew out the candles. He'd just reached the foyer when a knock sounded at the front door.

Because of the late hour, Flannaghan didn't open the door to see who was there. He peeked out the side window first, recognized his employer's friend, and then unbolted the latch.

Morgan Atkins rushed inside. Before Flannaghan could explain that both Colin and Alesandra had already retired for the night, Morgan said, "I know it's late, but this is an emergency and I've got to see Colin right away. Sir Richards will be here in a few minutes."

"But milord has already gone to bed," Flannaghan stammered out.

"Wake him," Morgan snapped. He softened his voice when he added, "We have a crisis on our hands. He'll want to know what has happened. Be quick about it, man. Richards will be here any moment now."

Flannaghan didn't argue with the earl. He immediately turned to run up the steps. Morgan followed him. Flannaghan assumed the earl wished to wait in the study. He half turned to ask him to take a seat in the salon.

A blinding light exploded inside his head. The pain was so intense, so consuming, it overwhelmed him. There wasn't time to shout a warning, or enough strength to fight. Flannaghan was whirled into darkness the second the blow was delivered to the back of his head.

He fell backward. Morgan grasped him under his arms so the unconscious man wouldn't make any noise falling down the steps, then propped him against the banister.

He stood there staring down at the butler a long minute to make certain he hadn't just stunned him, then, satisfied he wouldn't wake up anytime soon, he turned his attention to the more important task at hand.

He crept up the stairs. In one pocket was the dagger he planned to use on Alesandra. In the other pocket was the pistol he would use to kill Colin.

His eagerness didn't make him less cautious. He'd replayed his plan over and over again inside his mind to make certain there weren't any flaws.

He was glad now he hadn't given in to his urge and killed her sooner. He'd wanted to . . . oh, yes, he'd wanted to, but he hadn't given in to the urge. Why, he'd even taken out the contract with Morton and Sons, naming Colin as beneficiary of course, so that the husband would be the only one who stood to gain from her death. Oh, yes, he'd been clever about what he was going to do. The princess had intrigued him from the moment he'd met her. Would there be a stronger rush killing royalty?

He smiled in anticipation. In just a few minutes he would have his answer.

He knew which bedroom belonged to Alesandra. He'd found out that interesting fact when he'd called on Colin that first time. He'd met Alesandra in the hallway outside the library, heard her mention she needed to get something from her room, and then watched her hurry down the hallway, past the first doorway and through the second. Oh, he was the clever one, all right. He'd filed that information away for possible future use and now it was going to give him the edge he needed.

He wanted to kill Alesandra first. There was surely a connecting door between the two bedrooms, and if not, then the hallway door would serve him just as well. He wanted to make Alesandra scream with her terror and her pain and watch as Colin rushed into the bedroom to save his beloved wife. Morgan would wait until Colin had taken it all in, had seen the blood pouring from Alesandra's body, and once he'd feasted on the horror and the helplessness in Colin's eyes, then he would kill him with one shot through his heart.

Colin deserved to die a slow, agonizing death, but Morgan didn't dare take such a chance. Colin was a dangerous man, and for that reason alone he would kill him quickly.

Still, the look on his face when he realized his wife was dying would be treasured in Morgan's mind a long, long while. And that would have to be enough, he decided as he slowly made his way down the dark hallway.

He passed the study, then the door to the first chamber, as silent as a cat now, barely breathing at all until he reached the door he'd watched Alesandra open.

He was ready now, composed . . . invincible! And still he waited, more to tease himself with the anticipation of the reward soon to be his than anything else. He listened to the silence for long minutes . . . waiting . . . letting the fever catch hold of him, burn him, strengthen him.

They both deserved to die—Alesandra because she was a woman, of course, and Colin because he had ruined his chances for success with the War Department. Richards didn't trust him anymore, and it was Colin's fault he hadn't succeeded. If Colin had gone along with him on the assignment, he wouldn't have given in to the fever raging inside him when he'd spotted the Frenchman's sister. He wouldn't have thought about how smooth her skin had looked or noticed the innocent vulnerability in her eyes. He would have been able to control the need to touch her with his blade in his hands. . . . But Colin hadn't gone with him, and luck hadn't been on his side that time. The brother returned from town earlier than scheduled and had come upon him while he was sliding his blade in and out, in and out, in his own mating ritual that gave him such a rush of pleasure. The screams had alerted the man—those necessary, thrilling screams that fed his passion—and if Colin had been there both the sister and her brother would still be alive. He would have been able to control himself—yes, yes, he would have—and, oh, God, she'd been so sweet. . . .

Her body had felt like butter against his steel erection, and he knew Alesandra's body would feel just as soft. Her blood would be hot and sticky as it spurted over his hands, as hot and sticky . . .

He didn't dare wait any longer. After Richards told him Colin and he had both come to the conclusion he wasn't suited for their line of work, Morgan had pretended disappointment. Inside he raged with fury. How dare they think him inferior? How dare they?

He'd made up his mind then and there to kill both of them. He'd been so terribly clever with his plans, too. Colin and Richards would both die in tragic accidents, of course, but the plans changed today when he'd taken Colin's sister riding in the park and she'd told him Alesandra had tried to talk her out of going.

The stupid chit told her every thought. Morgan knew then that they were becoming suspicious of him. There wasn't a shred of proof to link him to any of the women . . . was there? No, no, it was wrong of him to think of himself as vulnerable. He was far too cunning to ever give in to self-doubt.

He had immediately changed his plans, however. He'd worked every detail out. He would kill Alesandra for the sheer pleasure involved, then kill Colin, and on his way out he would make certain the butler never awakened.

No one was going to be able to point the finger at him. He had the perfect alibi. He was spending the night with the bitch Lorraine, and she would tell anyone who asked that he had never left her bed. He'd given her a large dose of laudanum mixed in with her drink and slipped out the back window of the whore's cottage. When she awakened from her drug-induced sleep, he would be back by her side.

Oh, yes, he'd thought of everything. He allowed himself to smile with satisfaction. He pulled the dagger out of his pocket and then reached for the doorknob.

Colin heard the squeak of the door as it opened. He was already awake and was just about to get out of bed to walk off the throbbing cramping in his leg when the muffled sound gained his attention.

He didn't waste any time waiting to hear any more noises. His instincts were screaming a warning. Someone was inside Alesandra's bedroom now and he knew it wasn't any of his staff. His servants wouldn't dare enter either bedroom without begging entrance first.

Colin moved with the speed of lightning, yet didn't make a sound. He removed the loaded pistol he kept in the drawer of the nightstand, then turned back to his wife. He clamped one hand over her mouth and dragged her across the bed. His gaze and his pistol stayed centered on the connecting door.

Alesandra came awake with a start. The moonlight filtering through the windows was bright enough for her to see the look on her husband's face. His expression was terrifying. Her mind instantly cleared. Something was terribly wrong. Colin finally removed his hand from her mouth and motioned for her to go across the room. He never looked directly at her. His attention continued to be focused on the door to her chamber.

She tried to walk in front of him. He wouldn't let her. He grabbed hold of her arm and gently pushed her behind him. He followed her across the bedroom, his back to her all the while, then pushed her into the narrow corner between the wall and the heavy wardrobe. He stood in front of her, protecting her from direct attack.

She didn't have any idea how long they stood there. It seemed an eternity to her and yet she guessed only a few minutes actually had passed.

And then the door slowly opened. A shadow spilled across the carpet. A blur followed. The intruder didn't creep into the chamber but ran with a demon's speed and determination.

The low, guttural cry he made sent chills down Alesandra's spine. She squeezed her eyes shut and began to pray.

Morgan held a knife high above his head in one hand and a pistol in his other hand. Because he'd run into the room he'd almost reached the side of the bed before his mind registered the fact that it was empty. The sound he was making, that god-awful mewing, inhuman sound he couldn't seem to control, suddenly turned into an outraged roar very like that of an animal being denied its prey. Morgan knew, even before he started to turn, that Colin was there, waiting for him. He knew without a doubt he had only a second at best to save himself, but he was so very clever, so superior . . . he was certain the second was all he needed.

He was, after all, invincible. In one fluid motion he whirled, his pistol at the ready, his finger caressing the spring . . .

His death was instantaneous. The shot from Colin's pistol entered Morgan's head through his left temple. He collapsed to the floor, his eyes wide open, his weapons still clutched in his hands.

"Don't move, Alesandra."

Colin's command was harsh, clipped. She nodded, then realized his back faced her and he couldn't see her agreement. Her hands started aching. She had been clutching them tight against her bosom. She forced herself to relax.

"Be careful," she whispered in a voice so low she doubted Colin could hear her.

He walked over to the body, kicked the pistol out of Morgan's hand, then knelt down on one knee to make certain he was dead.

He let out a long sigh. His heart was pounding a furious beat. "Bastard," he muttered as he stood up. He turned back to Alesandra and reached out his hand to her. She scooted out of the corner, her gaze locked on Morgan Atkins, and slowly walked over to her husband. Colin pulled her into his arms, blocking her view.

"Don't look at him," he ordered.

"Is he dead?"

"Yes."

"Did you mean to kill him?"

"Hell, yes."

She leaned into his side. Colin could feel her trembling. "It's over now, sweetheart. He can't hurt anyone else."

"You're sure he's dead?" Her voice shivered with worry.

"I'm sure," he answered, his voice still harsh with anger.

"Why do you sound so angry?"

Colin took a deep, cleansing breath before he answered her. "It's just a reaction," he said. "The bastard had some grand plans, Alesandra. If you had been sleeping in your chamber . . ."

He couldn't go on. The thought of what could have happened to her was too terrifying for him to think about.

Alesandra took hold of her husband's hand and led him over to the bed. She gently pushed against his shoulders so he would sit down. "But nothing happened to me because of your instincts. You heard him in the other room, didn't you?"

Her voice was a soothing whisper. Colin had to shake his head. His wife was actually comforting him . . . and, damn it all, he actually needed it.

"Put your robe on, sweetheart," he told her. "I don't want you to get chilled. Are you all right?"

He pulled her onto his lap when he asked her that question. "Yes," she answered. "Are you all right?"

"Alesandra, if anything ever happened to you, I don't know what in God's name I would do. I can't imagine life without you."

"I love you, too, Colin."

Her declaration soothed him. He grunted his pleasure while he lifted her off his lap to sit on the bed beside him.

He took another deep breath, then stood up. "I'm going to wake Flannaghan and send him over to Richards. Sit here until . . ."

He quit his order when she bounded to her feet. "I'm going with you. I don't want to stay here with . . . him."

"All right, love." He draped his arm around her shoulders and started for the door.

She was shivering again. Colin didn't want the fear to catch hold of her again.

"Didn't you say you thought Morgan was a real charmer?"

She let out a gasp. "I certainly did not say such a thing. Catherine thought he was charming. I never thought so."

Colin didn't contradict her. He didn't think now was the time to remind her she'd added Morgan's name to her list of marriage candidates. She'd just get more upset.

He'd made the remark to take her attention away from the dead man they had to walk around to get out of the room. The ploy worked. Alesandra barely spared Morgan a glance. She was fully occupied frowning up at her husband. The color had come back into her face, too.

"I was suspicious of Morgan from the moment I met him," she announced. "Well, almost from the moment I met him," she added when Colin looked incredulous.

He didn't argue with her. They reached the hallway before he realized he wasn't wearing any clothes. He went back inside, put on a pair of pants, then pulled a cover off the top of the wardrobe and tossed it over Morgan. He didn't want Alesandra to see the bastard's face again. He didn't particularly want to look at him either.

Flannaghan wasn't in his room. They found him sprawled out on the steps near the foyer. Alesandra was far more upset over her butler's condition than she had been over Morgan's demise. She burst into tears and clung to Flannaghan's hand until Colin convinced her that the servant had just been knocked into a deep sleep. When Flannaghan let out a low groan, she was able to gain control of herself.

An hour later the town house was filled with visitors. Colin had flagged down a passing hack and sent the driver to fetch Sir Richards, Caine, and Nathan. The three men arrived a scant five minutes apart.

Richards questioned Flannaghan first, then sent him up to bed. Alesandra sat on the settee, flanked by Nathan on one side and Caine on the other. The two men were competing with one another in their bid to comfort her. She thought their concern was terribly sweet and therefore put up with Nathan's awkward, stinging pats and Caine's sporadic words of sympathy that didn't make much sense.

Colin walked into the salon and had to shake his head in vexation when he saw the trio. He could barely find his wife. Caine and Nathan had literally pinned her to the settee with their wide shoulders.

"Nathan, my wife can't breathe. Move. You, too, Caine."

"We're comforting her in her time of need," Caine announced.

"Damn right we are," Nathan agreed.

"It must have been quite a fright for you, Princess."

Sir Richards made that evaluation from the doorway. He hurried across the room and sat down in the chair across from her.

The director was barely put together. He'd obviously been in bed when the summons came, for his hair stood on end and his shirt was only partially tucked into his pants. His shoes didn't match, either. They were both black, but only one had the Wellington tassel. The other was bare.

"Of course it was a fright," Caine announced.

Nathan patted her on her knee again in a bid to soothe her. Alesandra looked at Colin. The sparkle in her eyes told him she was close to laughing. He thought she might be smiling, but couldn't tell, for the lower part of her face was hidden behind Caine's and Nathan's shoulders.

"Get up, Nathan. I want to sit next to my wife."

Nathan gave her one last whack before he moved to another chair. Colin immediately sat down and hauled her close to his side.

"How did you kill him?" Nathan asked then.

Caine motioned to Alesandra and shook his head at his brother-in-law. She missed that action. Since no one else seemed inclined to answer Nathan, she decided to. "One clean shot, directly through the left temple," she said.

"Colin has always been extremely accurate," Sir Richards praised.

"Were you surprised it was Morgan, Sir Richards?" she asked.

The director nodded. "I never would have thought he was capable of such foulness. Lord, I put him to work for my department. The way he bungled the one assignment he was given told me he didn't have the instincts. A sister and brother were killed because of his ineptness."

"Maybe it wasn't ineptness at all," Colin said. "Richards, you told me the sister accidentally got in the way. Now I'm wondering if Morgan deliberately killed her. He did file the report, didn't he?"

Richards leaned forward. "I'll ferret out the truth," he announced. "By God I will. What set him off tonight I wonder? Why did he suddenly come out in the open to get Alesandra. He lured the other women to a secluded spot, but came here to get her. Perhaps he'd just become bolder," he added.

"Catherine is probably the reason he took the risk," Caine interjected. "She must have told Morgan that Alesandra tried to stop her from going riding with him. Catherine does like to tell everything she knows. Perhaps Morgan jumped to the conclusion we were suspicious of him."

Nathan shook his head. "The bastard was demented."

Colin agreed with that assessment. "The sounds he made when he came running into the bedroom makes me think he was out of his mind."

"He'd taken a real liking to it."

Caine made that statement in an emphatic tone of voice.

Alesandra was appalled at the very idea that anyone could gain pleasure from another person's pain.

"We might not have ever found out the truth if he hadn't come after Alesandra tonight," Nathan said. "Neil could have gone to the gallows for two crimes he didn't commit."

"What was Morgan's connection with Lady Roberta? Was he involved with her or was she chosen at random?" Alesandra asked.

No one had a quick answer to her question. Richards decided to speculate. "It was common knowledge the viscount and his wife were having difficulties. Perhaps Morgan pounced on Roberta's vulnerability. Notes and gifts from a secret admirer were probably flattering to her."

"We would have caught Morgan eventually," Caine said. "He would have made more mistakes. He was out of control."

"Catherine thought he was charming."

Nathan made that remark with a dark scowl. Caine nodded.

"Yeah," Colin drawled out. "He was a real lady killer."

# Chapter

# 16

∽⟡⟐

**T**hree months had passed since Morgan's death, and Alesandra still thought about the horrible man at least once a day. The mother superior had taught her to pray for the souls of sinners, for they needed prayers far more than saints did, but Alesandra couldn't quite make herself pray for Morgan yet. She tried to put the horror of that night behind her. She never wanted to forget Victoria, though, and did say a prayer for her soul every night before she went to bed. She prayed for Roberta, too. She wanted to believe that both women had suffered their purgatory while on earth and in Morgan's cruel hands and that they were now at peace with their Maker in heaven.

Nathan and Sara were preparing for their journey back to their island home. Caine had invited Alesandra and Colin over to their town house for a farewell dinner with the rest of the family. The food was elegant but also quite rich, and Jade turned green by the time the second course was served. She suddenly bolted from the table and ran out of the dining room. Caine didn't show much sympathy over his wife's obvious distress. He actually grinned with male arrogance.

It wasn't like Caine to be so insensitive, and when Alesandra asked him why he wasn't a bit more concerned about his wife's health, his grin widened into a full-fledged smile. Jade, he explained, was pregnant again, and while she was thrilled over her condition, she disliked her husband hovering over her while she went through the ritualistic morning and evening sickness.

There was a good deal of pounding done to Caine's shoulders. Toasts were given as well, and then Nathan and Colin, with their wives at their sides, went into the salon.

Sara was called above the stairs by Sterns to feed her impatient daughter. Alesandra sat next to her husband and listened to the talk of business between the partners. The topic of the large entry into the company's banking account came up. Nathan wanted to know where in thunder the money had come from. Colin was surprised by the anger in his friend's tone of voice. Alesandra understood Nathan's reaction. She knew he believed Colin had gone back to work for the director.

Colin explained Alesandra's feelings about her inheritance and how she had felt slighted because they had been willing to use Sara's money but not hers.

"The entry is the exact amount Sara would have received if our greedy ruler hadn't decided to keep it for himself," Colin remarked.

Nathan shook his head. "Alesandra, your gift for Joanna was quite enough," he argued. He glanced up to look at the beautiful golden replica of his favorite ship, the *Emerald*, sitting in the center of the mantel.

Colin also looked up at the treasure. He smiled because Nathan had placed the gift there. "It is beautiful, isn't it?"

"You can quit lusting after it," Nathan countered with a grin. "We're taking it home with us."

"I'm pleased you like it," Alesandra said. She turned to her husband to offer the suggestion that she ask the craftsman to fashion another ship for him, but Nathan interrupted her thought when he told her neither he nor Colin needed any money from her inheritance now. They were financially sound enough.

"Put the money into the town house Colin purchased for you," he suggested.

She shook her head. "My husband used the money he received from the insurance contract for a hefty payment, Nathan, and the castle needs very little work. I wish you could see the inside before you leave. It's only a block away from our rental and it's so large and roomy."

Colin turned his attention back from the ship to look at his wife. "It isn't a castle, sweetheart."

"Oh, but it is," she argued. "It's our home, Colin, and therefore our castle."

He couldn't fault that confusing bit of logic. "So I now have two castles," he said with a laugh. "And a princess."

He stretched his legs out and put his arm around his wife. Nathan wanted to continue to argue about the money, but it didn't take him long to realize Alesandra wasn't going to bend on the issue.

He finally accepted defeat. "Hell," he muttered.

"What now?" Colin asked.

"If I'd known about the gift from your wife's inheritance I never would have suggested we sell stock. Have you found out who owns the shares yet? Maybe we could buy them back."

Colin shook his head. "Dreyson isn't telling," he explained. "He says it would be breaking his client's trust."

"Let me talk to him," Nathan suggested. "Just give me five minutes alone with Dreyson and I promise you he'll tell us."

Alesandra immediately tried to soothe Nathan's temper. "Dreyson's extremely ethical. My father never would have done business with him if he hadn't believed he was honorable. I'm my father's daughter, Nathan, and I therefore follow in his footsteps. I also have complete confidence in his integrity. I would wager every coin I have that you would never be able to get him to break a confidence. You might as well give up."

"Colin and I have a right to know who the owner is," Nathan argued.

Colin closed his eyes and let out a loud yawn while he listened to the conversation. A comment his wife had just made suddenly gained his full attention.

She was her father's daughter. Colin opened his eyes and slowly turned to look at the ship again.

He was reminded of the castle perched on his father's mantel . . . and the bit of trickery Alesandra's father had played when he tucked the notes inside.

And then he knew. She was her father's daughter, all right. The stock certificates were hidden inside the ship. Colin was astonished by the revelation. The expression on his face when he turned to his wife showed his surprise.

"Is something the matter, Colin?"

"You wouldn't lie to me, would you, sweetheart?"

"No, of course not."

"How did you do it?"

"Do what?"

"You don't own the stocks. I asked Dreyson and he told me you weren't the owner. You also told me you didn't own them."

"I don't. Why in heaven's name . . ."

She stopped when Colin pointed to the ship. She knew then her husband had finally guessed the truth.

She was well into her sixth month of confinement and getting more awkward every day, but she was still quick when she needed to be. She hastily stood up and started for the doorway. "I believe I'll see how Sara's doing. I do so love to hold little Joanna. She has the most delightful smile."

"Come back here."

"I'd rather not, Colin."

"I want to talk to you. Now."

"Colin, you shouldn't get your wife upset. She's pregnant, for God's sake."

"Look at her, Nathan. Does she look upset to you? She looks damned guilty to me."

Alesandra let her husband see her exasperation. Nathan winked at her when she walked back to the settee. She folded her hands together and frowned at her husband. "You better not get angry, Colin. Our baby might become upset."

"But you're not upset, are you, sweetheart?"

"No."

He patted the cushion next to him. She sat down and smoothed her gown.

She stared at the floor. He stared at her. "They're inside the ship, aren't they?"

"What's inside the ship?" Nathan asked.

"The stock certificates," Colin answered. "Alesandra, I asked you a question. Please answer me."

"Yes, they're inside the ship."

Relief fairly overwhelmed him. He was so damned happy the certificates hadn't been sold to a stranger he wanted to laugh.

A faint blush crept up Alesandra's face. "How did you do it?" he asked.

"Do what?"

"Are they in my name? I never thought to ask Dreyson that question. Do I own them?"

"No."

"Are they in Nathan's name then?"

"No."

He waited a long minute for her to confess. She remained stubbornly silent. Nathan was thoroughly puzzled.

"I just want to talk to the owner, Alesandra, to see if he might wish to sell the stocks back to us. I won't use intimidation."

"The owner can't talk to you, Nathan, and it really isn't legally possible for you to purchase the stocks—not now anyway."

She turned to look at her husband. "I will admit I did interfere just a bit, husband, but I would remind you that you were being very mule-headed about my inheritance at the time and I had to resort to a bit of trickery."

"Like your father," he countered.

"Yes," she agreed. "Like my father. He wouldn't be angry with me. Are you?" she asked again.

Colin couldn't help but notice that his wife didn't appear to be overly concerned about that possibility. She smiled, a radiant smile that made his breath catch in the back of his throat. She was definitely going to drive him crazy one of these days, and he couldn't imagine anything more wonderful.

He leaned down and kissed her. "Go and say good-bye to Sara. Then you and I are going home to our castle. My leg needs some of your pampering."

"Colin, that's the first time I've ever heard you mention your leg," Nathan interjected.

"He's not nearly as sensitive anymore. The ache in his leg did save our lives, after all. If the throbbing hadn't awakened him, he might not have heard Morgan. Mother Superior told me there was a reason for everything. I believe she was right. Perhaps the shark took a bite out of your leg so you would be able to save me and our son."

"I'm having a son?" Colin asked, smiling over how matter-of-fact Alesandra sounded.

"Oh, yes, I believe so," she answered.

Colin rolled his eyes heavenward. "Have you named him yet?"

The sparkle came back into her eyes. "We should call him Dolphin or Dragon. Both names are appropriate. He is, after all, his father's son."

Alesandra left the room to the sound of her husband's laughter. She patted her swollen middle and whispered, "When you're smiling at me and showing your gentle side, I'll think of you as my dolphin, and when you're angry because you aren't getting your way, I'll know you've turned into my dragon. I'll love you with all my heart."

"What's she whispering about?" Nathan asked Colin.

Both men watched Alesandra until she turned and started up the steps. "She's talking to my son," Colin confessed. "She seems to think he hears her."

Nathan laughed. He'd never heard of anything so absurd.

Colin stood up and went to the mantel. He found the latch cleverly concealed by a trapdoor fashioned into the side of the ship and opened it. The stock certificates were rolled into a tube and tied with a pink ribbon.

Nathan watched him pull the papers out, unroll them, and read the name of the owner.

Then Colin burst into laughter. Nathan bounded to his feet. His curiosity was killing him. "Who owns them, Colin? Give me the name and I'll talk to him."

"Alesandra said the owner wouldn't talk to you," Colin replied. "She was right about that. You're going to have to wait."

"How long?" Nathan demanded.

Colin handed his partner the certificates. "Until your daughter learns how to speak, I imagine. They're all in Joanna's name, Nathan. Neither one of us can buy the stock back. We're both named as joint executors."

Nathan was astonished. "But how did she know? The stock was sold before she even met Sara or Joanna."

"You gave me your daughter's name in your letter," Colin reminded his friend.

Nathan sat down. A slow smile settled on his face. The company was safe from intruders.

"Where are you going, Colin?" he called out when his partner walked out of the room.

"Home to my castle," Colin said. "With my princess."

He started up the steps to collect his wife. The sound of her laughter reached him and he paused to let her joy wash over him.

The princess had tamed the dragon.

But the dragon was still the victor. He'd captured a princess's love.

He was content.

# An Exciting Interview With Julie Garwood

Heartbreaker *is a contemporary romantic suspense novel. This is something new for you. What made you decide to make the transition from historical fiction to contemporary suspense?*

The deciding factor is always the story. The idea for this book came to me a couple of years ago. I was attending a church service in London, and—I hesitate to admit—my mind began to wander, as it sometimes is prone to do. I was glancing around at the incredible architecture surrounding me, and I noticed the ornate confessional against the wall. That's when a story began to take shape. I've been letting it percolate ever since that day. It's a thriller and a mystery and a love story all at the same time, and while I love the historicals, this is a story that could be told only in a contemporary setting.

*Do you think that the type of characters you create, in a fundamental way, are the same in both the historical and the contemporary?*

It's my belief that human nature hasn't changed all that much over the centuries. The people of the Middle Ages had the same basic concerns that we do now. They wanted to find love; they cared and worried about their families, etc. —It's just the world outside that's changed.

*Tell us a little about the characters from* Heartbreaker. *Where did you get your inspiration?*

My characters are created from the initial scene that inspires the book. Once I've visualized that particular scene, the people who will play a part in the story begin to come to life. In *Heartbreaker*, the two main characters are Laurant and

Nick. Laurant is a strong woman, but she is also quite vulnerable and looking for some stability in her life. Having grown up in Europe virtually alone, she is searching for the one place she feels she truly belongs. She believes she's found it in Holy Oaks, Iowa. Nick, on the other hand, comes from a large, nurturing family, and his roots are deep and strong, but as a result of his work with the FBI, he's developed calluses on his heart and has learned to guard his feelings. When danger brings them together, the lives they've chosen are turned upside down.

*The plot of* Heartbreaker *is very gritty and edgy. How did you research the book?*

I've been reading as many books on profiling and the criminal mind as I can find. I've also interviewed FBI agents, psychologists, and priests, and they've been very helpful and patient as I pester them with endless questions.

*Do you find the Internet to be useful in your research?*

I still go to books for in-depth research, but the Internet gives me immediate answers when I'm looking for a quick response to a detail question.

*Speaking of the Internet, do you have your own Web page?*

Yes. For some time I've had an ongoing Web site at **www.simonsays.com/garwood** but I'm in the process of developing another one and I'm really excited about it. The new site—**www.juliegarwood.com**—is going to have lots for the viewers to see and do, and I'm hoping they'll want to visit it often.

*Your Irish Catholic upbringing seems to have played an important role in your life. Is there a little piece of you or those you love in all your characters?*

I think it's inevitable that writers put a little of themselves in every book they write. I've often been accused of passing on my warped sense of humor to my characters. And, since I grew up in a large Irish Catholic family, I think it's only natural that their influence shows up in my work.

*Now that you've written your first contemporary novel, do you think you'll ever go back to writing historicals?*

I love history, and I love writing stories set against exciting historical backdrops. So I don't think I'll ever stop writing them. But I also have a number of contemporary stories I'm dying to tell. I just hope I can find the time to do them all.

*Speaking of more books, what is the next project you are working on?*

I have two ideas I'm working on. One is a follow-up to *Saving Grace*, a medieval I wrote several years ago. And the other is a contemporary that involves the brother of Nick, the hero in *Heartbreaker*. As I was creating the characters for the book, something funny happened. Nick's large New England family of six brothers and sisters began to fascinate me. Even though they don't play a large part in *Heartbreaker*, I know them inside and out. Some of them have already had incredible lives, and some of them have some real adventures ahead of them. I'd love to write one of their stories. I'll keep working on both ideas until one of them pushes its way to the front.

The Duke of Bradford, Jered Marcus Benton, is the wealthiest, handsomest, and most arrogant duke in all of England. Bradford could have his pick of the women in London, but his eyes—and desires—are set on Caroline Richmond, a mysterious beauty from Boston who can give him the same fiery wit he employs. Bradford is sure he cannot submit to her, no matter how determined she may be.

But when a deadly intrigue unites them against a common enemy, they discover the latent passion between them that ignites into a burning desire and blazing love.

Keep reading for a sneak peek of

*Rebellious Desire*

On sale now!

*England, 1802*

GUNSHOTS SHATTERED THE SILENCE, disrupting the peaceful ride through the English countryside.

Caroline Mary Richmond, her cousin Charity, and their black companion, Benjamin, all heard the noise at the same instant. Charity thought the sound was thunder and looked out the window. She frowned in confusion, as the sky above was as clear and blue as the finest of fall's days. There wasn't a single angry cloud in sight. She was about to comment on that fact when her cousin grabbed hold of her shoulders and pushed her to the floor of the hired carriage.

Caroline saw to her cousin's protection and then pulled a silver pearled pistol from her drawstring purse. She braced herself on top of Charity when the vehicle came to an abrupt halt along the curve of the roadway.

"Caroline, whatever are you doing?" The muffled demand came from the floor.

"Gunshots," Caroline answered.

Benjamin, seated across from his mistress, readied his own weapon and cautiously peered out his open window.

"Foul play ahead!" yelled the coachman with a thick Irish

brogue. "Best wait it out here," he advised as he hastily climbed down from his perch and raced past Ben's view.

"Do you see anything?" Caroline asked.

"Only the groom hiding in the bushes," the black man replied with obvious disgust in his voice.

"I can't see anything," Charity remarked in a disgruntled voice. "Caroline, please remove your feet. I'm going to have shoe prints all over the back of my dress." She struggled to sit up and finally made it to her knees. Her bonnet was around her neck, tangled in an abundance of blond curls and pink and yellow ribbons. Wire-rim spectacles were perched at an odd angle on her petite nose, and she squinted with concentration while she tried to right her appearance.

"Honestly, Caroline, I do wish you wouldn't be so vigorous in your need to protect me," she stated in a rush. "Oh, Lord, I've lost one of my glasses," she added with a moan. "It's probably down my gown somewhere. Do you think they're robbers, waylaying some poor traveler?"

Caroline concentrated on the last of Charity's remarks. "From the number of shots and our coachman's reaction, I would assume so," she replied. Her voice was soft and calm, an instinctive reaction to Charity's nervous prattle. "Benjamin? Please see to the horses. If they're calm enough, then we'll ride ahead and offer assistance."

Benjamin nodded his agreement and opened the door. His imposing bulk rocked the vehicle as soon as he moved, and he had to angle his broad shoulders to clear the wooden doorway. Instead of hurrying to the front of the carriage where the stable horses were harnessed, he turned to the back, where Caroline's two Arabians were tethered. The animals had come all the way from Boston with the threesome and were presents for Caroline's father, the Earl of Braxton.

The stallion was fretful and the mare no less so, but Benjamin, crooning to both in the musical African dialect only Caroline fully understood, quickly settled the animals. He then untied them and led them to the side of the carriage.

"Wait here, Charity," Caroline commanded. "And keep your head down."

"Do be careful," Charity replied as she climbed back up onto the seat. She immediately poked her head out the window, completely ignoring Caroline's order of caution, and watched as Benjamin lifted Caroline onto the back of the stallion. "Benjamin, take care too," Charity called as the huge man settled himself on the nervous mare's back.

Caroline led the way through the trees, her intent to come upon the robbers from behind, with the element of surprise on her side. The number of shots indicated four, possibly five attackers, and she had no wish to ride into the middle of a band of cutthroats with such uneven odds.

Branches tore at her blue bonnet and she quickly removed it and threw it to the ground. Thick black hair, the color of midnight, pulled away from the inefficient pins and settled in curly disarray around her slender shoulders.

Angry voices halted them, and Caroline and Benjamin, well hidden behind the thickness of the dense forest, had a somewhat unobstructed view. The sight on the roadway sent a chill of apprehension down Caroline's spine.

Four burly men, all on horseback, surrounded one side of a beautiful black carriage. All but one wore masks. They faced a gentleman of obvious wealth who was slowly dismounting from the carriage. Caroline saw bright red blood flowing unchecked from between the man's legs and almost gasped aloud with outrage and pity.

The injured gentleman had blond hair and a handsome

face that was chalk-white now and etched in pain. Caroline watched as he leaned against the carriage and faced his attackers. She noted the arrogance and disdain in his gaze as he studied his captors, and then saw his eyes suddenly widen. Arrogance vanished, replaced by stark terror. Caroline was quick to see the reason for the swift change in the man's attitude. The attacker without the mask, obviously the leader of the group from the way the others were looking at him, was slowly lifting his pistol. The bandit, no doubt, was about to commit cold-blooded murder.

"He's seen me face," the man said to his cohorts. "There's no help for it. He has to die."

Two of the robbers immediately nodded their approval, but the third hesitated. Caroline didn't waste time to see his decision. She carefully took aim and pulled the trigger. Her shot was true and accurate, a reflection of the years of living with four older male cousins who insisted on teaching her self-defense. The leader's hand received her shot, his howl of pain her reward.

Benjamin grunted his approval as he handed her his weapon and accepted her empty one. Caroline fired again, injuring the man to the left of the leader.

And then it was over. The bandits, yelling obscenities and warnings, took off at a thunderous pace down the road.

Caroline waited until the sounds of horses faded and then nudged her mount forward. When she reached the gentleman, she quickly slid to the ground. "I don't think they'll return," she said in a soft voice. She still held the gun in her hand but quickly lowered the barrel when the gentleman backed up a space.

The man slowly came out of his daze. Incredulous blue eyes, a shade darker than Caroline's own, stared at her with dawning comprehension. "It was you who shot them? You shot . . ."

The poor man couldn't seem to finish his thought. The event had obviously been too much for him.

"Yes, I shot them. Benjamin," she added, motioning to the giant standing behind her, "helped."

The gentleman tore his gaze from Caroline and glanced over her head to look at her friend. His reaction to the black man worried Caroline. Why, he looked ready to faint. He appeared befuddled but Caroline decided that fright and the pain from his injury were the causes for his slow wit. "If I hadn't used my weapons, you'd now be dead."

After delivering what she considered a most logical statement of fact, Caroline turned back to Benjamin. She handed him the reins to her stallion. "Return to the carriage and tell Charity what has happened. She's probably worried herself sick by now."

Benjamin nodded and started off. "Bring the gunpowder just in case," Caroline called after him, "and Charity's medicine satchel."

She turned back to the stranger then and asked, "Can you make it back inside your carriage? You'll be more comfortable while I see to your injury."

The man nodded and slowly made his way up the steps and into the carriage. He almost toppled back out, but Caroline was right behind him and steadied him with her hands.

When he was settled on the plush burgundy-colored seat cushion, Caroline knelt down on the floorboards between his outstretched legs. She found herself suddenly embarrassed, as the injury was in such an awkward place, and felt her cheeks warm in reaction to the intimate position she was in. She hesitated over exactly how to proceed, until a fresh spurt of blood oozed down the fawn-colored buckskin breeches.

"It is most awkward, this," the man whispered. There was more pain than embarrassment in his voice and Caroline reacted with pure sympathy.

The wound was right at the junction of his legs, on the left inner thigh. "You're very fortunate," Caroline whispered. "The shot has gone straight through. If I can just tear the material a little, perhaps—"

"You'll ruin them!" The man seemed outraged over Caroline's suggestion and she leaned back to look up at him.

"My boots! Will you look at my boots!"

He appeared, in Caroline's estimation, to be bordering on hysteria. "It will be all right," she insisted in a quiet voice. "May I please tear your breeches just a bit?"

The gentleman took a deep breath, rolled his eyes heavenward, and gave a curt nod. "If you must," he stated with resignation.

Caroline nodded and quickly pulled a small dagger from its hiding place above her ankle.

The gentleman watched her and found his first smile. "Do you always travel so well prepared, madam?"

"Where we have just traveled from, it's a fact that one must take every precaution," Caroline explained.

It was extremely difficult to edge the tip of her blade beneath the tight breeches. The material seemed to be truly molded to the man's skin, and Caroline had the vague thought that it must be terribly uncomfortable for the man to sit at all. She worked diligently until she was finally able to tear the material at the junction of the man's legs and then split the fabric wide, until all of the pink flesh was exposed.

The gentleman, catching the unusual accent of the beautiful woman kneeling before him, recognized the colonial pitch in her husky voice. "Ah, you're from the Colonies! A barbaric place I'm told." He gasped when Caroline began to probe around the edges of the injury and then continued, "No wonder you carry an arsenal with you."

Caroline looked up at the stranger, surprise registering in her voice when she replied, "It *is* true, I am from the Colonies, but that isn't why I carry weapons, sir. No, no," she added with a vigorous shake of her head. "I've just come from London."

"London?" The stranger assumed his confused look once again.

"Indeed. We've heard stories of the mischief that takes place there. Why, the tales of countless murders and robberies have reached even Boston. It's a den of decadence and corruption, is it not? My cousin and I promised that we would take every care. A good thing, too, considering this treachery on the very day of our arrival."

"Ha! I've heard the same stories about the Colonies," the gentleman responded with a snort. "London is far more civilized, my dear misguided woman!" The gentleman's tone sounded very condescending in Caroline's opinion. Oddly enough, she wasn't put off by it.

"You defend your home, and I suppose that is honorable of you," Caroline replied with a sigh. She returned her attention to his leg before he could think of a suitable reply and added, "Would you please remove your neckcloth?"

"I beg your pardon?" the stranger replied. He was biting on his lower lip between each carefully enunciated word, and Caroline assumed that the pain had intensified.

"I need something to stop the flow of blood," Caroline explained.

"If anyone hears of this, I will be humiliated beyond . . . to be shot in such a delicate place, to have a lady see my condition, and then, to use *my* cravat . . . My God, it is all too much, too much!"

"Don't concern yourself over your cravat," Caroline soothed in a voice she used when comforting small children. "I'll use a portion of my petticoat."

The gentleman still held a rather crazed look in his eyes and continued to protect his precious neckcloth from her grasp. Caroline forced herself to maintain a sympathetic expression. "And I promise that I'll not tell anyone about this most unfortunate incident. Why, I don't even know your name! There, see how simple it all is? For now I shall call you . . . Mr. George, after your king. Is that acceptable?"

The wild look in the man's eyes intensified and Caroline gathered that it wasn't acceptable at all. She puzzled over it a moment and then decided that she understood this new irritation. "Of course, since your king is indisposed, perhaps another name will better suit. Is Smith all right? How about Harold Smith?"

The man nodded and let out a long sigh.

"Good," Caroline stated. She patted his kneecap and quickly climbed out of the carriage, then bent and began to tear a strip from the bottom of her petticoat.

The sound of horse and rider making a fast approach startled Caroline. She froze, realizing that the pounding noise was coming from the north, the opposite direction from Benjamin and their hired carriage. Was one of the bandits returning? "Hand me my pistol, Mr. Smith," she demanded as she quickly replaced the dagger in its hiding place and threw the strip of petticoat through the open window.

"But it's empty," the man protested in a loud voice filled with panic.

Caroline felt the same panic try to grab hold of her. She fought the urge to pick up her skirts and run for help. She couldn't give in to such a cowardly thought, however, for it would mean leaving the injured gentleman alone, without protection. "The pistol may be empty, but only you and I need know that," Caroline insisted with false bravery. She accepted the weapon through the window, took a deep, calming breath, and said a silent prayer that Benjamin had also heard the approach of this new threat. Lord, but she wished her hands would quit shaking!

From around the curve, horse and rider finally came into view. Caroline focused on the animal, a gigantic black beast at least three hands taller than her own Arabians. She had the wild thought that she was about to be trampled to death and felt the earth tremble beneath her. She held her pistol steady, though she did back up a space, and dangerous though it was, she had to close her eyes against the dirt flying up into her face when the rider forced his mount to stop.

Caroline brushed one hand against her eyes and then opened them. She looked past the magnificent beast and saw a gleaming pistol pointed directly at her. Both the snorting animal and the pistol proved too intimidating and Caroline quickly turned her attention to the rider.

That was a mistake. The huge man staring down at her was far more intimidating looking than either the horse or the weapon. The tawny brown hair falling against his forehead didn't soften the man's hard, chiseled features. His jaw was rigid and clearly defined, as was his nose, and his eyes, a golden brown that didn't give the least hint of gentleness or understanding, now tried to pierce through her, undermine her good intentions. His scowl was hot enough to burn.

She wouldn't allow it, she told herself. She stared back at the arrogant man, trying not to blink as she held his gaze.

Jered Marcus Benton, the fourth Duke of Bradford, couldn't believe what he was seeing. He calmed his stallion while he stared at the lovely vision before him, the blue-eyed beauty who held a pistol aimed right at his heart. The entire situation was difficult to take in.

"What has happened here?" he demanded with such force that his stallion began to prance in reaction. He was quick to get the animal under control, using his powerful thighs as leverage. "Quiet, Reliance," he stated in a harsh growl. Yet he seemed to contradict his firm command by stroking the side of the horse's neck. The unconscious show of affection was at great odds with the brutal expression on his face.

He wouldn't break the hold of his gaze, and Caroline found herself wishing that it had been one of the robbers returning after all. She worried that this stranger would quickly see through her bluff.

Where was Benjamin? Caroline thought a little frantically. Surely he had heard the approach. Why, the ground still trembled, didn't it? Or was it her legs that trembled?

Lord, she had to get hold of herself!

"Tell me what happened here," the stranger demanded again. The harshness in his voice washed over Caroline but she still didn't move. Nor did she answer, afraid that her fear would be apparent in her voice, giving him the advantage. She tightened her grip on the pistol and tried to slow her racing heart.

Bradford chanced a quick look around. His favorite carriage, loaned to his friend for a fortnight, stood at the edge of the roadway with several hideous bullet holes in his crest. He caught a movement inside the vehicle and recognized his friend's mop of blond hair. Bradford all but sighed with relief. His friend was safe.

He knew, instinctively, that the woman standing proudly before him wasn't responsible for the damage. He saw her tremble slightly and seized the opportunity.

"Drop your weapon!" It wasn't a request. The Duke of Bradford rarely, if ever, requested anything. He commanded. And under usual circumstances, he always received what he wanted.

Bradford was forced to decide that this didn't qualify as a usual circumstance when the chit continued to stare up at him, ignoring his order altogether.

Caroline concentrated on trying not to tremble as she studied the man looming above her like an angry cloud. Power surrounded the scowling man like a winter cloak, and Caroline found herself frightened by the intensity of her reaction to him. He was, after all, only a man. She shook her head and fought to clear her thoughts. The stranger looked arrogant and pompous and, from the apparel he wore, was obviously very wealthy. His waistcoat was a rich burgundy color, styled in the identical manner as Mr. Smith's forest-green jacket. His golden buckskins were just as fashionable, and as tightly fitted from the way his muscles bulged through the material. The Hessians shone with polish and attention, and the cynical-looking man even wore the same type of neckcloth.

Caroline remembered the injured man's worry that one of his acquaintances would hear of his awkward situation and remembered too her promise to tell no one. The stranger glaring at her definitely looked the type to spread stories, in Caroline's opinion. Best to send him on his way.

"Madam, do you suffer a hearing impairment? I told you to drop your pistol." He hadn't meant to yell but he felt captive, both by her weapon pointed at him and, he admitted to himself, by her eyes, daring him. They were the most unusual color.

"You drop your pistol," Caroline finally replied. She was pleased that her voice didn't tremble overmuch and thought that she sounded almost as angry as he did. It was a small victory, but a victory all the same.

Caroline's back was to the carriage and she therefore didn't see the injured gentleman wave a greeting to the stranger trying to frighten her to death.

Bradford acknowledged the wave with a curt nod. His eyebrow arched in a silent question to his friend and his gaze suddenly lost its cynical look. It was as if a filled chalkboard had suddenly been erased, and Caroline found herself wishing his intimidating aura of power would also disappear as quickly.

She wasn't given more time to consider her adversary's change in disposition. "It appears that we have a standoff," the man stated in a deep, rich voice. "Should we shoot each other?"

She wasn't amused. She saw the corners of his hard mouth turn up a bit and felt her spine stiffen in reaction. How dare he assume such a bored and amused attitude when she was so frightened.

"You'll drop your weapon," Caroline insisted in a soft voice. "I won't shoot you."

Bradford ignored her order and her promise and continued to study her with lazy appreciation as he patted his stallion's neck. It was obvious that he valued the animal, and Caroline suddenly realized she possessed a new weapon.

He, of course, would never give in. He would bend to no woman! Bradford had seen his opponent tremble a moment before and knew that it was just a matter of time before she crumbled completely. He reluctantly admired her courage, a quality he had never encountered in a female before, but considered that, brave or not, she was still a woman, and therefore inferior. All females were basically the same; they all . . .

"I won't shoot you, but I *will* shoot your horse."

Her ploy worked. The man almost fell off his stallion. "You wouldn't dare!" he bellowed in pure outrage.

Caroline's answer to his denial was to drop her arm so that her empty pistol was aimed directly at the proud beast's head. "Right between the eyes," she promised.

"Bradford!" The voice, calling from inside the carriage, put a halt to the duke's overwhelming desire to leap from his horse and throttle the woman before him.

"Mr. Smith? Do you know this man?" Caroline called out. She never took her gaze off the angry stranger now dismounting and watched with great satisfaction as he replaced his pistol in the waistband of his breeches. A wave of relief overtook her. He hadn't been too difficult to convince after all. If this Englishman was a typical example of the fashionable *ton*, then Caroline considered that her cousins just might be right. Perhaps they were all pansies.

Bradford turned to Caroline, interrupting her thoughts. "No gentleman would ever threaten—"

He realized, even as he made the rash comment, how totally absurd it was.

"I've never claimed to be much of a gentleman," Caroline returned when she realized he wasn't going to finish his sentence.

Mr. Smith poked his head out the window and let out a small groan when the quick movement caused him pain. "Her pistol's empty, man. Don't get all apoplectic! Your horse is safe." There was a snicker of amusement in his voice and Caroline couldn't help but smile.

Bradford found himself temporarily sidetracked by the woman's beautiful smile, the mischievous sparkle that radiated in her eyes.

"You were certainly easy to convince," Caroline noted. She immediately wished that she had kept her thoughts to herself, for the man was now advancing upon her at an alarming pace. And he wasn't smiling. He obviously suffered from lack of humor, she considered, as she backed up a space.

His scowl removed any possibility of attractiveness. That, and his size. He was much too tall and too broad for her liking. Why, he was almost as huge as Benjamin, who, Caroline was relieved to note, was quietly stalking up on the stranger behind his back.

"Would you have shot my horse if your pistol was loaded?" The stranger had developed a rather severe twitch in his right cheek, and Caroline, lowering her pistol, decided that it was best to answer.

"Of course not. He's much too beautiful to destroy. You, on the other hand . . ."